No, Wallace Daltry's decision didn't make any sense to her. With a son like him—Angel recognized the grudging respect for Jack inherent in those words—why leave the Circle D to her? Why come looking for her and save her, only to toss her into the middle of the heartache and mystery here? Just like Jack said, they were missing something—a fact, a bit of knowledge—that would clear up everything. Still, no matter how strong her compulsion to ask Jack what had caused the bad blood between him and his father, Angel knew she wouldn't. Because to do so invited confidences.

And there was just no sense in getting to know Jack Daltry any better than she already did. Because the day loomed when she'd likely have to throw him off her land. Just how she planned to achieve that, given their difference in sizes, if not temperaments, she couldn't even begin to fathom. But another question—how to get him to *stay* off—occupied most of her waking thoughts, it seemed. *Would* she have to kill him or marry him to hang on to his father's legacy to her? Angel didn't know which idea she hated the most . . .

"What a tour de force. CAPTIVE ANGEL grips you from the get go and never lets go. Cheryl Anne Porter [is] at the top of her form. This is a top-notch romance; [a] not-to-be-missed read."

—*Romantic Times*

Captive Angel

Cheryl Anne Porter

St. Martin's Paperbacks

CAPTIVE ANGEL

Copyright © 1999 by Cheryl Anne Porter.

All rights reserved. No part of this book may be used or reproduced in any manner whatsoever, without written permission except in the case of brief quotations embodied in critical articles or reviews. For information address St. Martin's Press, 175 Fifth Avenue, New York, N.Y. 10010.

ISBN: 0-312-96906-6

Printed in the United States of America

St. Martin's Paperbacks edition / April 1999

St. Martin's Paperbacks are published by St. Martin's Press, 175 Fifth Avenue, New York N.Y. 10010.

10 9 8 7 6 5 4 3 2 1

To C.L.M., the poet in my heart.

One

Angel Devlin never even got a chance to mourn her mother's passing before she found herself being strung up, the torn and bruised guest of honor at a necktie party. Threatening voices and brutal hands reached out of the mob that surrounded her, hoisting her aloft and holding her suspended for a dust-choked second over the enraged men's heads. In the next instant, she was slammed down on the lathered back of a sidestepping white-eyed cow pony. The men's heartless handling of her pitched Angel forward, had her gasping in spine-jarring pain, with barely the presence of mind to sit the animal and clutch its tangled mane.

Scared, panicked, as mistreated as the innocent roan under her, her heart pounding, her long hair hanging in her eyes and tangled all about her face, Angel relied on her gut instinct to save her hide. She knew, from lifelong experience, that no one standing back by the assorted log cabins and shacks that comprised Red River Station, or over by the Silver Star Saloon, would lift a hand to help her.

Because, to them, she was of no consequence. They knew what her mother'd been. And they knew what Angel had done today. So now, as always, it was up to her. She had only one chance to escape the lynching that awaited her. But that was all she asked for—a chance. It was all she'd ever asked for. And unlike every other moment in her abrupt eighteen years of life, maybe this time she'd win that chance.

So, sensing the loosening of the hands that gripped her,

and judging this to be her moment, she grasped the pommel tightly and dug her boot heels into the horse's ribs, gouging him and yelling, "Yee-haw. Git up!" The roan under her—held in place by the men but urged by his rider to take flight—froze into a stiff-legged posture, as Angel expected he would. She braced herself, held her breath. All hell was getting ready to bust loose. And she'd see that it did. Again she dug her heels into the horse's ribs, again she yelled for it to git up.

This time, the roan complied. Over the men's yells of "Hang on!" and "Watch out!", the horse fought to lower his head, fought the hands that gripped his bridle, that secured his unwilling participation in his rider's last moments on earth. Angel's grunts of effort matched her mount's bellows of outrage as he twisted and jerked, fighting as much, she knew, to unseat her as he did to free himself.

In his bucking efforts, he nearly succeeded in both. Angel's grip on the pommel broke. Teeth gritted, she clutched spasmodically at it, couldn't get her fingers to lock around it. Instinctively, she gripped tightly with her knees, turning in her toes, the better to circle the roan's ribs. Just when she thought she'd be thrown, her grasping fingers captured the coarse and reddish mane. She held on, despite the flailing, whiplike punishment the thick hair delivered to her exposed arms.

Just then, the horse pranced sideways, bumping against the nearest of the determined men and scattering them. Then, in its panic, it tried to rear, tried to bolt from under the heavy, low-hanging branch of the gnarled scrub oak that had proven, time and again, to be sturdy enough not to break under a body's weight. Something rough slapped against Angel's cheek. She jerked, cried out, snapping her head up . . . only to see her destiny.

A knotted rope. A noose. The cowhands had tied a thick rope around the tree's trunk, had snaked its taut length up the bark, finally slinging it over a branch. At the rope's other end, the dangling noose now swung in the rain-dampened wind.

No. Angel's breath came in tight gasps. *No.* She relinquished her hold on the horse's mane, clutched the pommel and kicked out again. But this time, in her fear and rage, she aimed her kicks at the pitiless men imprisoning her. Finally, she connected. The howl of pain and the crunching of cartilage in some unknown cowpoke's nose brought a snarling smirk to her face.

But with that act, her chance died, just as did the early-spring breeze. One second it was there . . . and in the next, it wasn't. The vengeful trail crew prevailed, maintaining their hold on the horse. They stopped its bucking and clutched at the muddied length of Angel's coarse-spun skirt, effectively keeping her atop her winded mount. The ruckus further settled as two men, now straddling the branch above Angel and facing each other, shoved the noose over her head and began pulling it tight around her neck, tangling her hair in the rope's grip.

Angel stiffened, sucked in a breath through flared nostrils, and sought, in her final desperation, a sympathetic face among the twelve cowhands surrounding her and so intent on ending her life. But there was none to be seen. Only hard, angry eyes greeted her, leaching from her any fight she had left. Sudden defeat, a constant companion to her bravado, had her bowing her neck, had her lowering her gaze until she stared at her white-knuckled hands, still fisted around the pommel.

Her vision blurred. Angel sniffed, hating the fear in her heart and the tears in her eyes. She wasn't a sniveling coward who'd go to her death begging for her life. That conviction made her clench her jaw in a resurgence of defiance as she willed herself to do this one thing . . . this *dying* . . . right. And that meant going out with squared shoulders and a curse for her killers. Her spine stiffened with intention. She straightened up, ready to deliver her last words.

But it was a whimper that escaped her, that betrayed her. A whimper and a plea. "No. Please . . . no."

At that moment, a large callused hand seemed to come out of nowhere to cover hers. Angel stiffened, ready for yet another fight. But the man tightened his grip and said, in a low, gruff voice, "It's all right, sweetheart. I won't let them hurt you."

She should have sought his face, should have looked upon her would-be savior. But all Angel could do was stare at the hand sheltering hers. And try to believe him. Time seemed to stretch into thin, gauzy moments, marked by a rippling tide of sudden quiet that flowed outward from the man nearest her, out to the fringes of the gang . . . perhaps all the way to the men observing from a distance, as if they too had heard the man's words and also waited.

The growing silence, the men's waiting, all suited Angel. Because while they did so, she was alive and drawing her next breath. But finally, she angled her head, peering through the dark and tangled waterfall of her hair, trying to make out the man's face. Most likely the last face she'd see in this life. And thus, she studied him. And saw him watching her do so.

Under his wide-brimmed hat, which revealed graying side-burns, the stranger's face was broad and weathered, lined by life and by wind, a face that had seen too much of the outdoors and too much of human nature. Dominating his craggy features were blue eyes with the saddest glint in them that Angel'd ever seen. She didn't know why he'd involved himself, why he would risk his own life to save hers. Nor did she care. Because right now she'd bargain with the devil himself, if need be. Then the man spoke again. "Did you hear me? I said I won't let them hurt you."

Angel stretched her neck against the rope's cloying grip and rasped out, "From where I'm sitting, mister, it appears that they're more likely to kill me than they are just to hurt me."

The barest of nods from him, and perhaps a ghost of a grin, accompanied his words. "I always figured you for one with some grit inside you, Angel."

With that, the big man turned his attention to the lynch mob, drawing his gun with one hand and relinquishing his grip on her to hold the skittish horse's reins with his other. He called out to the men for calm, began trying to get to the bottom of the lynching. And that was when Angel realized that he'd called her by name.

Frowning, her eyes narrowed, she riveted her gaze on the man. Forcing a calm born of hopefulness onto her thoughts, she tried to reason. He'd called her Angel. But he'd also called her sweetheart. So maybe his saying *angel* was just a coincidence, no more than another pet name to him. It had to be. Because she'd never seen this man before in her life. But then she recalled his exact words. *I always figured you for one with some grit inside you.* Always figured? He'd have to know her to figure anything about her.

But he could've just seen her around the station. He didn't have to know her to watch her from afar, to make conclusions about her nature. That was true enough. But whoever he was, she felt certain in that moment that she would never forget him.

The two cowboys perched on the limb above her quickly abandoned it when the stranger poked a hole in the air with his raised pistol and fired off a round to silence the men's renewed protests. "All right, you listen to me and you listen good," he was bellowing to the men surrounding them both. "I don't know what she's done. But—"

"Stay out of this, Daltry. She killed Jeb Kennedy. Our trail boss. And in cold blood. Stabbed him right through the heart with his own knife, she did," a skinny, scraggly cowboy called out. "That ain't mud all over her. That's his drying blood."

The man called Daltry jerked his disbelieving gaze back to Angel, sweeping her torso with one glance before looking directly into her eyes. She knew the damning blood was there for him to see. Yet she refused to look away. She returned his stare, but with the assessing solemnity and cool detachment that she reserved for those foolhardy enough to stand with her and try to defend her. She raised an eyebrow, as much as asking *Are you still so all-fired ready to help me?* As if this were a test he had to pass.

"See there? She don't even deny it. And now she's got to pay for it," another of the trail crew said. Daltry turned to face the speaker, who continued his tirade. "We all know you, Mr. Daltry, and our quarrel ain't with you. But it will be, if you don't step aside right now."

Thus incited, the men surged forward, calling for her blood and raising their fists in open threat. Angel tensed, as did the roan under her.

But her protector, this stranger named Daltry, leveled his pistol until it pointed right between the eyes of the man who'd spoken last, startling them all into stopping short. Then he cocked it—a loud, metallic sound in the sudden stillness— and drawled, "One more step, and you'll be the first one to die, Evans. Like you said—you know me. So you know I ain't bluffing. Tell 'em to back off."

But Evans didn't. He didn't say anything, nor did he budge. Angel didn't even dare breathe. Then, "All right. Have it your way," Daltry said. "And tell your friends what you want 'em to say about you on your headstone."

The air crackled, burned with an acrid scent, as if the gray-haired man's words were bullets he'd fired from his weapon. Finally, into the tense silence, Evans blurted, "Okay, I give." He pivoted to face the other men and raised a cautioning hand. "Hold up right there. She ain't worth dying over, no-how."

Angel raised her chin a notch at the man's words. She wasn't worth dying over. She'd heard that said about her before. Maybe a thousand times. But in this particular instance, her lack of worth just might save her life. A grim irony tugged at her lips, had her shaking her head, even as the men melted back some. Could it be that they really were going to give up, maybe let her live?

She glanced over at Daltry in time to see him relaxing his gun hand. Maybe so. Maybe she would make it through this day, would see the sun set. As she watched, Daltry lowered his pistol to his side, but didn't holster it as he told Evans, "Smart man."

Swallowing as best she could around the noose's scratchy thickness against her windpipe, and feeling hollow inside, An-gel remained silent and kept her gaze on the stranger. She couldn't figure him out. At risk of his own life, he'd challenged the mob with no more than a cold stare and a steady gun hand. All for her. But why? She had no answers, only questions, as he continued to speak.

"This girl's no more a cold-blooded murderer than any of you are. So, what the hell happened here?"

"I'll tell ya—if'n you'll first tell us how come you're so all-fired concerned with what happens to a dead whore's daughter." This from the skinny cowboy who'd first challenged Daltry.

A dead whore's daughter. The man's words bounced off Angel . . . because she willed them to. But a muscle jumped in her jaw, her gut tightened. She refused even to blink, as Daltry holstered his gun and bowed out his chest, warning, "Watch your mouth, Sully, or I'll watch it for you."

"All I did was speak the truth," the man whined.

"Truth or no, keep it to your sorry self." Daltry's warning came framed in a grimace of disgust.

But was his distaste really for Sully? Or was it for her? Angel wondered. Shame had her lowering her head, had her staring at her white-knuckled hands. This particular slur— *whore's daughter*—had been flung at her all her life. Surely it should've lost its sting by now. And perhaps, on any other day, it wouldn't hurt. But not today. Because only this morning, in the driving rain, alone except for the grumbling gravedigger, she'd buried her mother next to her long-dead father.

Just then, breaking into Angel's thoughts, Daltry's hand once again covered hers, once again startled her. She met his gaze, but allowed nothing of the inner turmoil that roiled her guts to show on her face. The man's grip tightened with his question. "Is it true, Angel? She's dead? Mrs. Devlin—your mother's dead?"

The note of regret, of caring, in the man's voice pierced Angel's armor. Her throat worked. The barest of nods had to suffice as her answer. Daltry's grip tensed, loosened . . . his hand finally slipped away from hers. He took a deep breath, let it out, turned a hard stare on the men, and stepped away from Angel's side to go talk with them in quiet tones.

Although she felt better with him closer to her—since she still had the noose around her neck, and no one held the skittish roan in place—Angel couldn't have been more grateful for Daltry's turning away. She hated that he'd broken through to her. Hated it. And hated him for doing it. She'd fought too hard not to feel anything for her mother's passing. Fought too hard to deny she did or could feel anything for the woman.

And she'd be *damned* if she would allow grief a place in her heart now. She would be *damned*—would take it to her grave first—before she would let the pain of it show on her face. Especially in front of these men.

And so, lost and alone, she sat there, bereft of words, willing instead that the hardness in her heart would firm her features, would settle itself on her face. Another thing she hated was having no say in her own fate. She could do nothing to free herself, even given the men's present inattention to her. Surely, if she were to raise her hands to work the noose free, she'd spook the danged horse and end up killing herself. And she had no intention of doing that. She was too ornery to die by her own hand, to give up like that.

And so, with no choice, no course of action—only patience—open to her, she fumed and waited for the men to decide her fate. Would they allow a peaceable end to this scene? Or would they hang her? Right now, she didn't care which because she was getting mighty tired of being a public spectacle atop this roan. Tiring now even of her own thoughts, Angel focused on the men, settling her gaze on Mr. Daltry's back, on his oilskin slicker.

And found that, quite unbidden, her mind wandered again to the note of caring that had saturated his voice and his words only a moment ago. Then it hit her. Her spine stiffened. Devlin. Her surname. He'd used it. Her mind leaped to further conclusions. His calling her Angel a moment ago hadn't been a coincidence.

Her heart pounding, she frowned, narrowed her eyes at the man's back. Who was he that he would care what happened to her? Because now she knew—he did care. That much was obvious. His actions were not those of a mere stranger possessed of compassion for her plight. Because he didn't just know *of* her . . . he *knew* her. Knew her mother, too. Angel cocked her head, carefully brushed her hair out of her eyes, and wondered about him, about a man who would call the town whore Mrs. Devlin.

Then it came to her. That was it—the town whore. The saloon. That's how he knew her. Maybe he was just one of the more polite customers her mother'd . . . entertained. A stab of soul-deep disappointment made Angel slump in the saddle. But instantly, the noose around her neck tautened, cut off her air, reminded her to sit up straight. Angel did, taking the rope's reminder as good advice.

Stiffening her spine again until she sat erect, she watched Daltry come back to her side. Watched him stare blankly at her skirt-covered leg. Watched his mouth work in a way that spoke of pain, of an aching hurt in the middle of the soul, one that Angel knew all too well . . . even if she did refuse to acknowledge it.

Just as she did her own grief, Angel discounted his, too, calling it a show for these men, a play on their sympathy to help him win her life. Because surely the death of a sick whore couldn't be upsetting him this much. Angel exhaled, suddenly deciding she didn't care who he was or why he hurt. Because the truth had to be that he'd been her mother's customer. Missing his comings and goings from the back room at the Silver Star would've been easy for her, she knew. Because it'd been years since she'd passed her time at the dingy saloon, watching the sideshow that was her mother's life.

Just then, cutting into Angel's thoughts, Daltry shifted his stance, looked up at her, and again met her gaze. "What happened to your ma?"

Angel felt the weight of the surrounding men's stares. Daltry's question had her jaw working around the truth, which she spat out. "You did. You happened to her." With her gaze, Angel swept the crowd of twelve gathered around her. "All of you. You and your kind. Every one of you who laid his money down and crawled into her bed and gave her his diseases. You happened to her. You killed her.''

The men set up a fuss, but Daltry quelled it with no more than his raised hand. He then jerked to her. Under the wide brim of his hat, the man's blue eyes narrowed. "I never laid down with your ma, Angel. Never. I always—'' He cut off his own words to take in a breath and exhale it. Then he said, "I'm sorry for your loss. Truly sorry. I know how it feels to lose someone you love.''

Angel turned a heart-of-stone look on the man and his sympathy. "I never said I lost a loved one. Just my mother.''

Daltry's eyebrows shot up, he opened his mouth, meant to say something. But no words came out. Then, as if he'd changed his mind, he firmed his lips together and stared up at her. From the horse's height . . . with a hangman's noose around her neck, with Jeb Kennedy's blood dotting her bodice . . . Angel leveled a challenging look right back at the man, daring him to tell her she should love a mother who'd made herself and her daughter the outcasts they were in this forlorn and godforsaken trading post called Red River Station.

But all Daltry did was look away and then down, as if concentrating on his muddied boots. After a moment, he raised his head, avoiding Angel's steady gaze as he again turned to address the waiting men. "I've had about all of this I can stand. You men—the same as me—know Jeb Kennedy's ways with women. He liked to force himself on 'em. Now I'm asking you . . . *is* that what he did to get himself killed today? Did he force himself on Angel—and her no more'n a grievin' girl?''

No one answered. Daltry focused on the tall, rangy cowhand named Evans. "I asked a question. Is that what your good-for-nothin' trail boss did?''

Sitting as still as death, moving only her eyes, Angel searched the faces of the men. A few of them—catching her gaze directed his way—had the decency . . . or felt guilty enough . . . to look away, to look at his boots, or at the man standing next to him. So it was up to her, she realized, to say the words. In a voice no more than a whisper, she said, "That's what he did.''

Daltry flinched, as if he'd been punched. He pivoted to face her. His blue eyes squinted against the sudden illumination of a lone shaft of sunlight that pierced the bruised rainclouds overhead and bathed them all in its weak yellow glow. For some reason, Angel felt compelled to add, "Or tried to do, anyway. I got him before he got me."

"Good for you," was Daltry's response. Beyond that, he didn't move or say another word. Instead, he held her gaze, seemed to stare right through her, seemed to be searching for her very soul. Angel wondered if she had one for him to find. Then—as if they were alone in a parlor somewhere, as if she weren't sitting here with a dead man's blood coloring her clothing—he said, "Tell me what happened, Angel."

Angel's stomach quivered, making her shiver. The remembered fear, the feel of the man's hands on her, his mouth groping, hurting . . . *No.* She didn't want to talk about it. She opened her mouth to tell Daltry just that, that she didn't owe him an explanation. But a new voice inside her screamed not to do that. *For once in your life*, it echoed, *let someone help you. Tell him*, it said. *Tell him and live.*

This clamoring inside her that willed her to reach out for help, to accept it, halted Angel's rebellious thoughts. And focused her attention inward. What was happening to her? She never questioned herself, never doubted the validity of her gut reactions, the one thing that had kept her alive thus far. So, what was this she now felt? Every nerve ending screamed at her to cooperate with Mr. Daltry, just as the men who comprised this mob were doing. The mob was slowly turning into individual men . . . all of whom appeared relieved that someone was stopping them.

So, given that, why shouldn't she cooperate? Why shouldn't she tell these men what their precious trail boss had tried to do? Why, indeed? Angel decided to speak. "I was in the back room of the Silver Star . . . clearing out my mother's things . . . when he—Mr. Kennedy—came in, all liquored up and feeling randy. I told him to go away, that Virginia Devlin was dead."

"But—" A ragged breath escaped Angel, surprising her

and cutting off her words. She swallowed, tamped down her emotions, and hurried on. "But Mr. Kennedy said . . . one whore's the same as another. I told him I wasn't like my mother. But he kept coming at me. I told him to stop. And he said he'd kill me if I . . . didn't let him. Then he jumped me." Angel closed her eyes against the memory, realized what she was doing and opened them again, and caught sight of Mr. Daltry, and finished. "When he did, we fell to the bed. And in the struggle, I got his knife. And I killed him. As for the rest . . . well, it's sitting here looking at you."

In the ensuing silence, Angel willed herself not to look away first. Finally, Mr. Daltry blinked, nodding as if acknowledging her words as he turned again to the men. "It seems to me that if Kennedy did what she says, and she killed him for it, then he had it coming. Anyone care to see it differently?"

He stopped . . . waited. Angel's heart thumped leadenly. When no one offered an opinion either way, Mr. Daltry broke the silence. "I'll give you two minutes to think about it and speak your mind. Then I'm cutting her loose. So if you got something to say to me, or to her, say it now."

Again, Angel held her breath, certain she could hear the seconds ticking by, like the hollow booming cadence of an Indian war drum. But no one in the mob said a word or made an abrupt move. They just shifted their weight . . . eyed a neighbor . . . shrugged a shoulder. Angel sat up straighter in the saddle, sought Daltry's profile, and kept her attention focused on him. If she walked away from this ruckus, it'd be because of him.

As if he felt the weight of her stare, Mr. Daltry flicked a glance her way. The glint in his eyes clearly counseled caution, told her it wasn't over yet, said she need look no further than the rope knotted around her neck for the truth of that. Renewed apprehension caught at Angel's breathing. With only the briefest of nods she let him know she understood. But tell that to her mind, which raced with thoughts of the immediate future, ranging from what she needed to collect before she got out of Red River Station forever . . . to where she would go . . . and to what she would do when she got there.

"Time's up," Mr. Daltry said, his words shattering the leaden silence that had fallen on them. "Seeing as how you don't appear to have any objections, I'm guessin' you all agree that Miss Devlin is free to go." He pointed to Evans. "Get that rope off her. Now."

Evans immediately stepped around him and began climbing the hangman's tree. Daltry pivoted, watched him a moment, as if making sure the drover was carrying out his orders, and then turned to the eleven remaining men. "Whose cayuse is she sitting on?"

Angel's legs tightened reflexively around the roan under her, the horse in question. After a moment's hesitance, a young wrangler whom Angel'd heard brag more than once about having been with her mother, called out, "It'd be mine, Mr. Daltry."

Daltry swung his gaze to the kid. "How much you want for it?"

The boy's face clouded. "I don't want nothing for it, 'cause it ain't mine to sell. That's a top cow pony and belongs to the Henton brand. I'm just the horse wrangler. An' if I sold that horse, Mr. Henton would have my hide."

"Is that so?" Daltry drawled, drawing his pistol from its holster, ignoring the cowhand while he fiddled with the weapon's chambers . . . all to make a point, a loaded one not lost on Angel. Or on the trail crew facing her, she could see.

Done with his gun play, Daltry again leveled his blue-eyed gaze on the hapless wrangler. "I know your Mr. Henton. A fine, upstanding cattleman. He won't be none too pleased with the news you men've got to bring him. That your trail boss got himself killed and then you and your crew involved yourselves in the near lynching of a young girl who'd done nothing but defend herself. But since you're letting her go—and you are—the way I see it is, all you've got to report is you need a new trail boss . . . and you're short one horse."

He paused, cutting his gaze from one man to the next, until he'd looked each of them in the eye. "Is that the way you see it? Or do I need to go talk to John Henton myself?''

Angel was so enthralled with the conversation between Mr.
Daltry and the trail crew that she only belatedly realized that
Evans had lifted the noose from around her neck. Now all
she needed to do was reach forward, grab the dangling reins,
dig her boot heels into the horse's ribs, and send him in a
tear through the loose knot of men surrounding her. If she
did, they'd both be free, her and the roan. Her muscles
twitched, aching with the desire to do just that. But she didn't,
couldn't. And had to wonder why.

Then, it hit her. Some insane sense of loyalty that she
hadn't known she possessed. Could it be that she figured she
owed Mr. Daltry her life and should stick around to make
sure the guilt-wracked, and therefore still dangerous, trail
crew didn't turn on him? If they did turn, she told herself,
she could use the horse as a weapon, maybe even the odds
out a bit by wedging it between him and them, or urge it into
a charge that would scatter them. Is that what she was thinking . . . that Mr. Daltry might need her?

Angel examined that notion for a moment and realized that
. . . yes, she was thinking that. No one had ever needed her
before. But Mr. Daltry did. And she intended to stick by him.
So there it was. She *could* stick by someone, even if her
mother couldn't. Virginia Devlin'd pushed her child away,
telling her it was the only way she could keep her safe. Well,
Angel hadn't accepted that then, and she wasn't about to accept it now in herself. She, for one, would stay with this
man—until she knew he was away safely.

And after that, she had her freedom and would disappear
into the Western wilds and begin a new life for herself. A
good life, free of the stench of cattle and saloons and
liquored-up cowhands. Free of the scorn heaped on her by
decent folks because of who her mother was. And free of
want, of never enough clothes to wear or food to eat. Or her
own roof over her head. Yes, she'd have all that. She'd see
that she did. But for now, she sat her horse, a free woman,
one with a debt of gratitude keeping her in place.

In the space of time it took for all this to occur to her, Mr.

Daltry had continued to address the men. Angel listened in, knowing that whatever passed between them . . . affected her directly. "I believe you men have made the right decision here today. I know if I heard the same tale about my men—men I was prepared to trust with thousands of dollars' worth of steers—that they'd kept their heads, buried my trail boss, and got back to work, I'd be most likely to think highly of them. And not worry one bit about one lost cow pony."

With that, Mr. Daltry reached into an inside pocket of his oilskin slicker and pulled out some silver coins, which he threw at the wrangler's feet. "That's more'n that roan's worth. So do yourself a favor, kid—pick the money up and count the horse gone."

For a moment, the young wrangler didn't move, except to stare at the money in the mud and then to exchange glances with his fellow drovers. Angel's throat constricted. The air seemed to thicken. She inched forward over the roan's neck, meaning to grab for the reins, the better to control him, should she need to assist Mr. Daltry. But in the next second, urged on by his friends' gestures, the kid picked up the silver coins, scooping the pieces up with more mud than bravado.

Angel exhaled her relief. It was over.

The now peaceable cowhands turned and wandered off in the general direction of the Silver Star Saloon. Angel couldn't believe it. She was alive. Only moments ago, she'd been as close to dead as she'd ever been. But now, she could go. Even though she'd never thanked anybody for anything before in her life, she thought to thank Mr. Daltry.

But her words no more than tipped against her tongue before they were cut off by Daltry's called-out question to the departing men. "Hey, kid?" The horse wrangler, along with the other men, turned as one and waited for him to continue. "Buy a round at the Silver Star and have everyone drink to Virginia Devlin's memory. You owe her that much."

A heavier quiet seemed to settle over the men. They stared back in silence. A few of them sought Angel's gaze. She raised her chin a notch, willed her solemn, unforgiving expression to speak for her. Then, the young wrangler tipped his wide-brimmed hat in acknowledgment to Mr. Daltry . . . and then to Angel.

Her guts tightened, her jaw firmed. If her mouth weren't so dry, she told herself, she'd spit on the ground to show her opinion of his gesture. Did he mean it as an apology? She doubted it. Mocking disrespect? Most likely. Or could it be he sought her forgiveness? Is that what he and his friends wanted? Forgiveness?

Well, they'd not have it from her. They'd all die first before they'd see that day. And probably would. Because she had no intention of returning to Red River Station. Ever.

Two

The Henton cowhands finally turned away, fading into the backdrop of dingy, muddied, clapboard buildings.

Her eyes burning, her heart full, Angel exhaled. And then—without warning—reaction set in. Realization dawned. Today, she'd lost her mother. Killed a man. And nearly been lynched for it. She could right now, this moment, be dead herself . . . her neck broken, her lifeless body swinging limply from the scrub oak branch.

Bile rose to her throat. Angel clamped a hand over her mouth, swallowing convulsively. She gripped the roan tightly with her legs, clenched a fist around the pommel. The merest wisp of a breeze could have blown her off the animal, so weak with fear was she. With her eyes closed, she breathed in and out . . . deeply, slowly . . . refusing to acknowledge either the abject wail that tore through her soul, or the big, warm hand that gripped her thigh.

"You okay, Angel?"

She nodded, unable to speak—not even to the man who'd saved her life . . . for reasons still known only to him. But right now, it didn't seem important what his reasons were. Because all she wanted was for him to take his hand away so she could go off by herself and empty her roiling stomach of its sickness. Then, she'd get her few belongings together and ride out of this hellhole that had never been home to her since she and her parents had arrived here when she was five years old.

But Mr. Daltry's hand stayed where it was. After another moment or so, he squeezed her leg gently. And asked again, "Are you really okay?"

This time, realizing she *was* breathing easier, that she was more in control, but mostly that he wasn't going to let her be, Angel lowered her hand, opened her eyes, and met Mr. Daltry's concerned gaze. "I've been better."

His abrupt chuckle greeted her words. "I expect you have." He patted her leg and then removed his hand, gesturing to indicate her neck. "That's a nasty rope burn. I might have some salve that could help it along."

Grateful for his practical words, when sentiment or sympathy would have unseated her, Angel put a hand to her throat and rubbed the raw skin there, wincing as she did. "No need to trouble yourself. It'll heal on its own."

He nodded. Under the wide brim of his hat, his blue eyes earnest, he frowned and looked around, as if he didn't know how to proceed from here, what to say to her, what to do. This awkward moment, Angel knew, was as good as any to say her good-byes—to him and to Red River Station. But she had some questions first. She put the first one to him. "You stepped in for me with those men. Why?".

Mr. Daltry sobered, stared up at her. His answer was slow in coming. "Why? Because I had to. I owe you. It's as simple as that. Hell, Angel, saving your life is the least of what I intend to do."

Angel cocked her head at a challenging angle. "It's best you not have any intentions where I'm concerned, Mr. Daltry." She meant to leave it at that, but heard herself blurting, "What is it you think you owe me? What'd I ever do for you? I don't even know you."

The tall, gray-haired man, suddenly looking haggard, slowly exhaled. "You know me. You just don't remember me. And you didn't do anything for me, Angel. It's what I did to—Well, all you need to know is I owe you more than I could ever pay back. But even so, I'd like to try . . . the best way I know how."

"The best way you know how?" Angel chuckled, a sound

that had nothing to do with humor. "How do you intend to top saving my life, as worthless as it is?"

He looked up at her. "I'm going to give you a home you can live out that life in."

Angel was stunned. Finally, she recovered enough to speak her mind. "You're just going to give me a home? Just give it to me?" Her words dripping with derision, she shook her head. "Everyone and everything has a price, Mr. Daltry. And I don't have a hankering to know what yours is."

Having had her say, Angel leaned over the horse's neck, intent on gathering the reins and wheeling the animal around to head for her small room at the back of the clapboard hotel down the street.

But Mr. Daltry, moving with a swiftness that belied his years, caught up the leather reins first. Angel stiffened, but then retreated to an upright position. Wary now, she readied herself to swing her leg over her mount's other side, drop to the ground and run, should it become necessary. But she hoped it didn't . . . because she needed the danged roan to get out of Red River Station. Preferably before sundown. And certainly before those drovers got drunk enough to change their minds about setting her free.

Thinking all this, weighing it, and seeing that she was trapped, Angel gave every appearance of relaxing, despite the tension that thrummed at her temples. "All right," she managed to drawl. "Say your piece. I'm listening."

Mr. Daltry's relief showed on his face. "I appreciate that." He added, "I didn't mean to scare you just now. I wouldn't hurt you for anything, Angel, but it's important to me that you hear me out."

He stopped, watching her, perhaps waiting for some assurance from her that she believed him when he said he wouldn't hurt her. But Angel said nothing, her sober expression did not change. However, what he saw in her face must've settled his mind some, because he added, "I know it sounds crazy, what I said about giving you a home. But I mean it. In fact, I swear it."

That caught her attention, had her cocking her head and

drawling, "You *swear* it? Did someone make you?"

He shook his head. "No. No one made me. I promised myself I'd do it. I vowed that when the day came, I'd take care of you."

Angel chuckled . . . at her own expense, her own dilemma. "Well, I've got to admit that day sure seems to be here. But why in the world would you make that promise? Are we kin to one another? Or are you just plumb loco?"

He shook his head. "None of those."

Angel huffed out her breath. This was the most vexatious conversation she'd ever had. She had a million questions, but figured he already knew what every one of them was, since he held all the answers. So, silently she watched him, as he wrestled with what he wanted to say.

But as she watched, she realized that he appeared weak and shaky. As if he were sick. Sudden concern coiled in Angel's belly. Not for herself . . . for him. That sat her up straighter in the saddle, had her fussing with herself.

She 'd never cared before about another living being. Her mother's face popped into her consciousness, as if to put the lie to her assertion. Angel forced the image back into oblivion, refused to acknowledge it. It *was* true. She'd never given another living soul, *including* her mother, this much of her time, much less her thoughts. So why this man? And why now, on the very day she'd buried the one person she was supposed to care about? Okay, so he'd saved her life. But it wasn't as if she'd asked him to. Still, she supposed she owed him for that.

But this concern of hers? No. She didn't owe him that. Didn't want to feel it. Didn't want to care. She firmed her jaw, preparing to harden her heart against him. But before she could tuck her emotions away, before she could fade away inside herself . . . he raised his head. His gaze met hers.

Angel's stomach muscles clenched with what she saw there. Death. Reflected in the man's eyes. His own death. She knew this because she'd seen this same look, only more pronounced, in her mother's eyes as she lay on her bed, wasting away. Angel swallowed, didn't know what to say. Just knew she felt sad for him. And hated it. *All right, fine*, she thought. But it was because he'd saved her life, and for no other reason.

"As you can see," he began suddenly, but speaking slowly, deliberately. "I don't have . . . a lot of time left. Which is why I came here today. I wasn't expecting to find your mother . . . gone. Or to see you being lynched. But that doesn't change anything. For me . . . it's time. So I'm offering you everything I have. My holdings are considerable, Angel. Considerable. And they're all yours, if you'll just come with me and claim 'em."

Go with him? Concern and sadness fled. It was wariness that now edged Angel's chin up. "Just like that? Just go with you and claim it?" She stared at him, waited. He said nothing. Angel had to wonder why he didn't, even as she added, "Nothing's that simple, Mr. Daltry. Nothing. How do I know you're telling the truth, that you even have this . . . this home you're so willing to give away?"

"Why would I lie?"

Angel's expression hardened. "I can think of ten reasons. For one, you might want the same thing from me that Kennedy did."

Shaking his head, Mr. Daltry looked disappointed. Although Angel felt guilty, she refused to flinch, even when he said, "I expect I know why you'd think that, seeing what your mother—Well, seeing her circumstances. But Angel, not all men are like that. I'm sure as hell not."

With those words, he held her gaze, a diamond-cold glint in his eyes. Angel refused to acknowledge her growing conviction that he spoke the truth. A moment passed. Then another. Finally, Mr. Daltry's expression changed, he looked defeated, resigned. When he next spoke, his voice was soft, his words hard. "But beyond that . . . I'm dying. So, please, let me do this one last thing for you. Let me give you everything your folks couldn't."

A beautiful speech, she had to admit. But Angel persisted in their staring match. Then she blurted, "Why? Tell me the why of it."

To her surprise, Mr. Daltry exploded, his face reddening. "Because I *owe* you, dammit. Can't you leave it at that? I owe you. Let me do this—please, Angel. Hasn't anyone *ever* given you anything before? Hasn't anyone ever been kind to you in your *whole* life?"

Even as the roan started at the man's outburst and he reined it in, tears sprang to Angel's eyes. "No," she cried out. "No, they haven't. And I don't want them to. I don't *need* things. Or kindness. I just need to be left alone. That's all I want. To be left alone." *And not to hurt or be afraid all the time,* added that inner voice.

Mr. Daltry put a hand up to her, but didn't touch her. "I'm sorry, Angel. I never meant to upset you. I'm sorry."

Angel glared down at him, her every breath coming rapidly. She struggled for control . . . and finally gained it. Now that she could, she spoke evenly. "You didn't upset me. You can't."

"All right," he agreed readily enough. "Then, will you just take a minute to think about what I said?"

Angel stared at him, realizing she was doing just that. Thinking about what he'd said, what he'd offered. Her mind raced, considering the facts. If what he said was true—and it was a big if, she knew, but she was coming to believe it—then he was offering her a prime chance at the kind of life she wanted, one that otherwise she'd have to fight and scratch for. And could still fail to attain . . . unless she married to get it. That thought hardened something inside her. She wasn't willing to marry. She'd been around men enough, had seen enough of their handiwork, to know she'd never hand her life over to one in that way.

So, she thought, what if he *was* telling the truth, what if his wealth *was* now hers, with no strings attached? She hated herself for it, but she glanced down at him, studied him under the sweep of her eyelashes. Yep, he looked sick enough, was probably dying. So, she couldn't be foolhardy enough just to walk away, could she? No, she couldn't. But her next thought had her cocking her head at a questioning angle and remarking, "It seems to me, Mr. Daltry, that a man such as you would have a family."

He squeezed his eyes shut, looking as if someone had slapped him openhanded. Angel's stomach clenched against the emotions she had obviously unleashed in him and against whatever grisly tale she might have to hear. But all she could do was wait for him. Finally, he nodded, opened his eyes, and said, "I did. I had a family. But they're . . . all gone."

Beyond grateful for his simple statement of the facts, Angel all too eagerly rushed to say, "I see." She then changed the subject, realizing how painful it must be for him. "What would I be claiming? And what would I have to do to get it?"

A sudden, unexpected smile played around the corners of Mr. Daltry's mouth. His eyes brightened. "You wouldn't have to do a thing but ride with me to my place. I've got the papers there, all drawn up. All you have to do is sign them. And everything I own is yours. Free and clear."

Angel nodded, liking the sound of that, but she had yet another question. "Again, Mr. Daltry, what exactly would I own?"

Now he grinned. "Oh, I forgot to say, didn't I? I'm talking about a real home, Angel. A big spread. A cattle ranch. With a house. And money—a lot of it. Something you've never had before."

Something you've never had before. His words of sympathy ate at her. She couldn't allow them to stand. "That's what's eating at me, Mr. Daltry. See, you're right. I haven't had any of those things. But how do *you* know that? How do you know so much about me and my life? And why do you care? Because I don't believe anybody's that good, that giving. Not without a reason. And I'd like to hear yours."

But he didn't answer right away. Instead, he fiddled with the brim of his hat, adjusting it lower over his eyes. Only then, when he apparently had his hat the way he wanted it, did he look up at her and say, "I want to tell you the why of it, Angel. And I swear I will. But not now. Not here. First, I want you to know me better before you hear my story."

Suddenly, his whole demeanor changed, as though he were imploring her to believe him. He shifted his weight, put a hand out, as if he meant to touch her. But didn't. ''I know what I'm asking you to do is hard. But . . . I need you to come with me on faith alone. I'm asking you to trust me. Can you do that?''

Still seated atop the roan, which stamped a hoof as if to signal its impatience with this standoff, Angel leaned over, abruptly hooked the reins from Mr. Daltry's unresisting hands, and gathered the leather leads into her own. She straightened up and shoved her tangled hair out of her eyes. ''No. I can't do that. I haven't kept body and soul intact by trusting strangers, Mr. Daltry. I'll be collecting my things and leaving Red River Station. But not with you.''

She tensed, preparing herself for action should he try to stop her again. But he didn't. He just stood there, looking up at her, his sick old heart in his blue eyes. Angel bit back a yelp of frustration. This was why she didn't get involved with folks . . . this right here, this feeling of being obliged, of *owing* someone what she couldn't afford to feel. And she didn't like that one bit.

''Dammit,'' she blurted, looking away as she broke the heavy silence between them. Then she turned on him. ''It was a foolhardy thing you did, stepping in like that with those men. But I'm much obliged to you, Mr. Daltry, just the same, for doing it. And that's more than anyone else has ever gotten from me in my life. So count yourself lucky. But seeing the way things are here at the station, I think I'll be riding on before sunset. Good day to you.''

To hell with feeling like this. To hell with him. Angel yanked the reins, dug in her heels. The roan responded, began to turn at her command.

''Wait,'' Mr. Daltry cried out. ''Please, Angel.''

She bit back another curse, but reined her mount, sat rigidly, arrowed her gaze down to meet his, and . . . waited.

His mouth worked, he stumbled over his words. ''I want to—I mean, I need to—''

''You need to what, Mr. Daltry? I've said my thanks. And

I meant them. But now I'm ready to get my things from the hotel, cut my losses, and move on." Again she urged the roan away.

"Wait!" he again cried out. Angel instinctively pulled back on the reins. As soon as she did, Mr. Daltry blurted, "I paid for your room at the hotel all these years."

His words split the air like the snap of a bullwhip. Angel recoiled, shook her head. "That's not true. I've worked there since I was twelve. I cleaned—"

"Yes, you did," he agreed. "You cleaned the rooms and cooked. And I paid for your upkeep. There was no job, Angel. Saul didn't need the help, didn't have that many customers. I paid him to keep you hired on. And gave him money to pay you with. Enough to live on—just enough so's you wouldn't be suspicious of the amount. I always wished it could be more."

Sickness washed over Angel. She'd been so proud of her independence. It was the one thing she thought she'd done on her own. Her eyes narrowed at this deception, this seeming betrayal. "There was plenty of work. I—"

"There was no work."

He said it so quietly that, again, Angel believed him. Her throat seemed to close on her, even as her heartbeat faltered. She swallowed, her mouth worked. "Why?"

"Because I owe you," came his quiet answer. Then, "Go on, if you want, Angel. I wouldn't blame you one bit. But just tell me, where will you go? What will you do?"

Angel considered him. And his questions, the same ones she'd posed to herself only moments ago. The same ones she still had no answers to. All she knew was she didn't intend to accept his offer. And so she gave the only answer she could. "That isn't any of your business, I expect."

Mr. Daltry nodded, firmed his lips. "Maybe not. And neither is my next question, but—do you have *any* money, enough to get you anywhere?"

A guilty flush warmed her—she had *no* money. There'd been some with Virginia's things, but she'd left it, wanting no part of coins earned that way. Still, Angel managed to keep her expression neutral as she considered this man standing next to her horse. A horse *he'd* bought for her, she suddenly remembered. That realization did nothing to warm her heart toward him, though. Instead, hard as nails, she leaned over, bracing her hand against her knee, putting herself almost in his face. "Why're you asking? You still wanting to pay for me?"

He neither moved nor flinched. But his expression hardened. "I am."

Taken aback, Angel straightened up in the saddle and glared down at him. He shook his head, saying, "But not in the way you're still so willing to think. If you don't want the home I'm offering, then fine. I'll give you the money to start over somewhere else. Only I didn't bring the kind of cash you'll need. It's at my ranch."

A cynical burst of laughter erupted from Angel. "Your ranch. We're right back where we started." Angel shook her head, looking away as she considered the bleak horizon, the one she could see in the distance, and the one she couldn't see in the future. And decided, *Oh, what the hell . . .*

She looked back down at Mr. Daltry. "I tell you what, old man, tell me one thing now, and maybe I *will* go with you. Maybe I'll be there to hear your whole story."

"Ask it," he said.

"All right. Tell me why . . . to you . . . my life was worth saving."

Mr. Daltry's quiet consideration of her ruled the next few moments. Angel had the distinct impression that what he had to say would not please her. Speaking as if the words had been forced out of him at gunpoint, he said, "Because I owed your father. Not just your mother."

Angel tightened her hands on the reins, pressed her legs around the roan's ribs. She stared at the gray-haired man, noticing again how haggard, almost gaunt, he looked. But it was his words, not his appearance, that finally commanded her attention. "You owed *my* father—Tom Devlin, dirt farmer? You have to *know* someone before you can owe them anything, Mr. Daltry."

His jaw firmed. "I did know him. And your mother. I knew them together, when you were a little girl. There. I've answered your question. I owed them, but they're gone now. So, therefore, I owe you."

As confused as she was curious, as tired as she was edgy, Angel just gave up and shrugged. "So . . . pay me, if you're so all-fired determined to do it."

Chuckling ruefully, he said, "That's what I've been trying to do—all afternoon and most of your life before that. But now . . . well, I don't have much time left. So what do you say?"

She didn't have anything to say. Not just yet. All this talk of leaving, of debts owed, of setting things to rights . . . The man was dying. Angel exhaled a breath. It'd been that kind of a day all around. A day for dying. Still, when she spoke, it was with more caring than she would've thought possible. "Want to go with a clean slate, huh? With no marks against you?"

He nodded. "Something like that. So, will you go with me?" He stopped, frowned, and then added, "To my ranch, I mean. I expect that up yonder"—he pointed to the heavens above—"they don't let you bring guests with you. Leastwise, I've always heard you have to be personally invited."

Despite herself, Angel chuckled, a rarity for her, born as it was of pure humor, and not cynicism or derision. "I tell you, Mr. Daltry, the way things were going today—had it not been for your interfering ways, I'd be in a position to get you a real answer to that."

He grinned back at her. "See there? Now *you* owe me. So, will you come with me?"

Angel's grin widened, came near to being a laugh. She tried to tame it, even looked away, taking in the man-made, muddied sameness that was Red River Station.

Finally, she looked back down at him, admitting to herself that while pleas or force would never have worked with her, humor had. "All right, Mr. Daltry. You win. I'll go with you to your ranch."

*   *   *

Angel knew she should have asked Wallace Daltry more questions. Like just how far away his ranch was. They'd been traveling west for two nights and three days now, over the rolling and hilly land of north Texas's central lowlands. They'd crossed long stretches of sandy prairie and kept the raging, rain-swollen Red River on their right. And they'd fought to keep themselves dry for the entire length of their trek. Spring was proving, on a daily basis, to be stormy and vengeful.

But as time wore on, and despite the almost constant deluges, which were followed by steamy, spirit-drooping lulls in the downpours, Angel's amazement grew. Amazement at the open country. Amazement that she was indeed away from Red River Station—for the first time since she was five years old. But most of all, amazement that she was alive at all—thanks to Mr. Daltry—to enjoy this growing sense of freedom.

And that was another thing. She'd decided that, given the distance and the timing, mere luck had had nothing to do with Mr. Daltry's arrival in Red River Station less than one minute before she was swinging from that now distant scrub oak. No, it had to be something else, something more than fate or good timing.

Mr. Daltry had said God led him there. But Angel had her doubts. Sure, she knew her Bible. Hadn't her mother taught her how to read and how to form her letters using the Bible? And hadn't she held her young daughter and read to her, and talked with her about the stories and the lessons in the Good Book? At least, she had until Angel'd been old enough—nine or ten, she recalled—to understand what it was her mother did for a living. And what the names people called Virginia Devlin meant. After that, the closeness between them had evaporated, along with the lessons.

Just then, the roan stumbled, yanking Angel out of her memories. Steadying her horse with a pat, and realizing where her mind had wandered, she frowned at this dim memory from the before times. Before her father was killed. Before Virginia began selling herself for money.

"You okay?"

Angel looked over at Mr. Daltry. Every time she got quiet, he asked her that. A sigh escaped her. "I'm fine. My horse stumbled."

He nodded, said, "Up here a ways, we'll stop for the night. I know just the sheltered spot, in case it rains again. You'll be glad to know that tomorrow, about half a day's ride west of here, we'll be home." With that, and without waiting for any response from her, he retreated back into his thoughts.

Knowing it'd do her no good to question him, Angel returned to her own thoughts, thoughts about God, she recalled. She supposed that when she'd been a little girl, she'd believed in Him. But not so much now. No, she couldn't call herself particularly religious or pious. Never saw a need to be. Never saw the proof, as she grew up, that anyone beyond herself—and sometimes not even herself—gave a damn what happened to her.

Well, except for Mr. Daltry. She threw a glance in his direction. He was looking into the hazy, wavery distance. Probably searching for that sheltered spot for their night's rest. Angel took advantage of his preoccupation to continue her scrutiny of him. He certainly seemed to believe in God, she decided. And she was coming to believe in Mr. Daltry. So, maybe she could give God some thought one day.

Just then, Mr. Daltry turned his head, trapped her with his gaze. "You know your mama didn't really have any choice, don't you?"

Angel's belly tightened. Every other word out of this man's mouth seemed to be about her personal business. She shifted her weight in the saddle and cleared her throat, delaying her answer. Finally, she asked, "No choice about what exactly, Mr. Daltry?"

"About what she did . . . had to do. For a living. She had you to feed. And there was no other choice open to her."

Angel firmed her jaw and held tight to a lifetime of shame and derision. "There's always a choice. She could have left."

"And gone where? And how? You weren't much more'n a baby when your pa died. And the only money she had was from selling the wagon and team. She had no kin to help her. And no reason to continue on out West with your father gone. So, there she was . . . a woman alone with a child. What should she have done when her money ran out and you were crying for food?''

Angel looked down at her fingers, now knotted around the reins. And hated him for putting this sick feeling back in her stomach. And for this new image in her head of her mother— a young widow, alone, afraid, a small child in tow. But Angel was not ready to concede anything. So she shrugged. ''She could've done other things, made do with what she had at the station.''

''Like what?''

Exasperated by his questioning, she blurted, ''I don't know. Maybe take in wash. Teach school. Work at Chisholm's. Anything but what she did.''

Mr. Daltry stared at her and then stretched in his saddle and fiddled with his hat. Angel gritted her teeth at the man's slowness in answering. But after three days of dealing with him, she knew he was ordering his thoughts and couldn't be rushed. And so, she waited, thinking that he seemed to take great care with each word he said to her, as if he were guiding her gently to certain conclusions. Which only made her that much more wary of every word he uttered. She didn't like being led. By anybody. For any reason.

After another reflective moment, Mr. Daltry finally said, ''Not in those days, she couldn't. Red River Station wasn't the growing town it is now. Back then, it wasn't nothing more than a stopover, a way station. Nothing too permanent. Certainly no school. And Chisholm didn't need any help. Hell, *nobody* back then had a need for a decent woman.''

A decent woman? Angel raised an eyebrow and made an abrupt noise at the back of her throat. Mr. Daltry's eyes narrowed. He said, ''Your mother *was* a decent woman. Right up to the end.''

Each of his words rang with the weight of a sacred conviction. Angel's bottom lip puckered stubbornly against her top one. She hated these conversations, hated the plodding pace and the unchanging scenery. "That's easy for you to say, Mr. Daltry. But you didn't live with her decision. I did."

The words were no more out of her mouth than Mr. Daltry made a strangled noise that alarmed Angel, because she now knew what came next. Sure enough, the poor man's body was racked with another coughing fit that bent him double. Angel bit at her bottom lip, telling herself that her fear for him was more a fear for herself. She just knew, with each fit, that he'd die on her and leave her out here with only the vaguest of ideas about where she was and where she was headed. After a minute of watching him, and of feeling helpless, she asked, "You okay?"

He nodded, despite his coughing spasm, and strangled out, "I'm fine." When it finally eased, leaving him red-faced and weak, his blue eyes tearing up, he said, "You're wrong when you say I didn't live with her decision. Because I did. And still do. After your father . . . passed on, I tried to help, tried to give her enough money so she could resettle. But she wouldn't take it, said she'd die first before accepting my charity."

The man's unexpected words had Angel reining in her horse. Mr. Daltry followed suit, met her questioning gaze. "So she did have a choice," Angel challenged.

Mr. Daltry shook his head, saying, "No. No, she didn't."

To Angel, time seemed to slow. She let a moment or two pass. Then . . . "Mr. Daltry," she began, speaking slowly, "if I had a gun right now, I'd shoot you for being closemouthed with the truth when it suits you."

He nodded, said, "I believe you would, Angel." Then he chuckled and ran a hand over his mouth. "And maybe you should. If you'd like, you can use my gun. It'd be a mercy."

Angel huffed out her breath, shook her head, ignoring his offer. "Tell me why my mother would turn down your money. Why she would let pride prevent her from accepting help and instead turn to whoring to feed me." Then something she'd missed before pelted Angel's consciousness. She narrowed her eyes. Suspicion had her cocking her head. "What'd you do to her, that she'd refuse your help?"

Mr. Daltry winced, as if he'd had a sudden pain. But not a physical one. "I didn't do anything to her." With that, he turned his face away from Angel and put his heels to his buckskin horse, urging it past her and onward. Frustration exploded through Angel, tensing her every muscle. She wanted to yell at this old man, wanted to throw something at him.

But just as suddenly, she let go of it and went limp, slumping in her saddle. Exhaling, firming her lips together, she looked after his back. It'd been like this for the past three days. Their talking always stalled when she asked why. Why he wanted to help her. Why he'd wanted to help Virginia Devlin, a young widow with a daughter. And why she had refused it. And why Angel should accept it.

But learning now of her mother's refusal of help only hardened Angel's heart that much more. Virginia Devlin had been offered a chance at a decent life. But hadn't taken it. For whatever reason. To Angel's way of thinking, no reason could be good enough. Not pride. Not any injustice done her. It couldn't warrant the life she'd therefore given her daughter, the victim of her decision. So what else could Angel think?

Virginia Devlin had evidently preferred to wallow in mud and to drag her daughter right along with her. Angel's features stiffened as she reached her rough-edged conclusions. She watched Mr. Daltry a moment longer before shaking her head in dismissal and urging her roan after the man's departing back.

She was surely glad to know they'd be at that danged ranch of his tomorrow. Because she needed answers. And he wasn't giving any until she signed some legal papers he had waiting for her. Only then, as he'd said maybe fifty times, would he tell her what she needed to know, what she had a right to know. Angel watched him, tensing when yet another coughing spasm—they were coming quicker and harder today, she noticed—seized him. This one, like all the others, arched his back and then bent him over his horse's neck. This man wasn't long for this world, Angel knew.

That thought settled a frown on her features. She was surprised to realize she wanted to help him, to do something, even if it was just to pat his back or say a comforting word to him. She knew she should do something, but a lifetime of doing without comfort herself rendered her unable to do much but hope he'd live long enough to bring them both safely to his home.

And once there, she'd sign those papers. And have her answers from him. Then, she supposed, they'd live there together until he . . . died. She looked over at him. His coughing eased, he straightened up. Angel winced at the image of herself as a nursemaid to a dying man. Well, she knew a few sickroom things from tending her mother during her last days . . . not that Virginia'd even known her daughter was there most of the time.

A stab of pain lanced through Angel's heart. She immediately firmed her jaw, pulling her thoughts away from that seedy little back-room scene, and forcing them to the future that Mr. Daltry was offering her.

And that was exactly what it was. A future. His home would be hers. But of more importance to Angel was the realization that her life would be her own. A rare and fleeting smile found its way to her lips. Her life would be her own. She liked the sound of that. Liked the sound of living on her own terms. Without hiding. Without running. Without fear. Finally.

And it all started tomorrow. Just half a day's ride west, Mr. Daltry had said earlier. A giddiness Angel didn't know she possessed tickled her stomach, had her biting down on her bottom lip, had her hoping, and looking toward the future. And the ever-closer horizon.

Only good things could happen to her from here on out, she just knew it.

Three

Yesterday's hope fled. In its wake followed yesterday's moment of giddiness. Because Angel's future was this new day . . . this dew-dampened early morning. A pink and red sky filled the vast blue canvas above, overshadowing the sun rising beyond it. Angel lowered her gaze from the sky, stared again at Mr. Daltry's still form next to the cold, ashy remains of last night's campfire. She swallowed, the motion more mechanical than voluntary.

Behind her, the precariously poised jumble of boulders she'd stumbled back against, only moments ago, pressed against her spine. Their impersonal coldness seeped through her clothing, cooled her fevered emotions. But her knees, she knew, could give at any moment. So could her stomach, were it not already empty. Her palms scraped across the rough, cold rocks behind her, as if she sought their solidness, as if she needed to feel their bulk. And still, she pushed against them, wanting to force herself through them.

This was madness, her hammering heart warned with each tripping beat. Angel knew the truth of that. She willed herself to breathe . . . in and out . . . in and out. Then, she blinked. Listened to her blood rush through her veins. Tried to deny that she'd awakened to the sight of Mr. Daltry lying there . . . in his blood-soaked bedroll . . . with a bone-handled knife protruding from his chest. But she knew—somewhere in a tiny corner of her mind—that it *was* true. Because here she stood . . . still staring at him, unable to look away.

Then, as if possessed of a will of its own, Angel's right hand crept its way up her clothing, up her neck, until it found her mouth and cupped itself tightly over her lips. A fresh surge of panic shivered through her, had her breathing hard through her nostrils. She hadn't heard a thing. And the horses . . . they hadn't raised so much as a nicker of a fuss all night. Angel pictured herself sleeping across the campfire from Mr. Daltry. That close, she'd been. And yet, she hadn't heard a thing. How was that possible?

Who could have done such a thing . . . and so quietly? Indians? Certainly. Outlaws? Maybe. The prairie was lousy with them. But this killing . . . done like this, with all their belongings still here, and her left alive? She shook her head. It just didn't figure with what she knew of outlaws and Indians. But what about those Henton drovers from Red River Station? Could they have followed her and Mr. Daltry and picked their moment? Immediately she discounted that notion. No, they'd have killed her, too—if not instead.

Angel pursed her lips. She knew enough of the world to realize that she—a lone, unarmed woman—would not be alive right now to tell about this cold-booded murder, if it'd been Indians or outlaws or even the Henton drovers. But Mr. Daltry's murder *wasn't* the result of a cold-blooded, random act. No, it was personal. And something that had nothing to do with her. Which was why she'd been left alive. Was it so she *could* tell about it? But tell who? And why. Mr. Daltry'd said he was a rich rancher. But since he had no family left, who would care?

Angel found herself focusing on the unknown murderer. She frowned, tried to figure out what type of person would just sneak in and kill a man in his sleep. A cowardly type, she reckoned, lowering her hand from her mouth. This murder spoke of a grudge. A wrong that had needed righting.

She stared at the body that had been Mr. Daltry's, at the blood that no longer flowed from his chest but stained his blankets. Now she'd never have her answers from him. Yes, it was a cold thought, she knew, and one that decent folks would have gasped at. But then again, no one had ever accused her of being decent, now had they? But what about Mr. Daltry? Was he decent? What could that old man have done to someone to bring this on himself? It had to be something awful.

What had he been capable of? And what, after all, did she really know about him? Nothing. Except what she'd seen with her own eyes. She couldn't speak for how he treated other folks. Or could she? He had faced down that lynch mob and saved her life when he didn't have to. That said something for the man. So did the respect with which those drovers had treated him. Angel weighed all this, decided that, yes, Mr. Daltry was a somebody. That much had been evident.

All those facts added together, she knew, were why she'd placed her trust in him . . . for the first time in her life. And now look what had happened. He'd saved her life four days ago, only to lose his now. And once again—twice in one week—her life had been spared. It had to mean something. And she couldn't say why or even how she felt about that. So, what was she supposed to do now? Because before this— meaning Mr. Daltry's murder—she'd looked to him for direction.

But he was no more forthcoming in death than he had been in life. Angel cocked her head. Had he been a good man? she asked herself. Or had he deserved to die like this? She closed her eyes against her own thoughts . . . and called herself a fool for not thinking this through before now. Although he had prevented her from being hanged, she had no firsthand proof that anything he'd said to her was the truth. Did he even deserve this awful feeling of loss that had settled rocklike in her belly?

That thought forced her to consider new and frightening possibilities. That ranch of his might exist only in his head. Those legal papers awaiting her signature could be nonexistent. Angel's heart pounded with sudden fear for herself, for her immediate future. Her tongue flicked out to moisten suddenly dry lips. What would she do if had lied to her? Where would she go? She had nothing but the roan she was riding. No money. No help. No direction.

Just like your mother.

A surge of anger squelched that comparison. She was *not* like her mother. Never would be, either. Never. She'd take charge of her life, would live it clean. She'd show Virginia Devlin. For long seconds, Angel breathed hard and glared at . . . nothing—until her anger finally subsided, leaving her, surprisingly, feeling better about herself. She *could* do this. *Do what?* she asked herself. *Find that ranch,* came her answer. Yes, that was good. Finding the ranch was *doing* something. It wasn't standing here being scared and doubting everything she knew to be true.

Angel pushed away from the boulders, looked westward. A half-day's ride west, he'd said yesterday. She turned to Mr. Daltry's body, and grimaced. She knew what she had to do. Take him along. It was the only decent thing to do. Bury him on his own land. Well, it was her land now, she supposed. If it existed. If she believed him. And then, she realized that she did believe him, she knew the ranch existed, and when she got there, those papers—and a new and a good life—would be waiting for her. Just as Mr. Daltry had promised.

Straddling his big brown horse with the ease of one born to the saddle, Jack Daltry directed his gelding's steps across the fenced-off stretch of north Texas prairie that fronted the ranch house he called home. He didn't like the look of things as he rode in and surveyed the yard. Too deserted. Too quiet for a sunny afternoon. Where was Pa? And Lou and Boots? Those two old hands always stayed behind when the drovers took the herd north to Abilene.

That wasn't to say he'd expected a welcoming committee. After all, no one even knew he was coming home. And might not even be glad he had. But, hell, *somebody* should have been here. Somebody besides the few disinterested chickens roaming free and scratching at the barren ground. Jack's eyes narrowed as he became certain that the place was deserted. He reined Buffalo in, started to dismount . . .

Then . . . he saw it. The front door of the house, as if in confirmation of his fear, hung open.

His heart skipped a beat. He resettled himself in the saddle, patted his gelding's shoulder when it sidestepped at his mixed signals. "Whoa. Easy there," he crooned absently, all the while trying to deny the sudden, skin-crawling certainty that he was being watched. By hostile eyes. As casually as possible, he made a visual sweep of the yard, looking for a furtive movement, or sunlight glinting off gunmetal. But he saw nothing. All remained calm and quiet.

Emboldened, Jack pivoted this way and that in the saddle, putting a cautionary hand to the six-shooter holstered at his right hip. But he didn't draw his weapon. Not yet. Didn't want to provoke someone into firing. Damn, he cursed himself, he shouldn't have stayed away so long. Never should've said the things he had four months ago. Never should have told the old man he was through with him, that he could just run the spread however he saw fit. *Leave me out of it. I don't want any part of it.*

Jack could still hear himself yelling that over his shoulder as he made for the door last January, the same door that stood open . . . and—*whoa!*—now had the business end of a rifle poking out of its darkened gap of a frame. The long rifle was aimed right at his heart.

Son of a—Jack's fist tightened reflexively around his horse's reins. Under cover of his stiff-brimmed hat, he watched the doorway, tried to size up his situation. From what he could gather, there was only one person inside. And it sure as hell wasn't Pa. They'd left off badly together, but not this badly. But whoever it was, one was enough. Because, sitting out in the open like he was, Jack knew he was a ready target.

So, with no choice, not if he wished to see the sun set, he remained still, didn't test the mettle of the stranger in his home. *The bastard had just better hope he isn't pointing Pa's Winchester at me,* Jack fumed. As galling as that notion was, Jack had lived most of his twenty-eight years knowing that the man with the bigger gun—and the drop on you—made the rules. So, he might as well make his peace now and find out later what was going on, where Pa was.

"Hello, in the house," he called out. "I don't mean you any harm. Show yourself."

The words were no more out of his mouth than a metallic crackling sound split the air and echoed against the windless sky, heralding the bullet that scudded into the ground mere inches from where Jack sat his horse. The startled gelding shied, tried to rear, bellowed his displeasure. Cussing through gritted teeth, losing his hat, Jack tensed and hunched over Buffalo, fought to keep his seat in the saddle, fought to haul down on the reins. A dusty battle ensued, but finally he bested his mount, bringing the prancing, circling horse under strict control.

Again he faced the house—*his* house, dammit—ready this time to return the favor to the son of a bitch who'd shot at him in his own front yard and had nearly gotten him thrown. He reached for his pistol—but then . . . he saw her. Jack stilled, smoothed his hand away from his tooled-leather holster, and stared openly at the woman standing in the sun-dappled shadows cast across the covered verandah.

He frowned. There was something naggingly familiar about her. He couldn't say exactly what, though. Who was she? And more importantly, what was she doing here? Then, it hit him—the only explanation there could be. Jack relaxed, even chuckled, shook his head. *Well, I'll be. Pa got himself a woman.*

The realization had him turning a critical eye on her. She appeared to be a young woman, too. He surveyed her again, and frowned at what he saw. A mighty young woman. And given the wild look of her and the reception she'd given him, a spirited one. Her long black hair tumbled past her shoulders, brushed against her narrow waist. There wasn't much else, at this distance, that he could see . . . except that she was slender and tall. And again raising what Jack could now clearly see *was* his father's Winchester.

"Whoa, ma'am," Jack called out, gesturing to match his words. "You can put that rifle down. I don't mean you any harm."

She didn't relax her hold on the weapon, but she did call

out, "You've got ten seconds to state your business, stranger."

Her voice, low and husky, was enough of a warning. But it was her challenge that went right through Jack, had him yelling back, "*My* business? I don't have to state anything, lady. I live here."

The woman stiffened, the Winchester dipped, but was instantly refitted to her shoulder. She called out, "It seems to me . . . being the one who stepped outside onto the porch just now . . . that if you lived here, I'd have run into you inside this house. So you'll have to do better than that, mister. Because *I'm* the one who lives here. Alone."

Jack didn't like one thing she'd just said. Especially *alone*. That gnawed at his stomach and had him calling back, "Where's Wallace Daltry?"

Again, she didn't say anything right off. That had Jack's pulse hammering. Was bad news what lay behind her slience? He wasn't sure she'd answer at all, or even that he'd want to hear what she had to say. But when she did speak, it wasn't to answer his question. It was to pose a question of her own. "Who wants to know?"

"I do," was all he felt like divulging. Up until now, he'd been thinking that, most likely, Pa'd accompanied the men and the herd up to the Abilene railhead and had left her here to look after the place. *And a damned fine job she's doing of it, too,* he thought sourly. But now, he wasn't so sure. About anything. Obviously a lot had happened since he'd left four months ago on that cold January day.

And still, Jack realized, she hadn't answered him. "Well?" he called out.

"Well what?" was her questioning response.

This was about the last thing he needed, Jack decided as his eyebrows descended down over his nose. He'd been a long time on the trail home from New Mexico. A long time. He was tired, hot, dirty, thirsty—and more than a little concerned about his father. All things considered, he wasn't someone she wanted to mess with right now. "You always answer questions with another question, ma'am?"

She shrugged. Or at least, the Winchester wavered momentarily before again finding the bull's-eye she obviously saw painted over his heart. "Depends on the question," was her only comment.

Jack's gut clenched. He scrubbed a hand over his growth of bristly beard. But a calmer part of his brain reminded him that he'd never killed a woman before. And she probably wasn't a good one to start with, since this contrary creature could be his father's wife. And his stepmother. Now *that* got a mirthless chuckle out of him.

"Something funny, mister?"

Jack sobered, stared pointedly at her. "Not a thing from where I'm sitting, ma'am. Pardon my lingo, but just who the hell *are* you, anyway?"

"Who the hell are *you*?" came her mimicking retort.

Jack huffed out his breath, looking away while he searched for control. Finally, he returned his gaze to her standing there on the verandah, and decided she was about as forthcoming as a tree stump when it came to giving out information. Still, he complied with her question. "I'm Jack Daltry, that's who the hell I am."

He expected she would lower the gun. And apologize. And welcome him. He should have known better. Because she tensed even more and told him, "I haven't heard any mention of a *Jack* Daltry."

Jack sat up straighter in his saddle. Pa hadn't even mentioned him? *Whew.* He'd left things worse off than he thought. But he wasn't about to tell her that. "That may be," he drawled. "And yet . . . here I sit."

"Says you."

Damned contrary woman. "Maybe we ought to start with who *you* are."

She didn't say anything. Jack waited her out. Finally, she said, "The name's Angel."

"Angel?" Humor laced his voice. "Pardon me, ma'am, but you don't look like any angel to me."

"Yeah? How many you seen, cowboy?"

Caught off guard, Jack chuckled. "Well, you got me there. Angel what?"

"Devlin."

Her full name hit him with the force of a fist to the gut. The humor fled from his face. *Angel Devlin? The wild-child daughter of Virginia Devlin?* The man-talk around Red River Station had it that this girl—an untouched, untamed beauty— was someone no man in his right mind would dare approach . . . at risk of his own life, as the stories went. He'd heard that she'd used a knife on more than one man who'd tried. Somber as a hanging judge, Jack cocked his head, considered her, wondered what she was doing here.

"I see you've heard the name."

Her words had him smoothing his expression and saying, "Yep. I've heard the name." If she was still calling herself Devlin, then she wasn't hitched to Pa. *Just warming his bed, most likely.* Jack shot her a look hardened by what he knew of her, by what he thought of her.

It was that lack of respect, and his resulting disregard for the threat she posed—rifle or no—that had him nudging his horse forward. She *was* only Angel Devlin, after all. And this was *his* land, no matter that she claimed to live on the Circle D. *Not if I have anything to say about it,* Jack thought. With each step of Buffalo's hooves, with each sway of his horse's gait toward the hitching rail that outlined the verandah, Jack's mood darkened. What a day this was turning out to be. He had hoped, in coming home, to mend fences with Pa. But now?

He kept his gaze on Angel Devlin. And realized he harbored a growing certainty that the long-awaited fence-mending was unlikely. He also believed without proof—it was only a gut feeling—that somehow she was partly responsible. And yet, he continued to approach, knew he was daring her to shoot him. But no rifle fire rang out to stop him. He told himself that was just as he'd figured. And then willed his heart to stop thudding.

But he never let his apprehension show on his face. Not when he reined in his horse. Not when he dismounted and tied Buffalo to the rail. Not when he turned his back on Angel Devlin and ambled over to fetch his black felt Stetson. Not when he scooped it up and hit it against his thigh to dust it off. And not when he settled his hat on his head, his back still presented to her as a broad target, as a way of showing her he considered her no threat.

Only then, his hands to his waist, did he turn to face her. She hadn't moved or given an inch. Still had the rifle aimed at him. Jack shook his head, not knowing which outweighed the other—his growing respect for her grit, or his exasperation with her obvious mule-headedness. "Well? What's it going to be, Miss Devlin? Why don't you just put down that Winchester of my father's, and we'll talk?"

He paused, giving her a chance to comply. She didn't. Obviously, she wanted no part of his peace offering. Jack looked down to study his boots as he collected himself, and then raised his head, sighting on her. "All right. It's your call, ma'am. But one thing you should know . . . if you shoot at me again, I'll shoot back. Woman or no."

She snorted. "Mister, I ain't shot at *you* yet. That bullet hit the ground because that's where I aimed it. But if I do shoot at you . . . well, you won't be in any shape to shoot back at anyone." She raised the rifle a fraction, and added, "Woman or no."

She dared fling his own words back at him. With long, angry strides, Jack crossed the distance between them, walked up the two steps that led to the raised porch, advanced on her. He expected her to retreat a step or two, to yield the rifle to him. But his momentum was such that he was upon her and grabbing the rifle she still clutched before he realized she'd stood her ground, had no intention of giving up her weapon. Still, he snapped, "Give me that damned thing before you hurt someone."

But still she didn't. She continued to resist, to hold on. Jack's gaze locked with hers. Logic told him he was much bigger than her, told him he could free the weapon with one good twist. Yet, for some reason he couldn't name . . . he didn't. Instead, he stood there, joined to her as they both gripped the loaded gun, and watched her features harden, her black eyes narrow. Then, he saw something in their depths, something ancient, something beyond them both. A shock of fear coursed through him when he realized what it was.

He'd seen that look before . . . on a she-wolf stalking her prey. Surprised, he was ready to let go of the rifle first. But then, inexplicably, she relaxed, complied. Gave over the gun. And silently stared at him, never blinking.

Jack couldn't look away. He didn't know what to think, what to do. She'd shut him down with one look. He swallowed, hunted inside himself for the anger that had carried him up here to her . . . thought of his father . . . and found it. Then, just to show her he wasn't afraid of her, he gripped her arm, turning her to face the open front door. As he marched her across the threshhold, he gritted out, "Inside, Angel Devlin. I want some answers from you. And I want them now."

The front door slammed closed behind them as the man calling himself Jack Daltry kicked it with his booted foot. Angel refused to struggle against his one-handed grip on her arm. She'd not give him the satisfaction of dragging her across the room. No, she'd go with him . . . but on her own terms. So, matching her stride to his as best she could, but still falling short, she accompanied him over to the gun case that stood sentrylike against the same wall as the door.

Once there, he opened the case door without releasing his hold on her, jammed the rifle into a notched space, closed it, and tugged her over to a cowhide sofa. There he let her go, but with a shove that had her sprawling across the cushions.

Angel landed in a heap, but quickly pulled herself upright, fishing her tangled hair out of her eyes. She meant to jump up and make him pay for his rough treatment of her. But she saw she was too late.

He sat leaning forward on the low polished split-wood table that fronted the sofa, his long and muscular legs straddling hers, his hands folded in the breach between his thighs. She looked him up and down. He really was a big man, she was

forced to admit. One she had no chance of besting. Which
was why she'd finally handed the Winchester over to him ...
once she'd seen him up close and had gauged for herself his
resemblance to Wallace Daltry.

Not that she felt better about him because he looked like
his father. No, him being kin—if he truly was—only made
her situation worse. But when he'd ridden up, she had thought
he must be Mr. Daltry's murderer. She feared that the murderer had had second thoughts about leaving her alive, and
had come to finish the job. But this man, unlike the cowardly
killer, had ridden right up to the front door in broad daylight
and had asked questions. Which told her he wasn't the killer.
Because if he was, he wouldn't be sitting here wanting answers. He'd want blood.

And so, deciding she was safe enough for the moment,
Angel melted back against the cushions, her hands folded
together in her lap. And waited. After all, if he was Daltry
kin, as he said he was, then she held the last ace in the deck.
If it was answers he wanted, let him dig for them. Let him
ask the right questions.

He looked her up and down, his gaze finally settling on
her neck. Angel's pulse raced. She knew he'd see: the healing
rope burns. The last thing she wanted to talk about. Sure
enough, he asked, "What happened to your neck?"

But Angel knew how to deflect such questions. She cocked
her head, asking, "You got nose trouble, mister?"

He stiffened, sat up straighter. "Meaning?"

"Keep yours out of my business."

His eyes narrowed. "All right. We can talk about *my* business. Where is everyone?"

Angel shrugged, looking him squarely in his blue eyes ...
eyes she again had to admit were the same color and shape
as Mr. Daltry's. "Who's 'everyone'?"

A muscle jumped in the man's jaw, telling her he didn't
like her answer at all. "My father ... Wallace Daltry. And
two of the hands—two old men—Boots Cornwell and Lou
Montana. Are they here?"

Angel shook her head, didn't bother to brush a strand of

hair obscuring her face. "I've been here a week, mister, and you're the first living soul I've seen."

His eyebrows rose a fraction as he studied her face. Clearly he thought she was lying. But Angel knew the truth of her words. She'd been here a week. Mr. Daltry hadn't been alive when she got here with him. And the place had been deserted otherwise. No live folks. No dead bodies littering the place. No one but her and a couple of horses and some chickens. And there were now fewer chickens than there'd been a week ago.

"A week?" he finally asked, breaking his reflective silence and frowning. When he went on, he sounded to Angel as if he didn't realize he still spoke out loud. "But they had to leave with the herd for Abilene longer than a week ago. Or they'd never make it in time for the sale and the shipment. Which means they—you . . ." He stared at her. "A week? Then you can't be my father's—" He bit back whatever he'd been about to say.

Angel sat up, leaned forward. "Your father's what?"

He leaned into her, his nose almost touching hers. "That's what I don't know, Miss Devlin. Why don't you tell me?"

Forced, at this close range, to look deep into the man's blazing-with-suspicion blue eyes, Angel found she couldn't look away, realized her heart was thumping with the intensity of his scrutiny. The tense seconds ticked away until she gave in first and sat back, staring at him.

"Don't make me ask you again where my father is. But you take your time, get your story straight," he drawled. "I can wait." To prove it, he shifted his weight and propped his hands against his denim-covered thighs.

Angel blinked, hating him. His questions were a trap. She hadn't been absolutely certain, until he rode in, that she was even squatting on the right piece of land. But now, thanks to this man, she knew. And the knowledge only increased her desire to hold on to the only decent home she'd ever known. Under the folds of her skirt, her hands fisted in response to her inner turmoil. If only she'd been able to find those legal papers she was supposed to sign. But there were none here.

Not any, of any sort. Nothing to say who had ownership of this land. And that was strange, she knew.

But worse, until she did find the documents, sign them, and then file them in the county seat at Wichita Falls, she had no real claim to the place. But the man sitting in front of her did . . . *if* he was who he said he was. Her spirits sagged as she had to admit to herself that she believed he was Mr. Daltry's son. Not only did he look like a younger version of his father, but he knew too much, and cared too much, not to be related. And given all that, he had every right to toss her out.

So once she answered his question, and thereby acknowledged Mr. Daltry as his father, this Jack Daltry would have her where he wanted her. But knowing all this didn't stop Angel from stalling. "Who'd you say your father was? And how am I supposed to know if you're lying or not?"

Jack Daltry reared back in surprise and then his expression hardened. "Goddamn you!" he snarled. He jerked forward, catching her off guard as he grabbed her by her arms, pulling her roughly to him. His beard-circled slash of a mouth only inches away, the man's hot breath blasted Angel's face.

But she refused to yield, even though his grip hurt her. All her life, when faced with terror and helplessness, she willed away the slightest show of pain, of vulnerability. And in its stead, she drew on a hardness of the soul that could break rocks. A hardness no one could penetrate, not with fists, not with words, not with threats.

"I've never hurt a woman before in my life," Jack Daltry was telling her. "But I'll break every goddamned bone in your body if you don't start answering my questions right now." His threats hissed through clenched teeth. "I know who you are. And what you are. So don't play coy with me, *Miss* Devlin." He made the title of respect a slur. "*Where* is my father? And you know just who in the hell I'm talking about, too. What'd you do to him? That's all I want to know."

Angel swallowed, certain the lump in her throat was her fear-frozen heart. This time her fading away into herself wasn't working. She remained aware of her blood rushing through her veins, of the weakness of her limbs. She still felt the pain of his grip. Able only to breathe shallowly, her words limped out on short gasps. "I didn't . . . *do* anything . . . to your father . . . I swear it." She stopped to suck in a series of shortened breaths.

Jack Daltry's blue eyes darkened, his grip tightened, almost forcing a scream from Angel, one she would have died before emitting. "Keep talking. You know more. And I'm listening," he assured her with deadly calm.

"You're not . . ." she began, but couldn't finish. The pain . . . it glazed her consciousness. Then he shook her. A cry was wrung from Angel. And a confession. "He's dead," she yelled into his shocked face. "He's dead. But I didn't do it. I swear it."

With his mouth open, his eyes unseeing, he loosened his grip some, as if he weren't aware he still held her. Only then did tears spring to Angel's eyes. And she hated him all the more for making her feel something, anything . . . even if it was pain. "You stupid bastard," she gulped out, crying and shaking now in earnest. "Your father's dead. I buried him out back. Go look for yourself."

He didn't move. She wasn't sure he'd heard her, or understood her words. Because he just sat there, staring at her. Angel's tear-watered gaze clashed with his for long moments. And then . . . it was all too much. All of it—beginning with the morning her mother died and ending right here, right now. Too much. Against her will, against her nature, Angel wilted in his grip. Her forehead slumped against his shoulder.

And he held her like that . . . close to him but still apart from him. Through her tears, Angel could see his chest rising and falling in heaving breaths, breaths that were coming faster, that foretold the building of further reaction. She braced herself for whatever it would be.

She didn't have long to wait. Jack Daltry suddenly pushed back, his motion shoving her away from him. On her back, she hit the soft cushions behind her, fought for a grip on them and wrenched herself up on her elbows. Through the shadowed curtain of her hair, she stared up at the man standing over her and pointing down at her.

"I don't believe you—that you had nothing to do with—" He closed his eyes, took a deep breath, again looked down at her, and started over. "But if what you say is true . . . and my father's . . . dead—"Again he paused, took several deep breaths. "I'm going to go out back and see for myself. If I find what you say I will—" His blue eyes blazed black "When I come back inside—trust me—you'll want to be gone, Angel Devlin. Because if you're not, I'll kill you."

Four

More composed now, her unruly hair pulled back and captured between her back and the cushions, Angel sat on the cowhide sofa and waited. She didn't think Jack Daltry would be out back that long. Clutched in her hands again was the fully loaded Winchester. It lay across her lap, atop the same skirt she'd had on the day she was nearly lynched. Her skirt was clean now. She glanced down, looking past the rifle to the worn brown fabric that covered her legs.

Yes, it was clean. Along with her other things . . . her blood-soaked blouse and unmentionables. She'd washed them all that first day here. After burying Mr. Daltry and then bathing herself. Then, using a needle and some thread she found, she'd sat at the drop-leaf table in the kitchen and mended those places torn by the Henton drovers. It wasn't so much that she liked this skirt, she told herself as she smoothed a still-shaking hand over the rough fabric. It was just the only one she owned. So, what choice did she have but to patch it?

When Angel realized the direction of her thoughts—back to that day, and then to something as silly as her laundry—she raised her head, tightened her grip on the rifle, and trained her gaze across the way. In silence, she stared at the wood-framed doorway on the far side of the great room. She knew, from a week of living here and exploring the place, that if she exited there and turned left, she'd be in a narrow hall that led past the furniture-crowded study, then on to the dining room, and finally ended at the kitchen. And the back door.

And it was that back door that held her attention. She sat there, listening. Listening for that distant door to open and then close. Listening for heavy, booted footsteps to sound on the wood flooring. And waiting. Waiting for Jack Daltry to step into the empty frame that now filled her vision and her consciousness.

Angel exhaled, her breath leaving her in a warm gust. She fully intended to kill him before he killed her. She didn't really want to. She wasn't a cold-blooded killer. And she felt that her sitting here and waiting on the man, giving him a chance to walk away—instead of getting up and going out back and filling him full of lead while he wasn't looking—proved that. But beyond that, she'd killed one man already and, though she wasn't sorry that Jeb Kennedy was dead—he'd deserved it—she didn't like having his or anyone else's blood on her hands. Or her soul. If she had one.

But Jack Daltry *would* force her hand, she knew it. Because she hadn't lied to him about what he'd find outside, about who he'd find buried next to a woman whose hand-lettered headstone simply proclaimed her to be Lily Daltry. Was she Jack Daltry's mother? Sister? Wife? Angel had no way of knowing, couldn't even suppose. Nor did she think *he* was lying, or even exaggerating, about what he'd do to her if she hadn't already hightailed it before he came back inside. Angel pictured herself fleeing astride that roan, in full retreat.

A chuckling snort escaped her. Then she shook her head slowly, promising herself she'd never run again. Up until now, she'd always had to, in order to keep body and soul together. And she'd hated it, hated the way it made her feel. But no more. She wouldn't go back to the old ways. This right here, this Circle D land, was a fresh start, a new life. And it was here she chose to make her stand. She wasn't leaving.

So, if Jack Daltry didn't back down, she'd just have to kill him. It was that simple. Because this house, this cattle ranch, was the only home she'd ever known. And Mr. Daltry wanted *her* to have it, not his son. That point confused her. Why wouldn't a man leave his property to his own son? Angel shrugged as if someone else had asked her that. Maybe there was bad blood between the two. How was she supposed to know? One thing she did know was she didn't care. Couldn't afford to care. Especially about someone she was maybe getting ready to kill.

Just then, she heard the back door jerk open. She tensed at the sound. Then she heard—felt it too in her chest—the same door slam against the wall behind it. All her senses were on alert. The next sound was the door slamming closed.

Jack Daltry was back inside.

Angel listened a moment . . . swallowed . . . then slowly slid the Winchester toward her body. Inadvertently she captured her skirt, pulling its length up her legs. No doubt she was exposing her lace-up boots, stockings, and some bare leg, she thought, as she listened to footsteps scuffing across the wood flooring and advancing toward her. Angel blinked, figuring that her exposed limbs probably would be the last thing the man would notice about her. Especially with the Winchester in her hands. She hefted it, sighted down the barrel— and aimed at where approximately his heart would be when he stepped around that corner.

With his murderous grief under tight lock and key, Jack turned into the great room, where he'd left Angel Devlin, and came to a sudden stop. There she was. Right where he'd left her. He stood there, framed in the arch of the doorway, his legs spread, his weight distributed evenly on his feet. His hands hung loosely at his sides. A gunfighter's stance . . . one Jack was all too familiar with of late.

Jack stared at her, silently cursed her. She'd gotten the Winchester out of the cabinet and had it pointed at him again. The long rifle was a deadly enough weapon, one he respected. And he didn't doubt for a minute that she'd not hesitate to use it, if he gave her enough of a reason. *Enough of a reason?* An abrupt, derisive sound escaped him. "You're still here."

She nodded. "It would appear so."

Jack continued to stare at her, his gaze repeatedly drawn

to the marks banding her neck. Only one thing, in his experience, could cause marks like that. But still, silent minutes passed, during which he decided he ought to kill her just for being so damned stubborn. But then he realized that, given all he'd ever heard about her willfulness, he shouldn't be surprised that she was still sitting here. Shouldn't be surprised she'd armed herself, either. Not that he really cared that she had. Not that he cared about anything at all at this moment.

Except having a drink. A man ought to be able to have a drink in his own home on the day he finds out his father is dead. On the day he realizes his father died thinking his first-born son didn't give a damn about him. The thought almost drove Jack to his knees. Instead, keeping his feet under him, he spat out, "That rifle getting heavy yet? I'd think it would be."

She didn't respond in any way. Not a word or gesture to indicate she'd heard him. Jack captured her gaze, held it. Saw no fear, no skittishness in her eyes. A muttered curse escaped him, had him shaking his head and speaking his mind. And meaning every word. "Go ahead and pull the trigger. See if I give a shit."

With that, and not waiting for her response, he turned his back to her, making his way over to the hulking walnut liquor cabinet in a corner of the room. Opening the beveled-glass doors, he sorted through the selection of brandies, whiskies, rums, and ryes, finally settling on one of many unopened bottles of first-quality whisky.

He yanked it off the shelf, inadvertently upending a smaller bottle that crashed to the floor and shattered. Jack looked down at the mess, at the hard spirits staining his denims and his worn, dusty boots. His nose twitched at the alcoholic fumes that wafted upward. But otherwise, he couldn't have cared less . . . about either the mess or the loss of the liquor. Because it just didn't matter. And he couldn't say if anything ever would again.

With his whisky selection fisted in one hand, he snatched up a squat cut-crystal glass from a lower shelf. Then he turned, crunching the broken glass under his feet, to face Angel Devlin. She'd lowered the Winchester. An aching cynicism had him chuckling and shaking his head, had him flinging his arms out to his sides. "What—no guts? You disappoint me, Angel. Go on . . . use that Winchester. Take your best shot. God knows, I am, too—but with these." He indicated the whisky and the shot glass.

Still she didn't say anything. But her gaze slipped from his face, traveled down the dirt-caked front of him. So she knew he'd thrown himself on his father's grave. So what? He'd also cried like a baby. Her gaze stalled at his feet. Jack looked down at himself, at his boots, saw that he stood in the middle of the still spreading stain of . . . what? He sniffed the air, trying to guess what type of liquor he'd spilled. When he had it, he looked up at her and said, "Rum," as if she'd asked. Then he added, "I'm waiting."

She cocked her head. "For what? Me to join you in drinking that bottle?"

Ah. He'd won a response. Grim but triumphant, Jack made an abrupt gesture with the shot glass. "Hell, no, I don't want you to join me. I'm just waiting to see if you mean to shoot me. Wouldn't want to waste all this fine liquor, if you are." Then he felt a need to prod her, even at the risk of his own life. "I still don't know what you're waiting on. Especially since you've been itching to fill me full of lead from the time I rode up."

"Yep. I reckon I have," she agreed instantly. But her expression could only be called somber. "Still, I'm not one to shoot a man when he's down."

" 'When he's down?' " Jack repeated. His eyes narrowed as he set himself in motion. With the slow, unhurried gait of a man used to setting the pace, and having others follow it, he approached her, stopped in front of her—almost on top of her—and looked down at her. "You think I'm down, Angel?"

She sank back, away from him, as if she meant to pull into herself. Jack's gaze slipped to her hands, saw them tighten around the rifle, whitening her knuckles. Again, he searched her expression, expecting finally to see fear shad owing the black eyes staring back up at him. But there was none. Nor did it flavor her husky voice when she spoke. "Yeah. I do. I think you're way down."

As he stared at her, as his mouth and his chin quivered with a fresh stab of grief, Jack knew she was right. Knew he wanted nothing more than to forget who she was, what he thought she'd done, and throw himself down at her knees, bury his face in her lap, and hold on to her. Knew that in his gut-wrenching pain, in his need for the simple warmth and solace of another living soul . . . any living soul . . . he wanted to cry out to someone.

But . . . like hell he would. Jack locked his knees, stiffening his stance and his resolve against such an unforgivable act. Because this *was* Angel Devlin he was talking about. Seek warmth and solace from her? Under these or any other circumstances? No.

Having thus put an iron-clad lock on his feelings, and seeming more in control of himself, Jack said, in a conversational tone, one that belied the volatility of his emotions, "You know what, Angel? You're right. I am down." He hefted the whisky bottle and the crystal glass, gesturing with them. "But with the help of these two friends here, I'll soon be down a lot lower."

He paused, cocked his head, and ran his gaze over her. Angel Devlin. Sitting in his house, all prim and properlike. It was actually funny, in a way. He grinned, and with the casual cruelty of one pushed too far, one whose soul was tearing apart, one who truly did not care about anything, told her, "What I said before . . . about killing you if you were still here when I came back inside? Well, I haven't forgotten that. Still intend to do it, too. Because I do believe *you're* the one who—well, you know what I think you did. But . . . I'm a fair man, Angel."

With that, he stepped around her and sat down beside her on the sofa, his shoulder all but touching hers. Propping the whisky bottle between his legs, against his crotch, he crossed an ankle atop his opposite knee and lay back against the cushions. Then he rolled his head until he was looking at her profile. With a slow swivel of her neck, Angel faced him.

She hadn't moved over. Or away. Jack respected that. "I like you, Angel. You've got grit, a lot of spirit. So I'll give you another chance to save your worthless skin. See, I'm taking my friends here with me to my room upstairs—"

He cut off his own words when an errant thought sidetracked him. Using Angel's face—she really was a goodlooking woman—as a focal point for his concentration, he tried to recall what had flashed in and out of his mind too quickly for him to grasp. Then, finally, he had it again. With his elbow, he poked her arm, making sure he had her attention. "We never did settle to your satisfaction just who I am, did we? Well, I'm Jack Daltry, all right. Son of Wallace Daltry. Pleased to meet you."

She didn't react in any way, not even to say a word. But he saw the quick intelligence in her eyes, knew she absorbed every word he said. So he gestured broadly with his glass, making a sweeping pass of the room. "I know the layout of this entire house, Angel. Hell, the entire spread. Every one of these hundreds of acres. I can tell you about each hill . . . where every drop of water is—and isn't. And if you've been snooping around upstairs yet—and I suspect you have—then you'll know that in the first bedroom . . . on the left . . . at the head of the stairs . . . are *my* belongings, the ones I left behind four months ago."

He then shifted slightly, looked right into her eyes . . . the widest, shiniest eyes he'd ever seen, he had to admit. "You convinced yet? Or do I need to haul your ass up there and show you?"

Obviously one to pick her battles carefully, Angel said, "I'm convinced."

Jack nodded. "Good. Now where was I?"

Angel nodded toward the liquor and the glass fisted in his hand. "You and your friends were going upstairs to your room. And then, something about killing me."

A chuckle escaped him, had him taking yet another look at her. "That's it. Thanks for reminding me." Now he noticed the feminine fineness of her features. And all that dark hair, thick and soft-looking. That high forehead, and black-winged eyebrows. The straight, slender nose, the full reddish lips. And that stubborn jaw. "All in all, Angel Devlin," he surprised himself by saying out loud, "you're one good-looking woman. I'll give you that much."

Jack's words hung in the air between them, seemed to thicken, to wrap around them like a caress. But then, her voice cool and distant—and dismissive—Angel said, "You'll give me nothing."

Poof. The wispy moment of intimacy evaporated, leaving Jack wondering what the hell was wrong with him, that he'd say such a thing to her, of all people. "Okay, I was going upstairs," he said abruptly, taking up his tale again. "Where I'm going to drink this entire bottle of fine grain alcohol. And then . . . I'll probably get some more. And drink it, too. But eventually, I'm going to sleep it all off. Now when I do, and I come to, and come back downstairs—however long that takes—you make sure you're gone. You hear me?"

She nodded. "I hear you."

He nodded, too. Realized he was again staring too long into her eyes. Realized that somewhere in the depths of those dark pools, she too knew it was more than just a look. He wondered if she also knew that he was starting to feel something he shouldn't, something that had a lot of heat to it, something that manifested itself in the vicinity of the whisky bottle leaning heavily against the button-fly opening of his denims.

But still, he didn't look away. No, he wanted her to see it. In fact, he felt a driving need to know what her reaction would be. He was soon rewarded. The longer he held her gaze, the more her mouth turned down. The more she blinked . . . and swallowed.

Jack chuckled, breaking the spell. Made her edgy, did he? Good. It was enough for now. He pulled himself upright and quipped, "You'd kill me if I even tried, wouldn't you?"

Her reply came with a slow nod. "Yes, I would. Ask anybody."

*   *   *

It'd been three days now. Angel didn't know what to think as she stood there on the second floor of the Circle D ranch house and faced Jack Daltry's closed bedroom door. Just as he'd said, it was the first one, on the left, at the head of the stairs. Twice now she'd put a hand out, meaning to test the brass knob. Was it locked or not? Both times she'd pulled her hand back without trying it. She grimaced fleetingly as she realized she'd been undone by something as simple as a doorknob. But the man hadn't come out of his room for two days now. Except to get more liquor and act more belligerent.

On his last pass late last evening, he'd been all slack-jawed and weaving. And had smelled to high heaven. He'd also sported a heavy growth of beard. At the rate he was drinking and grieving, Angel figured, she'd be burying him next to his father in a day or so. And that's what she told herself she was doing outside his bedroom door . . . checking to see if he was dead and needed burying.

But she knew different. She was concerned. Concerned he *would* drink himself to death. And that's what had her flum-moxed—her concern. Why should she care if he drank him-self to death? Or finally just stumbled and fell and broke his fool neck? If he did, her problem would be solved. There'd be no one left to dispute her claim to the Circle D. At least, no one else had shown up yet to lay another claim to it.

So, that should have settled it for her. Yes, if she had any sense, she'd leave him lying in his own filth until he died and thereby saved her the trouble of having to kill him. That was what she ought to do.

But *ought to* didn't seem to cut it today. Because what she was *going* to do—she still couldn't believe it herself—was go in there and get the man back on his feet. *Why?* Angel tried to tell herself she was doing no more than she had for the horse he'd left tied to the railing out front. Hadn't she had enough compassion to lead the helpless animal to the barn, brush it down, and turn it out to the corral with her roan and the other horses already there? If she'd do that much for a dumb critter, why shouldn't she do it for a dumb man who wouldn't even help himself?

But Angel's shoulders sagged with the truth, with the answer to the question she'd wrestled with repeatedly over the past two days . . . why was she so danged intent on saving the man from himself? *Because,* she railed at her rebelling conscience, *it's the right thing to do.* Because, no matter how much she'd wished for it or longed for it in her own growing-up years, she'd never had anyone do the right thing by her. Until this man's father came along.

So, quite simply, she owed Wallace Daltry one good deed, one act of human kindness. Something that, before him, had never been extended to her. Something that she'd never thought herself capable of doing for someone else. Or even caring about doing for someone else. Until Mr. Daltry. So, it seemed pretty straightforward. She would try to save the life of the son of the man who'd saved her life.

Angel shook her head, still resisting this high-and-mighty notion that had taken hold of her. But the hard truth was . . . if Wallace Daltry could grieve a bit for her mother, even when she herself couldn't, then she should see his son through his grieving for his father. She grimaced, pulling her lips tight against her teeth. Just the idea of soothing another's hurt went against her independent nature. But try as she might not to like it, she knew this was the only way she had left to repay Mr. Daltry.

Returning to the moment, Angel realized that not only was she staring at the doorknob, she was gripping it. This time, feeling more sure of her intentions, she didn't let go. Instead, she exhaled a deep breath, tested the knob . . . felt it give. Felt her heart lurch. *May as well get it over with.*

Fine, I'll do it. But it didn't come easy. She needed a hedge, she knew, against this nasty streak of caring that had apparently lurked, unbidden, unheeded, inside her until now. She thought a moment, and then came up with it. She promised herself that once Jack Daltry was back on his feet . . . well, *then* she'd kill him.

Why? Because she surely didn't see him just letting her have the Circle D, his home. Would he just hand it over and ride away, after thanking her for her help and telling her he was sorry for the bother of the past few days? Hardly. But, by God, neither would she leave for him. So this galling mission of mercy she was on, she now recognized, was no more than a delay of the inevitable, a tiny bandage stuffed into a cannonball-sized hole in the man's heart. And in hers.

Enough thinking. Get in there and do it. Pushing her body forward as she came to a decision, Angel twisted the brass knob as far as it would go. The door opened, her momentum swept her inside. She took a breath, preparatory to announcing her presence, but the darkened room's smell took her by surprise, and she reeled back a step and gagged. Reflexively, her hands sought her mouth, covered her nose, bent her forward.

Spilled liquor, man-sweat, unwashed body—and other noxious odors she didn't care to identify—had Angel gagging and running for the closed window, one hand still covering her mouth. Trying her best to hold her breath, fighting the tearing of her eyes, she ripped aside the heavy drapes and fought and fumbled with the latch until she could shove the lower casing up and stick her head outside. Bracing herself against the sill, her mouth agape, her lungs burning, she took in gasping, grateful breaths of fresh spring air.

And ignored the slurred grumbling and mumbling coming from the man lying atop the dirty, disheveled bed behind her. But finally, when she felt stronger, Angel turned around and stared at the pitiful sight the big man made, sprawled there on his bed, on his back, one arm and one leg hanging off the covers. He surely did not look anything like the determined stranger who'd ridden in here a few days back. He wasn't full of piss and vinegar anymore. Well, not vinegar, anyway, she decided, wrinkling her nose against the acrid miasma of odors that still pervaded the room.

Some mighty powerful demons ate at Jack Daltry. Angel understood that. Could even respect it. After all, hadn't she lived with some of the same all her own life?

She cut that thought off at its inception. She wasn't here to dwell on her own problems. Nor did she want to. She wasn't one to give in to pity for herself. But she could pity the snoring jackass on the bed who needed some help. Angel bit at her bottom lip, felt her skin crease between her eyes as she frowned. This was going to take some doing, she realized.

And some scrubbing and some bathing. She pulled away from the window. Her . . . bathe him? She headed for the door. *No.* And then stopped.

Yes. She fisted her hands, wanted to stomp her foot. *Yes.* She gritted her teeth to keep from screaming out her frustration. She couldn't help the man if she couldn't stand to be near him. So there it was. She had to clean him up. It was that simple. And that hard. Well, then—she squared her shoulders—so be it. She just needed to get some things, didn't she? Yes, she did. And it was reason enough to hurry out of the room. Things like soap and water, she assured herself. *A lot of soap and water.* And some towels. And clean clothes for him.

And a razor. Angel's knees weakened at the thought, had her groping with her outstretched hand for the support of the solid wall to her left. Her other hand found its way to her thumping heart. A razor. She'd seen one in another bedroom, probably Mr. Daltry's. She also recalled a shaving mug and a brush beside a porcelain basin and a pitcher on a dry sink there. She'd get that one.

Again she rushed off, heading to the other end of the hall, to the large bedroom facing her. She'd get a razor. A sharp one . . . to cut Jack Daltry's beard—if not his throat for putting her in this position, damn him.

When Jack woke up—or more likely, came back to consciousness—he was suprised. True enough, plenty of times in the past he'd awakened sprawled on a bed. Sometimes, like now, even his own. But always before—and there were a lot of befores—he'd been raunchy dirty, sweat-soaked, and in a mean mood. But not this time. His sense of smell, his awareness of himself, the physical sensations, all told him he was clean. Him, his bed, his body, and—He felt under the sheet . . . where were his clothes?

He smoothed his hand up to his bare chest and rested it

there as he tried to pull up the memory of cleaning himself and his bed. And found he had no such recollection. Well, what about his mood? He focused inward, checked that. Nope. Not even the meanness to see him through the hangover. Just the aching headache, the roiling gut . . . and the brightest damned sunshine he'd ever seen in his life.

He grimaced against the pain of the light hitting his pupils and brought a shaking hand up to rub over his eyelids and then down his jaw and his neck. Over his Adam's apple, his hand froze as he realized what he felt. Clean-shaven skin. *What the*—? Now, wait just a damned minute . . . he'd been too drunk to risk shaving. That much he knew. What was going on here? He edged his eyes open, glimpsed again the bare ceiling, the glare of sunlight, and immediately squeezed his eyes shut again.

"Sorry about the nicks and cuts on your throat. I never—"

Jack's entire body jerked at the sound of the female voice. He wrenched to his left—paid the hefty physical price of a pounding heart and burning muscles—and saw Angel Devlin pulling up a chair to sit beside his bed. "I was just saying I'd never shaved a man before," she finished.

Jack stared at her and considered her words. She'd shaved him? And undressed him and bathed him, too? Why? But beyond that, *how'd* she do all that, and even change the linens, with him in the bed? He blinked, tugging on the top sheet, trying to distribute it more evenly over his lower regions. Even that bit of movement hurt. Still, he managed to croak out, "You'd never shaved a man before? And you just thought you'd start with me?"

"Yep," she drawled. "Thought I would."

"Why?" he asked as he rolled onto his back. He winced, and his gut clenched. It hurt just to talk.

"Why? Well . . . because you needed it," came the practical response from the woman in the chair beside his bed.

Jack remained silent for a moment, concentrating on breathing, until he felt equal to the task of turning his head to see her. "I did?" he got out, taking in her appearance as she nodded her answer.

Her hair was pulled back behind her ears and tied at her nape, making the marks around her neck, though fainter, more stark in appearance. Her longish bangs brushed against her eyelashes, making her blink. And her attire . . . it was all his. His blue chambray shirt, which was much too big for her slender form, was open at the throat and unbuttoned enough to expose a white bit of her undergarment. It'd taken about three turns of the sleeves, he noted, to expose her hands and wrists.

His gaze slipped down to her belted denims. Well, his denims . . . which were also too big. The belt fit her. It must be hers, he concluded. This was mighty interesting. He'd seen women in men's clothes before. The prairie and mountains were full of women making do with what was at hand. He'd been surprised early on by the sight, but hadn't given it too much thought after that. Until now. Angel Devlin looked good in his clothes. And he liked it.

Afraid his scrutiny of her had given away his thoughts, Jack sought her gaze, saw she'd calmly been watching him notice every detail about her. And yep, he'd given himself away, if her slightly raised eyebrows were any indication. In sudden irritation, Jack wondered why she wasn't the least bit embarrassed or squeamish about him gazing at her. After all, most young girls her age—he judged her to be about eighteen or nineteen—would be.

Then he realized it was hardly surprising. Angel Devlin wasn't most young girls. She hadn't led the protected life they usually did.

And that only made him wonder what thoughts did lurk behind those wide and amazingly black eyes of hers, whenever he raked his gaze over her. To his surprise, especially given his present state, he found he really meant that. He really wanted to know. And couldn't have said why. Or didn't want to own up to why. And so, in an effort to avoid his own awareness of her, he asked, "How long have I been out?"

She shrugged. "Off and on since late last evening. It's mid-afternoon now, so I expect you'll live. But before that, you'd been drinking for two days."

Two—no . . . *three* days, all told? He'd lost *three* days? Damn. What had put him on this bender? He tried to come up with the answer, but couldn't. It hurt too much to think. But still, he'd known instantly who she was. So, at some point, they'd been introduced. Introduced? Was that all they'd been? Jack flicked a glance her way. He *was* in bed naked. And she didn't seem the least bit concerned that he was. Shouldn't his conclusion be the obvious one?

Damn. Me and Angel Devlin. Whew. Jack wished he could remember that. But with every muscle—every hair even—aching and burning, and his abused stomach threatening to empty itself with his next movement, all he could do was lie there. And settle for deep, gentle breathing. After a moment, when he was more able, he licked his lips and swallowed, then asked, "What the hell is going on?"

Her answer was slow in coming. Her very silence did nothing to relieve Jack's mind. He rolled his head just enough to see her, just enough to send her a questioning look. "You don't remember?" she finally answered . . . with a question.

Exasperated, Jack answered, "If I did, I wouldn't be troubling myself right now with conversation."

"Fair enough. You've been drinking to forget."

"Well, I must have done a good job because I *have* forgotten. What exactly have I forgotten?"

Angel Devlin firmed her lips together and stared at him. Jack's senses went on the alert. Whatever she had to say, he wasn't going to like it, he could tell. Finally, she spoke, saying, "I hate to be the one to tell you again but . . . your father . . . well, he's dead."

Jack stared at her, tried to absorb her words, and their meaning. *Your father's dead.* What did that mean? He'd expected her to tell him that they'd had themselves quite a time together right here in this bed. But not this. He'd never expected this. Then, like a gut punch, it hit him, came rushing back at him. All of it . . . everything since he'd ridden up three days ago. He squeezed his eyes shut, fought back the pain.

"I see you remember now. I'm real sorry," she said.

Jack didn't—couldn't—respond. His father was dead. His

mind couldn't stand the words and flitted to another reality. *She* was still here. He opened his eyes. She hadn't moved. She sat there, her hands clutched together in her lap, her expression composed. "Why are you still here?" he said.

She cocked her head, raised her chin. "You mean on the ranch? Or in this room?"

"I mean on the Circle D." Then he thought about it. "Well, both, I guess. Neither one makes much sense. Not to me."

Her first response was a careless shrug, which annoyed the hell out of Jack. Did she always have to appear so calm and unruffled? But her attitude didn't prove half as upsetting as did her simple answer. "I'm on the Circle D because I live here. I told you that. And I'm in this room because I felt a need to save your sorry ass from your drunken self."

Jack bolted up onto an elbow, forcing himself to ignore the throbbing that pounded at his temples. "If my sorry ass needs saving, I'll do it," he all but snarled, adding, "And like hell you live here. You do *not*."

Her eyes narrowed. Her lips firmed. But she didn't say anything. Jack concluded that she didn't have a comeback. A slow grin of triumph curved his lips, but then she said, "We'll see about that, Mr. Daltry."

Jack's grin fled. A challenge, if ever he'd heard one. Then, she added, "Once you're back on your feet, we'll straighten this out." With that, she made as if to rise from the chair.

Jack snaked out a cautionary hand, grabbing her arm and holding her in place. "Wait. I'm back on my feet enough for you to answer my questions right now."

Frozen in position, she looked pointedly at his hand on her arm. Then she slanted her head until her gaze met his. Her long hair slithered over her shoulder. Something in her dark eyes glinted, warning him. Jack released her arm. Still holding her gaze, he waited on her, thought he knew her struggle. She'd said her piece. She should walk out. Her other option was to let her curiosity get the better of her and sit back down.

The moments dragged by. Then, she made her decision . . . and resettled herself on the chair.

Jack exhaled, realized he was relieved. A flash of surprise, almost subconscious in nature, told him he'd been holding his breath, hoping she'd stay. *Now that's crazy*, he chastized himself. He squinted to prove it, massaging a hand over his face and telling himself he'd closed his eyes against the sunlight . . . and not her stare. A little voice inside his head asked him if he was afraid of her. Jack's hand stilled. *Afraid of her?* He lowered his hand to his side and stared at the ceiling, telling it, *Hell no*. So ask her your question, the voice persisted.

Jack turned his head, found her again. She hadn't moved. *No big surprise there*, he told himself, as he—ever mindful of keeping the sheet in place—swung his legs over the side of the bed and struggled to a sitting position. He braced himself with his hands on the mattress and stared at his bare legs and feet until the room quit spinning and his stomach settled.

Then, he raised his head, met her gaze, felt his hair fall forward over his brow. "My father's dead, Miss Devlin," he began. "And you seem to know something about the why of that—something you're not telling me. I'd like to know what that something is."

She raised her chin a notch. "He was a sick old man, that's true enough."

Jack jumped on that. "Sick? With what?"

Angel eyed him, as if she didn't know what to make of his question. "I don't know. He coughed a lot, got weak all the time. But I don't know what it was. He never said." Then her expression deepened into a frown and she asked, "You didn't know he was sick?"

Jack wasn't about to go into family troubles with her, but he did say, "No. I haven't been home since January. Is that what he died of . . . that coughing sickness?"

She shook her head, looked hesitant. But then she said, "No. It would've taken him soon enough . . . but he—Well, I'm sorry to say it, but he was killed."

Jack's heart all but stopped. It seemed to hang heavy and leaden in his chest, like a weighted pendulum. His hands fisted around the sheets he gripped. "What . . ." He swallowed, stared at her, felt weak. He took several deep breaths, and tried again. "My father was *killed*? You mean like thrown from a horse? Or a wagon mishap, right?"

She bit at her lower lip—as if she were considering her next words. "No. I mean . . . murder. But I thought you realized that earlier—a few days back—when you accused me of being responsible. I'm not. I didn't do it."

Mute with renewed grief, hearing her as if from a great distance, Jack could only shake his head no, meaning that he had not been thinking of . . . murder. Not really. Perhaps he'd suspected it, but just hadn't wanted to think it, or know it. Or accept it. But here Angel Devlin sat . . . saying it out loud. He watched her gaze rake over him, until finally she looked into his eyes and said, "I wondered when we'd get around to this."

When, indeed. Jack closed his eyes, took a breath or two. His father had been killed. And she said she didn't do it. A rage swelled his lungs, gave him renewed strength, renewed desire for revenge. Clutching at the sheet, keeping it wadded around his front as he jerked it free and wrapped it around his hips, he stood up, weaved slightly, blinking and trying to get his bearings. Despite his dizziness, he managed to tell her, "Your wondering's over, Miss Devlin. Because we're there— we just got around to it."

Five

Her nerves tingling with wariness, every sense telling her to flee, Angel came to her feet when Jack Daltry did. But far from fleeing—no more running, she'd promised herself—she stood beside the chair in his bedroom and wanted to kick herself. Why in the world had she thought she needed to play nursemaid to him? And what had possessed her to sit by his danged bed and chat with him?

Watching him weave and gesture weakly, no doubt struggling to clear his head—and to keep that slippery sheet in place—Angel gripped her chair's slatted back with one hand and held her ground . . . despite her thumping heart. And despite the gunbelt that was slung over a post of the polished-wood headboard near him.

Seeing his weapon caused her to flash back to three days ago when he'd jerked the rifle out of her hands, marched her inside, and thrown her on the sofa. He was capable of hurting her, had already proven he wasn't above it. And too, he'd already told her he intended to kill her if she wasn't gone when he woke up. Well, he was awake, and she was still here. So did it make her stupid to stand here because of some dumb promise she'd made herself? The real question was, would he, the minute he got himself together, want to do some violence to someone?

If he did . . . the only someone hereabouts was her. Angel's expression hardened. He *would* have to kill her first, she knew that much. Because it seemed to Angel that when men got randy or even just upset with things, most of them got rough with women. She'd seen it all too often in her childhood years around the Silver Star, around her mother and the other women Virginia worked with. Even with herself, when she'd been a small girl who didn't understand, who'd only wanted her mother's attention, there'd been roughness.

Angel harbored ugly memories of being smacked away from Virginia, of being wrenched out of her arms—over her mother's protests, true enough, but still torn away—by her latest customer intent on having his paid entertainment to himself for a while. Angel remembered one man shoving her out the door and calling out, "Git now, young'un. This ain't no place for you."

Words Angel had taken to heart. Especially when, past her girlhood and into her teen years, she'd started drawing the men's notice in other ways. Since that time, she'd stayed away from the Silver Star altogether, promising herself that she would never be like those pathetic whores. Never. She'd never allow herself to be used like they were, to be helpless, to have to beg for mercy that never came. Yes, she knew what it felt like to be hit, to be on the other end . . . and helpless.

Angel's mouth dried with her renewed sense of her predicament. She spared a glance for her only avenue of escape, the opened door to the room. Could she make it before he grabbed her? She calculated his position, her own, and the distance. The odds favored him. Then she caught his gaze. Her belly muscles tightened. His head was clear enough now, because he was watching her real close like . . . as if he only waited for her to make a move.

Why hadn't she brought the Winchester up here, she railed against herself. Well, she had once or twice during the past two days. But she had decided she was just being silly. After all, the man had been passed out colder than a high-plains January day. But not now. No, he was definitely on his feet. And mad at the world. But not as mad as he was going to be in a minute, she knew. Because he was right—she did know the truth. And he wasn't going to like it one little bit.

Angel's mind raced. Maybe she could stall his questions somehow, put him off until she was downstairs . . . closer to the guns. And out of this room. Because that was another thing she didn't like. It *was* the man's bedroom. That hadn't bothered her half so much while he was sleeping off his liquor. Or even when she'd had to undress him and bathe him. Angel entertained a fleeting image of his muscular and naked self. All she was willing to admit right now was that he had the right parts in all the right places. Suddenly, she recalled rolling him around while she changed the sheets under him.

A burst of heat reddened her cheeks. Of course, she'd seen her share of naked men before, first in the back rooms of the Silver Star and then over at the hotel, although usually by accident. But this was different. This wasn't the saloon. Or the hotel. And he was Jack Daltry. Not some drunken drover trying to grope her as she went about her job. Angel swallowed, willing away the high color of her cheeks and wondering when it would occur to him that she'd . . . well, seen him in the altogether.

Suddenly, given her thoughts and his silence, his scrutiny of her, the room felt too warm, the air seemed charged with the tension between them. Well, since he hadn't moved, she wasn't about to, either. No sense setting him off. Instead, Angel looked him up and down, assessing him as an adversary. Dark haired, muscled, tall. Blue eyes that looked right through a person. Nose a bit crooked. Some telltale scars on his face and arms that spoke of past troubles.

But even considering all that, some would say he was handsome, was finely put together, she supposed. And yes, she'd have to agree with them. But her concern right now wasn't his handsomeness. It was his size. He was most definitely a big man.

About six angry feet and two hundred fearsome pounds of big man. So . . . stall him? Exactly how? No doubt, the backroom girls at the Silver Star knew all the feminine wiles and ways of doing just that. But not Angel. Nor did she want to know them. She'd just have to rely on her wits, as she always had. But wits or no, she suddenly blurted, ''Before you set about getting down to anything with me, you might want to put some pants on first."

Jack Daltry froze, his hands gripping the sheet tugged around his waist. "You think so?" His question dripped with sarcasm. Then he added, "Give me those you've got on. They are mine—like everything else around here."

That did it. Angel's temper boiled over. Her cheeks heated with her anger, with her embarrassment—the clothes covering her body *were* his. "Everything?" she threw back at him. "I'm here, and I'm surely not yours. But the truth is, Mr. Daltry, not *anything* here is yours. And that's according to your own father."

His index finger pointing at her, he said, "Now, dammit, that's exactly what I mean. You listen to me—"

"No," Angel raged, cutting him off. "You listen to me. I've had all the threats I'm going to take from you. I'm here because your father wanted me to be here. Can *you* say as much?"

She'd stunned him with her outburst, she could tell. His expression hardened, but his eyes, in their blue depths, took on the shadows of deep pain. So . . . she'd struck a nerve. It was enough for now. Silently, Angel turned and began what felt like a mile-long trek as she crossed the room. She expected to be shot or at least grabbed and stopped. *Just let him try*, she prayed. *Just let him try.* She'd learned a few tricks along the way for dealing with this situation. And she'd be glad to show him what they were.

But he didn't stop her. A bullet didn't stop her, either. She made it safely to the open doorway and meant to turn into the hallway and keep going, but realized she still had something to say to him. So she turned and faced him once more, resting a hand against the door frame. He still stared at her, his face now a stone mask of hurt and belligerence.

But Angel had no pity for him. Only an awareness of him as her foe. And that being the way of it, they might as well draw the battle lines now. And so she said, "From this moment forward, Mr. Daltry, my debt to your father is paid. Now it's every man for himself, with regard to the Circle D. You up to the challenge?''

His blue eyes became dark slits. Angel realized that any other man, standing there bare-chested and wrapped in a sheet, would have been laughable. But not Jack Daltry. No. Quite the opposite, in fact. Commanding, powerful, was more like it. Angel swallowed her fear of him and her awareness of his physical power. She thought he wasn't going to say anything—prayed he wouldn't, in fact.

But then he said, ''There's no challenge here to be met, Miss Devlin. The Circle D is mine, plain and simple. Free and clear. I have blood kin on my side. What do you have?''

Her eyebrow arched. ''What do I have? Your father's oath. Something you're bound to honor.'' With that, she turned and left the room. Her footsteps echoed on the hardwood floors and on the stairs that took her to the first floor.

Dressed now in clean denims and a flannel shirt, Jack made his shaky way downstairs. Once in the great room, he checked the time on the mantel clock. And got a surprise. Three hours, and a bracing nap—one that left him more capable of staying upright—had passed since Angel Devlin had as much as told him to get off his own land. He chuckled at that thought. The less-than-cheerful sound split the quiet air of the otherwise empty room and brought his surroundings into focus.

Jack scanned the great room's familiar spacious contours. He smiled as he examined the well-worn furniture, greeting each piece as an old friend. Then he noticed the long, dark fingers of the day's shadows creeping across the floor toward his boots. He even listened a moment, almost afraid he'd hear the echo of his father's voice. He couldn't have stood that. The pain was too new, too raw.

To his relief, no sounds met his ears. Not the sigh of a breeze. Not the howl of a coyote or the keening cry of a bird. And not a muffled rustling or hint of a sound that could verify for him that he wasn't the last person left alive on earth. And still, he listened. But for whom was he listening, if his father was gone?

Well, hell, there was only one other person hereabouts. But no sign of her presence. Assuming that she was still here. And he thought she was. There'd been nothing in her words or actions earlier that said quitter. No, she'd fight to the bitter end to stay here. It was the why of it—why she would fight—that eluded him. All he knew was, he was glad she hadn't left. Jack stiffened. *What the hell—? Where'd that come from? Glad* she hadn't left? He shook his head, denying his own unbidden thought.

This house was making him crazy. Or maybe it was the quiet. It had to be. Again he surveyed the room, turning his head with the slow, deliberate calculation of an eagle. Yes, it was too quiet. And yet too full. Full of the memories of people he'd never see again. Of the sounds of voices he'd never hear again. He glanced at the small framed picture to the left of the clock. His mother's youthful face gazed solemnly back at him.

She had been a beautiful woman, that much he could see. She'd died when he was so young, though, that Jack had no memory of the sound of her voice. And that saddened him, made the loss seem worse. His mind then flitted to Old Mother. No picture of her graced any mantel or wall in the house. But she was gone, too. Still, as he stood there bathed in dust motes dancing on the invading shafts of sunlight, Jack believed that he could hear the soft cadence of the Comanche woman's voice.

Not so old when she arrived, she'd come out of nowhere when his mother died. She'd just ridden up on her horse that day and said . . . she was here. And she'd stayed, never offering any explanation for her presence or how she knew they needed her. Over the years, she'd become more mother than nanny to him and the newly born Seth.

Seth. Jack shook his head, grunted with defeat. Where the hell could Seth be? It wasn't as if he hung around the place. Nor did Jack want him to. The kid was a hothead. And an outlaw. And made them all miserable with his selfish, lawbreaking ways. But still, Seth had a right to know about Pa . . . if he ever showed up again. How long *had* it been? Jack thought . . . Well, unless Seth had put in an appearance during Jack's four-month absence, then it'd been over a year since he'd ridden through with those worthless bastards he ran with.

Jack shook his head, exhaling his breath on a sigh. Seth was one little son of a gun best left alone. The less he knew of Seth's exploits, Jack told himself, the better he slept. But still· . . . Seth was his brother. And he loved him . . . faults, flaws, and all.

Just then, Jack became restless in his inactivity. Or maybe he was still suffering from the ill effects of the whisky. He winced. *Damn. Don't even think the word*, he warned himself. As if agreeing, his stomach rumbled. Jack rubbed it, trying to remember when he'd had his last meal. Couldn't come up with it. But still, the mere thought of food right now thickened his saliva, all but closed his throat, had him grimacing.

Food could wait. He had something else he needed to do. Something that held his grief at bay, something that stiffened his spine and his knees, that kept him from giving in to the abject sorrow that threatened to break his heart. And so, he locked it away, deep inside, refusing even to consider his loss. All he knew was his father had been murdered. Murdered. It was a cold word. An ugly word. Cold and ugly . . . like his mood right now. And in this mood, Jack wanted to know only two things. Who. And why.

He knew where to get those answers. From Angel Devlin. She was the key to what was was going on around here. *Go find her.* Liking the sound of that, the decisiveness of it, Jack crossed the room and turned left, proceeding down the hall to the kitchen's back door. She had to be outside. There was no place inside he hadn't searched. Hell, before he came downstairs, he'd gone out of his way to look into the other three bedrooms upstairs. Only to find she'd taken the one Old Mother'd slept in.

He opened the back door and stepped outside. The bright day greeted him with the warm kiss of spring. A slight breeze ruffled his hair. Blinking until his eyes adjusted to the light, Jack looked this way and that, searching the yard and the service court to the horse barn. And then, off to his right, out back . . . he found her. His eyes narrowed as he saw where she knelt. He set himself in motion, heading toward her. *Goddamn her.*

The hair on Angel's arms stood up. She stilled her hands, frowning in concentration as she listened without turning around. Jack Daltry was coming her way. Her pulse picked up. Was the man a force of nature that he could affect her senses so? For the muddy ground under his feet hadn't warned of his approach. Then how was it that she could *feel* him close to her?

No one had ever affected her this way before. And she wasn't the least bit happy to admit to herself that he did. Surely it had to be because she expected him to kill her at any moment. Surely.

But even so, and not really believing her own rationalization, Angel still didn't turn around or otherwise acknowledge the man's presence. She simply resumed her task, which was tending to Wallace Daltry's grave. Not that there was much to tend, given its newness. But with last night's rain, the mounded earth had settled some.

When she'd come outside and seen the indented ground next to Lily Daltry's grave, she'd felt a need to pile more dirt on, to level off the site again. And she'd done all that. But now she wished she hadn't traipsed out to the meadow to pick all these stupid little flowers to adorn the two graves. That was just plain crazy. She hadn't even known the woman buried here. But still, it hadn't seemed right to put some on one resting place and not the other.

Heckfire, Angel chastised herself, she hadn't gone to that much trouble for her own mother's last resting place. Not that she'd had much of a chance, what with having to kill that Kennedy fella and then the lynching and all. But Angel knew better. She wouldn't have searched for flowers to mark Virginia's grave if she'd had all the time on earth. Why? Because that would mean her mother meant something to her, that she was someone her daughter would miss.

Angel's muddied hands fisted. The earth squished through

her fingers. She stared unseeing at Lily Daltry's grave. Miss her mother? *Like hell*. She hadn't shed a tear yet over Virginia's passing. And she wasn't about to start now. Angel blinked, set her hands in motion again. But still, it was silly—this flower thing she'd done—and it seemed especially so now that the man's son had caught her here on her knees packing moist earth around the bunched stems of the blue flower clusters.

To her further dismay, her efforts went for naught. When she released them, the flowers drooped over, sagging to lay their tiny heads, with the yellowish centers, on the raw earth that held them in place. Angel gave up, sighing as she sat back on her legs, her muddied hands braced against her denim-covered thighs. By now, Jack Daltry stood quietly behind her. Yep, she could feel him. Her tempered flared. *Damn him*. Ducking her head, she cut her gaze to her left and saw the toes of his boots. She wondered what he was thinking, but didn't feel compelled to look up into his face to find out.

Instead, without preamble, she broke the silence between them, speaking over her shoulder. "What kind of flowers are these? I've never seen them before."

A wordless moment ticked by while Angel wondered if she'd surprised him by realizing he was there. Then, "Bluebonnets," he said. "Some call them the wolf flower."

As it always did, Angel's heart thudded at the sound of his voice. She now suspected that it wasn't only fear of him that caused its erratic beat. "Bluebonnets," she heard herself repeating. "That's nice. I like that. But the wolf flower? That's strange."

"I suppose."

Something in his voice made Angel pivot to face him. Looking up at him, she shaded her eyes with her hand. He didn't like her being out here by the grave. It was written on his face. She thought she could understand how he'd feel, thinking what he did about her. But still, she was of half a mind to point out to him that she was the one who'd carried his father's body home. She was the one who'd dug this hole. She was the one whose back and arms had ached with the effort, whose legs had given out with the constant working of the shovel. And she was the one with splinters in her palms from the tool's wooden handle.

But what good would it do? Instead, she heard herself blurting, "The bluebonnets . . . they're pretty. Not much of anything like them grows up around Red River Station."

"I know."

Angel nodded, returned her gaze to the flowers, and sighed. "I suppose you do. Well—" She pushed off the ground with that matter-of-fact word, her back to him, and stood. "I also suppose you'd like to be alone with . . . your father."

Rubbing her hands together, trying to rid them of the muddy earth that clung to her skin, she turned again to Jack Daltry. She met his gaze—his eyes as blue as the flowers she'd stuck on his father's grave—and froze at the stricken look on his face. Slowly, her arms sagged to her sides. She waited for him to speak.

He didn't at first. Then he gestured to indicate the grave behind her. "I suppose I ought to make a headstone of some sort."

Angel bit at her bottom lip and actually felt sorry for the man. "I suppose," she managed to say.

Slowly, his gaze shifted to her. He frowned, as if he hadn't realized until this moment that he was talking to her. "Why'd you do all that?"

Confusion reigned in Angel's mind. "Do all what?" Did he mean dig the grave? Surely he knew she'd had to, that his father was—

"The flowers. Why'd you do all that?"

"Oh . . . that." Again, Angel wanted to kick herself for having gathered the bluebonnets. She narrowed her eyes, tried to tough it out . . . but couldn't. She gave up, and turned toward the meadow where she'd found the pesky flowers. She shrugged as she crossed her arms under her bosom. "I don't know. Seemed like the thing to do." Then, with bravado, she pivoted to face him and said, "I can pull them up, if you—"

"No. It's okay. His entire demeanor shifted. "It was . . . nice of you to do that."

Well, she hadn't expected that. And it caught her off guard. Her breath caught, and again she looked away. "I owed him," she managed to get out.

"For what?"

Angel took a deep breath, raised her chin. When she felt more in control, she turned to him and said, "For stopping this." She rubbed at the fading rope burns that still ringed her neck.

He nodded his head slowly. "What happened?"

Unlike the last time he'd asked her that—when she'd told him to keep his nose out of her business—Angel gave a nonchalant shrug that belied the terror she'd lived through, and answered him. "Some drovers meant to lynch me."

He winced. "Damn. I figured it was something like that. But, you're a . . . a woman. What'd you do?"

Too late, Angel realized she'd steered the conversation in the wrong direction. Sweat sprang up at her nape and under her arms. She needed to choose her words carefully. "I . . . well, I killed a man. Defending myself."

Jack Daltry pulled himself up straight. Angel's gaze flitted to his hip. No gunbelt. But still she rushed on. "Not your father. Remember—I said he put an end to the lynching."

"Why would he—" he began but stopped, shifting his gaze to a point behind her. Then he nodded, looking down at her again. His expression showed sadness mixed with pride. "Yep. That sounds just like him. Always interfering. Is that how he . . . well, how he—"

"No," Angel had to tell him. "No. It was on the way here that it happened. I woke up that last day on the trail—it was just the two of us—and . . . there he was. He'd been—" The words wouldn't come at first. Her mouth worked, she frowned, mustered her courage. "He'd been stabbed. I don't know—"

Jack Daltry exploded, grabbing her arm, shaking her. "There was just the two of you—and he'd been stabbed? Don't play with words to try to save your skin. *You* killed him—is that how you repaid him for saving your life?''

His accusation, as much as his hand on her, angered Angel. ''I did *not* kill him,'' she yelled into his face, shoving futilely against the granite wall of his chest. ''Would I have brought him home and buried him, if I had? Would I even be here, facing you? Think about it, you stubborn fool. I said he'd been stabbed—because that's the truth. I woke up and found him like . . . like that.''

''What the hell difference does it make what you say?'' he snarled into her face. ''You could be lying. Lying about everything. Would you even *know* the truth if it bit you on the ass, Angel *Devlin*?''

He'd used her full name—no doubt to invoke her mother's reputation. ''You mean because I'm a whore's daughter?'' Angel raged. ''Is that it? You think because my mother spread her legs for every man with the price that I'd be worthless, too? That I'd be a liar and a murderer? Is that what you're saying?''

His face an ugly mask, he growled, ''Yeah, by God. I think it is.''

A cry of outrage erupted from Angel's innermost depths. With all her strength backing her, she balled up a muddy fist, reared back, and came around swinging, aiming for his jaw. But Jack Daltry caught her wrist before she could connect. And such was the immovable force of his grip that Angel was sure he'd jarred all her bones loose.

He held her and thrust his face toward hers. ''Don't you ever try to hit me, you hear me? I'll take you apart.''

With mounting fear and no caution left in her soul, Angel snapped right back. ''And what about you? Are you going to hit me? If you do, you better make damn sure I don't get up. Because I won't just take you apart, Jack Daltry. Trust me, I'll see to it that you're the *second* man I kill.''

His grip on her wrist tightened, as if in response to her words. Then, he released her. But only to clutch her one-handed around her neck. Angel gasped, her hand clawing at his as he increased the pressure. His voice no more than the low growl of a predator, he crooned into her ear. "Was my father the first man you killed?"

"No," Angel had to whisper as she stiffened against his hold. She emphasized each word with a deliberation born of desperation. "I didn't kill your father."

The need for air forestalled any further words. She tried to gulp in a breath, but couldn't. Still, she forced herself to keep her gaze locked with Jack Daltry's. She refused to yield, refused to look away. She could tell by the look on his face that he didn't see her, that he wasn't thinking, that he was beyond caring that he was slowly killing her. Angel felt the numbness creeping into her limbs, felt her knees give. If he didn't soon release her, she'd—

His head jerked suddenly, as if coming to himself, and his expression reflecting his shock and disbelief. He looked down at her, his eyes focusing, changing color, lightening. His grip instantly loosened. "Son of a bitch! What am I doing?"

Angel sagged, choking, gasping for air. To her surprise, Jack Daltry gripped her arms, helped her settle to the ground beside his father's grave. Then he squatted in front of her, rocking back on the ball of one booted foot as he brushed her hair out of her face . . . and apologized. "Good God, Angel, are you all right? I'm . . . I'm sorry. I don't know what came over me. I've *never* handled a woman that way. Never. I just—I don't know. It must be what happened to my father. I'm sorry."

Angel heard him, but didn't want his apologies. Or his hands on her. But she couldn't speak, couldn't say a word. And so she sat there, helpless and terrified . . . with tears streaming down her face.

In the next moment, Jack Daltry gripped Angel's chin, gently raising her head until she looked into his eyes. "I'm so damned sorry, Angel," he said softly.

Glaring at him, Angel took a ragged breath, tried to speak. "Go . . ." Her voice was no more than a rasp, the one word only a gruff croaking sound. With both hands, she clutched at his sleeve, felt the hard muscle and warm skin under her fingers, knew his strength, and yet sought his blue-eyed gaze, clinging to it.

Finally, shoving his arm away, she managed, "Go to . . . *hell,* Jack Daltry."

Six

As Angel watched, Jack Daltry's eyes widened. But then his mouth turned down, as if in defeat. Releasing her, resting his forearm on his thigh, he considered her for a wordless moment. Through the fringe of her too long bangs, Angel observed him, much like a cornered mouse does the cat overtaking it.

"I deserve that," Jack said, "And I expect I *will* go to hell, Angel. But somehow I think you'll be there to greet me."

Angel's eyes glittered with hatred. When she finally was able to take a deep, fairly normal breath, she raised herself up and said, "Oh, I'll be there, all right—if only to hold the fiery gates wide open for *you*."

He chuckled, shook his head. "We're quite the pair, aren't we?"

Angel shifted her weight, suddenly uncomfortably aware that they'd just turned some sort of corner. Whether it was for better or for worse, she could only wait to find out.

"We're both stubborn as the day is long," he continued. "Both ready to kill the other one at the drop of a hat. But . . . okay, Angel, I believe you. I don't think you put my father in there." He pointed to the mound behind her. "Except for the burying part. And you've made your point about being here, too. You're not leaving. And I'm sure as hell not leaving."

Again, he stopped. He looked intensely serious as he stared

off into the distance. Thoughts and emotions shadowed his face, flitting across its planes, much as a stray storm cloud chases across the prairie. Fascinated despite herself—he *had* just tried to kill her—Angel watched him, telling herself she did so because she needed to. She needed to be aware of his every word, his every move. But instead, she found herself gazing at the chiseled features of his face. And how they all fit together into such a pleasing picture.

When he suddenly turned back to her, settling his gaze on her face, Angel blinked, hating the burst of heat on her cheeks that gave her away. "Go on. You sound like you're leading up to something," she blurted.

He nodded. "I am." Then, gesturing vaguely with his hands, hands that only moments ago had been around her neck, he seemed to wilt, like the bluebonnets on his father's grave. "I tell you, Angel, I don't know anything anymore. I have no idea what's going on around here, where everyone is. Hell, I can't even account for my own behavior." He ducked his head, sliding her a chagrined look. "What a bastard I am. *Damn.* I can't believe I—"

As he stopped himself and shook his head, Angel knew he meant her, the way he'd just treated her. He was truly sorry. The realization gut-punched her. And got her attention, as did his intimate opening up to her. There was no way she could have anticipated this. No way she would ever have thought he'd seek forgiveness from her, much less understanding. But what was she supposed to do with his confidences? Was she supposed to say something, somehow make him feel better? The man had just tried to choke the life out of her, so what did she owe him?

Suddenly Jack turned to her, saying, "Oh, the hell with it. I'm just going to spit it out. Look, Angel, whether I like it or not, right now I need you. I need answers. And I think you have them—at least, some of them." He arrowed her a questioning look, as if asking her to verify at least that much.

Angel swallowed, raised her chin. She'd never expected to live long enough to hear him—or any man—say he needed her. Even if it was only temporarily. And even if it was only for the knowledge she possessed. But denying that this revelation meant anything to her, she focused on his unasked question, saying, "I have those answers."

He nodded at her, but again looked uncertain of himself. Or was he uncertain of her? Did she unnerve him as much as he did her? "I thought as much," he went on. "And while I don't have any idea what you're doing here, or why you feel you own the place. . . ." Another pause.

Angel tensed. Was this an opening for her to explain herself? In silence, she stared back at him. No, let him play his cards first.

Finally, he said, "Fine. What I'm leading up to is this . . . we need to come to some kind of an understanding. One that won't have us at each other's throats, like a couple of fighting dogs, every time we're within touching distance of each other. You agree?"

Angel's gaze roved over the man's face, from his wide forehead, to his blue eyes and high cheekbones, from his almost straight nose to the firm set of his mouth and chin. She refused to admit how affected she was by the sight, but her breath left her in a sigh—and reminded her he awaited an answer from her. "I'm for that," she said, managing a deliberate drawl, despite her accelerated pulse. "So, what're you proposing?"

"I'm proposing that we declare a truce for now. That I quit trying to throw you off the place and quit trying to kill you." His voice softened, lowered, with his next words. "And that I start listening to you and believing you."

Angel cocked her head, considered his words. They were a declaration of respect. For her. The man was getting too close for comfort. Angel pulled back, if only emotionally, and spoke with forced bravado. "I like the sound of that, cowboy. But what do I have to do?"

He narrowed his blue eyes. "For starters, you can quit calling me cowboy and Mr. Daltry. The name's Jack. As for the rest of it . . . what *you* have to do"—he shrugged his broad shoulders—"I don't really know, to tell you the truth. Well, except just that . . . tell the truth."

Angel made a derisive sound. "I've been doing that all along," she let him know. But then she added "Jack," to soften her response, to test his name on her lips.

An emotion flared in his eyes—surprise? Or something else?—but just as quickly died, leaving Angel to wonder if she'd seen anything there at all. Finally, he nodded, distracting her with his frown, as if he didn't like their alliance, despite its being his idea. Well, neither did she. But he was right. The truth of what he said made a mutual understanding necessary. Because she didn't have the strength to battle him every time he walked past her.

So, like it or not, and unless she wanted to walk away— which she didn't—she had to agree. "All right," she conceded. "We have a deal. But I want to add something."

Another shrug, another gesture with his hands. "Fine. Shoot."

"Exactly. You keep your damned hands to yourself. Because the next time you lay so much as a finger on me, the deal's off. And I *will* shoot you."

An eyebrow rose, a slow grin spread across his face. "Deal," he finally said, holding his hand out. "Shake on it? And then I won't ever touch you again."

Angel stared at his hand as if it were a coiled snake. Then she raised her head to look into his eyes. Their blue depths glittered with a dare, one Angel couldn't let pass. She shifted her weight and wiped her right hand on her . . . well, his . . . denims. Then she held it out, meeting his grip. "Deal."

His handshake was warm and firm, not too much pressure. But still it seemed to travel up her arm, raising gooseflesh as it went. The deed done, her mouth suddenly dry, Angel tried to pull her hand away. But his fingers tightened around hers. She stiffened, barely stifling a gasp of surprise.

"In this new spirit of honesty, Angel," he said, "I have to tell you . . . keeping my hands to myself may be the hardest part of the bargain for me."

The sight of Angel Devlin in his kitchen stopped Jack in the doorway. Now why in the hell had he said that earlier? he wondered. About not being able to keep his hands to himself. He'd just said that to tease her, maybe shake her up some. But now . . . taking care not to give himself away to her as he rested a shoulder against the doorjamb and folded his arms over his chest . . . he wasn't so sure that he'd been teasing.

Grinning, not feeling the least bit guilty about essentially spying on her, Jack gave in to the sheer pleasure of watching her. With her back to him, she went busily about preparing a meal. And innocently excited Jack beyond anything he'd ever felt. It was true. He did itch to touch her. *And what man wouldn't?* he thought. She was a beautiful sight to see. Eyes and hair as black as night. Skin a light tan and soft-looking. Her body ripe with womanly curves that took his breath away.

And otherwise, damn her, she was all sass and daring. That was Angel Devlin. No doubt about it. With her words, her body, her attitude . . . she pushed him, challenged him. And he reacted every time. Strongly. Physically. *Damn* but he wanted her, he now admitted.

Jack shifted his stance, willed his body's reaction to settle. Wasn't this just the hell of it, he chastised himself? Of all the women in the world, he ached for the one he couldn't trust. Sure, he'd told her earlier that he didn't think she'd killed his father. But what he needed was to be *sure* of that. In his heart and in his mind. And where was the proof? He had none. Neither did she. Only her word. Only his willingness to accept it. Even if just for now.

So why in hell was he putting himself through this? he wondered. And then answered . . . because he *could* feel the tug of her, because he *did* ache to touch her, to hold her. But what if he did, only to discover later that she *was* guilty? In that eventuality, he'd have to shoot himself in the head. It was that simple.

But after an interesting afternoon spent in his father's office, searching for deeds and titles and such, and coming up empty-handed, he now suspected he could take that chance, could risk this unlikely partnership with her. Because from what he'd seen—and what he hadn't found—he now believed she was only a small part of the mystery that surrounded the deserted Circle D ranch. On that basis, if no other, he felt he could give her the benefit of the doubt. If she wanted it. If she cared. If she wouldn't laugh at him . . . and then carry out her threat to shoot him.

A bit of humor quirked Jack's mouth—and reminded him that, despite their handshake, she remained his adversary. She was someone who wanted everything that was his. *Yeah— everything but me.* The thought had Jack again mouthing a silent curse. Why did he care? Wasn't this a bit sudden, all these feelings he was having for her? Hell, he acted as if there were already something—something good—between them. When there wasn't anything at all between them. Except suspicion and distrust.

So why then did he feel as if he'd known her for years? That they'd experienced so much more than they actually had? Was it because of all the strong emotions they'd put each other through in such a short time? Strong emotions that arose from difficult circumstances? Could be, Jack decided. Maybe.

But suddenly he saw her as she'd been earlier that afternoon out at Pa's grave. Her eyes had widened. She'd risen slowly to her feet, and wordlessly turned and walked away. Then she'd stayed away from him the rest of the day. All because he'd said he'd have a hard time keeping his hands off her. But would he? Jack frowned at that question, his eyes narrowed. Angel Devlin was a threat to him and to the Circle D. He'd do well to remember that. So, the sooner he got his answers from her, and she was away from here, the better off they'd both be.

He could question her now, he supposed. No, he was too tired. And too hungry. So, instead, he stood there, quietly watching her every move. Like a silk shawl around a woman's shoulders, she seemed to slip around the room, to flow over the open space. And what was she cooking? He glanced over the meal's ingredients spread across the chopping block in the center of the room. Judging by the smells, she knew her way around a meal. In fact, it was the beckoning aromas wafting up to his bedroom that had finally drawn him down here, his stomach rumbling angrily.

But now that he was here, he didn't know what to say, what to do. Was she cooking for them both? Or just herself? Was he supposed to help her? Or stay out of her way? He would've asked her all that, except . . . she was Angel Devlin. She might move like silk, but she bit like a rattler. Jack knew her well enough already to know he'd get a fight for every word he uttered. He grinned. All that was true but, damn, right now she sure looked like her name, like an angel. Again, he raked her up and down with his steadily heating gaze. She was a *most* pleasing figure of a woman.

In his heightened state of awareness, Jack saw her as almost calculating in her innocence and her unguarded sensuality. Right now, he wanted nothing more than to reach out and pull her to him. He also wanted very much to nuzzle her neck, to pepper kisses down its column, across her shoulder . . . *Whew.* Jack shifted his weight, willing away his body's response to her. This was Angel Devlin he was lusting after. Again, that stopped him, cooled his thoughts and his body. Because she'd do exactly as she'd said she would. She'd shoot him if he touched her.

As if to prove it, his gaze winged to her left hip, where a gunbelt with a holstered Colt rode low and ready. One of his old guns, he recognized. So she'd use his own gun against him, huh? *Yep*, came his instant and amused reply to himself.

"You going to stand there all night staring at my backside? Or are you going to help get this supper on the table?" She never even turned around, just spoke over her shoulder as she pulled down the oven door and, her hand protected by a wadded-up bit of thick towel, lifted out a skillet of baked cornbread.

Caught—and feeling guilty for it—Jack straightened up, denying the heat of embarrassment that stained his cheeks. "I'm going to help," he declared, thinking he sounded silly just saying the words.

"Good," she said, hefting the hot skillet to the top of the

wood-burning stove, closing the oven door, and then finally turning to him. She now eyed him in that unnerving manner of hers as she pulled the towel off her hand and flung it to the drop-leaf table in front of her. Her hair was pulled back and an apron protected her white blouse and the front of her brown skirt. She'd changed out of his muddy denims from this afternoon. Actually, she looked wifely. Except for the Colt she'd strapped on . . . much to Jack's continued amusement.

She must have picked up on his assessment of her appearance because she glared at him, snapping, "If you don't help, you don't eat. At least, not what I cook."

"Fair enough. What do you want me to do?"

She eyed him a moment longer and then looked around, reminding Jack of a field general surveying his troops, before finally telling him, "Set the table."

"Yes, ma'am." With a slow grin, Jack came away from the doorjamb, intent on the china cabinet and the plates stacked inside it. "Is that a new rule? You don't help, you don't eat?"

"It is. And get those big bowls. We'll need 'em. It's a stew. A chicken stew with dumplings."

Once they'd sat down and had gotten past the awkwardness of their first shared meal together, once they'd eaten and were ready to push their now empty bowls away, Jack rested his elbows on the kitchen's tabletop, tented his fingers, and broached the subject that had been bothering him all during their meal—a most delicious and satisfying one, he had to admit.

"Earlier, Angel," he began, garnering her sober attention when he broke the quiet that, before now, had been punctuated only by the harmonious clinking of silverware on china. "You said something I didn't understand."

Warily, Angel stared back at him. Then she lowered her gaze to her plate, laying her knife beside it—just so, as if its placement were a matter of great significance. Finally, she looked up at him again. "And what was that?"

Jack watched her closely, realizing that his question was the first test of the bargain they'd struck only today. "Earlier, you said you'd made your own way in life. Or so you thought. What'd you mean by that?"

Angel's chin rose with her deep intake of a breath. She looked away and exhaled. Her hands slipped away from the table's edge, sliding down to her lap. After a moment, she turned back to him and explained. "All those years I worked at the hotel, I *thought* I was making my own way. But it turns out I was wrong. If we can believe your father."

Jack's jaw clenched. Gone was any notion of being smitten with her looks. Instead, he gritted out, "My father never told a lie in his life."

Her gaze steady, she said, "I'm not so sure about that, Jack."

Despite her quiet use of his name, outrage stiffened Jack's body and squeezed his heart. "Be careful what you say. A man is only as good as his word. And I won't sit here and listen to—"

"He was paying my way. Did *you* know about that?" she asked, cutting him off.

Into the charged silence between them Jack blurted, "What? Paying your way? What does that—how do I know you're telling me the truth? That he actually said that?"

She bristled, sitting up straighter and jutting her chin out. "Because I don't lie, either. Name one I've told you."

"I can't," Jack admitted readily enough, adding, "But neither can I name one truth you've told me. One that you can prove."

Angel leaned forward, holding his attention with the heated force of her black eyes. "I told you where to find your father."

He hated like hell doing it, but Jack was forced to concede that she had. "Yes, you did."

"Yes, I did," she came right back. "I didn't lie about that. And I'm not lying about this. Your father told me himself that he paid my way. And don't think I like the notion one bit more than you do. Because I don't."

"Well, we share that, then. Because you're right. I *don't* like it."

Apparently his words, or something in his voice, got to her. Because she settled back in her chair and, when she spoke, it was in a softer, more thoughtful tone. "I don't expect that you do. But I'm the one who's beholden to him for it." She looked down at her hands a moment before again meeting his gaze. "I was hoping you'd know why he'd put out good money on me."

"Well, I don't." Jack firmed his jaw. He hadn't meant to snap like that. He allowed a wordless moment to pass before asking, "What does that mean, anyway? He paid your way?"

"Just that. He paid Saul, starting when I was twelve, to let me work and sleep at the hotel, even when there was really no job. Saul paid me out of what your father paid him. That's according to your father."

"Unbelievable," was Jack's soft response.

"Yeah. So, either he paid out the money . . . and lied to you about it. Or he didn't pay it out . . . and lied to me."

Jack heard her, knew the truth of her words, but couldn't seem to stop himself from defending his father. "He didn't lie to me because he never told me one way or the other. In fact, I don't think I ever heard him even say your name. But I don't see how he could slip that kind of money, for that many years, past me." Mounting emotion had Jack hitting the tabletop with his fist. "I've done the accounting books for years. I would have noticed."

"Didn't he keep cash around?"

Jack caught and held her gaze. He saw where she was going with this. And he didn't like it. Because it was totally logical. "Yeah, he kept cash around and"—now he began to understand—"he made regular trips to Red River Station. . . ." He thought about it and stared at Angel, who looked as sorry as he was surprised. "Well, I'll be a son of a gun."

"Then, it's true," she said. "At the least . . . he had his secrets. And I'm one of them."

A sudden thought all but twisted Jack's gut. "Angel, are you telling me you're his . . . daughter?"

A strangled chuckle erupted from her. "No. I knew my father. He was a farmer and died at Red River Station when I was five. My mother didn't—well, she never . . . took up with men until after that." Then, after a long pause, she added, "I'm not your sister, Jack."

Relief . . . layers of it . . . coursed through Jack, warming him and dampening his skin. Relief because of his strong attraction to her, mainly. But relief also because of the life she'd led and the guilt he would've felt for her being unclaimed by his father. And even further relief—he wasn't proud of it, but there it was—because if she'd been blood kin, that meant he'd have to share the Circle D with her. He wasn't prepared to do that.

Jack looked at her. "This is too much, isn't it?"

She nodded, crossing her arms under her bosom and making her words sound like a dare. "Yep. A real can of worms."

Jack considered her, knowing she wouldn't give an inch, no matter how ugly it got between them. Anger and resentment exploded through him, his muscles bunched, begging for physical release, and he wanted to jump up and pace the room. But he was as good as glued to his chair by the emotional force of her revelation. His father had paid for her upkeep most of her life. Why would he do that? Jack decided to put that very question to her. "Why in the hell would he do that, Angel? And I mean pay your way."

She shrugged, looking awfully calm and collected. He hated that about her. Because around her, he was neither of those things.

"I don't know," she said. "I asked him the same thing. And he just said because he owed me."

"He owed you?" Bracing his palms against the table's edge, Jack leaned in toward her. "What'd he owe you? And why?"

Angel made a wide "who knows" gesture with her hands. "I asked him that, too."

"Well, what did he *say*, Angel?" Jack heard his abrupt,

even belligerent, tone but couldn't help it. This was crazy, what she was saying.

"Well, *Jack,*" Angel mimicked, "as I recall, he said the answers were all here."

"Here?" Now Jack sat back—with enough force that he nearly sent his chair over backward. He grabbed for the table's edge to steady himself. "Here? At the Circle D?"

Now it was Angel's turn to lean forward and place an elbow on the table. Despite his surprise, a detached part of Jack's mind insisted on pointing out to him just how wrenchingly sensual she was, even in the kerosene lamp's smoky light. Struck speechless, as much by her physical nearness as by her words, he could only watch as she rested her chin against her fisted hand and nodded.

"Yeah. Right here at the Circle D," Angel said.

Jack shook his head, feeling a need to clear it. He gestured at her with raised index fingers, holding them as if they were twin revolvers. "Wait. Does that explain your being here? A search for answers?"

She considered his questions. "Yes, it does. That, and he said he wanted me to own everything here. The cattle, the ranch house, the land, the money. Everything," she answered.

Jack jumped up, sending his chair tumbling over. "What? What the hell are you talking about?"

Angel came to her feet. "I'm talking about the truth." Her voice sounded as controlled as her movements.

Jack could only stare at her. Assaulted by questions—why had his father interfered in her lynching? Why had he paid her wages? Why had he said he owed her?—Jack wrenched away from her, kicking his overturned chair out of his way and rubbing at his throbbing temples as he muttered, "Jesus, what's going on here?"

From behind him came Angel's response. "I wish I knew. But Mr. Dal—your father—died before he could, or would, tell me anything. He said . . . he said there were some papers here . . . for me."

Lowering his hands to his sides, Jack turned to her, noting

her hesitations and her air of plunging forward with this bit of information. "Papers?"

"Legal papers. For me to sign."

"Legal papers for you to sign," Jack heard himself repeating as his mind raced. "So . . . you could make everything yours?"

"No. So he could."

Anger invaded Jack's soul, made him speak in a low, threatening tone of voice. "And did you sign them, Angel?"

She shook her head no, but didn't say anything. Jack thought that wise of her. "I see. You haven't signed them. But do you know where they are? Do you have them, I mean? Because I spent all afternoon in the office and upstairs in my father's room—"

"I know. I heard you," she interrupted.

But Jack went on, as if she hadn't. "—searching through his belongings and not finding one single scrap of paper. Not a ledger book, a will, a document, or even a deed of any sort. Even the safe is empty. Would you know anything about that?"

She swallowed, looked hesitant. A cold, sick feeling invaded Jack's gut. Was she trying to get her story straight before she answered? Finally, she shook her head and told him, "No. I searched . . . looking only for the papers to do with me. But everything, like you saw for yourself, was already gone when I got here over a week ago. The safe was open and cleaned out, too. I never had the combination."

Jack stared at her. Could he believe her? *Should* he? was a better question. After all, if Pa'd paid her way all these years and felt he owed her something—hell, *everything,* according to her—then he surely could have given her the safe's combination. Jack had to wonder if, in his four-month absence, his father had maybe lost his mind, like some old folks do. Her tale certainly made it sound like he had.

Either that, or the old man had deeper secrets than those concerning Angel Devlin. But if she was telling the truth, then *who* had already stolen every significant piece of paper on the place—as well as all the money? Who had, essentially, wiped him out . . . and left him with only Angel Devlin?

Another possibility presented itself to Jack. Maybe she had a partner. Maybe her job was to use her lies and her femininity to distract him and keep him from searching too quickly for the truth. And while she did, her partner got far away with the deed and the money. After all, they were talking about a lot of money here.

Things like this happened all the time, Jack knew. Some lonely rancher got taken in by a huckster female and ended up penniless. Or dead. Jack raked his angry gaze up and down her . . . and decided there was only one way to find out the truth about her.

Seven

Angel didn't much like the look on Jack Daltry's face because it had her name written all over it. For about the hundredth time today, she told herself she was sorry she'd cleaned him up. An image of his naked, muscular body, and her pulse-pounding reaction to the sight, leaped unbidden into her consciousness. She instantly squelched it, telling herself he'd been nothing but a pain in the ass since he'd been sober.

Yes, she should've left him to die and then buried him out back next to his father. And that was another thing. How'd a good man like Mr. Daltry raise a son as troublesome as Jack Daltry? Inching her hand down and over until she felt the pistol at her side, Angel commented, as calmly as she could, "I don't know what you're thinking, cowboy. But let me remind you . . . I have a gun strapped on."

He straightened up. "Part of our deal was you won't call me cowboy."

Angel's eyes widened. She'd forgotten that, but she said, "I remember. And *another* part of it was you're not to lay a hand on me. Do *you* remember that?"

He spread his hands wide in a gesture of acquiescence. "I do. And I have no such intentions . . . unless you want me to."

Angel tipped her tongue out to moisten her suddenly dry lips. "Well, I don't. But I think you're lying. Your mouth says one thing. But your face says another."

"Does it?" His eyes narrowed, his features became wolfish. "And what does my face say, Angel Devlin?" He started toward her, coming around the small table.

Angel locked her knees to keep from fleeing. She'd die first before she'd turn tail and run. Especially since she was the one who was armed. She ripped the Colt out of its holster and poked its business end into the firmness of his shirt-covered abdomen. But his arms remained at his sides. True to his promise, he didn't touch her. *Damn him.* "Your face," Angel said, swallowing and looking up into his, "says you'd like me for dessert."

He nodded, smiling without showing any teeth. Angel believed that if she could see them, they'd be pointed. Because his blue eyes sparked fire and heat. And his voice rumbled low in his throat. "That'd be a sweet end to the evening."

Angel arched an eyebrow. "I don't know about sweet. But it sure as hell would be an end. A bloody one. And all of it yours." Never looking away, she used her thumb to cock the hammer spur on the six-shooter she held. "Your call . . . Jack."

"You won't pull that trigger, Angel."

She swallowed, feeling the sweat trickle down her spine. He was going to try her hand. The damned man was going to make her have to kill him. "Try me," she again challenged.

"I will. But there's something you should know first. That pistol you're poking into my gut is my old one."

Angel shifted her weight, and wondered why she was listening to him, even as she said, "Is that supposed to stop me?"

"No, but there's something wrong with its firing mechanism. Which is why I quit carrying it."

Angel hated herself for asking, but couldn't stop herself. "What's wrong with it?"

He chuckled, didn't look the least bit afraid of her and her—his—pistol. "Well, what's important to you is, if you fire it, you could end up shooting yourself. Instead of me."

A frisson of fear coursed through her at such a prospect, but Angel narrowed her eyes. "You're bluffing."

"Am I?" A wolfish grin spread his lips back over his teeth—which weren't pointed.

Nervously, Angel split her gaze between the gun stuck against his belly and the look of challenge in his eyes. "At such close range, how could anyone but you get shot?"

He never blinked, never hesitated. "Pull the trigger and see."

Angel huffed out a breath, finally admitting to herself that she wasn't going to shoot him . . . or herself, as the case might be. But she hated his guts the whole while she released the hammer spur and lowered the gun to her side. And even though it had to be obvious to him, she snarled, "I'm not going to shoot you. Not like this. But I ought to, you snake. I ought to. Because I still think you're lying."

"About what?" He hooked his thumbs into his waistband and grinned, adding in a voice lowered to a husky whisper, "What am I lying about, Angel?"

Her mouth dried. He was going to make her say it. Damn him. Suddenly, she didn't know where to look, and realized she was cutting her gaze this way and that. Not liking this sudden bout of girlishness that was heating her cheeks, Angel settled her gaze on him, peering at him directly, as if her eyes were weapons. "About . . . both things. Meaning, the gun. And . . . about—" Sudden anger at his teasing expression made her temper explode. "About putting your hands on me, you son of a bitch. You know exactly what I mean, Jack Daltry."

"No. I didn't," he said around a chuckle. "But I do now." With that, he reached out, gripping her by her arms. Realizing his intent, Angel stiffened, resisting his tug. But it was to no avail, as he used his superior strength to pull her against his chest. "And you're right," he said around his leering grin as he peered down into her upturned face. "I am lying. About both things."

To prove it, he lowered his head, covering her mouth with his.

His kiss . . . Angel's first . . . proved so startling, so hot and penetrating, so wet and swirling in its passion, that she stiffened—as much against the foreign feel of a man's lips on her own as against her own body's rebellious awakening. Her shocked protests—no more than muffled moans against his mouth's pressure, moans that seemed to incite him further— would have been bellows of outrage had she had her own air and some distance between their bodies.

Fighting not to give in to him—even as her pulse raced in time with her heart's pounding—Angel's fingers flexed angrily, involuntarily—and tripped the trigger on the forgotten pistol she still held. An explosion ripped through the room, pegging a bullet right through the wood flooring at their feet and accomplishing what Angel hadn't been able to do on her own. Getting Jack Daltry to release her.

And release her, he did. With a shove that had her stumbling backward, he yelped "Son of a bitch!" and sidestepped right into the drop-leaf table to his right. Dirty dishes crashed to the floor. Openmouthed with shock, Angel didn't know where to look first. At the food and crockery splattering the floor and the wall. At the neat little hole in the floor at the table's edge. Or at Jack, who bellowed, "You could've killed me with that damned thing. What the hell were you thinking?"

Angel pulled back at his tone and then stared at the smoking gun in her hand. Then, swiping her sleeve across her still wet lips, meaning her gesture as one of contempt, she wiped away his kiss. Her triumphant grin ruled the next moments as she held his gaze, and said, "What was I thinking? That I could've killed you with this damned thing. You think about *that* the next time you act on any suggestions that come to you—with regard to me—from below your waist, Jack Daltry."

Angel had more to think about than she could focus on. Her jumbled thoughts, and resultant sleepless night, had her awake and standing at her bedroom's narrow window early the next morning. Her hair was a sleep-ratted mess about her shoulders, with stray curls tickling her crossed arms. She hugged herself and stared into the distance—with all the expectant intensity, she suddenly realized, of someone awaiting a messenger who was already late.

What was she doing? she asked herself as she stepped back, denying the tension that banded her forehead and lifted her shoulders. Why, this was just plain silly.

But blaming a sudden shiver of anticipation on being clad only in her small clothes on this cool morning didn't seem to be the whole truth, either. There was more to this sense of dread that gripped her. The coming day held . . . danger. She just knew it. Could smell it, almost taste it. Someone was coming. Someone was out there. Almost immediately, though, Angel discounted her intuition. Again she called herself silly as she turned and stepped away from the window.

Just then, from outside, came the most mournful howl she'd ever heard. And it had her turning back to the window, the hair on her arms standing up. Could it be what she thought it was? A wolf's howl. And from very close by. She'd heard wolf calls before and they didn't generally frighten her, as she knew that wolves left alone those folks who didn't mess with them.

But this one—well, it was just plain crazy, but she felt sure this howl was meant only for her, that only she could hear it. Looking this way and that, holding back the curtains, she searched the yard, the barn's service court, the outer grounds. Nothing. Then she focused on the meadow, where she'd picked the bluebonnets. *The wolf flower.* And saw him.

A big white wolf stood among the flowers. And stared right at her. Angel's gaze locked with the wolf's . . . and held. Fear jetted through Angel, had her clasping her hands together over her heart, her breath leaving her in short gasps. The wolf seemed, somehow, to commune with her. Angel found herself reaching out to it, her hand encountering the closed pane of glass. With determined but fumbling motions, she jerked the window up and stuck her head out, searching for the spot—

The wolf was gone.

"No!" she cried out, not even knowing why, just feeling the loss. "No," she repeated, with a whimper of emotion. And then she stayed there, hoping, fearing, she'd see him again. But as time ticked by, and the sun continued its ascent, he didn't reappear. Angel finally drew her head in and closed the window. Turning around, she stared at the room behind her as if she'd never seen it before. She felt strangely out of place now. And not because she was in Jack Daltry's house. It was hers now. Not his.

That thought got her moving. She crossed the room to where the man's borrowed dirt-encrusted denims and chambray shirt lay across the back of a chair, where she'd left them yesterday. Angel reached for the shirt. But her hand stalled in midair. She stiffened, staring at the two garments as if they were coiled rattlers. The idea of putting these clothes on her back felt too much like . . . well, like wearing *him* all wrapped around her today. It must be that kiss last night that made her feel this way.

Angel grimaced at the remembrance of the man's lips pressed to hers, at his tongue swirling inside her mouth. Even as her knees weakened, threatening to give out and send her to the floor, even as her bones seemed to melt, Angel was clenching her jaw and telling herself that she hadn't liked his kiss . . . dammit. She hadn't. So the rest of it, her hesitation, her giving the kiss any meaning or power over her, was just plain silly.

With that, Angel's breathing slowed and she felt better about herself. There, that did it. With renewed determination, she scooped up the shirt, first settling it around her shoulders, and then slipping her arms into its rolled-up sleeves. As she buttoned it, and refused to think about whose it was, she forced her scattered thoughts onto perhaps more mundane but certainly more important things. Namely, coffee. The only thing she really wanted right now. Strong coffee. And lots of it. And after that?

Well, she had to admit, she didn't rightly know. Not with Jack Daltry here. In the week before he'd arrived, she'd gone about the business of settling herself in, of establishing her own routine, of deciding what needed to be done, and then doing it—her way. But with him here . . . well, she just didn't feel like she owned the place, like she had any right to proceed with her own plans for the Circle D. Not that she had any grand ones so far. Not that she was able to think beyond her next meal here. But still, it didn't seem fair or right, this notion that she had to consult with him before she did the least blasted thing.

But that was how she felt. Angel jerked up the man's denims and took the two or three steps to the bed. There she flopped heavily down on the sleep-mussed linens, clutching the trousers in her clenched fists and staring down at them. Too bad it wasn't his neck in her grip, she lamented. *Well, now what?* Huffing out her breath, Angel searched the room as if her answer lay hidden in the armoire or the chest of drawers. One thing she did know—she sure as shootin' wasn't sitting in here all day. He'd think she was hiding from him.

Her eyes narrowed. Well, he'd better think again. Angel flipped the pants out in front of her and stuck her feet and legs into them. She then stood and hiked them to her waist. Just as she did, the door to her bedroom burst open. A reflexive tightening of her fists around her pants, as she clutched them to her belly, accompanied her gasp of startlement.

For there stood Jack Daltry, fully dressed and glaring like a belligerent bull. The man filled the doorway. In his hand was the same Winchester she'd pointed at him the day he rode up. Recovering some, Angel yelped, "What the hell do you think you're doing? This is my—"

"Nothing here is yours," he barked. "Are you expecting someone?"

Expecting someone? Angel's gut clenched, along with her fists. She was reminded of the danger she'd sensed earlier. Her gaze riveted to his, and fearing she gave away her thoughts, she mutely shook her head and finally got out, "No."

The sudden downward tilt of his chin and his raised eyebrow clearly said she hadn't succeeded in keeping her fear off her face. He didn't believe her, not one bit. "You sure? A partner, maybe? Someone helping you?"

"Someone helping me?" Angel repeated. She didn't like

his inference one bit. "Helping me how? I don't have a—"

"Someone's coming. If you know who it is, and you care about him, you'd better speak up right now. Because I aim to shoot first and ask questions later."

Angel huffed out a breath, shifted her weight to one leg, and dared him. "Go ahead. Shoot him. Whoever's coming is no kin to me."

For some reason, one she couldn't fathom, her words stiffened him, had him releasing the doorknob. His gaze shifted to a point over her head and he muttered a name, which Angel barely heard. But it sounded to her ears like "Seth."

Sensing imminent danger, Angel didn't move, didn't say anything. Because she felt it, too. A presence. An evil one. She watched the play of emotions over Jack's face. Finally, his features hardened. He lowered his gaze to look into her eyes. Angel all but gasped as her heart lurched into an erratic beat. Jack's eyes, with their intense stare, were hot enough to scorch her skin. "Stay here," he rasped out.

With that, he stepped back and closed the door behind him. Stunned, Angel stared at the impassive solid-wood barrier. *Stay here?* Should she? Stiff-legged, her bare feet as good as nailed to the braided throw rug under them, she looked around helplessly. *And do what?* Who was this Seth? The more she thought about it, the more sure she was that was the name Jack had mumbled a moment ago. Angel bit at her bottom lip. And knew she couldn't just stand here. If Jack—no, the Circle D—needed defending from this Seth character, then she'd be the one to do it. Or the one to help do it.

Besides, *just who the hell did he think he was?* Angel June Devlin took orders from no one. And it was high time Jack Daltry learned that. Her decision made, Angel tucked in her shirt and buttoned and belted her denims with hurried but precise movements. Then, marching over to her stockings and boots—and Jack's old Colt revolver, holstered and hanging over an edge of the dry sink's framed mirror—Angel vowed she'd show him she was here to stay.

*   *   *

Standing on the verandah, a booted foot propped up on the hitching rail that fronted it, the Winchester held loosely in the hand that he rested against his bent knee, Jack watched his younger brother ride up. Alone. To all appearances, anyway. Jack flicked his gaze to Seth's left and right. No movement anywhere to forewarn of hidden henchmen. You wouldn't think someone coming home would need to be covered while he did so, but this was Seth.

Casually spitting on the ground to his right, Jack then focused again on the lone rider approaching him. And held all other thoughts and considerations at bay. This boy—how old was Seth now? Twenty-three, maybe, to Jack's twenty-eight?—warranted and deserved his strictest attention.

"Hello, Seth," he drawled when his younger brother reined in his big brown horse.

"Morning, Jack," Seth answered, adding a nod of greeting to his words. He stayed in the saddle, grinning. But there was no welcome, no warmth, in his expression. More of a dare, a try-to-figure-out-why-I'm-here look.

Not willing to play Seth's game, not this time, Jack cut to the heart of the matter. "What are you doing here?"

Seth chuckled as he notched up his stiff-brimmed hat. "In case you forgot, I live here, big brother."

His words had Jack fisting his hand around the Winchester. "Like hell you do. What do you want?"

Seth sobered, shrugging as he looked around Jack, as if he were searching for someone. "Thought I'd see Pa."

"Well, you can't," Jack said, garnering Seth's attention again.

"Why the hell not?"

"Because he's dead, Seth."

Seth stiffened, sat up straighter in his saddle. His eyes narrowed. "Dead? What happened?"

"That's what I'd like to know," Jack said, swallowing around the lump in his throat caused both by his father's death and his own failed relationship with his kid brother. And then he waited . . . in vain . . . for the least sign of grief from Seth. The empty moments ticked by. And each one ate at Jack. Did the kid just not care? But Jack already knew the answer to that. No. Seth didn't care. Never had. Not about anybody or anything . . . except himself. And sometimes Jack doubted that his brother even cared about his own hide.

Finally, Seth said, "I hope you're not accusing me."

Jack's gut twisted at the thought . . . a son killing his father. And how like Seth to be defensive. But Jack was glad he could shake his head in denial. "Nobody's accusing anybody of anything. But Pa *was* killed. He didn't just die."

"Is that so?"

Seth's reaction enraged Jack. His muscles bunched with a powerful urge to leap right off the verandah and onto Seth and beat the hell out of him. He acted as if Jack had just told him one of the horses, and not their father, had been killed.

"Do I have to fight my way past you, Jack? Or are you going to invite me in, so I can pay my last respects?"

"Respect?" Jack snorted. "The time to show respect for your father is when he's alive, Seth."

Seth chuckled. "You haven't changed a bit, have you, Jack? You were always the good one, weren't you? Always the one with your nose up Pa's sorry ass."

"Why, you little son of a—" An ugly emotion had Jack pushing himself away from the railing and setting aside the Winchester. "Is that all you've got to say about your dead father? Get down off that damned horse. I'm gonna kick your ass, boy. And it's high time I did."

"You can try, big brother," Seth said, swinging his leg over his horse's neck and ripping his Stetson off to send it sailing away from him. Like a cat, Seth landed lightly on his feet, already unbuckling his low-slung six-shooter from his right hip. "Come on. I've been wanting this day for a long time."

"Have you? Well, here it is. Hope you like it." Jack took the two steps to the ground in a single leap and grabbed Seth by his shirtfront, flinging him in a half-circle that had him stumbling to the hard-packed dirt of the gravelly yard.

In a flash, Jack—bigger and more muscled than his younger brother—jerked Seth upright and punched him in the jaw with a powerful right hook. Seth grunted and reeled backward, but kept his feet, recovered with a shake of his head, and came in a driving tackle at Jack. Crouched and ready for him, Jack sidestepped his brother's charge and sent another right to Seth's belly, which doubled him over and had him gagging. Reflexively Seth clutched at Jack's arm, but Jack jerked himself free, his heart pounding with anger and hatred, his fists balled and ready.

But as if he'd never been hit, and with a mighty grunt of effort, Seth suddenly came up, his hands fisted together into one pile-driving weapon, and caught Jack under his chin. Crying out, Jack flew backward, landing on his butt, jarring his spine. Stunned by the blow, unable to move, Jack saw Seth reeling around with the force of his own effort, saw his brother's knees buckle. *Good,* was Jack's one thought. He shook his head, tried to clear his vision, tried to get up. But his equilibrium wouldn't return. Nor would his arms support him. He fell back onto his elbows, tried to draw up a knee but couldn't.

Through the red haze of his pain, he looked down at his blood-covered shirt. And more blood spattered onto it as he watched in dread and fascination. *Where's that coming from?* a functioning part of his mind wanted to know. But he didn't get the chance to find out because just then a shadow fell across him. Jack, still dazed and fearing he was losing his grip on consciousness, looked up. Only to see Seth standing over him . . . with a gun in his hand, which pointed at Jack's chest.

Breathing erratically, Jack stared up at Seth. "So . . . this is"—he drew in a sharp breath—"this is . . . how it'll end, huh, Seth? You"—another breath around the pain exploding through his head—"going to shoot me?" Talking cost him. Jack closed his eyes, heard Seth pulling the trigger hammer back on his pistol.

And heard Seth say, almost pleasantly, "I suppose so, big brother. Say hello to Pa when you get to hell."

The next sound Jack heard . . . the last sound he heard . . . was a gun firing. And the world went black.

* * *

"That was the warning shot, mister. Now drop that gun and step away from your brother. He's passed out. You don't shoot a man when he's down."

Seth Daltry had spun toward her when she fired on him before he could kill his brother. Even now he was crouched into position and had his Colt aimed at her. Then a slow grin split his lips as he relaxed his stance. "Well, will you lookee here? Angel Devlin. You sure you want to come between blood kin like this, girl?"

Angel didn't even blink. "Blood kin or no, you aren't going to shoot him. Not before I can kill you." She got her words out, even as another part of her mind dealt with the fact that he knew her. But that wasn't so strange because more men knew her on sight, thanks to her mother's reputation, than Angel could ever count. But until this moment, when she'd heard all she needed to as she stood in the shadowed doorway behind Jack, she'd not known of the existence of Seth Daltry. But that was neither here nor there. What was important was facing him down now.

"Cat got your tongue, Miss Devlin? That'd be a shame, because if you're anything like your ma, you got a real nice tongue. And you'll know what to do with it."

A blazing anger mixed with outrage had Angel grimacing, almost snarling. Her entire body stiffened, her finger squeezed reflexively around the trigger, but she stopped herself from shooting and called out, "The only reason you aren't dead where you stand, Seth Daltry, is because I think your brother deserves the honor of killing you, should that fine day come."

Now he laughed outright. But it had a crazy kind of sound to it that stood the hair up on Angel's arms. "You're probably right," he called out, as cheerful as if he'd just accepted an invitation to dinner. Then he looked her up and down, saying, "Since you're not going to shoot me, why don't you put down that rifle and let me come pay my respects to my pa?"

"Like hell I will," Angel assured him. "But I do want you to drop *your* gun." She waited. But all Seth did was grin—as handsome and blue-eyed as the devil himself—and shake his head no. *Damn.* Angel's gut tightened. But she knew what she had to do. "Suit yourself. But should you change your mind, just call out."

With that, she swung the rifle down and to her left until it pointed to the ground directly in front of the verandah's steps. Immediately, she began firing, employing a smooth back-and-forward motion of the trigger guard. Bullets, dust, and noise skipped across the hard ground, lancing a path right to Seth Daltry's feet. Silently Angel kept count of the number of times she fired.

Only when Seth jumped back and yelled out did she raise the Winchester, pointing its noisy end at his chest, and say, "That was seven. Plus the one warning shot, which makes eight. By my count, I've got eight more shots. So . . . are you feeling lucky? Or are you figuring on dropping that pistol?"

Red faced and sweating, Seth Daltry threw his pistol down and jerked his hands up over his head. "You're a crazy bitch. Crazy!"

She nodded and drawled, "I'll add your name to the list of folks who've already agreed with you. Now get your mangy horse and your hat and clear out of here. Leave the gun."

"Like hell I will—"

Angel lowered the Winchester, aimed, worked the trigger guard, and fired, hitting the ground right between Seth's legs. He yelped and jumped back, this time nearly losing his balance. "I said leave the gun," Angel reminded him. "And I also said clear out. I meant that, too."

Without taking one step toward her, Seth Daltry exploded with anger, kicking at the ground and balling his fists up, one of which he shook at her. Angel remained outwardly impassive but, inside, her heart lurched and lunged about her chest, as if it were no longer anchored in place.

"I'm leaving. But only for now," Seth called out. "I'll be back, little lady. And when I am, you better watch yourself. Because I'll do worse than kill you. Worse. You mark my words."

Angel swallowed, nearly choking on the dryness in her

mouth and the tightness in her throat. She believed every word he said. She'd just made a powerful enemy. As Seth jerked around, stalking toward his hat and his horse, Angel spared a glance for Jack. He still lay on the ground, not moving. Was he dead? But she didn't get to decide how she felt about that possibility because at that same second, the sound of a horse's high-pitched whinny captured her attention.

Facing his horse, an enraged Seth Daltry had grabbed the animal's reins and was jerking them, trying to get his mount to stand still. But in the process, all he accomplished was scaring the fool critter to death as the loose ends of the leather thongs whipped this way and that, striking the frantic animal's chest. It tried to rear and got itself purposely whipped this time. Angel's lips firmed in anger. She stepped forward, her fingers tightening around the Winchester.

"Stop it!" she cried out, even knowing he couldn't hear her, not over the horse's bellows. With everything inside her, she wanted to help the big, terrified animal. But couldn't, not unless she meant to shoot Seth Daltry or put herself within his vengeful range. She wasn't prepared to do either of those things. Not today. Not that she'd mind shooting him. But she didn't much fancy the notion of telling Jack Daltry, if he was alive, that another of his kin was dead. And once again, she'd be the only person around.

Finally, and mercifully, Seth got the quivering animal to stand still long enough to mount it. As he settled himself in the saddle and again fought the lathered horse, Angel dragged a deep breath into her constricted lungs and, teeth gritted, tried to stare the man down.

As Seth Daltry turned his horse to face Angel, he yelled a warning. "Until the next time, Angel Devlin. Until the next time."

With that, he gave a war whoop like a Comanche's and dug his spurs into his horse's sides, turning it and racing away from the Circle D, away toward the low rolling hills of the prairie.

Angel's knees gave out. She sank to a sitting position on

the verandah, her legs hanging off it, the Winchester standing upended between her legs, her forehead resting atop her hands, which were clutched around its barrel. Only then did she realize there were tears coursing down her cheeks.

Eight

A moan from Jack finally made Angel raise her head from atop her hands. Moving the rifle out of her line of vision, she swiped one-handed at her tears and peered out into the yard. He was moving his legs and trying to sit up or turn over, she couldn't tell which. But instantly, she was on her feet and laying the Winchester on the worn wood flooring of the porch. Then she took the two steps as one and ran over to him. The sight of so much blood running over the man's neck and chest stopped her cold. She couldn't help but recall finding Wallace Daltry the same way. "Jesus," she whispered.

Beside Jack now, Angel dropped to her knees and folded her legs under her. She put a hand on his shoulder. "Just hold real—"

With a startled gasp, Jack Daltry jerked, grabbing her wrist and twisting it sideways. Angel cried out and hit at him, even as he rolled on top of her, his other hand to her throat. Crushed under him, pinned and helpless, she lay there stunned, staring up at him. In less than a few seconds, his expression changed from a snarl to shocked surprise. "Angel. What the—"

Now that he knew it was her, and not his brother, Angel let her feelings be known. "Get off me."

"What?" he said. But then he looked down at himself . . . atop her. And jerked up and away from her. He followed that with a gasp as he stared at her chest. "You're bleeding," he yelped. Then he gripped her arm, helping her to sit up. "Jesus, I'm sorry."

Angel wrenched her arm out of his grasp. "I'm sure He's right glad to hear that. And will take it into account, come Judgment Day."

Jack smoothed her hair out of her face, saying, "What?"

Angel batted his hand away. "Nothing." Then she pointed to his blood-soaked shirt. "You're the one bleeding. Not me. I think it's coming from your chin."

"My chin?" he repeated, sounding dazed, as he looked down at his shirt and held it out with a hand. "Damn. I am." He rubbed his chin, checked his hand, and saw what Angel did. A thick red smear. Then he captured her gaze, mouthing, "Seth." His eyes narrowed. He rolled to his feet but instantly bent over at his waist, clasping his knees with his hands and hanging his head down between his shoulders. "Whew. I'm dizzy."

"I'm not surprised." Angel came to her feet and gripped his arm, felt his warm, hard muscles quivering. "It's okay. He's gone." But about the last thing she needed right now, in case his brother did decide to show up again, was Jack passing out on her this far away from the Winchester. "Why don't we make our way over to the verandah so you can sit down?"

"All right," he agreed, as docile as a lamb. He then surprised her by putting an arm around her shoulders, which all but forced her to encircle his waist with one of hers and put her other against his chest. Under her hand, his heart beat steady and strong. And felt reassuring. But he was pale and sweaty. So Angel allowed him to lean heavily on her as she walked him across the yard and even held on to him as he— very gingerly—sat himself on the porch's edge. Once he was settled, she tugged his jaw up, telling him, "Raise your chin. Let me see that cut."

But Jack captured her wrist, forcing her to look into his eyes. "It's okay. Where's Seth?"

Angel wanted nothing more than to look away, but didn't dare. "I told you. He left."

A muscle jumped in his jaw. His mouth worked. "Seth doesn't just leave, Angel."

Angel huffed out her breath. There was no sense in telling him about his brother's warning. It was probably just an empty threat, anyway. And even if it wasn't, it was her problem, not Jack's. And so she just said, "Well, he did this time."

"Tell me what happened."

"You just don't stop, do you?" Angel's rising temper had her looking away. Taking his silence as his intention to outwait her, she turned back to him, ready to tell him what had happened. But her breath caught, her attention captured by the incredible blue of his eyes. In the space of a glance, she found herself riveted by the powerful effect his strong masculine features had on her. With a desperation born of reluctant awareness, she tried to shake off her reaction by focusing on how he looked now . . . dust covered, beat up, and bleeding. And on keeping her voice from betraying her confused emotions when she asked, "So what's the last thing you remember?"

His eyes narrowed, his expression hardened. "Seth standing over me with his gun in his hand. But what I want to know from you is how you stopped him. I know you did because Seth wouldn't stop himself."

She should have expected that he'd know his brother. Again, Angel contemplated him, focusing this time on the world of hurt that must lie hidden behind his matter-of-fact words. More of a reason not to add to his worries, she decided, saying, "What happened, meaning what I did or didn't do, doesn't matter. The important thing is he did leave. And what matters is . . . you're alive."

His eyebrows winged up. "It matters to you that I'm still alive?"

"I didn't say that. I just supposed your own hide meant something to you." Then she yanked her arm, tried to pull her wrist out of his grip. "Are we going through life joined like this, cowboy? Or are you going to let me go?"

Jack started to say something to her, but apparently

palms were sweaty, a part of her mind noted. "I've changed my mind, Jack Daltry. It's all yours. Everything. I'll be leaving now."

His eyebrows veeing over his nose, Jack bolted to his feet. "What? You can't leave."

And that was exactly what she needed for him to do. To dare her, to tell her she couldn't do something. "Watch me," she said, turning on her heel.

Behind her, he grabbed her arm and spun her around. All she could see, looking up at him, was the dried blood starting at his chin and coating his neck and shirtfront. "Why are you leaving? What happened? Did Seth lay a hand on—"

"No." Angel now looked pointedly at Jack's hand on her and then raised her head until she met his angry eyes. "He didn't touch me. If he had, he'd be dead. Or I would." And then she waited. He released her. "Smart," she assured him, as she again turned away from him and stalked toward the barn, speaking to him over her shoulder. "I'll be taking only what I brought with me. And that'd be my horse and the clothes on my back."

"Those are *my* clothes on your back, Angel Devlin."

Angel stopped, her eyes popping open wide as she stared straight ahead and absorbed his words. Then she looked down at herself. At his shirt and his denims. *Damn.* She spun around, jamming her hands to her waist as she stared into those glaring blue Daltry eyes of his. "You can't spare these?"

He slowly shook his head no—and meant it, she could tell. Angel bit at her bottom lip, felt her chin jut out. "Fine," she spat out. "Keep your danged duds."

In a towering anger that had her acting outside the bounds of cool reason and her normally overweening modesty—perhaps a backlash response to her mother's constant baring of her body—Angel yanked and tugged on the chambray shirt's tail, trying in vain to free it from the tightly belted denims.

Jack Daltry held his hand out, as if he meant to stop her. "What the hell do you think you're doing?"

Short of breath from her straining efforts in the day's

steadily warming sun, Angel stopped her tugging and said, "I'm giving you your clothes back."

"I don't want them back."

Defeated, Angel dropped her arms to her sides. "I'm burning daylight standing here and jawin' with you, Daltry. Make up your mind."

"I didn't change it," he told her. "I don't want them back. But you can't have them, either."

Angel thought she understood. And it stung. "What are you going to do? Burn 'em because I wore 'em?" Sudden tears sparked her eyes, had her swallowing. "They're too nasty to wear since they touched my skin. Is that it?"

Jack jerked angrily. "Oh, for—I've had about all of that I'm going to listen to. Get that damned chip off your shoulder, girl. You're not the only one who's had a hard life. Plenty of people have had it worse than—"

"Maybe so. I wouldn't know. But I don't give a rat's ass about any of them. Or you, either"—Angel stabbed a pointing finger at him—"Jack Daltry. So stay out of my business." She jerked around, took two steps toward the barn and her horse, but decided she wasn't through with him. She pivoted again to face him. He hadn't moved. "And I'm keeping your danged clothes. Mine aren't worth the putting-on anymore. And it's too bad if you don't like it."

That got him moving. He stormed toward her. Angel took a step back for every step forward of his, but his stride was longer, and he caught hold of her in three steps and pulled her to him. "Tell me why you're leaving."

Control of her temper a lost cause, Angel strained upward as if she meant to bite his nose off. "Tell me why you don't want me to."

"Because I—you never told me—" He frowned and stared at her a long time. Like wind-blown tumbleweeds, conflicting emotions ran across his face. Then . . . he chuckled. "ave no idea." He let her go and laughed. "Go, then."

ow Angel frowned as she tried to deny the stab of dis-
intment that he'd give up so easily. "Fine. I will." She

then tested him further, saying, "And I'm keeping your clothes."

He shrugged. "Fine. Keep 'em. You need any money? A gun? Food?"

Angel cocked her head to one side. Why was he being so cooperative all of a sudden? "Yeah," she said, hating the hesitance in her own voice. "I can use all that. And a bedroll."

"A bedroll. Okay." He shook his head and ran a hand through his hair. Then he grimaced and gingerly probed the open cut on his chin. "You think that before you go, you could sew this up for me? In exchange for your provisions, of course. And not because you're the least bit beholden to me."

"What?" Angel snapped, her hands again finding her waist. "I don't like the sound of that, cowboy. Me—*beholden*—to *you*? For what?"

He started ticking items off on his fingers. "For those clothes you're wearing. For the roof over your head—"

"Hah!" Stiff-legged, Angel advanced on him, stopping only when she stood toe to toe with him and had to crane her neck to meet his gaze. "A roof over my head? I had to use a gun to keep it there. You didn't do me any favors, Jack Daltry. *You* owe *me*. I cleaned you up. I saved your sorry ass when you were too drunk to care if you lived or died. I brought your pa home and buried him. I've done the cooking and the mending around here. And I just now saved you again from your own brother. So don't—"

"And that's another thing"—he now poked her chest with his finger—"you don't know where my brother is. He could be anywhere out there . . . just lying in wait."

Angel grabbed his finger, shoving it away, even as a shiver of fear coursed through her. Jack was right. But she wasn't about to give in. "I can take care of myself."

Jack spoke in a low voice, as if he didn't wish to be overheard. "Can you? Seth killed his first man when he was twelve years old. A harmless old drover by the name of Odie

Grossman. Just shot him in his sleep one night because he snored.''

Angel was appalled. "Well . . ." she said, casting around for something to say. "Too bad for Odie," she came up with. "He shouldn't have snored." With that, she again pivoted away from Jack. And again headed for the corral and her horse. Again she threw her parting comment over her shoulder. "And *I* shouldn't have come here."

She'd taken about four long strides, figuring she'd won the last word, when he called out, "Why *did* you come here, Angel Devlin? And what are you running away from now?"

A while later, as storm clouds gathered in the sky above, Jack stood outside the corral's split-rail fencing, his arms resting along the chest-high top rail, a booted foot against the bottom one. He had washed up some and changed his clothes, and now he quietly watched Angel Devlin saddle her horse. His gaze heated with desire and appreciation for the way her slim hips swayed and moved as she worked. Any other woman probably would have looked comical in denims as big as his were on her. But she didn't. Far from it. No, she was all woman. Jack mentally applauded God for His exceptional handiwork.

Just then, Angel's roan captured Jack's attention when it turned its head to stare curiously at him. This horse, Jack decided, was one of the finest-looking cow ponies he'd ever seen. Well muscled. Long legged. An intelligent look in its eyes. It also looked familiar. That star on its forehead . . . Hadn't Mr. Henton's young drover—what was that kid's name? Ben something?—been riding it the last time he'd been through?

"Angel," Jack called out, having finally seized on a legitimate enough reason to call his continuing presence to her attention.

Angel's hands stilled, but she didn't turn around, didn't ⸻ him. Not that he'd expected her to. She hadn't said a ⸻ o him since she'd stalked out here and set about the ⸻ s of leaving. Jack's gaze slipped to the ground, to the bedroll and neatly packed saddlebags he'd presented her with a few minutes ago. True to his word, he'd gathered together everything she'd said she'd need when she left. *If* she left. In his mind, that wasn't settled yet. He'd only collected it all to humor her. Because he still meant to talk her into staying.

Realizing she hadn't answered him yet, that she'd gone back to minding her own business—something he wasn't doing—Jack grinned, watched the swing of her long hair as she worked, and called out, "Hey, I'm talking to you."

"I hear you," she barked out, still not turning to him as she tightened the saddle's cinch under her horse's belly. "And I already said I wasn't sewing up your cut. So what do you want?"

"My cut's fine. It doesn't need stitching. What I want is to ask you about that animal. It looks familiar."

Again, her hands stilled. She turned just enough to send him a sidelong stare through that tangled hair of hers. For about the tenth time, Jack wished he could take a brush or a pair of scissors to it. He slipped his attention back to her face when she began speaking. "The animal looks familiar to you because it's a horse. You might remember riding in on one."

Caught off guard, Jack laughed out loud. Not only was she fast with a gun, she was one of the fastest wits he'd ever run across. He wondered if she knew that about herself. Or even cared. She glared another moment and then turned back to her roan. His laughter having now sudsided to a stray chuckle or two, Jack watched her backside with great appreciation.

But his humor was suddenly displaced by a solemnity that he couldn't explain. His gaze now roved over her slender, fragile frame as if he sought its breaking point, as if he sought a crack in her that needed to be repaired. *If she leaves here,* came his thought to explain his shift in mood, *she'll run into Seth.* Jack stiffened, felt the anger build in him, as if Seth already held her in his clutches. Like the thunder that rumbled closer and closer, Jack boiled with his emotions. And knew . . . he'd kill Seth, the little bastard, if he so much as laid hand on her.

Everything inside Jack told him he should be

dling a horse, preparing to ride after Seth. He'd like nothing better. But how could he? He had no idea at which of Seth's hiding places he could be. Or if he'd be at any of them. Furthermore, Jack knew, if he did go, Angel would be in danger, because Seth could come and find her here alone. That is, if Jack could convince her to stay. Say she did, he reasoned. That meant, if he went looking for Seth, she'd have to go with him. And it wasn't very likely she'd agree to that.

Gripped by an acute agitation brought on by his difficult choices, Jack swiped a hand over his mouth, irritating the raw cut there. He grimaced at the pain and fumed that his best course of action was proving to be . . . doing nothing. Which was how he saw sitting tight at the ranch and waiting for Seth to come back. Because Seth always did. Which was small comfort. But the next time, Jack told himself, he'd be ready.

But even if Seth hadn't existed, even if he wasn't a threat, Jack knew he still had reason enough not to want her to leave. As scanty as her knowledge about recent events here at the Circle D might be, she still possessed the only information he was ever likely to get about them. And about his father's untimely end. To Jack, Angel's knowledge represented his only starting point for setting things right in his life. Or as right as they could ever again be.

But there was yet another reason why he couldn't stand the thought of her riding out of his life. The truth was, he'd miss her like hell. Every contrary thing about her. From that long hair always in those black eyes of hers, to her slender, womanly form and her graceful way of moving about. And her stinging wit and quick intelligence. Divining his own thoughts, Jack stilled, as if he'd just heard a friend confess to being smitten with Angel Devlin. What would he say to such a friend? *Wave good-bye as she rides off*. That's what he'd say. So what was he doing?

Well, if he had any sense, he'd take his own advice. But Pa had always told him he didn't have any, that his Daltry temper and his acting-before-thinking always got the best of ——— Jack grinned, almost laughed at himself. Here he was, ——— up to that legacy by annoying her until he could think up some reason why she had to stay. He focused on her again, saw her slinging the saddlebags up behind her saddle. If he was going to keep her here, he'd better talk fast. "Where you intend on heading?"

"That's my business," she said, not looking his way.

Her answer was the match that lit the fuse on his temper. Jack fought to tamp the angry fire inside him. "You don't have any idea where you want to go, do you?"

She turned on her heel. "Don't you have something better to do, cowboy?"

"Yep," Jack said, nodding. "I do. But it'll keep until you're gone." Then, while he had her attention, he pointed out, "There're some mean-looking clouds rolling in, Angel. You noticed 'em yet?"

"Yep, I did . . . with the first grumble of the thunder."

Jack took in the challenging glint in her eyes. She obviously still expected him to try to stop her from leaving. Which was exactly what he was doing. "So you don't mind riding in the rain?"

She shrugged. "I did it before, on the way here. I dried out okay."

Again Jack nodded. "I bet you did. You got a slicker?" When she shook her head no, he persisted. "You want one?"

Angel eyed him the way wild horses do when they're boxed in and waiting for their captors to make a move. She looked around, as if trying to determine how to escape. "Why are you being so . . . nice and helpful, all of a sudden?" she asked.

He thought of his awful behavior toward her the entire time she'd been here. Trying to provoke a strong response from her, he said, "What do you mean 'all of a sudden'? When was I *not* nice and helpful?"

She took the bait, stiffening and glaring. But before she could do more, a booming clap of thunder rumbled across the prairie sky. Startled, Jack jerked away from the split-rail fence, glanced heavenward. Angel grabbed the agitated roan's reins and soothed the horse with pats and strokes down its arched neck. As the rumbling lessened, she called out, "Even

the Almighty had to call you on that lie. Nice and helpful?
Hah.''

Jack's mood darkened right along with the weather. As a
wind blew up and the landscape was blanketed in a deepening
gray, he no longer saw the humor in humoring *her* in this
ridiculous idea she had about leaving. She needed to stay.
That's all there was to it, and it was high time she heard it.
''You can't leave in this weather, Angel. Hell, go if you have
to. But just wait until this passes. You'll get yourself killed
out there.''

Stroking the roan's nose while she held down on its reins,
she laughed humorlessly at his words. ''Get killed *out there*?
My life's been threatened right here no less than three times
by two men. Thanks, but I'll take my chances on the trail.''

And that was all Jack needed to hear. In one easy bolt, he
was over the fence and stalking toward her. The closer he
came, the wider those black eyes of hers got. But she didn't
back away. Jack stopped in front of her. ''I knew it. Seth
threatened your life, didn't he?''

Briefly, she looked uncertain, perhaps even a bit fearful.
But as usual, she covered it with a thick layer of bravado and
a squaring of her shoulders. ''So what if he did? You did,
too. What's the difference?''

Damn her. When it came to words, she always had him
roped and tied before he even got out of the chute. ''The
difference is,'' Jack began, speaking slowly and deliberately,
hoping that she'd take his words to heart with regard to Seth,
''unlike me, my brother'll do it. He'll kill you.''

Angel slid her gaze away from his, but not before Jack
saw the fear there. She made a show of paying attention to
the roan and making soothing noises to it. After a moment,
she turned back to him. No fear remained in her eyes. ''I
believe you. I believed him too when he said it.''

''Why didn't you tell me?''

''It wasn't you he threatened.''

Jack's temper flared, making his eyes burn. He looked off
toward the barn and mouthed, ''Son of a *bitch*.'' Then feeling
more in control, he focused on Angel, contemplating anew

her smallness, her saddled horse, the packed bags behind the saddle, and her determined face. "You're not going anywhere," he said, sounding to his own ears like a judge handing down a sentence. "Not until Seth's had time enough either to get far away from here or to show up again."

"Is that so?" She jutted her chin out at him. "And how are you going to stop me?"

Jack exhaled mightily and looked her over. And knew what he had to do, as much as he hated it. "How? Like this," he said . . . as he fisted his hand and popped her in the jaw, knocking her out cold and catching her limp body up in his arms, all in one smooth move. Startled, her roan shied and skittered away to the other side of the corral.

"Shit," Jack cursed loudly as he settled her slight weight against his solid frame and turned toward the enclosure's latched gate. "I really didn't want to do that, Angel," he told her, speaking as if she could hear him. "But you just wouldn't listen to reason."

And I'm betting that I'd better not be anywhere around here when you wake up, either, he thought as he fumbled with the gate's latch and stepped outside the corral. Kicking the gate closed, he turned and strode toward the house, his bundle of female no more burdensome to him than a kitten. As he warmed to the feel of her in his arms, as he became aware of her warmth, of her curves, the first raindrop fell, landing on Angel's cheek and trickling down like a teardrop.

The sight stopped Jack in his tracks, sobering him. Emotion suddenly ran liquid through him. Tears pricked behind his eyelids. And scared the hell out of him. This feeling . . . so strange . . . as if he could look into the distance and see the future. It had something to do with her. He stared into her face. She was so beautiful. Her head lay in the crook of his arm. She could be sleeping. But the angry, swelling knot on her jaw said otherwise. Seeing how he had marred her flesh, Jack could only hate himself for what he'd done, even if it was for her own good.

But was it, really? Had he done her any favors by keeping her here? As if in answer to his questions, a feeling of overwhelming despair welled up inside Jack. The crushing emotions nearly sent him to his knees. *Angel!* Her name was a cry from his soul. He gazed at her intently. She couldn't be more delicate, more finely boned, more like the child she now appeared to be. Her body was all woman, her words sharp and cutting, but she was a wounded fawn otherwise.

Before he realized what he was doing, before he could think it through and perhaps stop himself, Jack straightened out his arms, raising them, holding her limp rag-doll body up to the heavens. As if this were its signal, the sky split asunder, sending cascading sheets of rain down on them in earnest. The stinging drops pelted them like lashes from a whip, soaking them. The wind, like circling vultures, skirted them, flapping and mocking. Jack heard the hoarse yells, realized they were his.

"Why?" he cried out. "Why is she here?"

No one answered. Sudden foreboding had him clutching her tightly against his chest as he crouched over her still form. Did he seek to hide her? To protect her? From what? The coming storm? *Yes.* But not this one . . . not the rain and the lightning that assaulted them. Another storm. Another danger . . . Seth.

From the corral, Jack heard the frightened roan's grunts and bellows, but he couldn't help the poor animal. No more than he could help the woman in his arms. Sudden defeat tore a jagged hole through Jack's being. He'd made a mistake in keeping her here. That sudden conviction clamped viselike around his heart. He should've let her go. He knew this now, just as he knew he too was lost.

He tried to attribute some of his emotion to his father's death, to his trying to hold it all in. But he realized that was wrong. Whatever this was, it had less to do with Pa than it did Angel. Again he lowered his head, stared into her rain-soaked face. Did she know she was lost? Whether she did or not, it was too late. Whether she stayed or not . . . it didn't matter. Because she'd never get away. She was caught in his destiny. Or he was caught in hers.

Either way, it didn't matter. The results would be the same.

Because keeping her here had set retribution in motion. It was that simple. That hard.

As if frozen in time, Jack stood there, his eyes closed, this innocent woman limp in his arms. And wanted to give up. Right here. Right now. But that didn't happen. His heart continued to beat. His brain to think. His blood to course through his veins. *Nothing could be crueler than to live.* Jack heard the words as if from outside himself. Frightened, gasping, he straightened up, stiffening his legs as he looked around. But he and Angel were otherwise alone.

Then he looked to the bundle in his arms. His breath left him in a hot exhalation. As if awakening from a dream, he looked around, realized he was standing . . . soaked to the skin . . . in the rain . . . holding Angel Devlin in his arms.

Just then, she stirred, whimpering like a crying child, mouthing something unintelligible as she raised her arm, as if meaning to stop the rain from beating upon her skin. But she was still weak, and her arm fell back, hanging limp.

The sight tore at Jack's heart. His hands fisted around her clothing, around the warm feel of her arm and her leg, as if he needed to touch her living body. As if he needed to assure himself that she still drew breath.

"*Oh, God, Angel,*" he cried out. He blinked away the teardrops of rain that ran in rivulets down his face. "I am so damned sorry. Can you ever forgive me?"

Just then, there was a sound Jack hadn't heard in years. He jerked his head up, his spine stiffened . . . he listened. There it was again. The hair on his arms rose in fear and warning. The mournful howling of a wolf. But not just any wolf. Jack's heart thundered. His blood coursed like lightning through his veins.

The white wolf.

Slowly, against every instinct in himself, Jack turned around. For an instant, the wind died, the rain ceased. And the earth held its breath. There . . . in the meadow, among the bent and fallen heads of the bluebonnets . . . she stood. Old Mother. The white wolf. Looming larger than life, seeming closer than she actually was, she raised her big head, her pointed ears pricking forward. Her eyes—the same blue as Jack's—bored into his. He swallowed, clutched Angel to him.

But even from a distance, the she-wolf reacted to his gesture. She raised her head, laying her ears back, and howled.

Nine

Angel jerked awake. She sat straight up, staring across the lamp-lit stuffy room. And wondered how she had got here. Outside, lightning cracked, thunder boomed. With a start, Angel turned her head, seeking the sound. Looking out the narrow window across the room, she saw the storm that raged outside. The wind rattled the glass panes, as if demanding to be let in.

Jerking away from the sight, bracing herself with her palms flattened against the soft leather cushions she sat on, Angel again took in her surroundings. She knew this room. She looked around slowly, taking in the three-shelved lawyer's bookcase to her left, and to her right, the big dusty desk with the worn padded chair behind it. This was Wallace Daltry's office.

Why was she in here? Angel tried to recall how she came to be here . . . but the last thing she distinctly remembered was being out at the corral and saddling that roan. Her frown deepened. She'd been talking to Jack Daltry. She remembered that. She looked down at herself, at her bare legs, and gasped. She'd been fully dressed then, too. And not in this clean white shirt and nothing else.

Shifting her weight, wondering what the heck was going on, she put a hand to her face, only to cry out in pain. *What the—?* She pulled her hand away, wondering why her jaw hurt. Then, she remembered. Jack Daltry had hit her. With great gentleness, she probed the area, feeling the tender lump there that met her fingers. The man had knocked her out.

And then he'd obviously . . . well, he'd undressed her and brushed her hair and—all the things she'd done to him only a few days ago. Well, his doing it to her wasn't exactly the same thing, she decided as she vowed revenge. Wait until she saw *him* again.

The room's closed door suddenly thumped open, banging against the wall behind it and rattling the pictures hanging there. Gasping in surprise and jerking her legs up, digging her heels into the leather, Angel nearly flipped herself over the back of the sofa, so startled was she. With her arms outspread, she clutched at the Indian blanket draped over the sofa's spine. In one neat swooping motion she dragged it off the cushions and threw it around her near naked self before straightening up to see—who else?—Jack Daltry entering the room. Butt first.

"Ah, I see you're awake," he said as he turned around to reveal his reason for entering the way he had. He clutched a food-laden tray in his hands. As if unsure of his reception, he just stood there, staring at her.

"Well, come on in," Angel drawled. "You already woke the dead." With that, she settled into a slumping posture and, with no small amount of malice in her heart, eyed the first man ever to see her naked. If she had any sense, she'd shoot him or cuff him upside the head or—she returned to being sensible—or leave it alone, not mention it, forget it happened.

He walked across the room, heading for a low table next to a wing chair. Angel's gaze followed him. It was bad enough he'd feasted his eyes on her, she argued with herself, so why make it worse by talking about it with him? After all, he could throw it in her face that she'd done the same thing to him. And had done it first. So what good could come of taking him to task over it? He couldn't take it back. Well, he could have the decency to gouge his own eyes out, Angel decided. But figured the odds of getting him actually to do that were awfully slim.

"You're pretty quiet over there," he remarked as he bent over the table.

Angel sniffed, now eyeing the man's denim-covered butt and his muscled thighs as he did so. Her eyebrows arched. She exhaled a sharp little breath. Finally she remembered to answer him. "Nothing to say, I guess."

He straightened up and turned around, barely giving Angel enough time to lift her gaze to his face. He stared at her, grinning, raking her up and down. Under the Indian blanket, Angel felt too warm. "You do nice things for that blanket," he remarked.

"I guess you'd know," Angel snapped before she could think better of her words, much less her moments-old decision not to bring up his having seen her naked. Instantly he sobered, but her face heated, afraid to hear what suggestive or downright dirty thing he might say. She'd heard such things all her childhood years when she'd lived at the saloon with her mother. And expected no less from him.

"I did only what I had to, what I felt needed to be done, Angel. Nothing more. I didn't do anything to you that you didn't do to me the other day."

Just as she'd known he'd say. But other than that, the man's comeback was a decent one. Angel lowered her gaze to her lap. How dare he be so nice as to make her feel ungrateful for his looking after her? Then she remembered. She wouldn't have needed looking after if he hadn't popped her in the jaw. Her head snapped up, she started to tell what-for, but—

He'd turned away, back to the tray he'd brought in, and was now ordering its contents to his liking. Angel caught herself again staring at his backside and exhaled another sharp breath, quickly forcing her gaze to the dishes from which an aromatic steam arose. The curling scent chased away the musty kerosene odor of the room. And made her stomach growl. Under cover of the blanket, she clutched at her belly, willing it to be quiet.

She flicked her gaze to Jack, fearing he'd heard it and would tease her. But he didn't turn to her. So she took a moment to scrutinize the man's appearance. And found herself wondering just how long she'd been out. Because he'd done plenty in the meantime. He too looked freshly washed and dressed. Just like her. But unlike her, he had on pants. And boots. His hair was wet and combed straight back off his high forehead. Angel's hair wasn't wet, but it was brushed back away from her face and secured at her nape.

As Jack began dragging the table over closer to her, Angel gave in to her curiosity, worming her hand out from under the blanket's folds to feel for what fastened her hair. A piece of ribbon. It was made of a soft fabric, something she'd never owned before. It felt like the satin she remembered fingering at Jesse Chisholm's trading post before he caught her and told her he knew she didn't have any money, that she was to put it down . . . and to keep her dirty fingers off his merchandise.

Angel stored the memory, wondering only why Jack Daltry had such a piece of ribbon, as he sat down next to her on the sofa and held out a spoon to her. Angel looked at the spoon, then up at Jack's face, saw the mocking challenge in his eyes. Huffing her breath out, and being careful to keep the blanket secured around her, she took the danged spoon—snatched it from him, was more like it—and directed her question to him. "What's this for?"

"The soup."

"The soup?" she repeated. He nodded. Warily, Angel looked from his face to the tray. Sure enough. Soup. And bread. Thick slices of it. She'd made this bread a couple days ago. But couldn't account for the other. Still clutching the spoon, Angel looked again to Jack. "When did you make soup?"

He gave her a sheepish look and then shrugged, saying, "While you were, um, out. I was beginning to get worried, you were out so long."

Angel's eyebrow rose. "You were so worried that you cooked?"

He chuckled. "It'd seem so. Hell, I just threw everything together and set it on the stove. I thought it might taste good to you—" He cut himself off as if he'd realized what he'd said. Looking unsure of himself again, he ran his hand through his still damp hair and said, "I don't know how good it is."

He'd made this for her? To make her feel better? Angel stared at him, long enough to blink a few times before she thought to check out the soup. Meat chunks and sliced spring vegetables swam around in a nice brown broth. It looked okay to her. But she held her spoon out to him and said, "You first."

He chuckled again. "That's fair." And took the spoon from her. Then he picked up the bowl and dipped himself some of his own handiwork. Then he eyed her as if she'd just ordered him to eat a writhing snake. Angel bit down on her bottom lip against the sudden bubble of laughter that welled up in her. *Stop that*, she scolded herself.

But evidently he'd seen the laughter in her eyes. Because he grinned wide and slurped up the spoon's contents. "Hmmm," he intoned, closing his eyes with a look of sensual delight on his face as he chewed and swallowed.

Delighted with his expression, Angel only belatedly realized her mouth was open . . . as if she'd taken the bite with him. She covered herself by asking, "That good, huh?"

He opened his eyes, his look baleful as he grimaced and put down the bowl. "No. It's awful. Trust me, you don't want to eat this." Standing, he picked up the tray and held it out to her. "Grab the bread and eat that. I'll go find something else—"

"No, Jack," Angel said, stopping him, her hand on his bare arm . . . and every nerve ending in her body aware that it was. "Wait. Put the tray down and sit. Please." Angel heard the new softness in her voice and hated it. She *never* said please. What was happening to her? Even worse, she had no idea why she'd asked him to stay. But she had, and now his gaze locked with hers. He studied her a moment. Angel willed herself not to look away.

Finally, he did as she asked. He put the tray down and sat down, bracing his forearms against his thighs and folding his hands together. Hanging his head between his shoulders, he angled a look over at her, obviously unsure of her intent but willing to wait until she told him. A defiant lock of his black hair slowly slid forward over his forehead.

Angel's heartbeat leaped. He was purely the most handsome man she'd ever seen, as well as the first one she'd ever remarked on in such a way. She took a deep breath and tried not to stare at him, tried not to give away her tingling response to him. Her hands fisted around the blanket's edges as she made a mental vow to herself that she would not have feelings for Jack Daltry. But just having to vow it told her it was already too late. *I have feelings for Jack Daltry?* She inhaled sharply, garnering a questioning frown from him.

"You okay?"

"Yeah, but no thanks to you," she shot back. And liked that response. Comforting, it was. Even familiar in its harshness, in its standoffishness. This was more like her. Angel rode the crest of that emotional wave, finally telling him, "I ought to shoot you for hitting me."

As if feeling guilty, he turned hurting blue eyes on her as the words poured out of him. "I figured you'd feel that way. I don't blame you. But I didn't have a choice. It was the only way I could get you to stay here."

"You think so? You think I'm staying now?" Angel tried to scoot forward on the leather, but her bare skin stuck to the fabric, wouldn't allow it. Nor would Jack's hand on her arm. She tensed, narrowing her eyes at him.

"Hear me out, Angel. Please. If you still want to leave when I'm done . . . then, fine. I won't try to stop you. Deal?"

What choice did she have? He still held her in place. He had a six-shooter strapped on. The storm still raged outside. She had no idea where she would get more clothes to cover herself. And even less of an idea where she'd go once she did leave. So, she was stuck here, as surely as her behind was stuck to the leather cushion under her. Given all that, she slumped back against the cushions and huffed out her breath, saying, "Deal."

Looking relieved, but not releasing her, he said, "Good. First of all, I want to say I'm sorry I hit you. I've never hit a woman before in my life. And I can't imagine ever doing it again." He paused, looking into her eyes.

Did he want her forgiveness? Well, she had none for him. Maybe when her jaw quit hurting. Angel said nothing, gave him nothing.

"Okay." He ran a hand through his hair and went on. "I just *couldn't* let you leave. I have several reasons why not, but the most serious one is Seth."

Feeling but otherwise ignoring the heated grip of his fingers still wrapped around her arm, Angel nodded, saying, "That's some brother you have there."

Something flickered in his eyes. "You have no idea. He—" Jack stopped and sprang suddenly to his feet, startling Angel into clutching at her blanket. Obviously agitated, he stalked back and forth in front of her. "What do you suppose is going on around here, Angel? I mean, where *is* everyone? Where're the cattle? The men? Have I been robbed? If not, where's the money? And where's all the paperwork for the ranch? This stuff's eating at me. It's making me crazy."

Without warning, he stopped right in front of her, his hands fisted at his waist. "And just what the hell *did* happen to my father? And why'd he tell you the Circle D is yours?" As if he didn't expect a reply, he set off on another round of the room. "See? I don't know what to make of any of this. I should be out looking for answers. But here I am—trying to shake them out of you."

"Well, don't let me stop you—"

"But you do." None too gently, Jack scooted the tray aside and sat in its place on the heavy little table. To Angel's further surprise, he pulled her hands away from the blanket and gripped them tightly, looking right into her eyes. "The last thing I ever want to do is hurt you, Angel. And yet I keep doing just that. So what kind of a sorry son of a bitch am I, anyway?"

"You're not a—" Angel bit back her words, couldn't believe she'd been about to defend him. Disconcerted, she looked down at his hands holding hers, suddenly aware of the strong, warm pressure of his fingers wrapped around hers.

Finally, she found her voice, and tried again, raising her head until she met his sincere gaze. "All those questions eating at you are some of the same I ask myself."

She paused, allowing that to sink in before going on. "But I don't have the answers you seem to think I do. And that's the truth. What's happened here at the Circle D—meaning, everything and everyone that's missing—was already done when I got here. I don't know who did it, Jack. Or why."

His hands squeezed hers as his breath came out on a heavily accented sigh. "I feared as much," he said, speaking with almost no emotion as his somber gaze sought hers. Then he said, "Angel, I need to ask you something."

A sudden wariness had her heart thudding against her ribs, had her pulling her hands away from his. "Ask away."

He held her gaze a moment, then looked down at his empty hands. After a moment or two, he redirected his blue-eyed gaze to her face. "What's your part in all this?"

She frowned, pulling back, stiffening. "My part? Beyond your father saying all this is mine, I don't know as I have a part. What do you mean?"

"I mean," Jack began, "exactly that. Your being here now, when all this is going on. Do you think it's just luck, just bad timing for you . . . or maybe something more?"

"Something more?" Angel repeated, thinking of almost being lynched, of killing Jeb Kennedy, of her mother dying. "I can't call it any kind of luck, except bad. But I never even heard tell of you or your father or this ranch until he came to my rescue and said he was bringing me here."

Jack threw his hands wide in a gesture of exasperation, startling Angel. "That's another thing. Why, Angel? Why did he bring *you* here? Why *you*? And not someone else? What's behind him doing that? Do you know?"

Angel stilled, felt her temper rising. "I've already told you I don't know why. I asked. He wouldn't tell me. He just said the answers were here."

Jack rubbed his hand over his jaw. "There's not a damned thing here except for me and you. And we don't know a blessed thing." Then he stared at her, his heart in his eyes.

thought better of it, closing his mouth instead and staring solemnly at her. Angel felt certain the air around them thickened. She edged her chin up and glared, lest he get some funny notion about kissing her again. But all he did was release her and say, "I'll let you go. Because I don't think anyone can hold you, Angel. Not for long."

"You got that right," came her instant retort as she lowered her arm. But her sharp words belied what she felt inside. What he'd just said hurt her. His words emphasized how far removed she was from him, from everyone. Until now—until she had met Wallace Daltry and his son Jack—she'd always thought of being alone as being free. But now she knew the truth. It meant . . . being alone. With no one to care.

Always before, that had been her badge of independence. No one cared for her, and she cared for no one. Only now did she clearly see how wrong that was. How empty that was. But, given her life, she feared it was too late to do anything about it. So why *was* she still standing here, she had to ask herself, as she watched Jack watching her. She needed to move away from him. But the truth was, he wasn't the one stopping her. She was.

She was too interested in watching his gaze rove slowly over her face. As if he searched a locked treasure chest for its key. Or for a hidden opening, some undiscovered way to unlock it. Maybe she'd been wrong about what he felt for her. When Angel suddenly swayed toward him—and caught herself—panic overtook her. Had she meant to kiss him? What was wrong with her? Her heartbeat thumped, her mouth felt dry.

This was wrong. She had to get away from here. She had to. If she didn't, he'd make her . . . care, dammit. No. She'd leave right now. Just turn around and go. Forget everything. The Circle D was his. The money, the cattle, his crazy danged brother and his threats. Everything. All of it. They were his headaches. Not hers. She didn't need a home. Couldn't miss what she'd never had. She'd just saddle that roan she'd ridden in on and skedaddle it out of here. Now. This minute.

Thus spurred, Angel stepped back, fisting her hands. Her

"I wish my father was here so I *could* ask him the why of it."

Caught off guard, Angel lowered her gaze, unable to look at him. This was the first time he had mentioned missing his father, grieving for him. She didn't know what to say, what to do . . . other than to pick at her own fingers.

"Don't you feel it?" he said suddenly into the quiet between them.

Angel looked over at him. His expression was no longer clouded with sadness. Relieved, although not understanding his question, she asked, "Feel what?"

"That there's more than one thing going on here. There's you. And my father going to get you. There're the things that went on here. All the ransacking and the missing money and papers. And the men and the cattle. I hope like hell they're just on the trail to Abilene. But my father being killed . . . all that. I have to wonder if any of those things—or all of them— are connected somehow."

Angel hadn't thought of the situation in those terms. But now she nodded thoughtfully and said, "You could be right. About a connection. Like maybe things were already set to happen, things your father didn't even know about until he started back here with me. That makes some sense."

"I agree. I just wonder what that connection is."

Angel watched him rub at his jaw, watched him avoid the angry cut on his chin. When she began to warm up to him too much for her own liking, she blurted, "We probably won't find it sitting here."

He cut his gaze over to her, his expression sobering into sincerity. "No, we won't. But whatever it is we're going to find out, Angel . . . it's going to mean something to both of us, I just know it. What I'm trying to say is we're in this together. Me and you. You can't leave."

Angel huffed out her breath. "I expect you're right," she said barely above a whisper, as she stared into those blue Daltry eyes of his. What he said was true. She felt it, knew it. They were as tightly bound to each other as wet was to water. She'd been just plain silly earlier to think she could ride away.

"So you'll be staying on? At least until we sort all this out?"

She raised her head a fraction. "I'll be staying." She meant for good, since Wallace Daltry had left the place to her. But she didn't see any reason to go into all that now, especially considering the look of relief on Jack's face. But still, this new partnership between them, no matter his need to keep her here, didn't excuse what he'd done earlier. She couldn't forgive that. So she added, "Now I have something I want to say."

"All right. Go ahead. Say it. Anything."

Watching his hands, fearing he'd take hold of hers again— and thereby turn her insides to butter—Angel tucked them up under the blanket. "Up until now," she began, speaking with deliberation so that she would be sure to get her words right, "I've only made threats about what I'd do to you if you laid a hand on me—"

"Say no more," he interrupted. "I won't, Angel. I swear it. Jesus, I'm sorry. I've already told you I won't ever do it again. And I mean it. At the time, I felt it was the only way— well, no. That's no excuse, either." He looked into her eyes, holding her gaze, speaking softly now. "I'm sorry."

Angel swallowed the sudden lump in her throat and watched him lean forward to plant his elbows on his knees. He lowered his head, as if the fate of the world rested on his shoulders, and then covered his face with his hands. Angel didn't know what to do, what to say. She only just barely stopped herself from reaching out to give a comforting pat to his shoulder.

And that—seeing her own hand stretched out to him—was when she knew she'd forgiven him. A first for her . . . with anyone. She usually held on to a grudge. Before now, hoarding hurts had been one of the things that kept her strong. So was she getting weak now? Weak or not, she decided he needed to know how she felt. Without asking herself why she cared if he felt better or not, Angel broke the silence with her simple words. "I believe you."

Jack's head came up. Wide blue eyes, full of guilt and hope, stared at her.

Uncomfortable in her role as forgiver, uncertain if he even understood what she'd meant, she tried again. "When you say you're sorry . . . I believe you." His expression didn't change. Angel quirked her mouth and arched an eyebrow. "That'll have to take, because I'm not about to say it again, cowboy."

A tentative grin curved his wide mouth. "Cowboy, huh?" Then he chuckled. "Now I know you mean it."

Then he stood up, acting as if none of this had happened, and offered her his hand. "Come on. It's still early. We'll go exchange that blanket for some better-fitting clothes and then see if we can scare up something decent to eat. After that, we'll decide what our first move should be, what we can do with the rest of the day."

Angel looked into his eyes, relieved to see, from his open expression, that he most likely didn't mean . . . *that*, when he spoke of what they'd do with the rest of the day. Only then did she tug the blanket around her legs, holding it secure at her waist with one hand, and raise her free hand to meet his.

When she did, as their hands met again, as his fingers closed around hers, she looked into his eyes. He smiled sincerely, one that seemed to come from his heart. A sudden warmth spread through Angel. She felt her mouth begin to curve with a smile that wanted to answer his . . . for being heartfelt.

The late afternoon air, swept clean by the earlier thunderstorm, smelled cool and fresh, like wet laundry hanging on a clothesline. Angel breathed in deeply of its rich, earthy scent. She'd almost forgotten what it felt like to be outside, to feel the wind against her face, to smell the prairie. She supposed some would say the prairie had no scent to it. But Angel knew better. It was like . . . dried wood, like warm sand, but with a faint touch of flowery perfume to it.

What am I doing? Remarking on nature was something she'd never done until now. Before, each day had merely meant more long, hard hours of work at the hotel. So what could be different about this particular day that made her feel glad to be alive?

Perplexed, Angel tried to get to the bottom of her emotions, tried to capture the real question she wanted to ask herself. What, she finally came up with, did she have now, that gave her this feeling of being glad to be alive, that she hadn't possessed before? There. That was what she wanted to know.

Suddenly, as if the answer lurked, waiting only for her to seize on it, it popped into her consciousness. It was this. Riding her own horse across the open prairie meadows. And what it represented. This was what was meant by belonging to the land. By owning a piece of it. By having something to call your own. She loved it. Loved the Circle D. Like she'd never loved anything before.

Thinking of the Circle D in such terms brought her riding companion into clear focus for her. Angel stole a glance to her left, her breath eclipsed by just the male and muscled sight of Jack Daltry. He paid her no mind, instead casting his sharp-eyed gaze this way and that, maybe looking for anything out of the ordinary, anything that might point them in the direction of the answers they sought. While the prairie held his attention, Angel found hers caught by the thoughtful expression on his face, by the air of quiet that enveloped him. By the way he sat his big brown horse, fitting his body's movements to the animal's natural gait.

Unexpectedly, Jack glanced over at her, caught her staring. He didn't say anything, but he didn't have to. Because a trace of a smile tugged at his lips and crinkled the skin at the outer edges of his blue eyes. Under that black Stetson of his, he nodded to her, acknowledging her. Angel shifted desperately, distractedly in her saddle, as if something besides her conscience pinched her. But giving no sign that he noticed her discomfiture, Jack looked away again, off to his left.

Relieved beyond measure, Angel jerked her own gaze

away from the man, sighting instead on a nearby scraggly stand of blackjack oaks that heralded a creek's watery course. Suddenly she wished Jack would talk. Why was he so danged quiet? came her question raised by irritation with him for affecting her so. Usually the man had plenty to say. But the one time she needed the distraction of his words, even if they did always come in the form of hard questions, he kept his own counsel.

Well, Angel consoled herself, maybe she didn't much feel like talking, either. Because she'd already talked to him more in the past few days, she believed, than she had to everyone else she'd ever known, all combined. Besides that, her jaw hurt like hell and talking only made it worse. As if to punctuate her thought, her jaw throbbed, seemed to pulse.

She winced, welcoming the cool sanity of the pain. But she was still losing her battle to keep from thinking about what had happened this afternoon. It was after the soup in the office. Again she saw herself standing in the doorway to Jack Daltry's bedroom and watching him sort through his clothes. Finally he'd come up with another pair of his outrageously big denims for her to wear.

Again, she saw him tossing her the pants in an offhand manner. Again she felt them hitting her in the chest. She'd had to catch them at the expense of loosing the blanket that covered her lower half. She'd fumbled to retrieve it but had lost. So there she'd stood, her feet and legs bared to his eyes. She didn't think she'd ever forget the hot look of wanting that Jack had sent her way as his gaze traveled the length of her and held her in its thrall. Angel remembered her breath catching, remembered expecting her usual response to such a look from a man.

But it hadn't come. She hadn't turned away, hadn't stiffened in rejection. No, far from it. She'd stiffened, yes. But with a burst of desire. With a need to feel his hands, his mouth, on her. And now she was finding it hard to forgive herself for that. And hard to forgive him for awakening that need in her. She didn't want to need anybody.

What she did want was to get through this life on her own.

Angel waited, expecting a sense of well-being to flood her, to confirm that she was right to hold herself aloof, just as she always had. But it didn't happen. Only a pervasive sense of loneliness greeted her. And frightened her.

With a catch in her breathing, Angel blinked, drawing herself back to the present moment, to her surroundings. To Jack. But again her defiant thoughts won out. Again she heard his earlier words that had made them both laugh, that had lightened the tension between them. He'd said something smart about the denims being so big on her, she could probably belt them around her neck and they'd still drag the ground. Angel now looked down at herself all but swimming in his folded-up, tucked-over trousers and admitted he hadn't been too far off the mark.

And given all those feelings, and the laughter, and how she was warming up to him—and not particularly relishing the thought of being alone with him in the house all afternoon, considering the way they kept staring at each other—she'd readily agreed to take this ride over the Circle D to see if they could find any clues. Or answers. Anything was better than her own confusing thoughts.

Thoughts that centered on the man riding next to her. All her life she'd said she didn't want anything to do with a man. And now, here was Jack Daltry catching her eye—the one man with the power, the blood right, to send her away, to deny her everything she'd ever wanted. Such as this grassy land they now rode over. And the ranch house, a place to call home, a place where she could belong. Two things she'd never had. A decent place where she could make her own way and live out her life however she saw fit. Lots of folks had all that. Why couldn't she?

As if to answer that question for herself, as if she needed to prove to some unseen someone that it wasn't so much to ask, she pictured herself happy and doing just that . . . running the house, doing the chores, buying provisions, overseeing ranch hands who tended to fat cattle, doing the books—something she'd learned a little bit about from Saul at the hotel—

and riding out to inspect her own land. Like she was doing now.

You think Jack Daltry's going to stand for all that nonsense you've built up in your head, Angel? she asked herself. *What about him? What about the Circle D's rightful owner, Jack Daltry? Where does he fit in to your plans, Angel? What's he doing while you're living out your dream life?*

Poof. That put an end to her little daydream. And left her wide-eyed and wondering.

Ten

Wondering about Jack Daltry. And his final intentions once they got through this mess. Angel finally admitted she didn't know where he'd be. Or what he'd be doing in this picture she had in her head. All she knew was the Circle D was *not* his. It was hers. If he could accept that . . . then maybe he could stay on. But out in the bunkhouse. After all, she could use his knowledge of the place and the cattle business.

Her nose wrinkled with her immediate rejection of that notion. He'd not stand for living in the bunkhouse while she lived in the house where he'd been born. Well, what was she supposed to do with him, if he wouldn't just go away? Which she didn't see him doing. And she sure as hell didn't see herself marrying him to keep the ranch.

She wasn't about to marry anybody. Ever. Because she knew what he could then expect of her . . . in the bedroom. She looked over at Jack Daltry. A hot thrill raced through her, pooling at the juncture between her legs. Dammit. *All right*, she argued with herself, *I don't have to marry him.* But could it be that she wanted him . . . in that way a man and a woman wanted each other? Ashamed, embarrassed, Angel ducked her head, hating herself for even thinking it. How could she want that? She'd seen what such goings-on with men had done to her mother. It had killed her.

But then, almost as if she couldn't help herself, Angel again sent a shy glance his way. Under his stiff-brimmed hat, his black eyebrows arched above those thick-lashed Daltry blue eyes of his. His profile revealed the almost straight line of his nose, his high cheekbones, the shell of his ear, and that stubborn jaw. His mouth was set in a straight line as he peered into the distance. It was then that Angel realized a few other things about the man.

She knew his touch. The way his hands felt on her skin. The memory gave her goosebumps. She knew his kiss. The way his mouth fit over hers, what his tongue was like. Angel licked at her lips, caught herself doing so, and sat up straight. *Heck*, she fumed, frowning and forcing herself to be practical. *So what if I liked his kiss?*

Not getting any argument from herself on that score, she then felt free to allow herself, for the first time, to dwell on how she knew firsthand what the rest of him looked like. Well, how could she not? she defended herself. How else could she have cleaned up the man, if she hadn't first gotten him out of his clothes? Well, she couldn't have, came her answer. And her absolution.

Given free rein, her mind insisted on replaying for her . . . slowly . . . just how he'd looked. Tight skinned. Perfectly formed. Long limbed. Impressively muscled. That dark hair on his chest that centered to a vee as it traveled downward below his waist to where his—Angel's breath caught. She took herself to task for such thoughts of Jack Daltry by recalling, *The man had been hairy and dirty and smelly. And drunk. What's so wonderful about that?*

Now she felt better. Or did, until she started considering his character. He seemed fair and honest. And tough. Like his father. His smile was okay. He didn't mind laughing, either, it seemed. But Jack Daltry had a temper, too. *So do you*, a nagging part of her mind accused. Angel quirked her mouth, ignoring her conscience, outrightly refusing to admit that she might want not only the Circle D and all it stood for. That she might also want the Daltry that came with it.

Angel's hand fisted around her roan's reins. No, she did *not* want him, she tried to convince herself. He wasn't a piece of property she could own, anyway. Wondering how he'd take to being considered property, much like women were, got an amused snort from Angel—and brought Jack's attention to her.

"You all right?"

"I'm fine," she blurted, her cheeks heating up. He continued to stare silently and solemnly at her. This time, with more deliberation, she repeated, "I said I'm fine."

Even though his hat shadowed his features, Angel could see his eyebrows arch. "Pardon me. As long as you're fine."

Angel felt ungrateful. For what, she didn't know. But still, she found herself saying—none too pleasantly, so she could live with herself—"I suppose I ought to thank you for seeing to my horse earlier today."

He chuckled, no doubt because her irritated tone didn't match her words. But then he quickly said, "No thanks necessary. He was left out in the rain because of my bad behavior."

Angel stared at him, wondering what he meant, but then realized the bad behavior he referred to was his popping her in the jaw. "Oh. I see what you mean."

That killed the conversation for a few plodding paces before Jack spoke up again. "I ought to be thanking you, instead. I just recalled that I left Buffalo tied up at the hitching rail my first day home. Since I didn't find him still there when I sobered up, I suppose you saw to him?"

Angel shrugged. "Who else? He wasn't near as much trouble as you turned out to be."

A hearty laugh burst out of Jack, catching Angel off guard, startling her. But an answering grin fought its way to her lips. She bit down on her bottom one, willing away the humor, but failing. Because she liked being able to make him laugh. And he always did. Even when her barbed words were at his own expense. This trait of his made her wish she could be more like him, instead of always being so quick to find offense, so quick to use words to hurt.

She knew why she was that way. The life she'd led before she came here. Words had been one of her only weapons to keep folks from getting close enough to hurt her. Sure, she'd done what she had to do. But still, she wished she could be different. Maybe now, maybe in this new life she had here at the Circle D, she could learn to let her guard down, could learn to laugh. Like he was doing now.

Just then, Jack levered himself up, his palm pushing against the pommel. About midway in his stretching, as the saddle leather groaned under him, he said, his eyes still brimming with hilarity, "Angel Daltry, you're a hard woman. But still, I'm beholden to you, ma'am." He then tipped his Stetson to her.

Fighting a bigger grin, fighting her warming up to him that she couldn't seem to stop, Angel retreated some, sobering her expression. "I guess you had just cause for your drunken actions that first day. I *did* shoot at you. And it's not every day you learn"—too late she realized where her words were headed, but could do nothing at this point except continue—"your father's been . . . well, you know."

The humor bled from Jack's face, as did some of his color. He winced as if against a sudden pain and then turned away, looking straight ahead. Angel wanted to kick herself. In the ensuing heavy silence, she watched his Stetson-shaded profile, watched him look down and eye his pommel as if he'd just now realized his saddle had one.

"I'm sorry," Angel blurted, even before she knew she was thinking it. Jack looked over at her, frowning as he did. She wondered why this had to be so hard. Quickly, though, before she lost her nerve, she explained. "About your father—I'm sorry. I don't know if I've said it yet. And if I haven't . . . well, I am. I'm sorry." No wonder she never expressed her feelings. Doing so hurt, like a stomachache.

A sudden, unbidden image of her mother came into her mind. She was the one who had taught her that folks were supposed to say something nice about the dead, had taught her good manners. But she'd had no sympathy, no kind words for her own mother. Angel blinked away the image and said, "Your father . . . he was a good man."

Jack nodded, looking uncomfortable as he shifted his weight in the saddle and directed his gaze to the far horizon.

"Yeah, he was. But there was a time, not so long ago, when I would have disagreed with you."

Angel's stomach fluttered. Full of unquenched curiosity, she stared at his profile. This was her opening, she realized. With only a few questions, she guessed, she could probably find out why Wallace Daltry hadn't left everything to *this* son. Seth Daltry spoke for himself. But Jack? She watched him now, watched him as he continued his silent scrutiny of the prarie around them.

No, Wallace Daltry's decision didn't make any sense to her. With a son like him—Angel recognized the grudging respect for Jack inherent in those words—why leave the Circle D to her? Why come looking for her and save her, only to toss her into the middle of the heartache and mystery here? Just like Jack said, they were missing something—a fact, a bit of knowledge—that would clear everything up. Still, no matter how strong her compulsion to ask Jack what had caused the bad blood between him and his father, Angel knew she wouldn't. Because to do so invited confidences.

And there was just no sense in getting to know Jack Daltry any better than she already did. Because the day loomed when she'd most likely have to throw him off her land. Just how she planned to achieve that, given their difference in sizes, if not temperaments, she couldn't even begin to fathom. But another question—how to get him to *stay* thrown off—occupied most of her waking thoughts, it seemed. *Would* she have to kill him or marry him to hang on to his father's legacy to her? Angel didn't know which idea she hated the most.

A grimace of indecision captured her features. Maybe she could have killed him—she'd certainly been prepared to—on that first day he rode up, when she hadn't known him yet. But now? Now that she knew his kiss, knew his laugh, knew his touch? Knew how much he was like his father, meaning kind and decent for the most part? Angel's jaw chose right then to throb and thereby remind her of yet another side of him. And to raise suspicions of him that she'd thought she'd put to rest.

Put to rest? What was wrong with her? Was she not allowed to doubt the man's sincerity? Angel mentally shook herself, disappointed with what she now realized she'd done. She'd placed on Jack's head all the respect she'd had for his father. And once there, it was hard to retract. Oh, this was awful. If she stayed, she'd have a showdown with Jack, as sure as the sun was about to set. But there was something else she'd better face: he might not be the one who ended up lying on the ground. It could be her.

And most likely—she eyed the serious six-shooter strapped to his hip—it *would* be her. She could handle a Winchester, all right. Back at the hotel in Red River Station, she'd sneaked Saul's away when she could and had taught herself to use it. And now, Jack had let her keep his old pistol, which rode her left hip. But she knew she wasn't a real gunhand, not like Jack Daltry was. Angel sighed in frustration. For the second time today, she asked herself *why* then—if it was this hard—why she didn't just ride away and forget the Circle D?

Because, she realized—and the thought stiffened her spine—for all she knew the papers weren't here because they'd already been filed, in her name, in Wichita Falls. Maybe she didn't really have to sign anything at all. Maybe that was what Mr. Daltry'd used to get her here. After all, she didn't know any of the fine points of the law.

So until she found those papers, or got to the county seat to see for herself if they'd been filed or not, she needed to behave as if she already owned this place. Just the thought, the idea, of owning all this land quickened Angel's pulse. But there was another reason she couldn't just ride away. And that reason rode to her left. Angel crooked her neck, pivoting to peer over at Jack and consider again the bad blood between him and his father. For all she knew, Mr. Daltry might not have wanted Jack to have the Circle D because of something horrible—perhaps something to do with Jack.

So who was she to deny the old man his last wish? Angel was too smart to believe he'd just been angry at his sons and, in a vindictive mood, had picked the first ragamuffin he crossed paths with to be his heir. No, there was more to it, she now knew, because of what Wallace Daltry had told her.

She wondered if it had something more to do with him and her parents than she'd credited before now. Some huge reason why Wallace Daltry, at the expense of his own sons, owed Tom and Virginia Devlin's daughter a world of wealth. But what could it be? Until she had *that* answer . . . she wasn't giving an inch.

Well, this is just plain crazy, Angel decided. The more she thought about her predicament, the worse it got. One minute she trusted Jack Daltry. And in the next, she didn't. One minute she trusted herself with Jack Daltry. And in the next, she couldn't. What was she supposed to—

"Angel," Jack snapped, his voice low as he grabbed her arm and reined in his horse. Startled out of her thoughts, her heart pounding, Angel pulled back on her own reins and looked over at him. His features hardened as he exchanged a glance with her and then fixed his concentration straight ahead.

Swallowing the lump of fear in her throat, Angel did the same thing. And found what had riveted his attention. Big, dark birds swooped and circled in the sky. Angel lowered her gaze. And a gasp was torn from her. She put a hand to her mouth, nearly retching. Sick inside, hot and heaving, suddenly sweaty in the day's coolness, she stared in horror.

Up ahead, a slight but measurable distance away, and scattered over the wet and rolling land like so many broken branches . . . were broken bodies.

A slaughter had occurred here. And now provided a feast for the coyotes and vultures vying for position and settling among the carcasses. The snarling, snapping, wing-flapping, and screeching were deafening. Angel couldn't seem to look away. Men. Cattle. Horses. Dogs. All dead. "Oh, my God," came her sickened whisper.

"Stay here," Jack said, not looking at her as he released her arm and drew his gun.

"No," Angel snapped. "I'm going with you. I can help. They're not going to give up their find easily."

Jack wasn't happy with her announcement. He contemplated her from under the low brim of his Stetson. Angel watched the ice-blue chips that were his eyes, saw no emotion, barely any recognition in them. Then he said, his voice flat, not brooking any argument, "That's why I want you to stay here."

His voice, chilling her, streaked fear through Angel. But she swallowed and shook her head, saying, "I'm going. How do you intend to stop me?"

Jack stared steadily at her, his gaze, his will, locking with hers. Finally he exhaled, saying, "All right. But stay behind me."

"I'll do that," Angel conceded. Nodding, Jack tensed, readying himself, Angel knew, to send his horse in a galloping foray right into the middle of the feeding frenzy up ahead. "Wait," she entreated, recapturing his attention. "Who do you think that is out there? I mean the men."

He blinked, firming his mouth as he turned to stare at the scene spread before them. Angel watched him, saw the hard lines form to either side of his mouth, and waited for his response. Behind her question lay her concern that he might have more family she didn't know about, family he could find among the victims. She told herself she cared only because she wasn't about to go through another three days with him being drunk and belligerent.

Finally, Jack gave a constricted shake of his head and turned back to her. "I don't know who they are. Not by name. We're too far away. But it's got to be my hired men and some of my cattle. Jesus, I just hope it's not the cows we meant to grow our herd with. If it is, I'm ruined."

He was ruined? Angel's belly tightened. This was her land. Not his. So if there was ruination to be had, it would be hers. Her mood bleak, Angel kept that observation to herself—now was not the time for that fight—and watched Jack stare at the scene ahead.

After a wordless space of time, he turned to her and said, "Come on. Let's go." He kneed his mount, urging Buffalo into a ground-covering gallop over the treacherous, rain-slippery ground.

Taking a breath for courage, Angel put her heels to her

roan and followed Jack, her heart pounding in time with her horse's hooves. All too soon, she was beside him among the carnage and mimicking his actions, firing her pistol into the air and yelling at the carrion eaters as she danced her roan in tight, dangerous circles. The coyotes cringed and snapped, showing blood-reddened muzzles. The vultures shot up in the air amid a flapping of wings and bared talons.

Within moments, though, the creatures had either slunk away or flown away. But only to the edges of the carnage, a chilling reminder of their sly patience, of their hungry intention to return when Jack and Angel left. In the death-quiet aftermath, sickened by all that she looked upon, by the rotting stench that burned her nostrils, Angel reined in her horse and, like Jack, sat there . . . numbly shaking her head as she tried to take it all in. But couldn't.

They were all dead. There was no doubt about that. Two men who, given their positions and those of their horses, had been shot right out of their saddles. And the cattle—all cows, that she could see—lay clustered almost on top of each other. Shot where they stood, apparently, with no time even to stampede. And the two cow dogs . . . Angel swallowed. Dead. Just shot down.

"God*damm*-it! Son of a *bitch*!" came the hoarse cry off to her right.

Tightly reining in her white-eyed roan, already skittish from the scent of blood and death in its nostrils, Angel turned the horse until she faced Jack. About twenty feet away from her, he was swinging down from his saddle, his face contorted, his gaze intent on the two fallen men. He knelt between them, going down on one knee as he felt first one rain-soaked, torn, and bloodied chest, and then the other. Was he checking against hope for a heartbeat?

Angel wanted nothing more than to stop him, to pull him away, but knew she couldn't, didn't dare. She supposed that Jack knew he wouldn't find any life here, but maybe felt he needed to make the gesture. Because he could see the signs as clearly as she could. What they'd happened onto here wasn't a first feeding. Angel swallowed the sourness at the back of her throat. She'd seen her share of dead men back at Red River Station. That cow town seemed to grow nothing but misery and death.

But this way of dying—she forced herself to look upon the ravaged bodies of the dead men, men who most likely had been in their prime—was the worst. To have the life forced from you . . . it seemed to be the worst way to go.

Like Mr. Daltry. Again she saw the older man with that bone-handled knife protruding from his chest. All that blood— *the knife!* Angel's breath caught. She hadn't thought about the blade since she'd pulled it from the old man's chest, had wiped his blood off it, and brought it with her, only to hide it under her mattress. She couldn't have said right then why she was thinking of Mr. Daltry now, except that his death was more removed, less immediately dreadful, than the murdered men facing her now.

But the knife. Under her mattress. It'd been such a natural thing for her to do. Because that was where, all her life, she'd kept those few things that meant something to her. And still did. It remained the safest place, since she still didn't intend to allow anyone close enough to her to share her secrets. Or her bed. Or her life.

Sitting there on her roan, surrounded by the ugliness of death, terrified by the reality of it, Angel recalled her treasures, her comforts. A small and tattered old rag-cloth doll from her childhood. A yellowed scrap of lace from a hat of her mother's. And her father's rusted-out pocket watch. Yes, they were all under the mattress, stuffed up against the bedboards and wrapped in some oilskin . . . together with the knife that'd been used to kill Jack Daltry's father.

Fear shot through Angel once more. How could she have forgotten to tell him about the knife? Because now she would look guilty, even to her own way of thinking. But they'd hardly discussed his father's murder, Angel thought in self-defense. And too much had happened in too short a space of time for her to think of everything. Truth be told, she'd simply forgotten about it.

But now, suddenly the knife loomed large in her mind.

She needed to show it to Jack. He might recognize it, might even know its owner . . . the man who'd murdered his father. Yes, she needed to show it to him before he, for whatever reason, under whatever circumstances, found it himself in her room. Angel worried what he'd think, what he might do, in that event. She'd seen his grief, his temper . . . so she figured he'd kill her, no questions asked.

Suddenly, Angel *knew* with gut-tightening certainty what she and Jack had only supposed a few hours ago. Wallace Daltry's murder and that of his hired hands were related. She put her knuckles to her mouth, rubbing them agitatedly over her lips as she focused on Jack's hunched figure. She wondered if he suspected what she did, or if he already knew it. She wanted to say something, to ask him, but didn't dare, fearing that her guilty feelings about the knife might be written plainly on her face.

Just then, as Angel watched, Jack's fist closed around a torn sleeve, the soggy material wadding, ripping under the onslaught of his grief-strengthened grip. Angel stiffened, forcing herself to be still, to let him work through this. Jack covered his face with his other hand. But still, his muffled cries carried to her. "Who could have done this? *Why?* Why, dammit? What the hell is going on here? Will somebody *please* tell me?"

Angel swallowed around the tear-clogged lump in her throat and blinked against the wetness invading her eyes. She wanted to go to him, to put her arms around him. She wanted to comfort him, as she'd never wanted to comfort anyone before in her life. But as hard as it was for her just to acknowledge this compassionate urge in herself, she knew that acting on it would be even harder. Because, her own considerations aside, she simply didn't know whether or not Jack would appreciate her doing such a thing. She wondered if he'd push her away . . . like her mother had, more than once.

Angel figured that if she didn't know him well enough to know how he'd react, it was best if she did nothing. Unable to help, she simply looked away from such raw emotion, leaving Jack his privacy with his fallen friends.

But immediately she wished she hadn't.

Her gaze lit upon the poor dumb cattle. She grimaced, eyeing the bloated bodies, counting them. Ten head. And the dogs . . . their bodies lying in sprawling heaps next to the cattle. Those two hadn't gone down without a fight. That was a cow dog for you. He'd give his life protecting his charges. Angel's heart, full of a special tenderness for the dogs, went out to them. She'd long admired the breed's fierce loyalty and hardworking spirit. And the way they loved you whether you deserved it or not.

But the dogs, the cattle, the men, none of them deserved the end they'd met. Someone—more than one someone, given the numbers—had just cold-bloodedly killed them. Angel silently wondered who'd do such a thing, and why. What was worth this? She inhaled deeply, and exhaled just as sharply. *What a shame—*

A hand grabbed her right arm. "Angel, get down—"

A yelp of fear tore through Angel, her heart pounded against her ribs. Her roan's head came up, his ears laid flat against his head. Angel pulled back on the reins and saw it was Jack who had grabbed her horse's bridle and held on, helping her regain control. When she had recovered, she put a hand to her heart and said, "You scared me out of ten years' growth."

"I know. I'm sorry. Get down. I need your horse."

Angel frowned at that. "You need my horse?"

Jack nodded, looking back over his shoulder at the dead men, and then turning again to her. "To get my men, Tex and Calvin, back home. I can't leave them here. They need to be buried. You can ride behind me."

Considering his clipped, emotionless tone, Angel eyed first him, then the bodies littering the ground. A good, practical solution. What else could she say? "All right." With that, she dismounted and, leading her trailing horse as she walked alongside Jack, sidestepped her way around the animals' carcasses. "What about the dogs? They shouldn't be left here."

Without breaking stride, Jack glanced over at her. "The dogs? There's nothing we can do—"

"I know that." Her voice hardened. "There's nothing we can do for your men, either. Except bury them. Those dogs died working for your father, Jack. Doing their jobs. Protecting his property. Same as these men did. Let the vultures and the coyotes have the rest. But the dogs . . . well, you owe 'em."

Jack stopped. Angel did, too, halting her roan as she stared up into Jack's face. He looked away from her. Then, apparently having made his decision, he looked down at her. "All right. Let's go. It'll be dark soon. We'll get Tex and Calvin . . . and then the dogs."

With a nod of her head, Angel silently agreed. She was glad he agreed with her, didn't think she was overly sentimental. Then she spared a glance at the setting sun, since he'd mentioned the day's end. Sure enough, in less than an hour, it would slip below the horizon. Angel looked for Jack, saw he'd already made his way over to the first of the men. She followed after him.

Working together, in short order they had the two men's bodies slung over the roan's strong back. On top of them, tied down by a *reata* of braided rawhide that Jack pulled from around his pommel, lay the two dogs' tongue-lolling bodies. A grim load, to be sure, but one her experienced cow pony seemed to take in stride.

Done with their task, her roan tied by a lead rope to Jack's pommel, Angel now stood beside his leggy brown gelding, reached for his hand and let herself be pulled up behind him. His superior strength lifted her as if she weighed nothing. Settling herself behind him, and then wrapping her arms around his waist, feeling the hard muscle and the warm shirt-covered body under her touch, Angel said, "I'm ready."

Jack's only answer was to prod his mount with his heels and set them off for home. Rocking along behind Jack, his every sway her own, Angel took a deep breath, inadvertently inhaling the warm, earthy scents of the man in front of her. She closed her eyes, realizing she'd probably never forget this moment, the musky way he smelled . . . and how very much she wanted to seek the comfort of his reassuring nearness, to rest her forehead, if only for a moment, against his broad back. But she knew she couldn't.

On that next sunshiny morning, as Jack stood on the verandah, a mug of coffee in one hand, his other gripping a splintery support beam, he pulled back and hit the beam with his fist. All this standing around was going to kill him. He needed to *do* something.

What he wanted to do—and the only thing he couldn't do—was saddle Buffalo and ride hell-for-leather to search for clues to what had happened here. Despite still being bone tired, despite the soreness that cramped his muscles, a soreness from his fight yesterday with Seth and from digging those two graves last night by the light of the moon and the kerosene lamp Angel had held up for him, Jack ached for . . . *just one damned clue*.

Anything that would free him from this feeling of being hog-tied. From sitting here and waiting for something to happen . . . again. Waiting for something to reach out of thin air and grab him around the throat. That's how vulnerable he felt, how exposed . . . just standing here, inviting disaster. As his impatience surged, Jack looked out beyond the low brown hills that rolled in gentle undulations away from the Circle D.

Once those hills had called to him, but now they seemed only to mock him. Not so long ago, only a matter of months, he'd craved the opportunities he imagined lay beyond them. But now he knew better. He knew what lay beyond their openness. It wasn't freedom. No, it was a drunken wasting of time that turned out to have been the last precious months of his father's life. And now, Jack had to live with knowing he'd squandered every last one of them on cheap liquor, cheaper women, and barroom fights.

He shook his head, wanting to turn away from the memories, from the hills, turn away from the pain he'd caused the old man, away from the last look of sad longing Jack had seen on his father's face. They had yelled at each other over differences about how the ranch should be run. In light of the fresh graves out back, in light of the slaughter of the breeding stock, and what that meant to the future of the Circle D, what difference did that make now?

Jack uttered another curse. He'd been so stupid, wanting to get away, fighting with his father about how he never took Jack's ideas seriously. Jack could still hear himself telling the old man that he could just forget it, then. *Just forget the Circle D. Do what you want with it. I don't want any part of it. There's a whole world out there, and I want to see something of it. And I can't do that sitting here. You don't need me. You don't care what I think, so the hell with you. I'm leaving.*

He'd wanted only to prove himself, to earn respect, like any man needed to do. But what had all that independence gotten him? *Then go. Just go on,* his father had said. *But don't come crawling back to me. Make your own way. Don't take what I'm offering you, son. Go.* And he had gone. And now he'd come back. To this. To an empty ranch. To questions with no answers. To a mystery with no clues. And already, he wanted to leave again. But now, Jack knew, he wanted to get away for different reasons, reasons having to do with answers, with making someone pay for what he'd lost . . . before he could reclaim it.

Again he looked around the only home he'd ever known. And asked himself what exactly he had lost. Men, cattle, the cow dogs, horses, money . . . all that. Sad. Senseless. But it was inside himself he discovered his real loss, when his father's face shimmered in his memory.

Jack closed his eyes, felt the moisture under his lids, and opened them, blinking away the tears. Grimacing angrily, he decided all he needed was one name. Someone who would pay for everything that happened here in the four months he'd been gone. Someone to take his guilt away, he finally admitted, for not being here when he'd so obviously been needed. But no name presented itself. Other than the roll call of the dead. Tex. Calvin. Pa. *Dammit, Pa, I never meant to—*

Shifting his weight from one booted leg to the other, Jack shied away from the swamp of emotion that threatened to drag him under. Instead, he concentrated on another part of the overall mystery that was the Circle D. Just where in the hell had Lou and Boots, those two old drover setting hens, gotten off to? *Hell, they'd never leave here.* Jack's expression hardened. *Not of their own free will.*

Don't think about it, he warned himself. Because, given everything else that had gone on around here, whatever their fate had been, it couldn't have been good. Using his free hand, Jack scrubbed at his jaw and chin, not sparing the fresh cut Seth'd given him yesterday . . . as if the physical pain could take away that of the soul. But he knew better. He also knew that with everyone else dead or missing . . . only Angel was left. She was his only link—and a weak one. She didn't seem to know—or wasn't telling—anything. *Which one is it? Does she not know? Or is she just not telling?*

Frustrated, agitated, locked into this forced inactivity that kept him standing on the verandah, Jack felt more like pitching his mug of strong, black coffee than sipping at it. But he continued to stand there. On the verandah. Staring at the chickens. Even those happily occupied birds out in the yard seemed to mock him with the direction and purpose in their lives, seemed to say that even they knew what to do next. Jack narrowed his eyes, venting his sour thought. *Yeah, keep on pecking. You'll be Sunday dinner soon enough.*

Just then, the front door opened behind him. Jack turned around, knew who he'd see. Angel Devlin. She stepped outside, a mug of steaming coffee cupped in her hands. She nodded when she saw him looking her way. Jack returned her greeting, noting—as she turned to close the door behind her—that she was all but swallowed up in his clothes from yesterday. Her long black hair hung thick and loose, curling at the ends that brushed her waist.

Jack swallowed his hiss of wanting . . . of wanting to run his hands through that hair, of wanting to feel it on his body, brushing over his naked skin . . .

Her sudden graceful movements broke Jack's reverie. Careful of her mug, and flinging her hair back over her shoulder with her other hand, she settled herself in one of the two wooden rocking chairs that adorned the verandah. Then she glanced up—and caught him staring. "Mornin'," she said, making it sound less like a pleasantry and more like a statement of fact.

Embarrassed to be caught staring, and still burning for her, but chuckling at her early-morning bad mood, Jack came back with, "Yes, it is."

Angel shot him a pissy glance and sipped at her coffee. But then, and without any preamble, as if she'd been inside and thinking, and had come outside only to ask him, she said, "Those men we buried last night, next to your father . . . Tex and Calvin? Who were they, Jack? How well did you know them?"

Jack stared at her, cocking his head, and wondered why she was asking. But deciding that talking to her was much better than entertaining his own thoughts, Jack stepped over to the other rocker and lowered himself onto it. Sitting next to her, careful of his coffee, but with his attention focused on the prairie landscape in front of his house, he shrugged, saying, "I knew 'em well enough, I suppose. They rode the grub line. Good men. Hard workers. Been showing up together every spring for the last three years and right on time for the drive up to Abilene. Why?"

Now she shrugged. "No reason, really. I was just wondering. Wondering if they had any family who might want to know."

Well, that surprised him for its thoughtfulness. Jack considered her, and the constant surprise that she was. One minute she was damning the whole world and in the next, she was playing nursemaid to it. Interesting. He sipped at his coffee and then said, "I don't know. Didn't know them that well, myself. My father hired the men. He might've known that answer but . . ." A sudden catch in his emotions had Jack's intended words—*he's gone now*—trailing off unsaid.

"It doesn't matter," Angel said. "Just an idle thought."

Jack doubted if she'd ever entertained any thought for idle purposes, but kept that observation to himself. In the ensuing quiet that seemed to invite his belated appreciation for the budding spring day, Jack rocked his chair back until he could stretch his legs out in front of him. Resting his booted feet atop the porch rail and nestling his coffee mug in his hands, he again looked over at Angel, noting now the tired look hovering around those black eyes of hers.

Damned if he didn't feel responsible. Again he saw her standing there last night, uncomplaining, holding that heavy kerosene lamp while he dug the graves, saw her helping him lay the blanket-rolled bodies into the deep holes, saw her trudging listlessly back to the house, heard her mumbled good-night. As if he couldn't stop himself from asking, Jack heard himself saying, "You sleep okay last night?"

She turned her head, staring at him, arching a black-winged eyebrow. "Yeah. Why?"

Her standoffish attitude had Jack feeling pretty silly for asking. "No reason. Just an idle thought," he drawled, using her own words and trying to keep himself from staring openly at her surprisingly delicate, dark-haired beauty. She was one of those women you could look at every day of your life, he decided, and never tire of the sight of her.

For a stretch of time after that, during which she sipped at her coffee and rocked her chair, its repetitious squeaking somehow reassuring, Angel said nothing else. Jack waited, figuring something bigger was on her mind. Then, looking straight ahead, she said, "Doesn't look much like rain today."

A faint smile tugged at Jack's lips. He glanced at the clear blue sky, at the hot yellow sun shining down from a cloudless sky. True. It didn't look like rain today. But curiosity had him wondering what was going on in that mind of hers. Because she didn't talk just to pass time. Hell, she spoke only when she had something to say. And answered him only when she felt like it, it seemed. And so, he looked over at her and cut to the heart of it. "What's wrong, Angel?"

With a sharp turn of her head, she was looking into his eyes. "Nothing."

Jack nodded, took a sip of his coffee, and called her bluff. "Liar."

Her black-winged eyebrows dropped low, matching the

frown of her expressive mouth. She leaned forward a bit in her chair. "What did you just call me?"

Jack narrowed his eyes, cutting her no quarter, but loving how her black hair, like so much soft velvet, fell forward, all but shielding her face from his view. "You heard me. I called you a liar. Now, tell me what's wrong."

With an unconsciously feminine move that had Jack's blood stirring, Angel swung her head in such a way that her hair slipped over her shoulder and trailed down her back, out of her way. Even glaring at him, as she did now, she was one striking woman. Then she blurted, "First you take that back—calling me a liar—cowboy."

Jack chuckled. Cowboy. So they were back to that. "Can't. Because I was right. You are lying. So, speak your mind."

She firmed her lips together until her bottom one was in danger of poking out. Jack was willing to bet a gold coin she did that as a kid, poked that bottom lip out. "All right, I will," she said, acting like she wasn't giving in. "There're some things around here I don't understand."

"Only *some* things?" Jack remarked, squinting as he took another sip of his coffee. "Hell, you're one up on me, then. Because I don't understand even one blessed thing going on around here. But give me a for-instance."

"All right," she said again. "For instance, your mother."

Eleven

Everything inside Jack, even his blood, seemed to still. He looked over at Angel. "What about her?" he said, hearing the tightness in his own voice.

Angel blinked, suddenly looking unsure of herself. Jack waited. Finally, she asked, "Is that her picture on the mantel above the fireplace?"

"Yep."

"She's . . . she's a pretty woman."

"Yep. She was."

"You favor her."

Sudden impatience, stirred with a dose of painful memory, had Jack snapping, "What do you want to know about her, Angel? Why are you even thinking about my mother?"

Angel's eyes widened a fraction, then she stared down at her coffee. After a moment or two, she again looked up at him, her black eyes wide and innocent. "I don't know. I just—what happened to her?"

His mother, the one person closest to his heart, was the last person Jack wanted to talk about. He turned away from Angel, seeking the quiet anonymity and the gentle washboard roll of the grass-covered hills. "She died a few days after Seth was born," he finally gritted out.

He meant for those words to be the only ones he said as he sat there feeling the warm and gentle breeze, like a kiss, brush across his face. But then he heard himself say, "And there wasn't a damned thing I could do to save her."

A wordless quiet passed moment by moment, deepening with each second. A sad-sounding sniff came from Angel. Then she spoke. "I know something about that feeling. But . . . save her from what?"

Jack huffed out his breath, ready to tell her to drop it, but then her words sunk in. Who'd she mean that she hadn't been able to save? His father? No, most likely her own mother. Now that he thought about it, he wondered what Virginia Devlin thought of her daughter being here . . . and why Angel hadn't brought her here with her. But then he remembered the stories—Angel and Virginia didn't get on well. No one had to tell him why.

Finally, and belatedly, Jack recognized Angel's words for what they were. A rare insight into her feelings. And felt— silly as it sounded, even in his own mind—honored. So, he returned her barest of confidences with, "I couldn't save her from bleeding to death."

Angel pulled back some, her color blanching, her expression showing that she looked inward as she repeated, all but whispering, "Bleeding to death."

Her reaction brought a frown to Jack's face. Why would talking about his mother cause her to—Jack's breath caught, his mind paused right there. *Something happened to her mother.* His frown deepened as his curiosity intensified. It was quite a leap, he knew, but one he felt more certain of, the longer he stared at Angel, the longer he entertained the thought. And began putting events together. Something had happened to her mother. His father went to Red River Station. And Angel was returning with him when he was killed.

Were these events connected to everything else that was happening? Was there a common thread he was missing? And if so, what was it?

Jack blinked, came back to the moment when Angel cleared her throat and took a sip of her coffee. In profile to him, her face revealed an arched brow, a high cheekbone, and a slender, curved jaw. Touched by her air of vulnerability, one not evident in her manner or her words, Jack felt a flood of compassion for her. He wanted nothing more than to hold her, to draw her over to his lap and wrap her in his embrace. But instead, he said "Angel?" and drew her black-eyed attention. "What happened to your mother?"

Her expression hardened, narrowing her eyes. But under her tan, she paled, a hurt cast settled itself around her eyes. Then she said, "She took ill and died. I buried her the same day I left Red River Station."

And you're going to act like you don't give a damn, came Jack's silent accusation. But what he said was, "I'm sorry for your loss. I didn't know."

She shrugged, sipped at her coffee. "No reason why you should."

Watching her, wanting to shake her out of her air of toughness, wanting to break her until she cried it all out and healed herself—*Look who's talking,* his inner voice railed—Jack cut off his thoughts and gave in to his own need to talk about his mother. And so, with no preface to his remarks, he said, "I was little more than five years old that spring. But I remember it well."

She turned to him now, her dark eyes acknowledging his opening up. "What happened?" was her quiet question.

Jack felt his chest constrict, felt his heart thud dully . . . just as it did every time he thought of those awful days. Suddenly he found he had to speak rapidly and not give anything but the barest accounting. "Pa was gone to Red River Station—more than a three days' ride away, as you know—when her time with Seth came early. I did what I could, what she told me. But . . . she lost too much blood. By the time Pa got home, she was all but dead. She died the next day."

"Jesus," Angel said softly. Then, "Who—Seth was just a tiny baby. Who . . . took care of him?"

"She did. Kept him in her bed, nursing him. Until the end." Jack swallowed a lump in his throat. He'd never talked about this before with anyone. And had to wonder again why he was spilling his guts to Angel Devlin, even as he continued . . . without looking over at her. "But then—and this is the hell of it—that afternoon, when Pa'd no more than buried her and had to be wondering what he was supposed to do with a hungry baby, over that hill right there''—he pointed to it, in the distance—''came Old Mother.''

"Old Mother?" Angel repeated, confusion evident in her tone.

"Yeah," Jack said, nodding and glancing over at her. "She wasn't all that old then, of course. But that's what she said to call her."

"Well, who was she?"

Jack could almost grin at her childlike interest in his story. For some reason, her unbridled attention made the telling easier. "A Comanche woman. Don't ask me where she came from. Or how she knew we needed her. But there she was. She walked in, like she knew the layout of the place, picked Seth up, and put him to her breast and fed him. It was the damnedest thing I ever saw. Pa and I just looked at each other."

"Then what happened?" Angel now braced her forearm on her chair's arm, her coffee mug all but dangling from her hand as she leaned toward him, her eyes wide.

"Well, nothing," Jack said, grinning now and hating to disappoint her. But hating more that he was at the end of his story—or the only part he was willing to tell—and would lose her undivided attention. "She stayed for the next ten years or so, raising me and Seth. And then, one day, she just up and saddled a horse, saying it was time she left. And then, taking nothing with her, not even provisions, she rode back over that same hill. We never saw her again."

Angel stared at him, as if he were lying to her. Then she blinked and fell back against her chair, mindful now of her coffee but slumping in her seat. "Well, I'll be," she commented, staring at the hills out front. "I don't believe I've ever heard such a tale as that. Old Mother, huh?"

Jack grinned. "Yep. Old Mother."

"Hmm," was Angel's final comment. Or so he thought. A moment later she broke the silence with, "You ever seen a big white wolf with blue eyes around here?"

Jack's gut tightened. "Where—" he tried, but couldn't say more. "What'd you see, Angel? Where?" he finally managed. If Angel—someone outside his family—was seeing her . . . then more trouble was about to come.

"Out back. In that meadow out there. Standing in the middle of those bluebonnets you told me about. Yesterday morning, I was looking out my window and saw it. I swear, it looked right at me and then howled. I felt like he—"

"She," Jack said, interrupting her. Instantly he was sorry he had. He'd just confirmed his knowledge of Old Mother. Had he kept quiet, he could have denied the wolf's existence. He could have told Angel she was imagining things. And then, he could have secretly watched over her, protecting her in a way she'd never let him do openly, he knew.

"She?" Angel finally repeated. "Then you've seen . . . her, too?"

"Yes. I've seen her." *I've lived with her,* he added to himself, leaning down to place his coffee mug on the verandah's worn wood floor. Then, with increased urgency driving him, Jack scooted his chair closer to Angel's, took her mug from her, set it on the floor, and startled her by taking her hands in his.

Alarmed, she tried to yank her hands away. But Jack held on. "Angel, this is important. You must tell me exactly what you saw, exactly what she—the wolf—did. Exactly. And leave nothing out. Nothing."

But Angel wasn't about to be that cooperative, not right off, not just because he asked. Jack should have known that, but still it irritated him when she shook her head. "I already told you what it did. It's just a wolf—"

"No, it's *not* just a wolf." Jack tightened his grip around her fingers, saw her brow knit, her mouth firm—no doubt with unremarked pain—and forced himself to relax some, even though he alone of the two of them knew the urgency needed. "She's not *just* anything, Angel. You have no idea. In Red River Station, you never heard anything about the white wolf Old Mother . . . and my family?"

Angel frowned, looking askance at him. "White wolf Old Mother? But that's the woman who—"

"I know."

One dead moment passed another as Angel stared hard at him before again finding her voice. "Are you telling me, Jack Daltry, that the Comanche woman who raised you and your brother just up and one day rode off over that hill"—she pulled a hand out of his grip and pointed to the hill, all without looking away from him—"and turned into a white-furred, blue-eyed wolf?"

"No, I'm not," Jack said honestly, soberly. After all, he had no real proof of that.

Angel lowered her arm, but only to grip her knee with her hand. "Then what are you saying?"

"I'm saying that if you'll think about it, you'll probably recall having heard about my family and Old Mother in Red River Station. About how the Comanche don't bother us. And you'll know I'm not lying. Now, think."

"I don't need to. I never heard such a tale as yours. Because if I had, I wouldn't forget it." Then she pulled her other hand out of his grip and stood up. "Folks in town didn't spend a lot of time chatting with me. But still, something this strange? No, I would've gotten wind of it. And I didn't. So I think you're telling a tall tale. And shame on me for sitting here listening to it." With that, she turned and stomped off, skirting around him and going inside, slamming the front door after her.

Jack flinched at the noise of the slammed door, but didn't blame Angel a bit. If he hadn't lived the story, hadn't lived with Old Mother and been brought up in her people's ways, and didn't know the spiritual things the Comanche knew, he wouldn't believe, either.

But still, Jack sat there staring out at the hills and trying to figure out what Old Mother's renewed presence in his life—and apparently in Angel's—meant for them both. One thing he did know, the white wolf's showing herself to Angel confirmed for him something he'd only suspected before now. Angel Devlin's fate was undeniably tangled up with the Daltrys'.

With that thought, Jack got up, picked up the two mugs, held them in one hand, and turned to go inside. But before he made it to the door, a prickly feeling stopped him, had his skin crawling, had the hairs at the back of his neck standing up. Awash with dread, almost afraid of what he'd see, given all their talk of the white wolf, Jack pivoted to face the open prairie beyond the ranch house yard. And found the source of his foreboding.

Surprise struck him in the gut, had him reaching for the firmness of a rough-cut beam that supported the overhanging roof on the verandah. He all but hung on to it for a long moment . . . watching . . . not believing.

Recovering some from the initial shock, he set the mugs on the floor, and then hustled down the verandah's steps, all but leaping to the ground as he took off running, heading for the approaching riders.

From the front of the house came the sounds of the heavy door opening and closing. Back in the kitchen, Angel's head came up, her hands stilled from her merciless kneading of the innocent bread dough rolled out on the floured chopping block in front of her. Cocking her head at an angle, she heard . . . sure enough . . . ever louder bootsteps scuffing across the wood floor, announcing his approach. *So he's come inside, has he?*

She couldn't have said how much time had passed since she'd left that lying Jack Daltry out on the verandah, but it hadn't been long enough, she knew that much. And she'd be glad to tell him so when he got here. Angel glared at the empty kitchen-door frame, preparing for him to be standing there. But her courage failed her when his arrival became imminent. Quickly looking down, she attacked the dough again, telling herself she'd changed her mind. And would be damned if she'd give him five minutes of her time. Just see if she'd listen to any more of his tall tales. *A Comanche woman who turned into a white wolf, for pity's sake.*

He'd probably sat out there on the verandah all this time, having a big laugh at her expense. Well, she hoped he'd enjoyed it because—*he's here.* Angel's breath caught, cutting off her thoughts. Even with her head down, and facing the entry as she did, she could see his boots and his legs, up to the knees. But not deigning to give him a word of acknowledgment, or an opening to tease her, she forced her attention back to her task and picked up the pace of her kneading, all but strangling the hapless dough.

"Angel?"

Her hands stilled, she kept her head down, concentrating on the breaddough . . . and feeling her heartbeat pick up. His voice sounded so flat. She hoped it was because of his guilt for stringing her along like he had. But a sixth sense told her something different. Even so, she didn't look up. "What?"

"We have company."

Now she raised her head, her eyes widening at his appearance. His face was pale, his knuckles white against the door frame he gripped. "Company?" she repeated, not liking the sounds of that, especially given the look on his face, and the way he'd said it. "Not Seth again?"

He shook his head. "No. Four Comanche braves. And two of my old hands. They're hurt. I'll need your help." With that he stepped into the kitchen and set their coffee mugs down on the drop-leaf table.

Angel's mind froze and her knees stiffened. *Four Comanche braves.* Just the words had the hair on her arms standing on end and her thoughts flitting to the renewed battles of late between the Indians and the U.S. Army. Her gaze flitted to his hip. No gun. "Shouldn't we be reaching for weapons?"

Jack shook his head. "No need. They won't harm us. I told you that outside."

Was this more of his teasing, since Old Mother was a Comanche, as he'd said? Angel wondered. But she dismissed that notion immediately. One look at Jack's hardened expression said he wasn't teasing. And that this was no time for hesitation on her part. He'd also said something about two of his men being with the Comanches and being hurt.

"You going to help or not?" came his impatient bark.

Angel snapped to, realizing she'd done nothing but stare at him. "Yes," she promptly replied, wiping her hands on her flour-dusty apron and reaching for its long ties at her neck and waist as she stepped around the chopping block. "I guess since the Comanches brought your men home, they're not the ones who hurt 'em?"

"You guessed right," Jack said. "Come on. Let's go. Standing Elk and his men aren't too happy about being here."

"I don't suppose they are," Angel murmured, knowing the Comanche had no particular tenderness toward whites and their reservations. "Do you know what happened to your men?"

Jack looked into her eyes but stepped aside to allow her to precede him down the long, narrow hall.. "No. I'm just glad these two are alive."

Angel nodded, figuring he was thinking of the two dead men they'd found yesterday on their ride. Just then, his hand captured her elbow. Angel flinched in surprise, looking up at him as he stepped up to her side and hurried her along beside him. "Sorry, but I don't want Standing Elk to get any unhappier."

Angel swallowed. Neither did she. Jack's long-legged strides carried them to the end of the hallway and into the great room, where they threaded their way around the furniture, working their way toward the ... open front door. Hadn't she heard Jack close it when he came in? Frowning, but not dwelling on that, Angel finally commented, "This is mighty curious, Jack. I've never heard of the Comanche carrying whites anywhere—except to an early grave."

A wordless moment passed. Then, "That's generally true. But Standing Elk said . . . Old Mother told them to take care of Lou and Boots and then to bring 'em here when they were able to travel."

That did it. He was poking fun at her again. Angel stopped, staring up at him. Her jaw jutted out, her voice was singsong. "The Indian woman Old Mother? Or the white wolf Old Mother?"

Exasperated, Jack said "Angel, I know you don't understand—"

"Which one, Jack?"

"The white wolf. In a vision their medicine man had. She

told him where the braves would find Lou and Boots.''

"Well, that was mighty kind of her.'' Angel's sour expression belied her words. She pivoted on her heel, intending to return to the kitchen and her bread-making—and get away from him. "Damn you, Jack Daltry,'' she threw over her shoulder. "With everything that's going on around here, I'd think you—''

"Angel!''

The imperative tone of his voice spun her around. Another angry rebuke tipped against her tongue. But when she saw what Jack meant for her to see, she swallowed her words, gasping instead. Sure enough, four Comanche braves were entering the house, coming in single-file with two older, injured, and bandaged white men carried between them by their shoulders and legs. Obviously, they'd reopened the door to get the men inside.

"Merciful heavens,'' Angel intoned, something she recalled her mother saying on more than one occasion. She then sought Jack's gaze, questioning, asking for his direction. "Where do you want them?''

"Upstairs,'' he said to her as he signaled to the braves and led the way.

Angel fell in line behind the tall, muscular Comanches, noting their long black hair, their air of silent superiority, and their careful handling of the two old men, both of whom were pale-faced and moaning. Grim of expression, not having the first idea what she could do to help, but knowing that, as a woman, she'd be asked to do so just the same, Angel hung back, giving the braves plenty of room to maneuver up the stairs.

As they carried the men up the stairs, the braves facing her glanced at her more than once. A tingling cold ran over Angel's skin. The Comanches' eyes could have been so much black glass for all they revealed of their thoughts or intentions.

Relief coursed through her when the injured men were laid together on the big bed at the end of the second-floor hallway and Jack turned to her, saying, "Stay here. I'll see them out.''

Angel had time only to nod her agreement with him before he stalked away, the four braves at his back.

She watched them file out, briefly entertaining the thought that she hoped Jack made it back in one piece. Then, she turned to the gray-haired and grizzled old men on the bed. And got a surprise. They were wide awake and pulling up to sitting positions.

"Them Co-manch gone yet?" asked the taller of the two, his voice gravelly but strong.

Somewhat taken aback, not knowing what to make of their apparently rapid recovery, Angel nodded. "Yes."

The two men—one tall and skinny, the other short and wiry—exchanged looks of relief. Then they faced her again . . . and stared, as if just now realizing they didn't know her. "Who're you?" the tall, skinny one finally asked, even as he began unwinding a bandage from around his arm, exposed under a torn-away shirtsleeve.

With his question, Angel's bemusement with their antics turned to stone. She hated to tell them her name. Would she have to endure sly looks and insults every time she said who she was? But, stiffening her spine, readying to defend herself, she said, "Angel Devlin."

Not one bit of recognition crossed either of their faces before the taller one reached up to tug at a hat that wasn't there and to say, "Pleased to meetcha, ma'am."

Angel exhaled her relief at their unquestioning acceptance of her presence on the Circle D. She watched them swing their legs off opposite sides of the bed and hobble with limping gracelessness over to the window.

As they went, the taller one said, "Where's Mr. Daltry? Not the boy, Jack. But his pa? He ain't still over to Red River Station, is he? 'Cause he ain't goin' to like one bit our being in his bed. I don't know what that fool kid was thinkin', bringin' us up here. We'll just lick our wounds out in the bunkhouse, once them Co-manch get shut of the place."

Angel had almost forgotten the question by the time the man finished speaking. Then she remembered . . . where was Mr. Daltry. "He's not still at the station. He's—" She caught herself. But they didn't seem to notice her abrupt ending since they now were staring intently out the window.

She bit at her lip, realizing she couldn't just blurt out that he was dead. Jack had said they were his drovers. But she suspected the two older men were much more than that to the Daltrys, given everything the tall one had just said, and given Jack's care with them. But what piqued her interest the most was that they knew Mr. Daltry had gone to Red River Station. But apparently not the why of it because they hadn't known who she was. Dang it. The one time she needed someone to know who she was, the one time their knowing could provide answers, they didn't have a clue. But what else was new in this whole stinking mess?

Just then, the taller one turned again to her. "Did you say yet where Mr. Daltry is?"

"He's . . . out back," Angel settled on saying. "He won't be back . . . for a while." Then, she just had to ask . . . "Who are *you*?"

Pulling back the curtains, one man to either side of the glass pane as they peered out, the taller one again spoke for them. "I'm Boots Cornwell. This here's Lou Montana. He don't talk much."

Probably just doesn't get a chance, Angel thought, nodding as Lou Montana spared her a sweet, gap-toothed smile and a wave of his hand before poking at Boots's arm and pointing to something outside. Boots nodded, remarking, "Yep, I see them heartless critters a-mountin' their ponies, Lou. I'll swear and be damned, them squaws of their'n liked to've killed us tryin' to cure us, didn't they?"

Not sure whether to frown or grin, Angel could contain herself no longer. "What's going on here? Are you two hurt or not?"

The men, dressed in tattered denims and equally dirty flannel shirts, pivoted to face her. "We sure enough were, ma'am. But not so much now," said Boots, his gray eyes wide, his expression respectful.

Amused again despite herself, Angel cocked her head and

arched an eyebrow. "What happened to you two? Why were you with those Comanche?"

"Well, hard as it is to believe, ma'am—even for me and Lou here—them Co-manch as good as saved us. Just rode right up on us like they'd knowed we needed their help . . ."

Exactly what Jack said, was Angel's startled thought. The hair stood up on her arms. *The white wolf. Could it be true?* Her mouth opened, the better to get air into her suddenly tightened chest. She blinked, coming back to the moment, to Boots's continued explanation of events.

". . . Now me and Lou know enough Co-manch lingo to get ourselves scalped, but I don't mind tellin' you, ma'am, that we couldn't recognize a word they was sayin' to us when they scooped us up right off the ground and carried us away. But you coulda knocked us over with one of them feathers they wear when all's they did was doctor us and bring us back here . . . alive." Wide-eyed, he stopped . . . apparently finished.

Angel exhaled her rising exasperation with his rambling tale. He still hadn't told her what she needed to know. She decided to try again, this time being more specific in her questioning. "Mr. Cornwell, what *happened* to you . . . *before* the Comanche came along?"

"Oh. We was ambushed, is what we was." Boots then turned to his friend. "Ain't that right, Lou?"

Lou nodded, looking a bit simple as he stared at Angel but pointed at Boots, as if to say he agreed with him. Then "Yep," he blurted.

Angel wanted to scream, and even feared she would. But she got no further than a frown with their names on it before the two men once again directed their attention outside, pulling back the curtain to peer down at the activity in the yard.

Just then, an unexpected tenderness—still a new emotion to her—assailed her, tugging at her heart. She exhaled her anger, ready to chuckle at them. Or perhaps, herself. How could she be mad at them? The poor old things were tattered, hurt, and scared breathless from their ordeal. And how many times in her life, Angel asked herself, had she been the same?

How many times had she needed someone to care that she was, only to have no one take pity on her . . . except, of late, Wallace Daltry?

And these were his men. She needed to return the man's favor to his hired hands. Yes, she still needed answers from them. After all, they represented the only links she had to what had gone on here. They might even know a name or a direction she and Jack could go to find answers. But she needed to ask gently . . . even if the notion of herself doing such a thing did go against the grain. But it was worth a try. Angel unfisted her hands and spoke up . . . kindly. "Did you see who ambushed you, Mr. Cornwell?"

Boots let go of the curtain to look back at her and scratch and rub at his balding pate. "No, I can't rightly say that I did, ma'am. Had their bandannas over their faces, they did. But there was a passel of 'em that showed up here. Rustlers, I suppose. After the cattle. Weren't no Injuns, that's a fact. But whoever them ornery critters was, they dragged us off when we told 'em the cattle was already on the trail and then they shot us up pretty good."

Even though her heart sank with his negative answers, answers that did not divulge the identities of the murdering thieves, skepticism born of Boots's allegation that he and Lou Montana had been shot up drew a skeptic frown on Angel's face. Her gaze slowly slipped over the two men. They looked hale and hardy enough to her. She met Boots Cornwell's suddenly wavering gaze and reddening face.

"Well, leastwise, they meant to shoot us up," he blurted. "Just nicked and grazed us some, is more like it, before them Co-manch rode up, a-yellin' and a-hollerin'. Plumb scared them rustlers off. But still, me and Lou got enough injuries to give us a gawd-awful fever, that's for sure. And I ain't never seen the like of them poultices and medicines them squaws forced on us and into us." He again turned to Lou for support. "Ain't that right, Lou?"

Not surprisingly, Lou's widened brown eyes and his frowning nod again verified Boots's version of events.

Gawd-awful or not, Angel suspected the women's remedies had saved these men's lives. "When did all this happen?"

Boots shrugged. "Well, I lost track of time, what with the fever and all, but near as me and Lou could figger, once we come to, it was a good ten or more days ago." Then he frowned, sending her a considering look. "Why you askin', ma'am?"

Angel heard his question, saw his waiting stare, but momentarily turned her thoughts inward, making some calculations of her own. So, Lou and Boots had been shot up right before she arrived here. Right about the time Mr. Daltry was killed. If she considered those two events and the missing men and cattle from the Circle D—and those men she and Jack found yesterday—then yep, all those things were happening about the same time.

And, no doubt, being done by the same men. But she didn't for a minute believe that cattle rustling was what lay at the bottom of events here. For one thing, rustlers who knew their business wouldn't have killed off the most valuable of the lot, the breeding stock. They might have killed the men and the dogs, but not the horses, valuable cow ponies. No, cattle rustling didn't explain much, especially the missing papers. Or Mr. Daltry's murder, which she'd always said was personal, like a revenge killing.

So, something else, something a lot worse, something just plain evil, was behind all this. Her fearful thoughts chilled Angel's blood as she entertained the question *What could it be?*

"Ma'am? You all right? You look a mite frownish around the edges."

The sound of Boots's voice snapped Angel back to the moment. "I'm fine. Just doing some figuring."

"Figuring about what?" asked a deep male voice from behind her.

Twelve

Startled, Angel jerked around. And was forced to pull up short, a hand to her chest, over her thumping heart. Jack was directly behind her, all but on top of her. Wide-eyed, her vision filling with his broad-chested presence, she stared up into his starkly handsome face. And instantly realized, from his expression, that yet something else—in the short space of time he'd been outside—had happened.

He looked away from her, directing his attention to the two old men by the window, and putting his hands to his waist. "Lou, Boots, what're you doing out of bed? About five minutes ago, I'd have said you two weren't long for this world, the way you were moaning."

"We done that for them Co-manch. They didn't mess with us too much if'n we carried on so. But don't you worry. We're still kicking, all right—just not as high," Boots assured him. Then he smiled broadly, revealing a mouth full of snaggly, yellowing teeth. "You shorely are a sight for sore eyes, boy. I figured after that yellin' match you and your pa had last winter over the way he was a-runnin' the ranch, we'd not see hide nor hair of you again. But here you are. I'll bet your pa is plumb tickled to have you here, too. Did you tell him yet that me and Lou was home? I figured as he'd be up here a-yellin' at us for layin' about with them Co-manch and not being here doing our jobs."

Angel's heart thudded. She could tell by Jack's softening expression that he wasn't ready to deal with what he had to tell them. So she jumped in with, "I told them he's out back, that he won't be returning for a while."

Jack looked into her eyes, nodding, as much as thanking her with a relieved lift of his eyebrows and a roll of his eyes. Then he looked again to the men, exchanging a few more words with them. With him thus distracted, Angel studied his face, noting the lines to either side of his mouth, the eagle-eyed intensity of his stare. Something was eating the man alive. What could it be? Angel fisted her hands against her sudden desire to reach up and smooth away the worry that lined his face. "Jack? What's happened?" she all but whispered.

He looked down at her again. Almost imperceptibly, he shook his dark head, indicating with a lift of his chin the two older men in the room with them.

Understanding, Angel nodded in return, even as she felt her belly muscles tighten. Whatever it was, he didn't want to speak of it in front of Lou and Boots. But as the moment stretched out, and he said nothing, simply stared at her, Angel blurted out the belated and the obvious. "You gave me quite a start just now, standing behind me like that."

Jack exhaled his breath and firmed his mouth until tiny lines, like mocking smiles, formed at either end. "I know. I'm sorry," he said, sounding weary. Then he pointed to Boots and Lou. "You get anything out of them?"

Angel nodded. "Yeah. Some. About ten days ago, they were ambushed here and dragged off by some yahoos wearing bandanna masks. Boots seems to think the men were cattle rustlers—"

"They weren't."

Angel frowned, narrowing her eyes, her mind working. The way he said it, the note of certainty in his voice. She was right. He'd learned something while outside. "Then who were they?"

Jack's answer was a riveting and blazing blue-eyed glare that all but turned Angel to ashes, had her stepping back, even though she figured it wasn't directed at her—thank the Good Lord—but was more for the men whose identities were now burned into this man's soul, no doubt. "I'll tell you outside," he said. "Hold on a minute." When Angel nodded that she would, he turned to his drovers. "You two get back in that bed and stay put, you hear?"

Even as he complied, even as he and Lou shuffled over to the wide four-poster, Boots shook his head. "Now, Jack, I don't think your pa's going to be too happy about that if'n—"

"It's okay for now, Boots," Jack cut in. "I'll be back in a minute to check on you and to . . . talk." That was one conversation Angel didn't envy him. It was obvious to her now that these two simple men were as good as family— well, maybe better than family—to Jack.

"All right, Jack, we'll do that. We'll wait right here for you," Boots again assured him.

"Good." With that, Jack gripped Angel's arm, turned them both, and escorted her out of the room, closing the door behind them and stalking down the hall with her . . . to his bedroom. Unceremoniously he led her inside and closed the door. Only then did he let go of her arm.

Angel took a few more steps into the airy room, looking around but knowing already, from her investigation when she'd first arrived here, what she'd see. No frills, solid furniture, and a wide bed covered with a colorful quilt. She pivoted to face Jack, her hand going to the place on her arm where he'd gripped her. He hadn't hurt her, but still she rubbed her fingers over where his had been.

"I'm sorry I rushed you out of there," he told her. "But I couldn't take any more of their questions about my father." He huffed out his breath, ran a hand through his hair. "That's going to be a tough one, telling them. They've been with the Circle D since I was a boy."

"I figured as much, watching you with them," she said. What she didn't say was how much her respect for him was growing, seeing as she had how he'd taken such care with the older men's feelings.

As if he hadn't heard her, Jack shook his head. "I've got to tell them about Tex and Calvin, too—the men we found yesterday.'' Then he frowned, looking around the room as if he hadn't realized until now where he'd brought her. He flicked his gaze to her. "You mind being in here?"

"No," Angel drawled. "One room's as good as another."

He gave her a considering once-over. Not a heated stare, just a measuring one. Then he shifted his stance, as if that signaled his change in subject. "All I had time for outside was a few words of greeting to get Lou and Boots over their surprise at seeing me home."

Angel remembered Boots's words. He'd said something about the fuss between Jack and his father being over how the ranch was run. There had to be more to it, though, for him to disinherit his son. But she didn't get any further than that in her thoughts before she realized he was quiet . . . and again staring at her. Discomfitted by his scrutiny, she blurted, "What?"

His expression and his voice softened. He pointed to her rubbing her arm. "I'm sorry I put my hand on you. I know I'm not supposed to. Did I hurt you?"

"No." Angel jerked her hand away from her arm and denied to herself the guilty warmth that crept over her cheeks. "It takes more than that to hurt me," she said, her voice sounding, even to her own ears, a little too high and less indignant than she'd intended.

"I bet it does," he said, managing to sound as if he felt sorry for her.

And that realization only increased her anger at herself, at her uncustomary reaction to his touch, his voice, his words. How did he do that . . . seeing inside her and making a mishmash of what he found there? Feeling as if somehow she'd been untrue to herself, Angel notched her chin up, looked him right in his concerned blue eyes, and chose a few sharp words as a salve to her abraded pride. "Still, you'd do well to remember to keep your hands to yourself—*before* the fact . . . cowboy."

Cowboy. With that one word, she probably just saved my sanity, Jack thought. She just saved him from the soul-deep, raw hurt and anger that tore at his insides. And all but drove him to his knees in defeat. He supposed he ought to thank her for that.

Hell, he admitted, he ought—no, *wanted*—to do more than that. He wanted to grab her to him. Wanted to hold her close, needed to feel her warmth and the comfort of her embrace. He needed someone—Angel—to touch him, to tell him it was going to be all right. Even when he knew it wasn't going to be. Not ever. Not after what he'd just learned from Standing Elk.

What his Comanche friend had told him tore at Jack's heart. *No,* he pleaded with himself. *Don't think about it right now. Think about Angel.* And he did, looking her up and down as she, for whatever reason—perhaps tiredness, perhaps impatience with his continued silence . . . turned away from him to take the few steps to the window. Once there, she crossed her arms under her chambray-shirted bosom and stood in slender profile to him, staring out at what he knew lay outside within her view. The service yard, the barn and corral, the prairie beyond.

Jack fisted his hands against the urge to go to her, to take her in his arms and just hold her. She'd never allow it. He needed to look away from her, needed to do something. Anything but stand here with his naked want hanging out. His agitation lending abruptness to his movements, he ran a hand through his hair, shifted his weight from one booted foot to the other. And again turned to her. The sight she made, here in his room, staggered him, had him all but crying out the questions in his soul. *Is it your touch I want, Angel Devlin? Or just anyone's right now?*

He had to consider both, weigh them against the ugly truth festering inside his heart and possibly clouding his judgment. Was what Standing Elk told him making him think he wanted things he didn't really? Couldn't it be, just like on his first day home when she'd told him about his father, that he simply needed the comfort of anyone warm? Or was it, in truth, her—and only her—he wanted?

A sinking feeling in Jack's stomach gave him his answer.

It was her he wanted. Angel Devlin. And only her. He wanted to fall into her arms and clutch her to him . . . and never let her go. He wanted her to hold him as much as he wanted to hold her. He wanted to feel her kisses on his face, her hands in his hair, her heart beating against his. He needed her to tell him he wasn't alone, that all would be okay. But he couldn't go to her. He couldn't ask her for that.

Because she *was* Angel Devlin. And she wouldn't welcome his touch. Or any man's, he suspected. Not after what she'd watched her mother go through. Hell, common sense said she'd probably seen only the worst side of men all her life. A sadness invaded Jack with his next conclusion. Those experiences had most likely hardened this girl's heart until no man could touch it.

This realization only added to his misery over what Standing Elk had reluctantly told him. And right now, Jack couldn't have said for whom he felt more sorry. Her . . . because she'd never admit to needing him or anyone else. Or himself . . . because he needed her.

Dejected by his thoughts, Jack fought what he felt as a growing truth inside himself with regard to her. How could it be, he fumed, that he could have such strong feelings for her? He'd known her only a few days. So how, in that short space of time, could he have such a certainty about how he felt?

Maybe, he decided, it was because of their being thrown together like this under such trying circumstances. Maybe it was what they were still going through together. He frowned, shaking his head, thinking no, they weren't going through anything *together*. They *were* going through the same thing . . . wanting to hang on to the Circle D, but from opposite sides. Then, how . . . ?

A sudden vision from yesterday—of the white wolf lifting her head in the rain and howling as he'd held Angel up in his arms—brought Jack his answer. They were meant to be, the two of them. He repeated it for himself, with a growing sense of conviction. *We were meant to be.* It really was that simple. Their being together had been written in the stars long before they'd ever walked this earth. Pulled back to the moment, Jack glanced again at her. She'd now turned completely away, her back to him, apparently as lost in her thoughts as he was in his.

He studied her back, noting anew her shapeliness, the slenderness of her frame, a frame that held so much strength, that kept so much inside. Just then, her long, curling black hair shimmered with a slight movement she made, a shifting of her weight. Then, a tiny sniff escaped her. As if that were his signal, Jack let out a breath he hadn't realized he'd been holding and called to her. "Angel?"

She pivoted to face him, her arms easing down to her sides. Her black eyes, bright with questioning, considered him, waited for him to speak. Jack then realized she hadn't been lost in thought. She'd been waiting for him to speak. Under her quiet scrutiny, faced with her vulnerable yet aloof beauty, Jack had to clear his throat, and still wasn't sure he could get the words out. But finally, he did, speaking haltingly.

"It was—" he began but stopped, choking off his words. He couldn't look at her as he said this. It was too ugly. He shifted his gaze just to her left, to the white-laced curtains of the window. And took a deep breath, preparing himself to utter the most evil, the most unbelievable words he'd ever have to say in his entire life.

"It was what, Jack?" came Angel's sudden yet soft prompting. "What's wrong?"

He glanced her way again. This time, her black eyes, the luminous depths, as always, captured and held his attention. "It was . . ." he began again. And again stalled. He clenched his teeth, fisted his hands, hating this hurt inside him. Instead, he should be feeling rage. A righteous and vengeful anger. He took a deep breath, firmed his lips together. And felt the first stirrings of those emotions deep within himself. As if he'd planted them in his soul, they sprouted, grew within him, came to his rescue.

Rage, vengeance, a need for justice. They belonged to him now. Jack exhaled, felt his heartbeat slow, his body grow in strength, felt a terrible peace befall him.

This time, as he thought about what he wanted to say, a grim self-assuredness that he hadn't possessed even a moment ago now gripped him, telling him he had nothing to fear from the words he had to say. The words meant nothing. Because the acts they spoke of had already been done. And that was what he needed to deal with. Retribution for those acts. So, all he had to do was . . . tell her. And then, he'd leave, go set things to rights. By himself.

With all that decided, Jack focused on Angel and said, "I spoke with Standing Elk . . . outside. It was Seth, Angel. My brother. He did it. All of it."

"Seth?" Angel repeated, not understanding . . . at least, not consciously. Perhaps some part of her knew, because her heart began thudding, her palms became damp, and her knees weakened. Still, she had to clear her throat before she could get out her next words. "Did what, Jack? What *all* did Seth do?"

His face a study in stark contrasts, in hardness overlaying an aching hurt, in a man's sharp planes and angles atop a child's rounded face, Jack looked away from her, directing his gaze to his boots, his hands to his waist. His dark head seemed to hang between his shoulders. Then he looked up, looking lost, and sought her gaze. "Everything. All of it. Shot up Lou and Boots. Killed Tex and Calvin. The horses, the cattle . . . the dogs."

Shock gripped Angel. She gasped, stiffening her knees, and protested . . . because her mind refused to accept what he said. "But he couldn't have," she cried as she took a step toward him. "Boots said there were a bunch of men. Seth's only one—"

"Seth has a gang he rides with, Angel. They helped him. And I can't account for them right now. Since he came here alone, I fear he may have sent them riding out after the herd by now. You need to know that if they catch up to them, if they kill the men and take the cattle into Abilene and sell them . . . then there is no Circle D. Because all the money's gone, too. There'd be no starting over. This place would dry up and blow away.''

"No." She couldn't even entertain such a thought. This was her home. "Why is he doing this, Jack? Why? What does he want?" she said angrily.

"The same thing you do. The same thing I do. The Circle D. He wants it. The land, Angel. It's about the land.''

"The land? All this killing's about the land? It's not covered in gold. What you're saying just doesn't make any sense.''

"It does to Seth.''

Shaking her head, confused, angry, Angel stared at him. Could simply wanting the land mean its death? Did coveting its rich grassy acres cost people their lives, kill its innocent creatures, and stain its ground with blood? No, she couldn't believe that. She wanted to build on it, wanted to make something good for herself on it. She wasn't like Seth. She wasn't. "But he's destroying it," she cried when Jack just stood there, a grim expression on his face. "What good would the ranch be to him then?"

Jack still didn't say anything. Angel wanted to shake him. Had he turned to stone? Was he waiting for her to figure it out on her own? But then, it came to her. She knew. And gasped with the truth that lay within her own words. A seeping coldness overtook her limbs and worked its way toward her heart. "My God, that's exactly what he wants, isn't it? He wants to destroy everything you've built here.''

Finally, Jack nodded and spoke. "Yes.''

"Why?" Angel's question, the one word, was no more than an angry cry.

"Because he hates us. Me. My father. He always has.''

Something about the way he said "my father" caught Angel's attention. "Oh, God, no . . . Jack, don't tell me. . . .'' Unable to look away from the awful truth darkening his blue eyes, Angel's knotted hands found their way to her chest and pressed against her lurching heart.

"He did it, Angel. He killed my father. His father.''

Angel swallowed, felt as if her throat were closing up on

her. But still she managed to get her words out. "What are you going to do?"

"Kill him," he said without hesitation. For all the emotion he exuded as he stood there, he could have been made of stone. Indeed, his voice was hard and flinty, his stance rigid. But then, and abruptly, with jerky movements, he turned and went to his bed. Sitting on its side and leaning forward, he braced his elbows atop his knees and cupped his face in his hands. No sounds came from him. His shoulders didn't shake. He just sat there . . . frozen.

An eye for an eye. Angel blinked, put a hand out to him, pulled it back. If she touched him, he'd shatter. She knew that. And she also knew better than to argue with him right now. Knew better than to tell him he couldn't go kill his own brother. That he'd be no better than Seth, if he did. Because this was a family matter. His family. He'd take care of it as he saw fit. She had no business interfering. Not that he'd listen to her, anyway.

But still, she wanted to ask him what had gone on in this house that had brought them all to this. What had made Seth into the monster he was? What was it that had caused the bad blood between Jack and his father? And the bad blood that had been evident yesterday between Jack and Seth, even before Jack knew anything about Seth's murdering ways?

And what in the living hell was it that made Wallace Daltry leave everything to me, and not to his sons, Angel railed. *Why involve me? What's behind all this?* she asked herself for the hundredth time.

It was just sick, was what it was. No, she didn't hold any particular love in her heart for her mother. But she sure as heck hadn't ever thought about killing the woman. What ate the worst at Angel now, though, was the notion that the old man had been killed for his kindness to her. It was so hard to accept, that what to her had been a mercy, a blessing— being given the Circle D—was to his sons a betrayal.

She saw that now. And could only stare at Jack's bent head and shake her own. And pray he was somehow innocent in all this. Because she was beginning to fear she could come to feel something for him. Something more than was good for either of them, given the battles yet to come. Just thinking of battles made Angel want to slump on the bed next to Jack. She'd thought her troubles were over the day she rode out of Red River Station. She'd thought her near rape and then the near lynching she'd been through were the worst things she'd ever be asked to endure.

Now she knew better. Because Seth Daltry was beginning to look like her worst nightmare yet to come. He'd killed two hired hands and had tried to kill those old men down the hall. Then he'd succeeded in killing his own father. A shudder ripped through Angel, when she thought of how close he'd been to her that night on the trail. Quickly she turned her thoughts away from that scene, away from that terror, and back to a litany of Seth's sins. He'd next tried to kill his own brother. But she'd stopped him. And then he'd threatened her.

Dear God. Now she knew he'd make good on that threat, if he got the chance. Angel drew herself up, telling herself she'd just have to see to it that he didn't get that chance, now wouldn't she?

Belying her bravado was a sudden sickness that invaded her soul. Her insides turned to cold stone, locking her muscles, stiffening her knees. She stared wordlessly at Jack. And thought again of Wallace Daltry. Again she saw the knife protruding from his chest, saw again his life's blood staining his bedroll. For a second, she closed her eyes, forcing her air and the sickness out, and inhaling a dreadful, numbing calm.

Then she looked again at Jack, watched him a moment. Felt for what he must be going through. "You all right?" she heard herself ask. But the voice sounded tinny, not at all like her own, even to her ears.

He looked up at her, dragging his face out of the shelter of his hands. His eyes were dry, bloodshot. He nodded, looking anything but all right.

Angel knew it was a stupid thing to ask—how could he be all right?—but she had no words of comfort to say to him.

Except his earlier words to her about her mother. "I'm real sorry, Jack."

Again he nodded, now dropping his hands between his knees. "Me, too. But not half as sorry as Seth's going to be."

Angel swallowed. She hated that he was going through this. Hated it. Not knowing what else to do, how to help him, but seeing that talking to him kept him from walking out the door and strapping on a gun, seeing that her words were keeping him from putting himself in harm's way, Angel asked, "You sure it was Seth? You sure that Comanche brave—"

"Standing Elk wouldn't lie."

"I wasn't going to say that," Angel rushed on. "I was going to ask how he knew . . . since he wasn't there. With your father, I mean." Instantly the opposite possibility crossed Angel's mind, and she gave voice to it. "Unless he *was* there, Jack. Think about it."

A flicker of emotion crossed his features. He blinked, a muscle in his jaw twitched, he shook his head. "I don't need to think about it. Standing Elk wasn't there. But he knows because Pa's murder, and everything else, was . . . seen."

It was seen. He didn't have to say how or by whom. Angel already knew. "The white wolf. The medicine man's vision." Skepticism had her pressing her lips together into a straight, firm line. When Jack nodded that she was right, Angel's heart sank. "Jack, you can't go kill your brother on the strength of what some Comanche medicine man says he saw in a vision."

With a heavy sigh of exhaled breath, Jack levered himself up, his hands pressing against his knees as he did so. Then he stood there, staring at her. "Yes I can. You don't understand their ways, Angel. I do. I was raised by one of them. And I know their visions to be true. You, yourself, have seen the wolf."

Further arguments—all of them logical—screamed to be voiced, but Angel held her tongue. Now was not the time. Jack was hurting too much. He wasn't thinking straight. But then a sudden vision of her own—of herself pulling the bone-handled knife from Wallace Daltry's bloodied chest—told her that now *was* the time to speak of that.

"Then there's something I want to show you," she said without preamble, already walking toward him. "Come with me."

"All right," he agreed readily enough, not touching her as she passed him, and falling in behind her, then reaching around her to open the door and hold it for her. In that way, him behind her, she walked him to her room.

Once they crossed the threshhold, Jack said, quite out of the blue, "This was Old Mother's room when she lived here. I'm surprised you don't feel her in here sometimes."

Angel's steps faltered, she gasped as her widening eyes sought Jack's when he stepped around her and looked the room over, touching things, turning them over. He acted as if he hadn't even noticed her reaction. So Angel glanced around with him, now seeing the square and inviting area through new eyes. Maybe that explained why she'd been so drawn to this room when she'd come upstairs on her first day here. She recalled again how scared she'd been, what with all the quiet and the abandoned look of the place. But this room had looked warm and sunny. And she'd chosen it— *Stop it*, she chastised herself. *Just stop it.*

I chose this room by pure chance and that's all there is to it, she insisted to herself, refusing to accept any other explanation. Angry at herself for giving in to silly daydreams, she stalked across the room to her narrow, Indian-blanket-covered bed, and without thinking too much about it, bent down and lifted the mattress—Jack said not a word, made not a sound—and reached under it to pull out her oilskin-wrapped belongings.

Allowing the mattress to flop back into place, she laid the pouch on her bed and opened it, exposing her treasures—for the first time in her life—to another person. She mentally defended her actions by asking her protesting half what choice she had in the matter, under the circumstances? "Here's what I wanted to show you," she quickly said over her shoulder as she moved aside her tattered rag-cloth doll to reveal the knife.

A sudden hissing intake of breath from beside her preceded Jack reaching in to grab up the long-bladed weapon. He eyed it, turning it over in his hands, and then sought her gaze. Anger blazed in the blue depths of his eyes. "What are you doing with this? Where'd you get this knife?"

Angel swallowed, suddenly hesitant to say where. "Then you know who this knife belongs to?"

"Hell, yes. It's mine. Where'd you—"

"It's yours?" Angel blurted, stiffening with surprise.

Jack stilled, as if he knew something awful was coming. He eyed her a long, dry moment before repeating, "That's what I said. Where'd you get it?"

"I found it," she blurted.

"Where?"

"Where'd you lose it?"

"I didn't. It was taken. Somebody took it. I haven't seen it for nearly a year. My father gave it to me, and a similar one to Seth a long time—" He stopped, as if he'd just heard himself rambling on. Then his eyebrows veed down over his nose. "Dammit, Angel, spit it out. The day's not getting any younger. Where'd you find it?"

"Just give me a minute, will you?" she crabbed, trying to hear herself saying *In your father's chest.* "Take some time, and make sure it's yours." He opened his mouth, no doubt to protest, but Angel beat him to it. "Please," she begged. "And I don't say that often."

Still annoyed, he nevertheless complied, lowering his gaze to the knife he held, turning it over and over in his hands, running his fingers over the deadly weapon's contours. Angel watched him. She'd expected him to say the knife was Seth's. But it wasn't. It was Jack's. Obviously the medicine man's vision hadn't revealed this detail. To further forestall answering him, Angel avoided his gaze and set about rewrapping her belongings.

It wasn't that she believed that Jack had killed his own father, she told herself. Because she didn't. But it wouldn't sit any easier with him, she knew, to learn that his knife had been used to kill the old man. A sudden low but hissing gasp, at just thinking the words, told her she couldn't say them. She just couldn't. Then she frowned, feeling her own eyebrows lower, her mouth pucker. This was just plain silly. *Why can't I? Why can't I just spit the danged words out and be done with it?*

Because . . . came the niggling response trying to worm its way into her consciousness . . . *you don't want him to hurt anymore. Because you care.* Angel's hands fisted around her father's old hat. She stared blindly at it. *No.* She refused to entertain the thought, refused to lend it credence. Hurriedly, she busied herself with rewrapping her belongings. Too soon done with her task, Angel turned back to Jack.

He was silently watching her now. Apparently had been for a while. She swallowed, flinching when he first spoke. "Well? For the third time, Angel, where'd you get this knife?"

His tone of voice brooked no argument, no further stalling. Finally, Angel said, "You might want to sit down first."

He shook his head, looking pale and grim, like death warmed over. "No. Just tell me."

"All right. I didn't really find it, Jack. I . . . pulled it from your father's chest. Seth—or whoever killed him—used your knife to do it."

"Oh, Jesus," was all he said. The knife fell from his hand, clattering harmlessly to the wood floor, and lay there, gleaming and deadly. As Angel watched him, feeling helpless, Jack again covered his face with his hands. Underneath his spread fingers she could see his reddening and contorted features.

Angel's heart flipflopped. Her own features twisted with sympathy. Again, she put a hand out to him. But this time—unlike all the other times in her life when she'd wanted to reach out, but had always stopped herself before the need became an act—she didn't pull back. This time, she didn't think of herself, didn't guard her heart against being turned aside. No, this time she allowed herself to reach out to another human being. To offer solace, comfort . . . understand-

ing. She took a risk with her heart. She touched his sleeve.
"Jack?"

In the next blurred instant, without really knowing how it
happened, she was a captive in his embrace . . . pulled up
against his chest and pressed tightly against him from her
head to her toes. His arms wrapped around her back and her
waist, capturing her hair. Angel circled his muscled neck with
her own arms. Nothing had ever felt so right before. She
melted against him, gave herself over to him, gave herself up
to the safety, the warmth, the strength of his arms.

His face nestled in the crook of her neck and shoulder. He
couldn't seem to get close enough to her, either. Acting out
of her own need, as much as his, Angel clung to him, held
his head to her, threaded her fingers through the black waves
of his hair. And crooned, "It's all right, Jack. It's going to
be all right. I'm right here."

He stilled, as if listening. And then . . . he cried. Great
wrenching sobs tore from him, he clutched at her, at her clothing. His hands kneaded her back, fisted around her hair.
Sweating with grief, with torn emotions, he pulled her closer
. . . his warmth and his brokenness tearing at Angel's long-
denied heart. Tears invaded her eyes. She blinked them back,
refused to think why—or for whom—she would be shedding
tears. After all, she was doing this for him. This big, strong,
fine man was undone. Not her.

Unbidden, her mother's words came to her. Virginia had
always said a broken heart could hold more love. Angel could
never understand that . . . until now. Now she knew. A broken
heart was open, so it had more room. A broken heart understood . . . and responded.

After a few more moments, he quieted, and pulled away,
his hands gripping her waist, his forehead resting against her
collarbone. Angel pulled back, too. Cupping his face with her
hands and lifting his head from her tear-soaked shoulder, she
looked into his face. She wanted to tell him again it would
be all right. Or perhaps she wanted to see for herself that he
would be all right.

But he stared down at her, his blue eyes bloodshot, and

spoke first, his voice hoarse with emotion. "Oh, God, Angel, I'm so sorry."

Frowning, she shook her head, asking him, "For what? You didn't do anything."

"Yes I did," came his response. He raised a hand between them . . . she released his face . . . he swiped away his tears and wiped his cheeks dry. "I kept you here. And now I can't keep you safe. I should have let you go yesterday. If anything were to happen to you because I didn't make you—"

"Jack!" she cut him off, again cupping his cheeks with her hands. "Look at me." Her palms still damp with his tears, she waited until he blinked, waited until she was sure he was paying attention to her. Only then did she speak her mind. "First of all, you can't make me do anything. And I would have come back. Even if I'd left . . . I'd have come back"—she faltered—"because . . . because I don't have any place else to go. This is *my* home, too. So whatever happens . . . would have happened anyway. And it won't have a blamed thing to do with you."

He shook his head, releasing her, turning away, again swiping at his face, wiping away evidence of his tears, tears that she suspected now embarrassed him. "I'd like to believe that, Angel. But I can't," he said, more to the bed he faced than to her.

"Then I can't help you," she said quietly. He pivoted to face her, his own face red, swollen around his blue eyes, his mouth downcast, white around the edges. "Because it's the truth. Look at me, Jack. I'm still standing here. No one's stopping me from leaving. Not you. Not those old men down the hall. And yet, I don't leave. What does that tell you?"

A ghost of a grin flitted across his features. He sniffed, rubbing a finger under his nose, looking somewhat like a little boy. "That you're too damned stubborn to save yourself?"

"Damn straight," Angel said, almost losing her battle to keep her own expression sober. "So, come on." She took a step toward the door. "Like you said, the day isn't getting any younger. And we've got some figuring and some work to do. Some answers to find."

Jack sobered, bent over to pick up his knife. Angel waited for him. He then stood tall—and maybe a little stronger, she decided, as if something on the inside were fixing itself as he stared at her. "Yeah, work and answers. And some men to kill," he said, ending the moment.

Thirteen

That evening, out in the long lamp-lit hallway upstairs, Jack closed the door to his father's room, leaving behind Lou and Boots to console each other. For a moment, he just stood there, his head hung forward, a hand to his waist, his other rubbing over his eyes and mouth. *Damn, that was hard.* Then he raised his head, looking toward the ceiling as he closed his eyes, swearing that when he found Seth . . . he'd tear him apart. That's all there was to it.

Soft footfalls sounded on the wood floor. Jack lowered his head, looking down the hallway, toward the stairs. Dressed still in his clothes, Angel was approaching him. At just the sight of her, Jack's heart raced, renewing itself, proving to him that he could still find a measure of peace, of happiness, in all this. He burned for her—he admitted it—his eyes couldn't get enough of her. A smile found its way to his lips. The truth was, she was the best thing he'd ever seen in . . . well, all his life.

"You okay, cowboy?" she asked when she stood in front of him, her somber gaze roving over his face, as if she meant to reassure herself, no matter how he responded.

"Yeah, I'm fine," Jack said. Her calling him cowboy somehow eased him away from the pain of his loss. And the pain of his brother's treachery that tugged at his heart. "How about you? Are you fine?"

She looked surprised by that. "Yeah. Why wouldn't I be?"

"No reason," Jack said, shrugging, wondering if she'd come upstairs just to check on him. That was a heartwarming thought, if it was true. "Did you need something?"

She blinked, her face colored, as if his question had caught her unawares. She *had* come to see about him. Jack had all he could do not to pull her to him and hug her tight for that. "Yeah," she finally answered, that chin of hers notching up, her black-eyed gaze wavering. "I don't mean to bother you, but I . . . I mean, I know you're . . . that you probably. . . ." Looking peeved with herself, she huffed out her breath and spoke abruptly. "I made some coffee. You want some?"

Jack smiled weakly and said, "I do now." Then he did manage a chuckle, garnering for himself her frown that dared him to say one untoward word to her about her kindness, just one. But what could he say? She'd deny—until the next century—any tender concern she might feel for him or anyone else. So he simply gestured for her to walk with him back to the stairs.

She fell in beside him, looking small and soft, despite being in his too-big clothes, despite her steady stride and self-assured ways. Even so, Jack felt his heart swell with a sudden protectiveness toward her. And wouldn't she laugh to know that? After a few paces, she glanced up at him, caught him watching her. He didn't look away. Her eyebrows rose, but all she did was ask, "How're Mr. Montana and Mr. Cornwell?"

Feeling his load lighten some, just being in her company—and how strange was that . . . Angel Devlin . . . he never would have dreamed it—Jack grinned. "You mean Lou and Boots? Don't let them catch you calling them mister. They'll think they're dying."

She grinned . . . finally. "I'll try to remember that."

As they walked on, now at the stairs and stepping down them, Jack behind Angel, he said, "I had a tough time convincing them to stay here and not go out to the bunkhouse."

She nodded her head, didn't turn around. Jack watched the sway of her long, black hair and had to control himself to keep from reaching out to stroke its softness. "I'm sure you did," she said over her shoulder. "How'd you finally get them to stay here?"

"I told them it was too dangerous right now for us to be scattered about. We don't know where Seth is, what might happen next. So we need to be in one place."

Angel turned to him, stopping him on the last riser, effectively holding him in place while she had her say. "A good argument, Jack. You ought to take your own advice."

Jack slumped. Not this again. They'd been at it all afternoon. "Look, the truth is, I told them a little lie. I do have an idea where Seth might be. I know his hideouts. Most likely, he'll be at one of them, plotting his revenge. So—"

"Well, I'll sleep better for knowing that," Angel quipped, heavy on the sarcasm.

A bit peeved, Jack ignored her interruption. "So all I have to do is make the rounds and find him."

"I hope you pick well. Which hideout, that is. It could mean all our lives."

Jack pointed a finger at her. "Now, that's enough, Angel. I know you don't want me to leave—"

"Want doesn't have a thing to do with it," she blurted, her color heightening. "You don't answer to me. You're your own man. So you do as you please. I just think what you're doing is foolhardy."

Jack clenched his jaw. "So you said earlier. But foolhardy or not, I've got to take care of my business. I can't just sit here anymore. Now that I know what to do, who's behind all this misery . . . well, I aim to go find him. And deal with him."

She nodded, saying, "I'd do no less. I don't fault you for that. And it's not my place to do so," she said, her voice sounding suddenly flat. "But what if you get yourself killed? What's Seth going to do then? Come here? And if he does, what happens to this place? To those two old men upstairs? And your drovers up in Abilene? Say they make it through and come back alive, expecting their pay and their jobs. What about them?"

Damn her for asking all the right questions. Jack stepped

down off the stair, forcing her back a step—but no more. She wasn't giving an inch. But he did notice that she hadn't included herself in his list of worries, in the list of his responsibilities she'd outlined. Which gave him his response. "What if I hadn't come home to begin with, Angel? What if I'd just stayed away? All this would still be happening. Only without me. So, the way I see it, it'd still all fall on your shoulders. This place and all its problems would be yours alone."

She ducked her chin, raising an eyebrow. "And the same is true if things had happened the other way around. If *you'd* come home and *I* hadn't been here. Everyone who's dead would still be. And the same person would still be responsible. So could you leave then, Jack? Just up and leave Boots and Lou and the Circle D to fend for itself? Could you?"

"Well, I'd just have to, wouldn't I?"

"Would you? It seems to me you're using me for your ranch hands and this spread while you're out looking for your brother—who could show up here and slip in the back door."

His worst nightmare, spoken aloud. Frustrated, feeling pushed into a corner, torn between what he should do—stay here—and what he felt honor bound to do—seek out Seth— Jack lost his temper, just threw his hands up, as if washing them of the place. "The hell with it all. I'm going. You want the Circle D so bad? Then you're welcome to it. Take it. It's yours."

Angel's eyes narrowed, her mouth turned down, her hands went to her waist. "It's not that easy," she told him, her voice low and level. "I need to know what it is I'm fighting for. I need to know if I have a real, legal claim to the Circle D. Something despite your father's just wanting me to have it. I need reasons, Jack. And I won't find them here. So tomorrow, same as you, I'm leaving. But for Wichita Falls."

Jack didn't know where to start answering all the wrongheadedness in everything she'd just said. But he knew she couldn't leave. She'd get herself killed out there. "What's in Wichita Falls?" he wanted to know. "You can't go there."

"Yes I can. And it's the county seat."

"The county se—" Then, suddenly, he understood. "You

want to see the deed of ownership for the Circle D.''

"Yep," Angel assured him. "I do."

He couldn't believe this. "You think it'll be in your name?"

"I don't know. That's what I want to find out."

"It's not. I've seen it. But let's say it is, that my father changed it somehow. What does that prove?"

"That the Circle D is worth my time. Maybe my life."

"Your life." Jack stared at her. "You won't have a life to worry about if you venture off this place and get caught by Seth before I deal with him."

Her expression hardened. "I can handle myself."

"I don't doubt that for a minute," Jack agreed with her. "But I also know Seth. He's a murdering son of a bitch. And you need to stay put until I . . . take care of him."

"You keep saying that. And I keep asking you—what makes you think he won't kill you first?"

Jack firmed his jaw. "That's a chance I have to take."

"Me, too," Angel said.

"Dammit, Angel."

"Dammit, Jack."

Jack huffed out his breath, ran a hand through his hair. They weren't getting anywhere like this. Nor had they all afternoon with this same rehash. And why was that? Because, as much as he hated to admit it, they were both right. And both wrong. A sudden chuckle escaped him—and had her raising her eyebrows. "All right, Angel, you win. We'll both either stay here. Or leave together. Deal?"

Angel raised an eyebrow. "No." With that, she turned on her heel and started for the back of the house, to the kitchen.

Dammit. Jack's teeth gritted against the emotion tearing at him, against the fit of temper itching at his skin. He started after her, focusing on her retreating back as he spoke. "Angel, I don't want to have words with you over this. We need to work together."

In the hallway now, she jerked around, forcing him to pull up short. "We? *We* need to work together? For what?"

"For—" He'd almost blurted *For us.* And realized he

wanted it to be true. Which only made everything else harder. And so, he amended his answer, saying, "For the Circle D, that's what. We may be knocking heads over who owns what, but the truth is, we could both lose it if Seth isn't stopped. He's already proven he's capable of anything, Angel. He could burn the barn down, even the house."

"Why is he like that?" Angel cut in, her voice strident with disbelief. "What happened to make him do the things he does?"

Her questions drooped Jack's spirits. "I don't know, Angel. A lot of things, I guess. Most of it to do with Pa. And my mother dying. Old Mother couldn't even get through to him. It's like something's missing in his head. Or his heart."

"I reckon so," Angel agreed. "Anyone'd who'd set his gang on two old men like Boots and Lou can't be all there in the head . . . or the heart, like you say."

"It's the truth. And it shames me even to be related to him. Those poor old men. Angel, we can't leave them here by themselves. Look what happened to them the last time."

She huffed out her breath, pursing her lips and staring helplessly at him. Was she wavering? Feeling encouraged, Jack pressed his point. "What do you say, Angel, since we both care about those two? And care about—" Again, he bit back his words.

"And we both care about . . . what, Jack?" came her question, in a voice achingly soft. Her big eyes, as round as full moons and as shiny as stars, called to him, begged him to step closer. Or was he just imagining it?

Jack's mouth worked. He knew what he wanted to say, but his heart pounded so hard and his palms sweated until he wasn't sure he could get it out. But he was bound and determined to try. "We both . . . care about . . . what happens to each other, Angel."

She all but recoiled, stepping back and shaking her head. "That's a lie. I don't give a rat's—"

"Yes you do," he abruptly cut her off, eliciting a gasp from her. But still, his heart sank. Could he have been that wrong? If someone had asked him, he'd have told them he'd been with enough women to know their signals. But with Angel Devlin . . . maybe not.

She recovered, her body rigid. "I said that's a lie. And I mean it."

"No you don't." To hell with that. He wasn't wrong. And he wasn't taking any more of her running away from the looks she gave him. From the things she said. From the many other ways she showed she cared. Like coming upstairs to check on him just now. "If you didn't care, you wouldn't have fussed with me all afternoon about leaving. If you didn't care, you'd be glad to see me ride away. Because if I do and I get myself killed . . . then everything you want will be yours. And that's the Circle D, right?"

Her body jerked, she glared at him. But Jack wouldn't give her a chance to deny it. Not able to stop himself, he reached out, grabbing her by her arms and pulling her to his chest. Looking down into her widened eyes, feeling the resistance in her body, but fueled by desire for her, by fear for her should she leave, he gritted out, "Say it, Angel. Say it again. Say you don't care. *Say it.*"

Tears sprang to her eyes. Tiny white lines formed at either corner of her mouth, no more than a grim slash on her face. But then her chin quivered, tears spilling over, coursing down her cheeks. "I. Don't. Care," she said, slowly . . . deliberately . . . through gritted teeth.

But still, believing he was fighting for something beyond the ranch, beyond his brother, beyond them both, something that would ultimately save them, he held on to her, looking deep into her eyes. "Then why are you crying, Angel?"

She had no answer for him. She held herself immobile, shaking her head, lowering it until he couldn't see her face.

Jack loosened his grip, circled her with his arms, now holding her tightly but with more tenderness. "I don't want to hurt you, Angel. I just want to hold you. And I think you want me to. I swear, you're killing me, girl. Do you hear me? You're killing me." He kissed the top of her head, felt her body begin to shake. A ragged sob escaped her. Jack rested his cheek against the top of her head. "I can't think about anything but you, Angel. I lie awake in my room at night, in my bed, and sweat for you. Just *ache* for you."

Now he pulled back, an arm still around her, his other hand tipping her chin up until he could see her face. "Aww, sweetheart," he crooned, seeing her tear-streaked cheeks and reddened face. She had a hiccupping sigh and stuttering breath for him that all but broke his heart. He pulled her to him again, holding her, wanting to protect her from all the hurt in the world. "Tell me you don't want me, Angel. Tell me you don't. And I'll never—" He stopped, frowning. He'd never what?

"You'll never what, cowboy?" came her muffled question. "Touch me again?"

Jack stiffened. Her voice. It wasn't tearful. Could it be—? A broad grin slashed across his features. He pulled back some, still holding on to her arms, afraid to let go of her. He looked down into her face, right now so womanly, so full of promise. And yet childlike and open, . . . and so trusting, for the first time since he'd known her. "What are you saying, Angel?"

"I'm saying," she repeated, lifting her chin and adopting that bravado she wore like a weapon, "that neither one of us will get any rest, or a single, solitary thing done until we . . . say we care what happens to the other one. One human being to another. And nothing more."

Seeing through her words, his heart soaring, like he'd never thought it could, and seized by a happiness long denied him, Jack said, "Angel Devlin, those are the most beautiful words anyone ever said to me."

Was the man plumb loco? Angel had to ask herself as she blinked up through her tears at Jack. She'd just admitted to as much heartfelt feeling as she'd have for a rabbit being chased for dinner by a coyote. And here he was acting as if she'd said she loved him. Well, she didn't. And it was high time he knew it. She opened her mouth to say as much—

And his head slanted down, his mouth covered hers.

Fourteen

As Jack's lips claimed hers, as his tongue pushed against hers, dancing with it in a swirling passion that tingled her to her toes, Angel pressed her palms against his muscled chest, felt sure her bones had melted. She'd never been kissed before, except by him that one time. But she liked it, liked the way his lips felt on hers, liked the way his arms held her close, the way his body pressed into hers. His strength and size sheltered her, yet demanded more of her, made her want more. Made her want to give herself to him in all the ways she'd never, ever thought she'd want to. Or could.

A moan escaped her, mingling with his breath, with the guttural sounds he answered her with. Angel knew what this was, this passion. It was a drug, a strong potion that could ensnare hearts, addle minds, cause men and women to behave in ways they shouldn't. But still, she wanted it . . . wanted Jack. But what she felt wasn't what the child within her heart cried out against. It wasn't, it couldn't be, her mother's betrayal, an elixir that killed. But a potion that healed, that held a man and a woman together . . . in love.

But even as she gave herself over to Jack, even as she molded her body more fully to his when his arms encircled her, when his kiss deepened, when the heat between them built, Angel involuntarily held back a part of herself, a portion of her heart that she felt sure she'd never give up. She couldn't help it, couldn't control it. Too long she'd been left on her own, too long she'd been denied simple compassion, a forgiveness for sins she'd never committed. Yes, there were parts of herself she'd give Jack, she knew. But there were also parts of herself, places in her heart, that he'd have to earn.

When Jack broke their kiss, he was left gasping, marveling at the sheer intensity of his desire for her. Never before had any woman ever stirred him as she did now. As she had since he'd first seen her. With nothing more than a look, a word, a touch from her, he'd been left sweating and sleepless.

And now, with her passionate but inexperienced kiss? Sweet Mary, every inch of him wanted her. And beautiful Angel—his heart went out to her—she was so brave. She clutched at his shirt and pressed her cheek to his chest, her breaths coming in gasps. But still, he suspected the battle within, the struggle and the sheer power of her will warring with her fears. She had to have fears, given her untouched state and her awful upbringing. She had to have strong misgivings about what he suspected was about to happen between them.

And yet, here she was facing them . . . essentially, for him. And that meant a lot to Jack, had his heart swelling with gratitude. What a gift her kiss was, her closeness was. He was humbled that she'd choose him, that she'd allow him next to her. Every man in Red River Station knew not to try. And here she was . . . in his arms. Perhaps he'd pulled her to him, perhaps he'd not given her much choice. But she wasn't pulling away, wasn't protesting. And it was this part of her, this unhappy, hurting part of her, that Jack wanted more than he did her physical love.

With every fiber of his being, he wanted to offer her healing. And yes, he needed her, too. He wanted to take tender care of her heart, if she'd allow it. And this, this loving tonight, if it happened, if it was what she wanted . . . would be only a first step, he knew that. This side of loving wasn't the struggle. He accepted that. The hard part followed, the building on the budding trust and respect between them. And he was more than willing to do his part, if she'd have him. He'd had enough of carousing, of drinking and wasting his life. Look what it had cost him—his father, perhaps his home, maybe his very life.

No more. He'd looked into her black eyes . . . and found everything he'd ever wanted. If she wanted him in return, then his life would be worth living. But it wouldn't be easy. No, nothing about Angel ever was. Furthermore, no one had to tell him that she might give her body, but not her heart. Not her real self. He'd have to earn that. But that was all right. He had all his life, and hers, to do that. And if that was how long it took, then so be it.

When Angel stirred in his arms, Jack pulled himself out of his thoughts and glanced down, only to realize he was stroking the length of her hair . . . down her back . . . to her waist. And still she clung to him, giving him as much of a go-ahead as he needed. Thus encouraged, Jack murmured the words he'd been wanting to say to her since he'd known her, tender words that spoke of desire, of wanting, of needing. He felt her shudder . . . a ripple of desire, he hoped, and not fear. Softly he soothed her, told her not to fear love, that it could make her whole.

Finally, Angel raised her head, seeking his gaze. Jack almost gasped with what he saw reflected in her eyes—everything he could ever hope for. The heat of desire, with a blaze of soul-deep wanting. An arm still encircling her waist, with his other he cradled her neck and chin, his long fingers curling gently around her jaw. "Oh, Angel, you sweet girl," he sighed, peppering her face—her eyelids, her nose, her cheeks—with hungry kisses and hungrier words. "I want you. Can you understand that? I need you. I want to hold you, to kiss you—"

"I want that, too," Angel answered, no more than breathing her words.

Jack stilled. Did she know what she was saying? Was she even aware that she had uttered those words, and what their impact could be? When Angel pulled back some—perhaps she detected the change in him—Jack slid his hand down to her heart. She tilted her head up, looking again into his eyes.

He hoped she could see the wanting, the caring there.

"*Do* you want me, Angel? Do you know what that means?"

She lowered her gaze, nodding. "I know. I want you. I do."

His gaze roved over her. With a feather-soft touch, he raised her head, stroked her cheek, a half-smile playing around his mouth. "Are you sure?"

Again, she nodded that she was. Jack's grin widened with what he saw. Her beautiful face was colored with a flush of embarrassment. Poor, sweet, innocent thing. She instantly lowered her gaze to his chest, stared at a button there. And shrugged as she admitted, "I mean . . . I think so. I've seen it a time or two."

Jack stiffened, knuckling her chin up until she was forced to meet his gaze. "You mean . . . your mother, the things she did?" Angel's gaze slid to his left, to his shoulder. She nodded. "Oh, baby, you poor thing," Jack sighed, pressing her to him, his hand now cupping her head as he held her to his chest. The way his heart was thumping for her, Jack suspected she could hear it under her ear. He hoped she could. And he hoped, for her, it was a reassuring sound. Perhaps it was . . . because her arms stole around his back.

Jack almost melted. Dared he hope that she needed his closeness, as much as he now admitted he needed hers? The very notion that she could want him, and the soaring love that burst through him for her, had him tightening his hold, kissing her hair, saying, "Sweetheart, what a gift you are, one I want to open."

"I'm scared," Angel finally admitted, her voice muffled by his embrace.

Jack's answering grin was tender. "I know you are. It's your first time, isn't it?"

Angel nodded, and shook with another shiver. He shifted her in his arms, laying his cheek atop her head and crooning more soft, seductive words meant to reassure her and warm her soul. "It's okay. I know how you feel. I won't hurt you, honey. I just want you to know that . . . well, it won't be like that for us, like it was for your mother. This is different. Because we care.'' Then he hitched his shoulder, forcing Angel to pull back. She looked up at him. He grinned, raising his eyebrows. ''We do care, don't we?''

''We care,'' she whispered.

Jack watched the play of emotions over her face. ''Good.'' Then, without another word, he scooped her up in his arms. Angel's arms instantly encircled his neck. He carried her down the hall that rounded onto the stairs . . . which led up to the bedrooms.

When he could, when his steps didn't need direction, Jack slipped his gaze down to her, down to Angel lying there in his embrace, her eyes closed, her forehead against his neck. He reveled in her soft warmth, in every breath that carried to him the delicate musk of her femininity. And still he wondered if she really realized what she was doing. She was giving herself to a man. What did that mean to Angel Devlin? And why him? Why now?

He knew enough about her life, had heard more in town, to know she'd sworn her heart and her body off limits. She'd held herself aloof, no doubt clinging to the hurt and the shock of her mother's life and its impact on hers. But what had it gotten her, he had to wonder? The bitterness that flavored her words, her deeds? A life alone, a life of loneliness? One lived apart? Had she thought all this time that what she had was strength? But now, in the shelter of his arms, in the warmth of his embrace, did she know better? Did she know that all she'd been was hurt . . . and scared?

Well, no more, Jack vowed, as he began their ascent up the stairs. If he had anything to say about it, she would never hurt again. This wasn't a child he held in his arm. She was a woman. And she wanted him, said she wanted everything that it meant. He had to believe her. Because, he now admitted, it was true . . . he'd been hurt as much by his family as she had been by her mother. Which only seemed, in some crazy way, to make what they felt for each other all the more right, all the more necessary.

At the top of the stairs now, on the second-floor landing,

Jack stopped. "Angel?" he called softly to her. She opened her eyes, giving him a wide-eyed, questioning look. Jack's heart leaped. What if she said no, what if she'd changed her mind? Could he set her down, allow her to walk away from him and into her room? Could he stand to see her close a door in his face? But still, he took that chance, accepted that possibility, and asked, "Are you still sure you want this?"

Her gaze steady, she looked into his eyes. "I'm still sure," she told him. "I'm very sure."

Jack's smile trembled, his expression softened, his heart thumped its relief. "Good," he said, "because I don't think I could stand it if I did something to hurt you. If I—"

Angel put her fingers against his lips. "Shhh. You won't. If I thought otherwise, I wouldn't be here . . . in your arms."

"Good." He nodded, smiling. "Good." He couldn't seem to say it enough, couldn't seem to move forward, either. Couldn't seem to take them into his bedroom. Not yet. He needed a signal from her, he suddenly realized, something physical, a reaching out to him. As if she'd read his thoughts, Angel reached up, shyly, wonderingly touching her fingertips to his mouth. Jack squeezed his eyes shut against the powerful rip of emotion that seized him with her simple act. And felt sure he'd crumple to the floor, taking her with him.

Locking his knees, steadying himself, he kissed her fingers. And finally accepted. "All right." Then, with a quicksilver change in mood, he sobered, felt the intensity of desire take hold of him. "I want you in my bed, Angel. I want to feel you in my arms. I want to show you what love is. It's so much more than you've seen, than you think you know."

Angel roved her gaze over his face, not giving away her thoughts. Jack wondered what she saw when she looked at him. Wondered if she could feel the thick trickling of desire for her that coursed through him, slowing his blood, pooling itself low in his belly, making him feel languid, almost lazy, as if he needed to stretch . . . but against her. Perhaps she could, because suddenly she pulled his head down to hers, his ear to her mouth. "I want you to show me," she whispered.

Jack stiffened, stared down into her face, feeling certain his eyes sparked fire as he muttered, "Damn." With a glance down the hall, reaffirming that the door there remained closed, that Lou and Boots slept on, he turned them into his room. And still, with the moment here, Angel clung to him, making Jack love her all the more for the trust she showed in him.

He set her on her feet, reaching for the kerosene lamp to his left, turning it down just a bit, softening the room's contours. Then he watched Angel, saw her looking around, saw her gaze locking on the bed. What now? he wondered. Would she have second thoughts? He waited, giving her that chance. When she didn't say or do anything, when she just stood there, Jack suddenly realized it was because she didn't know what to say or to do.

Well, he did. With that, Jack pivoted, closing the door behind them. Angel spun around. Sure enough, she looked scared. Jack stayed where he was, leaning against the door behind him . . . and waiting for her. Wide-eyed, unblinking, Angel felt for her pants, gripping the denim material in her fists.

Jack had to wonder if the scorching desire that fired his blood had found its way to his face and scared her. "What are you thinking, Angel?"

"Lou and Boots," she said. "Can they . . . hear us?"

Wondering if she was mapping strategy or simply stalling, Jack grinned. "Those two couldn't hear thunder at two paces. But their door's closed. And I can hear their snores from here," he assured her. Then he became quiet, his expression sobering. Still wanting to be sure, he again asked, "You still okay with this?"

Looking as if she were a deer about to bolt, Angel swallowed, notched her chin up. "Yeah. But are you going to ask me that every step of the way, cowboy? It could get tiresome."

Again, Jack grinned. "All right." He pushed away from the door, walking toward her, surprised his legs would carry him, so stiff with wanting was he. "All right, I won't ask again. I'll trust you to know your own mind." As he neared her, he held his arms out to her. "Come here, Angel Devlin. Let me hold you."

And then, she was in his arms, holding him again, clutching him to her, her fingers tangling in his hair as he again took her mouth in a hungry kiss that left no room for further talk, for anything but feeling. Spurred by her answering reaction to him, and almost before he even realized he was doing it, Jack had her belt undone, her denims slipped down her legs, and his hands under her shirt, under her camisole, smoothing them up her narrow waist, up her ribs. To her breasts. He wasn't sure he could wait, that he could be gentle with her. And she seemed to want him to hurry, too.

At just the feel of her silky skin, the way her full and heavy breasts felt in his hands, Jack gave himself over to the hot pricks of fire that shot through him, all but buckling his knees as his fingers slid over her nipples and gently tugged at them. Wrenching in surprised reaction, Angel gasped into his mouth. Jack ended their kiss, stared into her shocked eyes. She clutched at his shoulders, staring.

"That's supposed to happen. It's supposed to feel like that." With that, he smoothed his hands down to grip her waist, to steady her and give her time to get used to the sensations. Without a word, with a smile tugging at the corners of his mouth, he allowed her to stand there . . . as he unbuttoned her shirt. Angel looked down, watching his fingers work. He wondered what she thought of her britches pooled around her ankles, around her stockings and boots.

Looking up at Jack, she bit at her bottom lip. Jack wished he could spare her some of the fear and uncertainty she was sure to experience. But there was really no way to prepare her, except to touch her, to be gentle, and to talk to her . . . reassure her.

"It's all right," he crooned, smoothing the shirt off her shoulders, helping it slide down her arms until it joined the steadily growing pile of his clothes at her feet. All she had on now were her small clothes, a camisole and bloomers. Jack's blood heated, stirring anew, his breath caught. "My

God, you are beautiful, Angel.'' He looked into her eyes. ''Everything about you is perfect. Everything.''

Perhaps maidenly shyness attacked her because she again lowered her gaze. ''No,'' Jack protested, knuckling her chin up, wanting her to look at him. ''Don't be ashamed. This is how God made you. You're beautiful. And remember, I've already seen you without your clothes. You don't have to worry. I like what I see.''

Angel blinked, her mouth worked. Jack's heart melted. ''Come here, baby,'' he said, again lifting her, intent on carrying her to his bed. With her feet off the ground, the chambray shirt fell away, and she kicked herself free of the clinging denims. In his arms, her weight was little more than that little rag-cloth doll he'd seen when she showed him his knife. Once at his bed, he set her on its firm softness, her legs and booted feet dangling over the side. Jack knelt in front of her, unlacing and then tugging off her boots. He then slowly unrolled her stockings from her legs. Long and shapely. His gaze followed his hands, his breath caught.

And then he felt a shudder ripple through her, heard her gasping sigh, saw her clutch at the quilt she sat on. She liked his touch. Jack smiled, as relieved as he was uplifted. Her honest reaction meant more to him than anything she could have said, could have done. He excited her, too. He stirred her blood. Jack walked his gaze up the sensual length of her, until he looked into her desire-drugged eyes. She'd been watching him undress her.

Jack stood up, held his hand out to her. Angel took it without hesitation. He pulled her to her feet, held her close to him, feeling the rapid tattoo of her heartbeat. No doubt she was aroused, but she was also scared to death. ''It's your first time, honey. It's okay to be scared,'' Jack soothed. ''Everyone is. You'll be fine. Do you believe me?''

After only a moment's hesitation, Angel whispered, ''I believe you.''

Yes. Jack flung his head back, exhaling the breath he hadn't realized he'd been holding. Angel's fingers suddenly stroked his neck, smoothing up and down his skin, sending chills running over his body.

Jack tugged her forward and again claimed her mouth, heating the moment. She buckled against him. Jack tightened his grip, holding her up as his tongue sought and gained entrance into her mouth. Hungrily, eagerly . . . perhaps desperately she returned his kiss, allowed his onslaught. Afraid to overwhelm her, and despite what every male instinct he possessed shouted for him to do, Jack broke their kiss, pulling away, gasping.

But Angel surprised him, delighted him. She moaned, didn't want the kiss to end. Because she pulled his head back down to hers, eliciting a moan from him. Desire exploded through Jack. He had to get his clothes off. Now. With her directing the kiss, holding his face, Jack began tearing at his clothes. Within only seconds, Angel was helping him, all while still kissing him. His shirt came away. She had it in her hands, was tossing it aside. Jack couldn't breathe. Again he broke the kiss, barely gritting out, "Wait . . . a minute. Slow down. I have to—"

She undid his belt, ripping open the button fly on his denims. Jack froze. What the—? What was her hurry? She tugged on his britches—then Jack remembered his boots. "Shit." He jerked around to the bed—all under Angel's silent, watchful gaze—sat down and pulled them off, then his thick socks. Finally, he stood again, tugging his denims down over his hips, his body still covered by the white neck-to-ankles combination suit he wore underneath. He kicked free of his pants, began unbuttoning his long underwear, looking over at Angel when she gasped. "We can't do this with our clothes on."

"I know," she said quickly. "It's just that . . . I never . . . I—"

"I know." Jack stood there, all too aware of his . . . hardness under the cotton weave of his drawers, all too aware of its insistent throbbing and jutting. Now what? Knowing better than to let her think about it, he took her again in his arms, carrying them both to the bed and stretching out with her.

Instantly, as their half-naked bodies touched, full length,

the passion doubled. Their hands became restless, roving, their mouths questing, seeking, their hips thrusting, rolling. In only seconds, modesty was forgotten . . . and the remaining small clothes were discarded, thrown free of the bed.

Exquisite. She was like a pretty song with a melody you could whistle all day. Every part of her, every inch. Beautiful. Silky. Jack wanted to take his time with her, wanted to explore her, get to know her, gentle her to his touch. And allow her to become familiar with the contours of his body, too. But Angel would have none of it. As if fevered, as if time were running out for her, she urged him on top of her. Jack resisted, wanting to understand this new Angel, so full of urgent fire and wanting.

Lying half on top of her, he smoothed his hands up her arms, urging her to put them above her head. She did and he held her hands there, locking his fingers with hers, and kissing her mouth. Then he moved more fully over her, settling himself into the saddle of her hips and gently pushing against her. Her moan sounded inside his mouth, increasing Jack's sense of urgency. He released her hands, her mouth, and slid down her until he could capture a nipple, could suckle and lave it, could flick his tongue over its sensitive tip and . . . make her arch her back and cry out.

Angel writhed under him, only increasing Jack's desire, only fueling his lust. With nipping kisses, he worked his way over to her other breast—like its mate, a pinkish globe with a peaked and rosy nipple—and captured it, lavishing the same attention on it. As he did, and ever so slowly, he slid off her, lay at her side . . . and moved his hand down her belly, smoothing and kneading her velvet-soft, taut skin as he went. God, she tasted great. Like warm honey. His fingers sought the vee of her thighs . . . found it.

With feather-soft gentleness he stroked her there, up and down, in and out, each time entering her a little bit more . . . and withdrawing, entering and withdrawing. Until she was wet and moaning. And crying out his name. Only then did Jack pull himself up and over her. Instantly she wrapped her arms around his neck, clutching him to her warm body, instinctively bending her knees. Jack helped her, telling her, "Wrap your legs around my back, Angel. It'll make it easier, honey."

She complied, not asking what exactly this would make easier. Feeling she was ready, feeling her hips arch and buck against him, Jack positioned himself . . . and entered her. Slowly . . . paying attention to the suble changes in her body, to the tightening, the stilling, the stiffening. When he felt any of those things, he stopped, kissed her mouth, her eyelids, her cheeks, swirled his tongue in her ear, nipped at her neck . . . rubbed himself against her, ever edging inside.

And then, with one good thrust, he broke through, felt the tearing, refused to allow himself to revel in her slick tightness just yet, despite his muscles all but locking with intense pleasure. Because she'd stiffened, too, and gasped. Then Jack gasped himself when her fingernails dug into his shoulders. "It's okay," he soothed. "This is the only time it will hurt. I swear. Let me help you, Angel . . . let me help you."

She relaxed, still trembled, but she did exhale and nod vigorously. Jack took that as his sign and began the timeless dance that found its own rhythm. He rocked and thrust against her, inside her . . . finally allowing himself, once he knew she joined him, to feel the joy, the incredible pleasure of their mating. She was magnificent, even in her innocence. Ensheathed in her as he was, on fire for her, his every sense honed in on the feel of her body surrounding his, Jack maintained his pace, pushing into her, stroke after stroke that only built in intensity.

But still, and fighting it with every thrust, he held back, waiting for her, waiting for the subtle tensing signs he knew her body would give to tell him she was reaching her moment. And finally . . . it happened. She gasped, stilled, clutched at him, raked her fingernails over his back. A guttural sound, from the back of her throat—the sound he'd been waiting for—tore out of Angel. Her cry lifted in the still air of the room. Jack captured her sounds in his kiss—swallowing her desire, breathing her gasps, as he picked up the pace, only adding to their pleasure.

And then the explosion came, seemed to rip them in two while melting them together. Angel broke her mouth free, cried out again, buried her face in his shoulder as her hips worked rhythmically yet spasmodically against his. Her body now pulsed around him, grasping greedily at him, pulling him in deeper and deeper. The liquid fire of her satiation rent a hoarse and rasping cry from Jack. He could be dying, so intense was the pleasure. He jerked up, held himself rigid over her as he felt his life's force flow out of him and pulsate into her.

And then, it was over. Slick with a loving sweat, Jack slumped over her, lying atop her but supporting the brunt of his weight with his elbows. He smoothed her dampened hair out of her face, kissed her forehead, the tip of her nose, listened to her breathing, watched her closed eyes, watched her tongue slip out of her mouth to wet her lips.

Then, she cried . . . silently. But not so unexpectedly. Jack had seen this before. Reaction was setting in. Her face reddened, her features contorted, and the tears streamed from the outer corners of her eyes, ran across her temples and into her hair. Her shoulders heaved, she turned her face away.

Jack hurt for her as he roved his gaze over her wonderfully strong yet delicate profile, still smoothing away her hair, still kissing her. Her crying only intensified. Now Jack frowned, suddenly sensing that something else, something other than this irrevocable act between them, was making her cry.

And then, given what he knew of her, what he'd observed for himself—her sudden, almost frantic urgency—he came up with it, thought he knew what was wrong. A half-grin of sympathy and understanding, of hurting for her, curved his mouth, had him sliding out of the tight envelope of her sheath.

Rolling off her, lying at her side, and pulling her to him, Jack held her, wrapping his arms around her, draping a leg over both of hers. Angel eased a hand between his arm and his ribs, wrapping her arm around him. Her other one she nestled against his chest, the top of her head all but burrowed under his chin. Jack stroked her side, smoothing his hand from her waist to her hip and back.

"Angel," he finally said, hearing the whispery hoarseness of his own voice. "You tried to get through this without feeling anything, didn't you?"

Fifteen

Following the noonday meal that next day, a sunny but dampish one with a light wind, Angel pulled off her apron and wiped her hands on it, intent on escaping the house, and its many quiet rooms that seemed to mock her, to tell her she'd lost, that she didn't belong here. She needed to get away, away from Jack's weighted stares, his blue and questioning eyes. Away from Boots's incessant chatter and Lou's simple grinning ways.

Instantly, she regretted that thought. It wasn't the two old men. It was Jack. His life didn't appear to have changed any as a result of what they'd done last night. And who was he, anyway, to tell her what she did or didn't feel? What'd he know about anything, about her? Nothing, that's what. Nothing at all. And he was wrong. Because she did feel . . . had felt something. Wasn't she changed today? The blood smudged on her thighs last night proved that her life was now and forever different.

And it was that realization, minus a concrete understanding of what it meant for her and Jack, what came next, what he might expect, that made her want to run away, to be alone with her aching muscles and her troubled thoughts. She needed time to sort things out for herself, to see how she felt about them. And to decide what she was going to do about them. If anything.

Turning to the kitchen window, which looked out onto the barn, its service court, and the horse corral, Angel crossed her arms under her bosom and stared. What she saw brought a reluctant grin to her face. She chuckled, shaking her head. *Jack sure lost that battle.* Because there they all three were. Lou and Boots had filed out, right behind Jack, after eating a meal of beans and corn bread with her. Angel recalled the darting glances the two old drovers had shot her and Jack, who'd done no talking to each other. She remembered the men's subdued conversation, their lowered voices. As if she were asleep and shouldn't be awakened.

Those two old coots sure acted hell-bent on helping Jack make his preparations to leave, when the truth was they weren't doing much more than getting in his way and slowing him down. Then it occurred to her, they probably meant to do just that . . . slow him down. Angel's grin widened. She could respect that. Why, at lunch they'd even insisted he sit a spell, long enough to go over with them what was and what wasn't missing after all the goings-on around here, and what needed to be done in his absence.

Of course, Jack had protested at every turn. He'd told them to rest, had said he didn't need any help. *May as well have saved his breath,* Angel decided. Because Lou and Boots had followed him right outside, out to the barn, still stubbornly intent on helping him. As she watched, they were leading Jack to the barn, pointing and gesturing for all they were worth. *Must be time to figure out what was and what wasn't missing.*

As if it matters, was Angel's desultory thought as she finally turned her back on the scene outside and leaned against the sink behind her. She focused on the drop-leaf table across the way, but didn't really see it as she gave herself over to her thoughts. And found herself agreeing with Jack. What good would it do, he'd asked, to have a list of items needing replacement, if there was no place to bring them to? Because nothing was settled. They could all still be killed, and the Circle D could still just dry up and blow away.

Angel huffed out her breath, forcing herself to think the thought . . . *Jack's leaving. But I'm not.* She was staying put, right here. And there was the crux of the problem. All their lovemaking last night hadn't changed a thing . . . except her and her plans. Not that she'd . . . participated out of any hope of changing his mind about her owning the Circle D. She wasn't one to use feminine wiles to get her way. In fact, she wasn't even sure she owned a feminine wile. Or if it would work, if she had one and tried to use it. *What the heck am I thinking? Move on, Angel.*

All right. Adding to her frustrations was her demoralizing realization—arrived at after listening to Jack and his two old drovers, from hearing Boots's seemingly endless list of concerns and details to be seen to—that even at the best of times, she couldn't hold this place together without Jack, or someone like him. She didn't have the know-how, the years of experience, or even the muscles it took to make a go of a cattle ranch. What had she been thinking? She ought to just leave, was what she ought to do.

But she wouldn't. And how had he extracted from her a promise to stay put? Then she remembered. He'd done so after the second time they'd . . . made love, and before she'd gotten up, insisting on sleeping in her own bed. She'd expected him to say otherwise, but he hadn't raised a fuss. He'd said "Fine . . . go"—and something about her being as independent as a hog on ice—to her argument that she wasn't used to sleeping with anyone and saw no need now to start doing so.

To her way of thinking, it'd been bad enough she'd given herself to him. She stopped at that thought . . . why *had* she given herself to him? How had that happened? One minute they were arguing downstairs, and the next they were naked upstairs and in bed. Well, however it had happened, she didn't have to compound her mistake by spending the night in his bed and risk getting caught by Lou or Boots the next morning. Not that she cared what they thought. It just would have been . . . embarrassing. And none of their business.

So, *was* last night a mistake? Angel asked herself for about the tenth time today. Probably, she decided, and that led her to the next question for herself. If last night was a mistake, then could what they'd done together be called lovemaking? Because . . . was love ever a mistake? Grimacing, Angel put a hand to her forehead and rubbed hard. All these silly thoughts. Where were they getting her? Certainly not any closer to being outside.

And not any closer to answering the one notion that nagged her the most. And that was . . . no words of love, of loving each other, had passed between them. No words about today, about what last night meant for the future. But had she really expected such assurances? Angel now asked herself, thinking about it as she opened the kitchen door and stepped out back, breathing in the clean, fresh air. After all, it wasn't as if she loved Jack Daltry.

She closed the door behind herself and stood there on the enclosed landing a moment, considering her own question. *Do I love Jack Daltry?*

No, she decided, shaking her head. She didn't. But instantly another part of her mind—or was it her heart?—lodged a protest. Well, okay, she amended, she didn't *suppose* she loved him. But maybe she did. She quirked her mouth, thinking further. *How would I know? I don't know what love feels like, now do I? I've never loved anyone.*

The distant, fading echo of her father's gentle laughter haunted her a moment. He'd died so long ago, killed by that stray bullet as he'd walked past a saloon brawl in Red River Station. She was five when that happened, but she supposed she'd have to say she loved him. Didn't all children love their parents?

Angel sighed, thinking now of her mother. Okay, as a child she'd loved Virginia Daltry. She had memories of her mother's many tendernesses and her caring ways. Her quiet spirit and soft voice. But that was before Tom Devlin had been killed and Virginia'd taken to a life of whoring. Angel flinched at the cold, ugly word. Could it be, as Wallace Daltry had said, that her mother hadn't had a choice? That she'd had to sell her body, and her soul, to feed the child that Angel'd been back then?

It made sense, she now admitted . . . for the first time. But Angel suspected she'd always realized that. Just hadn't allowed herself to believe it. And why hadn't she? Because—

she took a deep breath, as if doing so would help her handle the truth, as well as her own private guilt—she'd not been able to pull her mother out of that life. She'd barely made enough money at the hotel to support herself. And the one time she'd haltingly asked Saul if she could have her mother stay there and work, he'd said "I don't want her kind around here. Got enough troubles as it is without the likes of her on the premises."

The likes of her. Her kind. His words ate at Angel, then and now. She recalled it was that day she really understood how other folks saw her mother—indeed, how they saw *her,* Virginia's daughter. It was after that—again Angel saw herself on that day, a skinny, ashamed fourteen-year-old—that she'd taken a step back from her mother, wouldn't accept her money, had hardened her heart toward her. Had left her there to die.

Angel grimaced, letting go of her disturbing thoughts. What good did they do? She couldn't undo what had happened. And then made up her mind to enjoy her moments of solitude. Dressed again in Jack's denims and his chambray shirt, she put one foot in front of the other, as if an act of will was required, and ambled down the back steps. As her booted feet touched the rain-squishy ground, she realized she wasn't done fretting over the question in her heart. Because here she was thinking about it again. Did she love Jack Daltry?

Suddenly angry with it all, she thought, *No, I don't.* But again, and immediately, her heart protested, thumped leadenly in her chest, stopping her and forcing her to turn her head toward the barn, to seek him out.

And . . . there he was. Her breath caught. Framed in the open doors of the hayloft, with a knee flexed, his arms crossed over his chest, stood Jack Daltry. And he was watching her. Even from this distance, she felt the weight of his stare, felt certain she could feel the blue of his eyes darkening as they had last night. Her gaze riveted to his, time and distance no barrier, Angel stood frozen.

Then . . . he turned away, disappearing into the barn's dark interior. In the same instant, Angel slumped, felt weak and clammy, as if she'd just been released from a spell he'd cast over her. Her heart now thumping, she wanted to turn and flee. But innate dignity and a huge dose of pride forced her to turn, head held high, and to stride evenly toward her destination. The meadow carpeted in bluebonnets. The wolf flower.

And suddenly, she was among them. As soon she walked into the field of silky-haired leaves and delicate blue blooms, Angel felt better, felt her cares begin to slip away. She didn't know how far or how long she'd walked among them—just that she was, exhilarated by the sunshine, by the quiet, by the openness—when an unbidden thought stopped her where she stood, shattered her. *He was right.* As if possessed of a will of their own, Angel's hands found her face, covering it. *I did try to get through the lovemaking without feeling anything. Why? Is it because of Mama?*

Mama? Angel gasped, lowering her hands, staring straight ahead, right through the undulating ocean of flowers sifted by the breeze. She hadn't called, or even thought of, Virginia Devlin as Mama since she'd been about ten years old. So why now? Maybe because now she was a woman herself? Because now she knew what it was like to be faced with hard choices? Because now she knew what it felt like not to choose well?

Not to choose well. Angel squeezed her eyes shut. She knew what that meant. Last night. Jack Daltry. Their . . . lovemaking. And that was exactly what it was. Love. She knew it now. And did it ever hurt. *Oh, Mama, help me!* The wail tore through her, echoing in her soul. As if she had no bones to hold her up, Angel dropped to her knees. The dampness in the ground, like so much blood, seeped through her denims, chilling her.

Close to giving up, to giving in, Angel fell forward, her palms flat on the ground, her hair cascading forward over her shoulders, brushing against her hands. She couldn't love Jack Daltry. She couldn't. There was too much about him, about his family and hers, about his father and her parents, that she didn't know. But the horrible twisting in her gut told her that whatever it was, whatever had happened all those years ago . . . was bad. Why else would her mother not accept Wallace Daltry's help? What could Jack's father have done to the young Virginia?

And if he'd done something so awful that her mother'd taken to whoring, then why was *she* here, accepting the man's guilt-offering? Angel looked up. With the sun's heat beating against her back, she stared into the distance, just above the flowers' heads. A guilt-offering. That's what this was—the Circle D and Wallace Daltry's insisting she come here to take over the place. But hadn't she thought as much, and even questioned him about it while they were still back at Red River Station? What had he said?

Oh, yes. He'd said something about the answers being here at the Circle D. He'd said he'd tell her once they got here, once she signed those papers. The missing papers. Did they even exist? And if they did, where were they? *Seth.* Angel gasped, sat back on her haunches, her hands gripping her knees, her gaze taking in the world but really seeing a hateful face, a raised fist . . . a threat against her. That murdering little bastard. *Seth.* He had them. She knew it, as surely as she knew she was sitting here and staring at—

Angel's heart almost stopped, her throat all but closed. Chills raced over her body. She couldn't seem to draw a breath.

The white wolf sat in front of her, had appeared out of thin air, for all Angel knew. Perhaps she'd been here a while because she was sitting, reposed on her haunches and so close Angel could reach out and touch her. If she dared. But she didn't . . . this *was* a wolf, after all. A big one. A flesh-and-blood creature of the wild. Angel could see that much because the animal's tongue lolled, her ears pricked, her fur was lifted by the restless wind. Unblinking, she stared deep into Angel's eyes.

Terrified though she was, Angel refused to believe that this fantastic creature was the Comanche woman, Old Mother, who'd raised Jack and Seth. It just couldn't be. People did not turn into animals. Or come back, like ghosts, to live inside them. They just didn't. So how to explain what sat before her now, as plain as day, and seemingly willing to give her time to think this through? The amazing part was that she could think at all, Angel decided. But still, she did.

She hadn't heard of this particular white wolf, or its connection to the Daltrys, but she had heard before of all-white animals occurring among types that weren't prone to be white. Like the white buffalo, which was a sacred Indian legend. *Just like this white wolf is, according to Jack. And to that Comanche brave who brought Boots and Lou home.*

Well, real or legend, Angel decided, it just didn't matter. Because there was still a wolf in front of her that could, solely with its keen blue-eyed gaze, hold her riveted in place.

"What—" Startled at herself, Angel swallowed the rest of her words, watching as the wolf's ears pricked forward. Was she letting Angel know she was listening, waiting for her to speak? *Well, this is just plain crazy*, Angel chastised herself. Had she actually been going to speak to a wolf? Did she think it would answer? But then again, the urge overwhelmed Angel, and this time, she gave in to it. "What do you want?"

The wolf's response again stunned Angel. She smiled . . . Perhaps it was more of an animal grin, just a lifting of her black muzzle that revealed more of her white and sharp teeth. Whatever it was, the wolf's blue eyes brightened, squinted pleasantly; her ears stood straight up, twitching. And then she stood, wagging her tail with an elegant grace as she backed up several paces. She was leaving.

"No," Angel blurted, a hand out, all but imploring the wolf not to leave. And why she didn't want her to go, Angel didn't know, couldn't say. She . . . just didn't want her to, was all. As if the wolf understood, she stopped, tilting her head . . . watching Angel. As Angel stared into the blue eyes considering her, she recalled Jack doing the same thing a little bit ago. Amazingly, the wolf's eyes reminded her of Jack's— they were the same blue . . . held that same quality of sizing someone up that his gaze had.

The wolf blinked. Angel jerked, seeming to come to herself. She held a hand over her thumping heart, calling herself addled as she wondered if maybe she had sun sickness. But that wasn't possible. It wasn't near hot enough, and she hadn't been out here long enough. Or had she? Was she just too sick to judge time, to know if any of this was really happening? That niggling doubt had her coming to her feet and pivoting around, seeking the barn, perhaps seeking Jack. Or just seeking reassurance that the barn and the ranch were still there, that any of this was real, that she wasn't sick, wasn't dreaming.

But everything was as she'd left it, was as it should be. Including the sun's position. It hadn't moved. Jack was nowhere to be seen, probably still inside the barn. But still she had her answer. She was wide awake, not suffering an illness. And this wolf was real. She turned to face the white-furred creature again, half expecting her to be gone. She wasn't. She was still there.

Before she knew what she was doing, Angel put a hand out, took a step toward the wolf, wanting—she didn't know what, except to touch her, to stroke her fur. Somehow, Angel knew that she needed to do that. And she also knew it would feel good when she did. The wolf remained where she was, her countenance sobering, her ears alertly pricked forward . . . again, waiting. Angel took another step. The wolf wagged her tail with a slow, mesmerizing sway that compelled Angel, made her want to cry.

But still, holding her breath, Angel reached out again, this time close enough to touch the wolf. Her fingers just brushed the soft and sun-warmed fur of the animal's square and regal head—

"Angel?"

A startled yelp accompanied Angel's spinning around to face Jack. Wide-eyed and speechless, she stared. Where had he come from? her mind screamed. She'd just looked a moment ago. He hadn't been there—

"You've been out here a while, Angel. What are you doing? Were you picking more flowers?'' His blue eyes squinted against the sun's brightness.

Angel shook her head, found her voice. ''No. Not the flowers.'' Then, she just had to know. ''How'd you get out here without me knowing it?''

Jack frowned, as if confused. ''I just walked out here, Angel. Like anyone else would.''

She was having none of that. ''But I just looked back toward the barn, and I didn't see you. That's where you were when I came out here.''

A frown marred his features. ''I left the barn a while ago. But I don't see why this is—''

''Just tell me.''

A silent moment passed, then Jack, clearly humoring her, drawled, ''All right. I came around the other way, on the other side of the house, where the bunkhouse is. I was talking with Lou and Boots and looking things over out there. Satisfied?''

For some reason, she wasn't. It disquieted her to be taken by surprise like that. But she kept that to herself and said, ''Yeah.''

''Good.'' Then a half-smile tried to capture his features. ''What's been holding your attention out here for so long?''

For so long? She'd thought it'd been only minutes. ''The wolf,'' she said, feeling suddenly out of place again, out of time.

Jack shifted his stance, tensed. ''The wolf? What about her?''

''She was here.''

Wide-eyed, Jack stood up straighter. ''What?''

''She was here.'' Angel pointed behind herself, half turning to where the wolf had been. Not surprisingly, given Jack's interruption, she was gone. Angel's hand drooped to her side. She stared at the trampled indentations the creature'd made, and was glad for them. They told her she wasn't crazy.

''Angel?''

Again she turned to Jack, desperate for him to believe. ''She was here. I saw her. I touched her, Jack. Look there''— Angel now pointed to the trampled flowers—''she did that.''

Jack glanced where she pointed, but his gaze immediately returned to her. His expression, as well as his tone of voice, could only be termed disbelieving. "You . . . touched her? The white wolf? You touched her?"

Angel frowned with a sudden spate of temper. "Isn't that what I said? Why is that so hard to believe?"

"Because she's—No one's ever—" Jack cut off his own words to eye her, to look her up and down. "She let you get close enough to touch her?"

Beginning now to doubt herself and her experience, given Jack's response, and feeling a bit silly, Angel stood taller, pretended the knees to her denims weren't muddy, and quipped, "I said I touched her, didn't I, cowboy? But then you came along and spooked her into leaving. So what is it you wanted? Why'd you come all the way out here?"

He was quiet a moment, his expression hesitant, his gaze not quite connecting with hers. "I'm ready to go. I'm leaving now."

The simmering anger that had carried Angel out here came to a boil. She stiffened . . . but fought to keep her feelings off her face. Feigning indifference, she shrugged, saying, "So . . . go."

Jack squinted, crinkling the skin at either corner of his eyes. "That's all you have to say? After last night? Just 'Go'?"

Angel raised her chin a notch, thinking of all that had happened, thinking of how her lingering fears and doubts had made her call out for her mama. "Last night doesn't have anything to do with this. Besides, it doesn't seem to be stopping *you* any."

Jack's eyes darkened. He stood there, glaring, his lips pressed together. "I don't *want* to go, Angel. I *have* to."

She knew he did, and she even understood why he did. "I know that. Seth has to be stopped. It's that simple."

He nodded, looking a bit relieved as he looked down at his boots, as if his blood ties to his brother shamed him. Suddenly, somehow—perhaps it was the play of the sunshine off his skin—he looked . . . all too human, all too capable of being hurt or killed. Angel wanted to cry. She just couldn't stand the thought of something happening to him, of maybe never seeing him again. And she hated worse that she'd be bothered by that.

Desperately close to giving herself away, afraid she might beg him to stay, and wanting him gone if he was going to go anyway, Angel blurted, "What'd you expect me to do, Jack? Burst out crying because you're leaving?" He glanced up at her, his blue eyes clear, light . . . easily hurt. Angel swallowed and went on. "Did you come out here thinking I'd beg you to stay? Well, not me. You got the wrong girl. You need to go, so . . . go. Saddle up. Ride away."

He exhaled, shook his head, saying, "I didn't want to leave like this, Angel."

"That's too bad, isn't it? Because the truth is, I don't give a damn what you do, Jack Daltry." With that, she pushed past him, leaving him standing there in the meadow. Among the wolf flowers.

About a half day's southwesterly ride away from home, and stiff with caution, Jack sat his horse, holding Buffalo's reins tightly as he surveyed the square, squat, rough-cut wood shack Seth sometimes used as his hideout. About fifty yards away, all but hidden among the afternoon shadows cast by a sheltering patch of mesquites and scrub oaks, the place appeared deserted. No horses outside, no movement inside. But still, he couldn't take the chance on being wrong. If Seth was here . . . then so be it. Jack knew what he had to do. And if Seth wasn't, perhaps there was some clue inside as to where the kid was.

He admitted that Seth had chosen his hideout well. The shack itself and the surrounding trees could hide any number of men and their mounts among them. Jack had known them to do just that. And on more than one occasion when he'd ridden out to confront his brother. So even now, he knew, it could be that he was being watched. And, goddamn, he hoped he was. He hoped that little son of a bitch was here. Just the thought of again facing Seth, given what he now knew his younger brother had done, given how it made his heart break to imagine Seth plunging that bone-handled knife into their father's chest, lifted Jack's lip into a snarl.

Righteous rage threatened to explode through him. He struggled to contain the emotion, gripping the reins tightly, his body tensing enough to make his legs hurt as they circled Buffalo's ribs. *I'll crush the little bastard. Just kill him without a second thought.* He again swept the hideout with his gaze, searching for a glimpse of his brother. *Come on, show yourself, Seth. I'll smell you out, you stinking rat.*

To Jack's feverish mind, the shack, the surrounding trees, even the very earth the ugly little house sat on, seemed to give off the stench of corruption that followed Seth, like an animal leaving its scent, like a skunk defining its boundaries.

His jaw clenching, his nose twitching against the odor, real or imagined, Jack forced a calmness on himself. Because riding in hell-bent could get him killed. He needed a cool, calculating mind to deal with his brother. And so, he sat there, thinking about how best to proceed. He decided that Seth wouldn't shoot him on sight. No, he was like a coyote playing with a wounded rabbit. Seth'd want to mess with his head, see what he knew. Which would give Jack a chance to get close enough to—he surprised himself to realize he couldn't complete the thought, even as determined as he was to see this through to its deadly end.

His breath left his body on an exhalation rife with sadness. *Kill my own brother. Shit.* Even thinking all this, though, Jack knew and accepted that it was time to act on his beliefs. Time to stand by his principles. Even when the easiest thing to do was to turn Buffalo around and ride away. That made more sense. But Jack knew he wasn't going to do it. He couldn't. Better to die trying than to live regretting. So, tugging his Stetson down lower on his forehead, Jack urged Buffalo from the cover of the stacked jumble of huge marble-shaped boulders he'd hidden behind.

Approaching the shack, keeping a careful watch for any movement, for a flash of sunlight glinting off gunmetal, Jack rode cautiously in, even though logic told him the place was empty, that neither Seth nor his gang of murdering thugs was here. But still, a part of Jack hoped his brother *was* here, that he was inside. And that the little scum *would* take a potshot at him. It'd be easier that way. Just shoot him. No entanglement, no words. Just simple gut reaction. Get it over with. And go home to Angel.

His last thought made him tense up. He gripped Buffalo with his legs, hauling back on the reins. What had he just said to himself? Go home to Angel? He stared at the shack, blinking, seeing instead a sweet, fine-boned face with black eyes and even blacker hair falling down across those eyes . . . eyes that sparked fire in his soul. And knew it was true. He wanted to go home to Angel. She was a part of him already. Son of a bitch. Jack notched his Stetson up, slumping in the saddle.

Now what? He may have held her body next to his, he may know what it was like to be warm and naked with her, may know what she felt like inside, but he still didn't know what was in her heart, what she wanted from him, what she felt for him. But he also knew . . . it didn't matter how she felt about him. Because how he felt about her would keep him going, would get him through this day—and the next and the next, if he needed them—until Seth was dealt with and he could get back to her. Then he'd tell her everything he was feeling.

And what was he feeling? Jack didn't try to kid himself. He was too old, too experienced for that.

He loved her. Plain and simple. Soul deep and heart-stoppingly so. With every fiber of his being . . . he loved her. Whether she felt the same or not for him, it really didn't matter. It wouldn't change how he felt. It couldn't. Jack knew you didn't ask for love, didn't go looking for it. It was there . . . or it wasn't. Couldn't court it, couldn't woo it, couldn't hope to win it. Especially in Angel's case. No, he had no illusions with her. A woman like her did the choosing. And a man like him would be blessed to have a woman like her. Strong and warm. Smart and funny. Determined. Stubborn. With so much love to give.

Again Jack exhaled, wondering why his heart wasn't soaring with his realization, wondering why he wasn't at least feeling happy inside. But he thought he knew the why of it even as he thought it. Again . . . Angel Devlin. She was also a hard woman, for all her tender years. She needed saving, he knew that. She needed tenderness and patience and understanding. She needed him. Now, how to make her see that?

Buffalo's impatient stamp brought Jack back to the moment, back to his squinting consideration of the shack. First things first. Seth. And then Angel. Stroking his mount's shoulder to reassure him, feeling the warm, hard muscle, the coarse hair under his hand, Jack straightened up, again urging his big-boned brown horse forward. Again he told himself that Seth might not be here, and probably wasn't, but there might be some clue left behind that would direct him in finding his brother.

But truth be told, Jack now admitted as he reined Buffalo in at the shack's entrance, he was so torn by what he wanted to happen that there still remained a part of him that wished like crazy that he didn't have to face his brother at all, ever again. He found himself hoping that Seth might harbor some fear for his older brother's reaction to his killing their father, that he might have just ridden away, never to return. Because to kill your own brother, no matter what he'd done . . . well, it just wasn't right. But letting stand the horrible wrong he'd done wasn't anything to be abided, either. Or forgiven.

As Jack dismounted and looped the reins over a crude hitching rail, as he kept an eye on the closed front door, he further admitted that this was quite the predicament Seth had handed him. One he had to end. So, exhaling, feeling the thudding of his heart, firming his lips and his resolve, Jack drew his gun and approached the door, hating that he knew enough of the world to know he'd face Seth again. And soon.

He opened the door, his gaze drawn immediately to a rickety table situated directly in the middle of the square room. Atop the table was a stack of papers . . . held in place with a long, bone-handled knife stabbed right through their middle. Jack's heart leaped, thumped wildly. The papers. No doubt, the missing ones from the ranch. The knife . . . Seth's own skinning knife. Jack suspended further thought, didn't dare form any conclusions. Not yet.

Hating like hell to do so, but knowing he had to, Jack stepped inside, walking slowly, mechanically, up to the table. As his gaze roved over the display, his features hardened, his chest hurt. Seth knew he'd come here, knew he'd come looking for him. And had left this for him to find. Holstering his gun, Jack then planted a hand atop the papers, and with his other grabbed the wicked blade's hilt, toggling it back and forth to loosen it and finally pull it free. With a vehemence born of fearful suspicion and towering temper, Jack flung it out sideways, his motion inadvertently embedding it in a wall.

He stared at it a moment and then picked up the papers, wanting to verify for himself that these were indeed the ones missing from home. But the top one caught his attention, freezing him in place as he read it. *She's right. Angel's right. Pa did mean for her to have the Circle D. Goddamn.* What he held in his hand was a document changing ownership of the Daltry land. It was made out to Angel Devlin. And it named her Wallace Daltry's heir. *But why?*

Jack flipped to an attached piece of paper, found a letter to Angel . . . in his father's handwriting. He skimmed the words, and finally had to clutch at the table, had to stop reading it. When he did, and as he held the papers up, another note, on a torn fragment of paper, fell out, floating to the crude wood floor. Jack bent over, picked it up, read it. It was in Seth's handwriting. The first lines read . . . "Me and Angel Devlin. And then, me and you."

Angel! Jack's stomach turned, shock and fear making him ill. He looked again at the note, read the remaining words. They too were for him. But not as important as Jack's instant calculations. Could he get home before Seth got there? Could he stop him? Could he save Angel? He didn't know. Because he had no idea how long ago Seth'd left here. Damn him! Such rage as he'd never known gripped Jack. He'd played right into his brother's bloodstained hands.

Seth'd drawn him out, had caused him to leave vulnerable

everything he loved. *Son of a bitch!* Angel'd called this one, too. Clutching the wad of papers in his hand, Jack jerked around, already running. He had to get home to her as fast as Buffalo could carry him. He couldn't spare himself or his horse. They'd have to ride on, even through the darkness.

Because Jack knew he had to get to Angel . . . before Seth did.

Sixteen

I hope you don't mind. But we just cain't sleep together no more, Miss Angel. Especially not in Mr. Daltry's bed, him bein' gone and all. It don't feel right. 'Course, if'n he was here, he wouldn't allow it none, neither.''

She knew what Boots meant. But the way he said it made it sound like more. Fighting a grin, she quickly reassured him. "I understand."

"A body ought to be able to rest where he feels most comfortable," the tall and wiry old man went on, as if she hadn't already told him—three times since Jack had left earlier today—that his decision to remove Lou and himself from the main house was fine with her. "I purely cannot abide another night of Lou's tossing and snoring. Why, I believe I'd have to shoot him to get him to stop."

Boots now leaned in toward her, speaking just above a whisper—as if Lou, having been banished to the other end of the bunkhouse, could hear his friend talking about him. "And that'd be a shame because you know the poor old soul cain't help it."

"I truly do understand, Boots," Angel again assured him, shooting a glance at the grinning Lou, and trying to keep from chuckling and thereby hurting the feelings of these two old-maid drovers. "It's okay. I'll be fine alone in the house. I have this gun. And I'm used to being on my own. But if I need you, I'll just holler or fire off a round."

Angel looked around the neat, airy bunkhouse and asked, "You got everything you need out here?"

"Yep," Lou all but belched, surprising her and Boots, both of whom turned to stare at him down the long aisle of empty bunks. His face coloring brightly, the short, skinny little man resumed making his bed. It amused Angel that Boots had made him take the one farthest down the line from his own.

"Well, then . . . if you're sure," she said, realizing she was hedging, that she didn't really want to leave, didn't really want to be alone in the house with only her thoughts of Jack to occupy her time. "You'll still take your meals inside with me, won't you?"

"Oh, yes, ma'am, we'll most certainly do that. We'd be honored to," Boots replied, so polite as to be practically bowing and scraping, which embarrassed Angel. "Why, my belly's still plumb tickled pink with them vittles you fixed for supper. Ain't that right, Lou?"

From his little corner of the world, Lou called out, "Yep."

"Well . . . good," Angel said, not comfortable with his compliments. And then, she stared at them . . . as they stared back at her.

The moments stretched out, became awkward. Boots sniffed, shifted his stance, was uncustomarily quiet. Lou simply stood in the background, bright-eyed, his hands to his sides, reminding Angel of a curious prairie dog. Much to her own consternation, she couldn't make herself leave. And it further annoyed her to realize she wanted their company, their comforting presence in the big house. But how could she tell them that? Why, they'd think she was just plain crazy. Or a sissy.

That thought spurred her to action. "Well, then," she blurted, startling Boots. "I guess I'll be going, then. Good night."

Boots reached up to tug on a hat that still wasn't there. " 'Night, ma'am. We're goin' to go lights-out right now. But we'll see you bright and early tomorrow morning, if'n that's okay with you."

"It's fine," Angel answered, forcing a buoyancy, a determination, into her voice and her steps that she didn't really feel as she, followed by Boots, headed for the door that would put her outside in the starlit twilight air. "Besides, I'll need some help eating all those eggs I robbed from the hens this afternoon. We'll have them for our breakfast."

"Yes, ma'am. That sounds mighty fine. Mighty fine." Boots reached around her to open the heavy door and held it that way as she stepped over the threshhold. "Good night now, Miss Angel."

Walking away, her back to him, her senses washed in the cool, sweet spring air, but upset by sudden tears of loneliness that pricked at her eyes, Angel didn't look back, didn't say anything, just gave a parting wave with her hand. She kept walking until she heard the door close behind her. Only then did she exhale . . . and stop . . . and look up at the night sky. Hands to her waist, a knee bent, she concentrated on breathing in and out, in and out, and wondered what the heck was wrong with her.

How, she demanded of herself, could keeping her own company suddenly not be enough for her? Why was she so afraid of being alone? Especially when she'd gotten this far in life by keeping to herself, taking care of herself. Except for those times when she'd been forced to go see her mother. And she'd done that only when Virginia had sent a note to her at the hotel saying "Please, please come see me, my baby."

Her mother's remembered words had Angel looking down at her boots. She didn't want to think about Virginia. Not after this afternoon when her heart had cracked, when she'd called out to her, had called her Mama. Raising her head now, Angel looked around at the moonlight-bathed Circle D. And had to stiffen her knees. All this emotion, this crying and wanting to be with folks. It was this place, wasn't it? Could it be that the ranch, those old men, and even Jack were really coming to mean something to her, like family . . . something she'd never had?

Shying away from thinking about what Jack meant to her,

and thoughtfully toeing the earth with her booted foot, Angel concentrated on Lou and Boots. She couldn't believe that those two—well, Boots, anyway; Lou didn't have the mental faculties, she suspected, to think anything through long enough to come to any kind of an intelligible conclusion—had never asked her what she was doing here, or why she was here. They just accepted her presence, just drew on her kindnesses—she hated to admit she had such impulses—and extended theirs to her.

It was true, they hadn't known who she was, or why they shouldn't like her. But she suspected that if they had, it wouldn't have made a bit of difference to them. Nor would it now. Because they seemed to think that everyone was just folks. Live and let live. Angel believed the same, perhaps always had. She'd certainly never bothered anybody, had never set out to hurt anybody. Her mother's sweet face, so much like her own, popped into Angel's head.

She blinked, not raising her head toward the moon's bright, accusing light, and finally admitted . . . she didn't hate her mother. In fact, maybe now, given the unpredictable turns her own life had taken, given some of the poor decisions she'd made, she understood her a little better. Maybe even . . . loved her. For all the good it did Virginia now.

At long last, a terrible sadness for her loss filled Angel's heart, swelling it. And somehow she knew it was still okay to say the words. Somehow she knew that Virginia would hear, would know. Angel put a shaking hand to her mouth, finally peering out into the dark to where the bluebonneted meadow lay under its blanket of night. And gave herself over to the halting, difficult words. *Mama, I'm so sorry. Thank you for never hating me . . . for never giving up on me. I . . . I love you. And I always have. Always.*

Then she stood there for a moment, feeling a warmth wash over her, a release, a letting-go. She sighed and looked around, savoring the peace inside her and the surrounding quiet of the night. And for a moment, Angel knew complete calm, complete peace.

And then, she set her feet in motion, walking slowly, contentedly toward the ranch house that anchored the Circle D. Her home.

Sometime during the course of the night, as Angel lay asleep on her back, her hands above her head, resting against her pillow . . . a big, rough hand clamped down over her mouth, wrenching her awake, eliciting an air-starved gasp from her. Her eyes popped open wide, saw a shadowy someone. His heavy body immediately straddled her middle, holding her pinned down. Gasping and thrashing, she instinctively fought back, clutching at the hand, scratching it, clawing. To no avail.

Her air was slowly being cut off. Her very life was in danger. Gasping, grunting, writhing, she gave no quarter, couldn't afford to.

But then, another hand circled her throat, clamping, squeezing. The man atop her leaned over her, hunched over her and snarled right into her face, "Stop fighting me. Or I'll kill you right now. I swear I will. I'll snap your neck like it's a fucking twig."

Angel froze, then went limp. She knew the truth of his words, the futility of struggling. She also knew the voice. *Seth's.*

He chuckled, a sound having nothing to do with humor. "That's better. I always said you were a smart one. But I got you, you bitch. I told you I would."

Angel's vision suddenly adjusted to the dim light of night seeping in through the open window. She blinked, focusing. Saw him above her, noted his blood-bloated, desire-suffused expression . . . and recognized his intent. A paralyzing fear further sapped her of strength, of will. Her soul cried out for Jack. But she couldn't move, could barely breathe.

Above her, Seth grinned, his face so much like Jack's that for a split second, Angel thought she must be dreaming. But then he spoke again. And she knew this was no dream. And there was no hope.

"Remember what I said I'd do, Angel Devlin? Remember?" he crooned into her ear, licking at its shell, finally clamping down on the delicate cartilage with his teeth. "Do you?" he mumbled, his voice garbled for having her flesh in his mouth. "Answer me, bitch, or I'll bite your ear off."

Chills spread over Angel. Her heart pounded, her blood raced. She grimaced in pain and finally was able to nod. A still functioning part of her brain took over, began talking to her. *Just stay alive, Angel. No matter what happens . . . just stay alive. No matter what he touches, or what he does . . . he can't reach you. Not your heart. Not your soul. Just stay alive.*

She wanted to believe it, tried to . . . but as Seth pressed down more fully on top of her, his superior strength pinning her to the bed, as he quickly moved his hands to grasp hers and pull them above her head and hold them there with one hand, as his other hand clamped her jaw open and his mouth assaulted hers, as his lips ground down on top of hers, as his teeth cut her lip, as his tongue forced its way into her mouth, she wasn't sure she could believe. Or that she wanted to live.

So forceful, so lightning fast was his onslaught, so terrified was she that she couldn't even think to bite him. Or even to close her eyes, to deny this was happening . . . or not to watch it. She whimpered. She cried. She felt the tears streaming from her eyes. She felt them running across her temples, into her hair. She felt the hot, sweaty fear reeking from her body. And Seth's knee pushing between her legs. She wanted to die.

Jack! His name was torn from her innermost depths, from the recesses of her heart. *Jack!*

And then Seth tore his mouth away from hers, and rose up, gloating and laughing, still clutching her hands above her head. The tender flesh of her mouth felt ravaged, torn and swollen. A metallic taste coated her tongue. "I used to kiss your mama like that, Angel, when I was with her. She liked it, too. Begged me for more. Just like you will."

This animal had been with Mama, had hurt her? At the same moment a piece of her heart died, rage exploded through Angel, giving her renewed strength. Clenching her stomach muscles, she jackknifed in Seth's hold, startling him, and spat full into his face. "You bastard," came her raspy words, from somewhere at the back of her throat.

Seth wrenched her down, slapping her face openhanded as his own contorted with a maniacal rage. Her face stinging yet numb, her sensibilities and her ears ringing, Angel watched— as if from afar—as he swiped his shirtsleeve over his face. "You whore, you nasty bitch," he snarled. "You'll pay for that—and live to regret it. You're just like your mother. All you women are. Whores."

He's going to let me live. Unexpected hope surged through Angel. She'd thought she wanted to die. *He's going to let me live.* She took in a breath cut short by his weight atop her, and believed she could stand anything, could take anything ... until he sat up and ripped at her camisole, until his fingernails raked over her flesh, scratching her, no doubt drawing blood. The ripping, tearing of the thin and worn fabric sounded all too soon.

"No!" Angel cried out. "No!"

"Shut up!" Seth snarled, clamping his hand around the bared flesh of her breast, kneading it, hurting it, pinching her tender nipple, leaning over her to claim it with his mouth, to lick at her, to suckle her.

"No!" Angel screamed, the sound welling up, seeming to fill the room. A gasping, desperate cry tore from her lungs. She writhed under him, or tried to, tossing her head, trying to buck and arch against his attack.

But all her resistance did was excite him further, inflame him, have him groping her more, sliding down on her, prodding, nipping her other breast, slobbering, biting at the flesh over her ribs, and urging her on. "That's it, baby. Fight me. Scream. Come on—do it! Tell me how you want it. Your mother did. You want money? I got money. Paid your mother, too, like the whore she was."

Mama! Sudden nausea—a cold, dark, sweating nausea— gripped Angel, taking the fight from her, leaving her weak and limp. It filled her throat, all but closing off her air. Her limbs as mushy as oatmeal, Angel lay there ... suddenly unable to fight, to think—to care. *Mama.* Angel stared at the ceiling, didn't really see it.

Then Seth shifted, loomed over her, his face a grimacing, sweating, grotesque and lusting mask. "What's the matter, Angel? You're just laying there. Don't you want it anymore? Don't you like this? Now, come on, honey, hasn't my big brother already done this to you?" Angel didn't say anything. She couldn't. She just stared up at him. "Cat got your tongue? Fine. I'll just find out for myself."

With that, he slid off her, still clutching her benumbed hands in his grasp and ripping at her bloomers, tugging them down over her hips. Wrenched out of her state of shock, Angel locked her muscles, pressing her legs together and pushing down as hard as she could onto the bed. With a snarled curse, Seth dug his booted foot between her knees, kicking at her, forcing them apart. "Don't do that, bitch. Don't make me hurt you," he warned.

Angel's legs gave, parted. She sucked in a gasping breath . . . as if this were her first-ever taste of air. When she did, Seth jerked up, staring into her face, and laughing. "That's right," he crooned, smoothing his hand over her bared concave belly, running his fingers under her undergarments' waist, clawing at her feminine mound. "I'm gonna have me an angel."

"No," she whimpered, surprised she could even form the word. If only her hands weren't numb from his powerful grip, if only his leg weren't thrown over both of hers. Her gun was under her pillow. If only she could get to it. *Keep him talking.* "Don't do this, Seth. Don't. Jack will kill you."

"Ah, so he *has* had you. I thought he had." Then Seth stilled, sobered. "Don't throw my big brother in my face. I'm not afraid of Jack. Never have been. He's the good one, you know. Pa always said so. Pa always said I was the bad seed. Said I killed my own mother getting myself born. Never let me forget it, either." Momentary hatred lit Seth's blue eyes, then his eyelids drooped, his hand continued its downward quest, down to the vee between her legs. "You think I'm bad, Angel? Huh? Do you?"

What did she have to lose? She may as well say it. "I think you're rotten, murdering, cowardly scum, you little bastard. That's what I think."

To her surprise, Seth merely swung his head back to her, raising his eyebrows and smirking, as if he didn't know she had it in her to curse him at this particular moment. "Is that so? We'll see what you think when I'm done with you."

His very calmness warned her, set her heart to thumping—which surprised Angel. She hadn't even realized her heart was still beating. How long had it been lurching about in her chest like this?

Then Seth was all over her. He fisted his hand around the thin cotton of her drawers, wrapping the cloth within his grip and tearing it, the rending sound as loud and shocking to Angel's ears as thunder-filled lightning. And then he was on top of her, shifting his weight, settling himself in the saddle of her hips, now holding her wrists in both of his. The crazy thought came to Angel that she'd never be able to use her hands again if they didn't get any blood soon.

Seth resumed his kissing and sucking and nipping over her body. His bites scored Angel, had her twisting and crying out, despite her all-out determination not to. Closing her eyes, she desperately arched and bucked against him, tried to roll, tried to unseat him, heard his sick laugh, heard his grunting, raspy words telling her that he loved her fighting him, felt his mouth on her breasts, felt him jerk her arms down to her belly, felt him hold them there, pinioned against her flesh as he—she opened her eyes, looked down her own length—dear God, opened the fly on his pants and jerked them down over his hips.

"No!" Angel screamed into the night. Over and over. Her chest heaved with her crying, her hair absorbed her tears. "No! Jack! Mama! Help me!"

But then, words failed her—only unintelligible sounds poured from her, only the hurting cries of a helpless, small wounded animal filled her throat, rent her soul, carried on the night air—as he forced his engorged self into her, as he thrust into her over and over, grunting, sweating, cursing, cursing her, cursing Jack, hating his brother, hating her . . . hurting her. Hurting her.

When Angel thought she'd die, when the pain was too much, when the humiliation overwhelmed her, when it seemed his bucking against her would never end, Seth finally tensed over her, held himself rigid, spurted into her. Only a whimper was left to Angel. All she knew was it burned, burned, burned as it ran out of her when he withdrew himself from her, when he pulled away from her, when he rolled off the bed, and impersonally—untroubled—stood up beside it.

Shaking, undone, dying inside, numb yet pain riddled, Angel immediately rolled to her side, clutching her hands together over her heart, and drawing her knees up to her chest. And then, she lay there, staring without wanting to see . . . because Seth stood in her line of vision, only inches away. All she could see were his legs as he hitched his pants up to his waist and rebuttoned his fly. She swallowed, felt her lungs take in air and push it out. But she drew no comfort from that, from this proof that she was alive. She just didn't care . . .

Not even when Seth leaned over, gripped her jaw in his hand and forced her face up until she looked into his eyes, so like Jack's that it was scary. His whole face was like Jack's . . . only without the kindness and the humor, without the goodness. "You listening, bitch?" Angel nodded, hoping he'd go away if she did, hoping he'd leave her alone. "Good. Tell my brother I was here."

With that, he leaned over and forced her lips to a pucker, again crushing them with a bruising, punishing kiss. Then he pulled away and said, "You're good. Real good. Like your ma. Oh, yeah—I was real sorry to hear she's dead. A right prime piece of ass, she was."

Then he released Angel's face, straightening up as he wiped his hand on his shirt. A bloody smear appeared there. She was bleeding, she realized, but felt detached from any emotion. Then she blinked, sniffed, curled herself tighter into a little ball, and lay there. Staring and breathing. And shivering.

After a while—she didn't know how long, but the night seemed to be lightening up, seemed to be making its way toward daylight—Angel snapped to with a sudden realization. Two realizations. She was alone. And the gun was still under her pillow, the very one her head rested against. *The gun.* Ever so slowly, as if she were being watched, as if she feared someone would try to stop her, she uncoupled her fisted hands and edged her left hand up under the feather-filled pillow. At the same time her hand connected with the cold metal and closed around it, she heard footsteps coming up the stairs, heard a voice calling her name.

Terrified it was Seth, that he'd come back to hurt her again, Angel pulled the pistol out, stared at it a moment, suddenly not sure how it worked. Then she heard the footsteps and the voice . . . getting closer and closer. Her heartbeat and her breathing picked up speed. *No. Not again.* Terrified anew, with hurried, desperate motions, she finally nestled the gun in her hand, finally settled it in her grip . . . and put it to her temple.

The sun was no more than above the horizon as Jack sharply reined in Buffalo at the hitching rail in front of his home. Cursing the sudden downpour in the middle of the night that had stopped him, that had made it all but impossible to proceed for endless hours, Jack bolted to the rain-soaked ground, his oilskin slicker billowing out around him. His heart still pounding with what he feared he'd find, he gazed hither and yon over the homestead as he took the steps to the verandah. Everything about the place looked normal. But too quiet somehow. As if the spread were holding its breath.

He barreled up to the front door, grabbing the knob, twisting it at the same moment he hit the wooden barrier with his shoulder. Neither the knob nor the door gave. Jack bounced off it, grunting his surprise and his pain. He held his shoulder and stared at the front door. *It's locked.* That couldn't be good. He stepped back up to it and pounded on it, calling out, "Angel? Where are you? Angel? Boots? Lou? Where is everyone? Goddammit, open this door!"

And then he waited. Silent moments ticked by. Nothing happened.

Desperate with fear, Jack jiggled the knob, pounding the door again with a fisted hand, calling out. Still no one answered. The door remained closed, locked, impassive. Ready to break out a window if someone didn't answer soon, Jack stepped back, stared at the door, his frown deep enough to contort his features. *They ought to be up by now.* And why they might not be, given the note he'd found at Seth's hideout, had Jack jerking around, had him turning away, had him staring out over the sandy-brown, rain-puddled yard, as if he expected answers out there.

He lifted his Stetson to run his hands through his hair, stared back at Angel's attentive roan in the corral attached to the barn, and resettled his hat. Then he sighed, admitted to himself that he was almost afraid to go inside, almost afraid to know. Tired as hell, his eyes gritty from lack of sleep, and soaked through where his slicker hadn't covered him, Jack willed himself to think, willed himself to calm down. *Calm down?* he argued right back. *How can I—*

"That you, Jack?"

Jack's heart leaped with a mingling of startlement and relief. He spun around, rushing the door, again jiggling the knob. "Yeah, Boots, it's me. Let me in. What's going on?"

"Hold on," Boots said, sounding tired. "Let me get this lock turned."

Jack stepped back, his gaze riveted on the closed door, his jaw muscles clenching with impatience as he listened to the sounds of Boots fumbling with the lock. But then, the door opened. Jack burst forward, pushing on the door, opening it and driving Boots back with it. He grabbed the older man's skinny arm to steady him. "Where is she? Where's Angel?"

Boots's mouth worked. Jack's heart sank. He now noticed details about the old drover. Unshaven. Clothes rumpled. Hair everywhere except in place. His eyes were bloodshot, watery. A shock of fear lanced through Jack.

"What's happened?" he demanded, hearing the suddenly hoarse quality of his own voice. Hot with fear, still eyeing

Boots, he shed his hat and coat, tossing them onto the coat rack to his left. "Well?"

Still the older man didn't answer. He looked away, slowly shaking his head, putting a long-fingered, knobby-knuckled hand to his face, rubbing his forehead. Only then did he volunteer, "Something most powerful awful happened, Jack. Most powerful awful. That poor little girl."

A confused second passed before Jack made the mental leap. The poor little girl was Angel. And something most powerful awful had happened to her. Dread rocked him, weighed him down, made him feel as if he were being pushed through the floor. He wet his suddenly dry lips and rasped out, barely above a whisper, "Is she alive, Boots?"

It seemed to Jack a heart-stopping eternity passed before Boots turned to him and nodded. "Yeah, but just barely."

Jack clung to that *yeah*. And *just barely* was good enough. Just barely was a heartbeat, was life . . . was hope. Like a raging river, relief coursed through him. As long as Angel was alive, he could deal with anything. Anything. "Where is she?"

Boots's thin, weather-lined, aged face remained impassive a moment. Bile rose to the back of Jack's throat with his certainty that there was something more the old drover wasn't telling him. He swallowed convulsively, ready to shake the truth out of Boots when the drover finally nodded his head toward the stairs and said, "She's upstairs. Lou's sitting with her. But it ain't purty, Jack. She's been through hell and back."

Through hell and back. Then why was he standing here talking? Overwhelmed with the need to see her, Jack lurched in the direction of Boots's nod. But the older man clutched at his sleeve, holding him in place, forcing Jack to look into his eyes. "Before you go up, son. . . .Just, well, take it easy. You . . . you look so much like him. . . . Just be quiet and slow. Give her a chance to see it's you."

His words and what lay behind them made Jack want to give up, just curl up in a ball and die. Seth. He'd kill that little son of a bitch. With that promise to himself a sudden, hateful, lifesaving anger ripped through him, held him upright as he asked, "It was Seth, wasn't it?"

Boots stared . . . and then collapsed with silent tears. His thin old shoulders shook. Torn, wanting only to see Angel, to assure himself that she lived, but needing first to comfort this hurting old man, Jack moved his hand up Boots's arm to squeeze his shoulder. "You and Lou okay, Boots? He didn't do anything to either of you, did he?"

"No," came the man's vehement reply. "But I swear to God I wish he had. Instead of hurting that pretty child like he done."

Jack swallowed thick saliva. "It's okay, Boots. Just tell me."

After sniffling for a moment, Boots wiped his sleeve under his beak of a nose and spoke. "Like you said, it was Seth. And we wasn't inside to help her none. We went out to the bunkhouse for the night. And I *hate* me for that. But that poor baby, Jack. He hurt her most awful, he did."

Jack's eyes narrowed, he wanted to kick something, to throw something. Shoot something. *He hurt her most awful, he did.* Goddammit! "All right, Boots. It's going to be okay. Come on," he urged. "You go first. Let her know it's me."

Boots nodded, wiped at his thin lined cheeks. "I'll try. But she don't move or talk none. Doesn't do anything. Just lays there. But there's more. She tried to. . . . Well, she put a gun to her head, Jack."

"Good God," Jack spat out. "Did she—?" He couldn't finish the thought.

"No. Me and Lou got her to give us the gun. But that's all. Like I said, she ain't talking none. And she don't want to be touched. She's just a-layin' there, Jack, all balled up on her side. And bruised and scratched. Like a hurt little kitty. It's most awful, is what it is. Seth ought to be shot for what he done to her."

Jack's heart squeezed in much the same way he now squeezed the old man's shoulder. "He will be. Don't worry. Now, let's go. I want to see her."

"All right. I don't expect it can hurt none." With that,

Boots turned, leading the way across the room and up the stairs. When they got to Angel's room, the same one Old Mother had used when she'd lived here, Boots paused in the doorway, blocking Jack's way. *Old Mother!* came Jack's sudden thought. Where had the white wolf been? Why hadn't she warned Angel? Why hadn't she appeared? But then he remembered . . . Angel said she had. And that the wolf had allowed Angel to touch her. It had to mean something, such different behavior for the spirit wolf. But what?

Boots turned to Jack, snapping him back to the moment with his whispering. "Speak a word or two to Lou, if you would, Jack. You know how ornery Seth was, how he used to taunt him and hit him. Well, just seeing Angel like this made Lou . . . well, you can see for yourself."

Dammit. Poor Lou. Angry beyond measure for yet another reason to damn his brother's soul to hell, Jack rubbed a hand over his day-old growth of beard. "All right," he gritted out, trying to tamp down the pent-up rage that threatened to eat him up, that made him want to hit the wall with his fist.

But apparently satisfied with Jack's assurances, Boots then stepped out of the way, stepping over the threshold, to one side of the open door, and stood against the wall. Taking a calming breath, Jack turned into the doorway, peered inside . . . and wished Boots hadn't moved. His heart sank and his stomach rolled. His gaze first found Lou. That poor old simple soul, not looking a bit better than Boots this morning, sat in a rocking chair beside the bed and held himself and rocked back and forth. He kept saying, "It's okay. It's okay. It's okay."

Jack wanted to die. He wanted to turn away, but refused to take the coward's way out. He needed to face this. His gaze slipped to the bed. Just as Boots had described, Angel— with a sheet thrown over her—lay on her side, curled up in a ball. A long lock of her hair had fallen across her cheek. But what he could see of her face was swollen, scratched, and bloodied. Dry eyed, she stared straight ahead . . . unblinking.

Jack's heart cried. He put a hand to his mouth, gripping

the doorjamb with his other, holding the wood so tightly that his fingers hurt. Every instinct in him said to go to her. Hold her. Cradle her. Whisper softly to her. Croon out words of love. But he didn't dare. He feared that touching her right now just might push her to a place in her mind so far away that he'd never get her back.

And so, he stood there . . . staring . . . hurting. And hating himself as he heard her last words to him, words as much as begging him to stay, telling him what bad things might happen here if he didn't stay. Why hadn't he listened? And now, how in God's name could he ever make this up to her? How? What could he do to make this better? Would she ever be better, whole again? Jack started to crumple—

"Jack?"

He stiffened, blinking, sniffing . . . as he turned to Boots. "Yeah?"

Boots gestured, urging him to step inside, pointing to Lou. "It'll be okay, son. Go on to Lou. Mayhap the rest will come to you."

Even though he wasn't sure anything would ever be all right again, Jack nodded and stepped inside. As softly as he could, given his boots and the polished wood floors, he walked over to Lou and sank to his haunches next to the rocking chair. Studiously he avoided looking over at the bed, avoided startling Angel. But she made not a sound, moved not an inch.

Hurting inside, as if he'd been punched, and acutely aware of her, of her open eyes, and knowing she had to see him, Jack put his hand on the older man—who started and immediately shrank away, his eyes widening with terror. Jack withdrew, gripping the chair arm instead as he softly crooned, "Easy, there. It's me, Lou. It's Jack. I won't hurt you. You okay, Lou? Are you? You okay? Can you talk to me?"

His mouth opened in a silent scream, Lou stared . . . then he frowned, closed his mouth, seemed finally to recognize Jack. He settled more in his chair. "She's hurt," he said. "Seth did it. Seth hurts."

Jack regarded the old drover with compassion. "I know.

Did he hurt you, Lou?'' Lou shook his head no. ''Good,'' Jack said, putting as much warmth as he could into the word, and again reaching out to touch the simple old man. ''I'm glad you're okay. You mean a lot to me.''

Behind Jack, softly, unexpectedly . . . maybe blessedly, Angel began to cry.

Seventeen

Still on his haunches, his weight balanced on the balls of his feet, all Jack had to do was pivot to see her. His heart melted at the sight she made, as her shoulders gently shook, as her face contorted with emotion . . . as tears cascaded from her eyes, running across her nose and down her cheek . . . onto her pillow. Jack's jaw clenched. He renewed his silent promise to himself—and to his brother. *Goddamn you, Seth. Your days are numbered, you little bastard.*

Jack forced Seth from his mind, wanting only to think of Angel. More than anything, he wanted to take her in his arms and hold her tightly to him. But he didn't dare. He comforted himself with knowing that her crying was good. It said her mind was working, that she . . . knew. And for now, that had to be enough for him, because the knowledge was certainly enough for her to deal with. And the last thing he wanted to do was force her to respond. He figured she'd been forced enough last night—and, in other ways, all her life—and so it'd be best to let her make the moves, let her show him what she wanted.

Praying to God that he was right not to do anything right now, he steadied himself by resting his fingertips against the sheet-covered mattress, mere inches from her face. And watched and waited. And hoped she'd reach out to him.

But still, staring down at her swollen face, seeing her hurt, feeling helpless, as if there were nothing he could do to take it away, Jack had to stop himself from reaching out to brush her hair back behind her ear. A soft half-smile of sympathy crossed his features. He made himself another promise. One day, he was going to take a pair of scissors to all that hair. Because not one inch of such a beautiful angel-face as hers should be hidden.

Just then, out of the corner of his eye, Jack saw Boots start in their direction. And divined the older man's intentions. He was going to get Lou and go. Jack looked up at him, nodding at Boots's gestures, which verified what Jack had just thought. When Boots drew even with him, Jack gripped the older man's arm and squeezed, trying to convey that he was glad Boots was here. Boots must've understood because he gave Jack a trembling smile and awkwardly patted his hand.

"Boots, will you see to Buffalo, too? He's all lathered up from our trip." Boots nodded, gesturing that he'd take care of the horse. Keeping his voice down, Jack rushed on, wanting to get all his orders in before Boots could wander off with Lou. "Be careful outside. I think you'll be okay. I have reason to believe that Seth won't be back. But take a gun, anyway. And keep your eyes open. Lock that front door again, too. And plan on staying in the house for now. Just keep a look out the windows for me. And call me if you need me. Or if you see anything. You understand?"

Boots nodded. "Don't worry. I'll settle Lou in downstairs and get that Winchester of your pa's and keep guard."

"Good. That's good, Boots." With that, Jack glanced back at Angel. She hadn't moved, hadn't responded to their conversation. His heart sinking because of that, Jack watched as Boots tenderly collected Lou and helped his buddy from the room. Then, finally, Boots quietly closed the door behind them.

And now, Jack was alone with Angel. Looking her over in the bed, his heart all but torn out—such a little ball she was, lying there—Jack suddenly realized that she was naked beneath the thin twisted white sheet. Her tanned skin showed through. And she was shivering in the morning cool. Annoyed that he hadn't noticed it before, but glad for this one thing he could do for her, Jack arrowed up to his feet.

Leaning over, he reached for the quilt at the bed's foot, drawing it up and over her, gently, tenderly settling it around her. Not one response from her did he get for his efforts. Grimacing in disappointment, Jack sat in the rocking chair Lou had just vacated and tugged it closer to Angel. Leaning forward, his legs spread, his elbows resting on his knees, Jack lowered his head to rub his face with his hands. *What a day. And the sun's barely up.*

After a moment, he raised his head, lowering his hands to hang loosely between his legs. He considered Angel, saw to his surprise that she'd quit crying. He didn't know if he should call that good or bad. But either way, her black eyes were wet and shiny, and she stared . . . but straight ahead, not at him. She blinked. Sniffed. Blinked again. And closed her eyes. A frisson of fear lanced through Jack. Was she dying?

Tensing, bunching his muscles, gripping the rocker's arms, he'd all but jumped up before he realized she was breathing softly, that her shoulders rose and fell with each steady breath. She was sleeping.

"Son of a bitch," Jack whispered in relief, wilting back onto the chair. He didn't think he could take much more of this without his own heart stopping. But seeing that she was okay for the moment, he gave in to his own body's demands for rest. Bone-tired and saddle-weary, he slouched down, resting his elbows atop the armrests, knitting his fingers together over his belly, and laying his head back against the rocker's headpiece as he closed his eyes. And nodded off.

Or thought he did. Because he suddenly jerked awake and couldn't say why. Nor could he say that the room's shadows were any shorter, that the sun's position had changed any. So, what had awakened him? His gaze sought and found Angel. Her eyes were open. She blinked, sniffed, shifted her gaze . . . as if looking him up and down, as if considering him. Did she recognize that it was him and not Seth? It appeared that way.

His heart racing, Jack slid out of the chair, again squatting next to the bed, his hands braced against the mattress. "Angel?" he said, speaking softly.

She blinked again, her nose twitched—Jack held his breath—she shifted her body, uncurled some, her shoulder edged up. What was she—? Her fingertips appeared out from under the quilt he'd thrown over her and smoothed their way across the sheet, stopping only when they touched his, when she closed her fingers around his. Overcome by such a simple gesture of trust, of a heart still working, of a soul still alive, Jack finally exhaled, felt the chills of emotion race over his skin, and finally allowed himself to believe. But still afraid of spooking her, he didn't move, just waited for her.

She looked up at him. A single tear spilled from her eye, coursing alongside her nose, down her puffy cheek . . . finally rolling onto her cut and swollen lips. Still staring at him, she tipped her tongue out and caught it, as if it were a sweet nectar. And blinked. Jack could stand no more. "Oh, Angel, I'm so sorry," he crooned. "You were right. I never should have left you. Can you ever forgive me?"

She swallowed, grimacing as if even that hurt. Jack saw the bruising around her neck, wanted to die. But then, the tiniest, barest nod he'd ever seen moved Angel's head up and down.

His heart soared. And, right or wrong, willing to risk it, he stood up, scooping her—quilt, undone sheet, and all—up into his arms. She didn't protest. Jack sat with her in the rocker, cradling her, holding her across his lap, as he would a baby. Her head rested just under his chin, her legs draped over his, her feet not touching the ground. Jack wrapped his arms her. She felt so damned warm and soft. And little. How could anyone hurt her?

And yet he had . . . he saw again himself hitting her. His father had hurt her . . . he recalled the contents of the letter his father'd written and that he'd read. His brother had hurt her . . . he held the evidence in his arms. And life had hurt her. He remembered the rope burns around her neck when he'd first seen her and conjured up a lynching scene. He'd seen enough hangings to know what one looked like. And before that, there'd been her life with her mother and her life on her own. He'd heard the stories, knew the tales of the little girl always being chased off, always shunned by so-called decent folk.

Well, damn us all to hell. She's worth more than the whole lot of us put together. It's the rest of us who should be licking her boots. It's the rest of us who'd be blessed to have her even speak to us.

Jack again looked down at Angel in his arms and kissed the top of her head, wishing she'd yell, or cry it all out. Or just speak to him. He supposed he wanted to hear her say she was all right. But he knew she wasn't. So how could she say it? And even if she did, it'd be her stubborn pride talking and not the truth of what she was feeling inside. She never spoke of that. He knew her that well already.

A sudden smile curved Jack's mouth. Right now he'd love to hear some of that sass coming from her. He'd give his gun hand to see her tilt that chin up and call him cowboy. A chuckle escaped Jack before he could guard against it.

He glanced down at her, wondering if he'd disturbed her. Apparently not. Because just as she'd been doing all along, she now stared straight ahead, blinking occasionally, sniffling . . . and nothing more. Forget about her not speaking, he told himself, tightening his grip around her, holding her closer. He had more than her words. He had her in his arms. She was allowing him to hold her. Even after everything she'd been through. Which meant she trusted him. And felt safe with him. Jack's mouth curved down with a newfound humility. He didn't deserve her. No Daltry did. All they'd ever done was hold her captive. And hurt her.

His expression clouded as he thought of the letter his father'd written. He could only wonder what her reaction would be once she read it. Of course, he didn't have to show it to her, came the sneaking thought. Which Jack immediately dismissed. *No, that's wrong.* Because he wanted Angel in his life for good. He glanced down at her, and his heart felt heavy, began to beat erratically. But in a good way. Forced to, Jack grinned at his lovesick self. Yes, he loved her. And he'd be a damn fool to let a woman like her get away from him. Which meant . . . once she was better—he clung to the hope that she would get past this—he had to tell her. But just picturing that scene sobered him. Well, it couldn't be helped.

Because she had the right to know everything the Daltrys had done to her. Everything. Only then could she make the right decision about him. Whether to stay or to go. Jack huffed out his next breath on a sigh. *Damn.* All this honesty and uprightness. The sacrifices he was willing to make. Standing ready to tell her the whole truth and then living with her decision, whichever way it fell. What was this? Was it love? Did love make a body want to do crazy things, take crazy chances with happiness?

It must. Because just the way he felt about her, how he ached for her, how his chest hurt when he simply thought about her, all told him . . . he'd never loved a woman before. He'd never been bound by such strong feelings of wanting to do the right thing. He'd never had notions of settling down, of waking up every day, for the rest of his life, to the same face next to him in bed. Of making something of himself and the Circle D. But now he sure as hell did. And look who was giving him these home-and-hearth tuggings. Angel Devlin. Amazing.

Jack shook his head, not sure how he felt about this, even after admitting it was all true. How did he feel? Well, a little sick to his stomach, actually. And weak. Probably because he'd ridden or huddled against the rain all night. Probably because he hadn't eaten since yesterday. No . . . probably because he was in love. With the one wrong woman in the whole world. Wrong for a lot of reasons. After all, what would people say? A Daltry—a respected name in the growing community of Texas landowners and cattle ranchers— marrying a Devlin, the daughter of a dirt farmer and the town whore?

Jack's eyes narrowed, he picked up the pace of his rocking, held Angel tightly. He didn't give a damn what anyone in town—in *any* town—thought. But just let some son of a bitch say that—to her, to him, to one of their kids. Just let him. He'd be picking his teeth up off the ground. Or find himself needing to be dragged off to the undertaker. Jack took a lot of satisfaction in that outcome. But then he slumped, wondering what some comment like that would do to Angel. She was his main concern. How would she feel, hearing someone say that, or holding it against their kids?

He knew it could, and probably would, happen. Well, there were just some things he couldn't fix. But, damn, what a cruel world it was that couldn't look beyond the circumstances of her life to see the goodness and the strength inside this girl who'd never hurt anyone. And that was another thing. How many people could say that? That they'd done no harm? Not too damned many, by God. He couldn't even lay claim to that himself.

Hearing himself defending Angel against imaginary detractors—when in reality he knew she was fully capable of defending herself—Jack felt an unexpected smile curve his mouth. She'd shoot their asses, and he knew it. A sudden bark of laughter filled the air. He was *so* blessed to have her trust. It was enough for now. Enough to build on. Warmed by this hope for the future, Jack spent the next few moments listening to her breathe, hearing her sniffs, feeling her subtle shifts of position against him. And loving her. Just loving her.

And wishing there were some way he could break through to her. Some way he could jar her out of this state she was in. He'd heard of this before, of folks who'd suffered such horrible things that they never recovered. They just went through the rest of their lives as if they were sleepwalking. Couldn't anybody touch their hearts or minds again. What if Angel was always like this? A wave of fierce protectiveness swept over Jack. Then so be it. If this was how she was for the rest of her life, then fine. He'd take care of her. He'd still love her. That wouldn't change.

It was true. He could do it, could live with that. But he wanted more than that for her. She deserved it. She deserved some happiness. Dammit, if she'd just get well, he'd give her the danged ranch. Just have her sign those papers he'd found at Seth's hideout and then file them himself in Wichita Falls. And take her with him to do it, just so she could see for herself, like she'd been so all-fired determined to do, anyway. So the Circle D would be hers, like Pa'd wanted, and if he— Jack Eugene Daltry—was lucky, she'd let him hang about the place . . . like some old chicken outside or some half-wild barn cat.

This whimsical view of the future had Jack chuckling, a happy sound that broke the silence. Until then there had been only an occasional chuckle from Jack, a sniffle from Angel, and the comforting squeaks of the rocker as he pushed it back and forth. *Well, maybe I ought to get her cleaned up and dressed. Maybe that'd make her feel better.*

Jack sat up, stopped his rocking, and looked down at Angel, at her scratched and bloodied body, at her tangled hair. What the hell had he been thinking to leave her cold and dirty and naked like this? Wasn't he the one who'd just said he could take care of her?

Yep. Well, then, time to prove it. Jack got up, handling her weight as if she were no more than a puppy, and set her on the bed. Her hands clenched the quilt, her upturned face begged for reassurance. All but undone, Jack smoothed his hand over her hair. "It's okay, baby. I'm not leaving you." She blinked, relaxing some. Only then did he go to the chest of drawers in the room and rummage through it, looking for suitable clothing for her . . . and hoping she had some, since all she seemed to want to wear were his clothes.

In the oven-heated kitchen, his shirtsleeves rolled up, Jack wrang out the washcloth again, glancing at Angel as she sat, still and quiet, gripping the sides of the hip bath filled with warm water. Her just-washed hair streamed down her back. And her bruised gaze never left him. Jack told himself that was good, that she needed his presence, that maybe she was clinging to him as she did her sanity.

He lifted her arm—so slender and fine boned, with its wrist so tiny that his big fingers more than closed around it—and washed it tenderly, softly. She watched him doing it, as she had every other detail of her bath, but still didn't say anything.

Clenching his jaw, forcing a smile for her, Jack tried to keep his Seth-directed rage off his face. Every scratch, every bruise, every toothmark on her . . . all had that bastard's death written on them. Goddamn, Seth'd hurt her. And Jack hadn't realized just how much until she'd whimpered and stiffened, breaking his heart as she clung to his neck when he'd lowered her into the water . . . when her privates had dipped into the wet warmth. Soothing her, telling her it was okay, figuring it stung pretty bad, Jack had knelt beside the tub, had held her suspended there, his muscles rigid with growing fatigue, until she'd relaxed, until he'd felt certain he could lower her all the way.

Even then she hadn't said a word. She'd just stared at him with those big, heart-wrenching eyes of hers. Just stared and trusted. Sighing, feeling the emotion-induced tightness in his chest, Jack decided to talk to her about anything that came into his mind. Maybe she just needed to hear another voice. And maybe, given how he always made her so mad, he'd happen onto something she'd feel a need to respond to.

Hoping like hell this new idea worked because he didn't know what else to do, Jack again smiled at her, lowering her arm back into the water and rinsing it. She didn't protest, just blinked and watched him.

"I tell you, Angel," he began, lifting her other arm, and washing it as he spoke. "I do believe, that for as long as I live, I'll never forget old Boots's red face and that embarrassed look he had when I carried you in here. How about you?" Nothing. Gamely, fighting disappointment, telling himself it was too soon and to keep talking, he went on. "It's a good thing you were still wrapped in that quilt, huh? Because I don't believe Boots has ever—" Jack choked back his next words. What the hell! He'd nearly said *I don't believe Boots has ever been with a woman.* That was the last thing she needed to hear about, someone being with a woman.

"I don't believe Boots has ever heated that much water that fast," he amended, feeling his own face heat up. "But he pretty much cleared out after that, didn't he?" Nothing. She blinked, watched his mouth move. Jack lowered her arm, rinsed it, began soaping her upper chest, dividing his attention between his task and her face. "Believe me, I'll hear about this. He and Lou love to tease me. But that's okay. I've been teased for doing a lot worse."

Jack paused as he soaped her to think a moment, rubbing his bared arm under his nose. Then he had the perfect story and focused again on Angel. "Once, when I wasn't much more than a kid, I thought it'd be fun to jump out of the loft and onto the back of my pa's stallion. Well, that ornery cuss just sidestepped like he knew I was on my way. Damn near broke my neck. Would've, too, if there hadn't been a loose pile of hay right there. I didn't think Pa would ever quit whipping my behind—once he knew I was okay."

Nothing. Discouraged, Jack fell quiet and washed her bobbing breasts, feeling only concern for the finger-shaped bruising on their full softness. But a part of him—as he lowered the soapy cloth down her belly, and washed her as best he could, as closely as he dared—couldn't help but note her beautiful pinkish skin and smooth, womanly body. With that thought, such defeat as he'd never known assailed him. How could anyone—Jack's temper surged, had him wanting to throw the wet washcloth across the room. Had him wanting to rage and scream against the injustice of it all.

How could Seth hurt her like this? What beat in his brother's chest where a heart should be? Some black and crumpled lump of a hard thing, was all Jack could figure. Because, damn, this was wrong. What he was looking at was *wrong*. As he fought for control, not wanting to spook Angel, Jack continued washing her, kept soothing her, continued talking about silly things. At long last, he finished her bathing . . . and his temper held, cooling as did her bathwater. He got up from his squatting position beside the tub and reached for one of the towels he'd laid across a chairback.

Suddenly, he realized he'd worked through his temper. He'd held it, had kept it in check. Was this some kind of turning point for him? Because always before, before Angel, he'd given in to his temper, had let everyone around him know he was mad, had gone off half-cocked and done some pretty stupid things, a few of which he'd barely survived to regret. But there'd been no explosion this time. Why? A good question. Suddenly reflective, Jack wondered what was different now. Was he just growing up finally? Or was it more than that?

With the soft toweling clutched in his grip, he eyed Angel in the tub. Her gaze was lowered to the sudsy water in which she sat. And then he knew. It was her. She'd made him different. For the first time in his life, how someone else felt, how they might be affected by his ranting and raving, had been more important to him than letting out everything he felt.

Jack exhaled and had a melting grin for her, had she cared to look. But she didn't glance up, just sat there, waiting. Sobering some, Jack approached her, touched her arm. She looked up. "Stand up, honey, I need to dry you. I don't want you to catch your death in this cool air."

Angel obediently stood up, water running in cascades and rivulets over and around her curves, down her firm and silky body. Despite his tender concern for her, Jack's very maleness had his breath catching in his throat, his knees weakening. He couldn't help it. She was so damned beautiful. So desirable. That word shamed him. Desirable. Why was he thinking such thoughts at a time like this? And poor Angel. Would she ever again allow a man, even him, to talk to her of desire? He feared her answer, but knew he wouldn't blame her if she didn't.

And if she didn't, what then? What of his love for her? What if she did get better in her head—he knew her body would heal, but what of her soul?—and never again wanted to feel a man's hands on her? Using the towel, Jack squeezed and rubbed the water out of her hair, trying his best not to tangle it. Done with that, he tossed the damp cloth onto the floor and reached for the dry one, wrapping it around Angel, tugging her hair free, and then holding her arm as she stepped out onto the other damp towel.

Well, he supposed, as he patted her dry—trying hard not to allow his male thoughts free rein, trying hard to ignore his

body's physical, almost involuntary response to her warm fe-
maleness—if she got right in her head and didn't ever want
to be touched again, he guessed he'd just have to do what he
could to make sure she was set up here at the Circle D . . .
and then leave. Because the way he felt about her, the way
his blood pounded through his body at just the thought of her,
he knew he couldn't stand being around her and not holding
her. No, he'd want to touch her. Do more than touch her.

Jack's mouth quirked with his troubled thoughts. This was
a tough one. But not really, he supposed. After all, he knew
how to live the kind of life that'd be left to him. Hadn't he
just spent four months wasting time and laying waste to his
health with drinking and gunfights, brawling and womaniz-
ing? He'd done it before, and he could do it again. Only this
time, if it came to that, his heart wouldn't be in it. He'd leave
that here with Angel. As if just now hearing his own thoughts,
and recalling his past selfish behavior, Jack paused in his
drying of Angel—she just looked at him—and shook his
head, wanting to chuckle. When had he become so good, so
willing to make sacrifices?

Again, the answer stood before him, blinking and sniffling.
"Ah, Angel," Jack sighed out, loving her. "Come on, let's
get you dressed, girl." He tossed the damp toweling aside
and reached for the pair of bloomers and a camisole—his
heart ached for how thin and worn they were—that he'd
found in a dresser drawer in her room. Helping her into
them—all too familiar with their workings—Jack then buttoned her into one of his own flannel shirts, a blue-checked
one that was too small for him.

But still, it engulfed her, hanging almost to her knees and
way past her fingertips. Three Angels could have worn it
comfortably. Jack didn't know whether to laugh or to cry as
he folded up the sleeves until he could see her hands. "I guess
it'll just have to do," he told her. "It's all I've got."

Then he stepped back to check his handiwork. And saw
her ruffled bloomers hanging out from under the shirt, her
bare calves below them, and did finally grin at her. "Teach
you to leave yourself in my hands, young lady. Now, sit

here''—he pulled a chair out from the drop-leaf table, positioned it with its back to the heated oven, and urged her onto it, holding her wet hair away from her shirt as she sat—''and let me see to that hair of yours.''

Angel sat obediently, her hands folded loosely in her lap. Standing behind her chair, Jack released her hair and eyed the long damp mass that dripped water onto the floor. What now? He'd never done this before. He crossed his arms, glanced at the tortoiseshell comb and brush reposing on the table, and then shifted his gaze back to her. Well, how hard could it be to dry it some more and rub it down and then brush it? That's what he did to his own. So, that's what he did to hers . . . dried it more, rubbed it gently, and then combed it, allowing the oven's heat to dry it.

Finally he parted it in the middle and brushed it until the rich and thick blackness of her hair crackled and shone almost blue in the day's light. As he worked and chatted amiably enough with her, Jack realized he'd never before felt so content in his life. Just doing something this simple for someone he loved, someone not able to do the same for herself, made him happy, made him feel . . . well, like a man, in ways he never had before. Angel. She was a woman of firsts for him. If he didn't take care, he thought, grinning, she'd wrap his heart around her little finger and render him as simple as Lou and as tractable as Boots inside of a month.

Stepping around in front of her, checking his endeavors with her hair, Jack grinned at her. Her mouth quirked . . . or seemed to. Jack's heart soared—Was that a grin? Was he getting through to her? Carefully, almost cautiously, as if the moment were a living thing he could disturb, Jack shifted the comb to one hand . . . and reached for the scissors with his other. Here was the real test. That too long, uneven fringe of hair that hung in her eyes, that she was always brushing away, only to have it fall right back into shaggy place. Would she allow him to cut it? Or would she cut his heart out with these same scissors, just for trying?

Only one way to find out, Jack decided. He squatted down in front of her, balancing his weight on the balls of his feet, feeling his denims stretch tight over his thighs. With the comb, he settled the hair over her eyes, heard her sniff under the silky waterfall he'd created. And then, gently, slowly . . . in case she cared to protest . . . began snipping, at first awkwardly, but then with growing confidence and sureness as Angel sat obediently, her hands still clasped together in her lap. Every now and then, she sniffled, but that was all.

In what seemed like only moments, Jack was done, and happy with the results. A delicate fringe of bangs now graced her forehead, cut level with her eyebrows. Clasping the comb and scissors in one hand, Jack cocked his head this way and that, smiling, nodding. Angel's clearly visible big black eyes stared back at him. And snippets of cut hair dusted her nose and cheeks. Jack grinned, and using his free hand, brushed them away as gently as he could, given his thick, masculine fingers. "There," he said. "What do you think of that?"

Tears sprang to Angel's eyes. Big, fat, wet ones. Her face reddened, crumpling. Jack's heart sank, his eyes widened. *Here it comes*, he warned himself. He laid aside the comb and the scissors, and reached out to grasp Angel's hands in his. She sat rigid in her chair, her whole body shaking with emotion, with her tears. She was really letting go now, as she needed to. Paralyzed in the face of such strong emotion, Jack didn't—couldn't—say anything. He just held her hands, stared at her bare feet, and ached for her, felt bad for her, felt bad for himself . . . for his part in all this. For his family's part in the bad life she'd had, was still having.

More than anything, Jack wanted to reach up and wipe away her tears, to stroke her hair, her face, tell her she was okay. But he didn't. How could he tell her she was okay? She wasn't. He just wanted her to be okay. And he couldn't reach out to her because she clung to his hands, gripping them tightly and sobbing. And thus, time passed. And Angel cried out her anguish. After a while, Jack began to worry. Could she stop? He wasn't seeing any sign of a letup. Should he hold her again? Would she want that? But most of all, he worried about what she might be going through in her mind. What were her thoughts?

"No one . . ." she hiccuped suddenly. Jack sat up alertly, his muscles tensing, his heart thudding. He watched her closely, craving her words, no matter what she had to say. But then she couldn't seem to go on, couldn't seem to get them out. She drew in a deep, shuddering breath and made a visible effort to calm herself.

"Take your time, sweetheart," Jack urged. "Just go slow."

She nodded, sniffling and staring at him. Somewhere in his heart Jack felt certain he was her lifeline, his presence was her sanity. And nothing in his whole life had ever made him feel better. Because this was his Angel. And she was talking. She was going to be okay . . . maybe. He supposed it depended on what she had to say.

"No one . . . what, Angel?" he finally prompted, suddenly dreading as much as anticipating her speaking her mind right now.

She looked up at him, her eyes deep and limpid pools, her chin dimpling with her stuttering sobs, her cheeks lined with watery rivulets. "No one ever . . . cared enough . . . about me to . . . cut my hair."

Eighteen

Angel couldn't believe she'd just said that. Not so much because she'd admitted such a thing. But more because she hadn't thought she'd be able to say anything ever again. Even now, as she sat there shaking, trying not to cry again, as she watched the play of emotion over Jack's face, watched the effect her words had on him . . . she couldn't shake the sense that she was awakening from a nightmare, one that had been followed by a deep and long sleep, one she'd entered into because she didn't want to be aware.

And yet, now she was. Aware. Now, in only a flash of a moment, she relived every second, knew every detail, felt every scratch and bruise, heard every ugly word Seth had said to her, felt every punishing thrust she had to endure. And found—surprisingly, reassuringly—that, despite it all, she wanted to live. And wanted to make sure that Seth didn't. Even as she looked into Seth's brother's eyes, even as she recalled Jack's many kindnesses, his warmth, his tending to her . . . she wanted to kill his brother. How would he feel about that, about her when she did it?

"No one ever cut your hair for you before?" Jack asked, pulling her out of thoughts she was all too glad to abandon.

Angel shook her head, shrugging as she loosened her grip on Jack's hands and reached up to brush away the wetness on her cheeks. "My mother used to, when I was a girl," she said, surprising herself because she couldn't seem to stop talking about this, couldn't seem to stop the flow of words. "But

then she . . . well, she couldn't, anymore, after . . . that. I tried
to, over the years, but I'm not too good at it. And there . . .
weren't always scissors around. And then it just didn't matter.
No one cared. Not even me.''

Jack stared at her with such warm sympathy that Angel
feared more tears. Why did she keep bawling like an abandoned calf? This wasn't like her. She didn't cry. And why
was she telling him these private matters to do with herself?
She didn't talk. She kept to herself, kept herself shut off . . .
frozen, she now realized. That stopped her. *It's no longer
good enough*, something inside her said, further capturing her
attention, making her sit up straighter. *No longer, Angel.
Reach out. Take this love offered.*

Love? Is that what this was that she felt? She blinked,
staring at Jack as he watched her, apparently content to talk
with her if she wanted to, or to be quiet and wait for her, if
that was what she needed. Her thoughts produced a frown,
which made Jack's eyebrows rise. But he didn't say anything.
Love. Is that, Angel wondered, what kept him squatted down
in front of her, kept him taking care of her, and talking about
silly things from when he was a boy? Was this love . . . this
sharing, this wanting to be here, this wanting to hear his
voice, feel his touch? Was this love?

She suspected as much, but just didn't know. It could be.
But she couldn't afford to find out, couldn't afford to need
him, to want him . . . not if she still planned on killing his
brother. Which she did. She still planned on it. Still fully
intended to do it. And that meant she'd most likely lose Jack.
Because no matter how much he might hate—and she suspected that he did, being the decent man he was—what had
happened to her, this was his brother she was talking about.
And blood was thicker than—

''What's wrong, Angel?'' Jack suddenly asked, again pulling her away from thoughts of Seth . . . as if he knew where
her mind had wandered and tried to interrupt her. ''Why're
you frowning like that? What were you thinking about?''

Angel looked at Jack. Should she tell him? Was she strong
enough right now to deal with his reaction, no matter what it

might be? And she had to admit, she had no idea what he'd do. He'd been tender with her so far, but as she'd just admitted . . . this was his brother she meant to kill. Just as she thought she'd decided to go ahead and say what she was really thinking, an unbidden image popped into her mind, stopping her words.

The white wolf . . . grinning, wagging her tail, letting Angel touch her fur. The memory had Angel blurting, "The wolf. Yesterday. What did it mean?"

Jack pulled back, stiffening but quickly trying to disguise that he had, Angel realized. Her senses went on alert as she watched him come to his feet and busy himself with cleaning up the kitchen from her bath. She sat where she was—waiting for him, waiting for him to speak—but pivoted in her chair to see him.

"What did it mean, Angel? In what sense?" came his offhand-sounding response as he picked up the towels and the comb and scissors.

She cocked her head, gripping the chair back with one hand, almost afraid to wonder why he'd not answered her right away. Still, sore as she was, it gratified her to be able to move, to function, to think. Feeling stronger by the second, and realizing that she did, Angel pronounced herself ready to deal with everything that had happened, and more than ready to get her life in order. She reached up, out of long-standing habit, to brush the hair out of her eyes, only to find there was nothing impeding her view. She lowered her hand to her lap and challenged, "You know what I mean, Jack."

Her words caught him on his way to the sink. He stopped and turned to her, staring, his expression changing with his thoughts. Angel drew a small measure of satisfaction from his reaction. She could tell that she'd surprised him. Could see— just by watching him, by the way he held himself—that he was realizing, as she had, that her time of weakness, of needing care, was quickly passing. She was back. And he would have to deal with her. "All right," he said, laying the things he held in his hands on the wood counter.

Then, again facing her, leaning his butt against the sink,

crossing his arms over his chest, and looking as if he were etched in stone, he said, "It means, Angel, that someone is going to die."

Angel clutched the chair back with both hands. "Someone? You mean me? Because she came to me and let me touch her?"

His expression impassive, he shrugged, saying, "I don't know." His voice was flat, his body rigid.

But Angel didn't believe that he didn't know and opened her mouth, meaning to tell him so, when he cut her off.

"No, that's a lie. I do know. But it's not you."

His answer made her slump down in her chair. She didn't want to ask, didn't want to know, but yet . . . she did. "Then who, Jack?"

He looked her right in the eyes, never changing his deadsober expression. "Me. Or Seth. Maybe both."

Angel's heart seemed to lodge in her throat. For long moments she could do nothing but stare at him . . . and be afraid for him. Then she burst out with everything she was thinking. "That doesn't make sense, Jack. Why would she come to me? I don't have anything to do with her. You do. She was as good as your mother for years—"

"I thought you didn't believe all that."

Angel clamped her lips together, raised her chin a notch. And realized that yes, she did believe it. How else to explain it? But still she wasn't ready to admit as much to him. "Well, let's just say I do."

"All right. She comes to you because . . . you're here and you have strong ties to us."

Angel cocked her head. "You mean the land, the ranch?"

Jack sent her an assessing, almost accusing, look that made Angel's face heat up. "It's more than that. And you know it."

She did, but felt shy about it. So she deflected his accusation with another question about the white wolf. "How come her coming to me, grinning, her tail wagging, has you thinking that you or . . . Seth is going to die?"

Jack shrugged, evidently allowing the change in subject.

"Well, it's hard to figure what lies in a spirit wolf's head. But now—and too late for you—I think I understand. Since Pa is already gone, Seth and I . . . well, we're the only ones left. So it has to be one or both of us."

Both of us. Angel ignored the sick feeling his words gave her and gestured her confusion. "I still don't get it, Jack. How you'd know that, I mean."

"Well, neither do I. But she comes either as a warning or as a comfort. And yesterday, for the first time, she was both, I believe. Her showing herself to you was a warning for me. To point me where the danger lay. She knew you'd tell me . . . and you did."

Suddenly, as if overcome, Jack jerked away from the sink, turning to it, pounding it with his fist, gripping its rim, and hoarsely crying out, "I should have heeded your words, Angel. But I was too damned stubborn and hell-bent on doing things my own way. I should have listened. I am so goddamned sorry."

Then, he became quiet, his body seeming to hang as he stood staring out the window for long, silent moments. Angel swallowed, didn't know what to say, what to do. Then Jack pivoted, staring at her with eyes burning, hurting. And suddenly, she knew. He wanted her forgiveness. Angel lowered her gaze, mumbling, "You did what you thought you had to, Jack."

"Yeah. And didn't it turn out great?"

Angel looked up at him, hating the bitterness wrapping itself around his words, and perhaps around his heart. This time, with more force, she told him, "You did what you thought you had to do."

His grimace said she might believe that, but he didn't. "Fine. I did what I had to do. To hell with me. I'm just grateful Old Mother came to you. At least you can count on her. Her tail-wagging and grinning . . . that was to let you know you'd be all right. Maybe she knew I wouldn't heed her warning. Maybe she already knew I'd be a hardheaded jackass."

Angel swallowed, fighting back the prick of tears edging

against her eyelids. "You don't have to be so hard on yourself. I'm all right." He didn't say anything, just continued staring at her as if she—with her scratches and bruises—were evidence enough of his own shortcomings.

Angel sighed out her breath, felt its warmness brush over her hands where they gripped the chair back. She could only wonder how, after what had happened to her last night, she could be up and around so quickly. She could only credit it to the way her life had always been, getting over hard knocks quickly, before the next one came. But too, this time, she had another reason for hurrying her recovery. She had someone outside herself to think about. Jack. Before Seth, he'd shown her what caring was, what it could be like between a man and a woman who cared about each other. To that, she would cling.

To that and to her fears for Jack, she would cling. She'd rather die herself than have anything happen to him. A part of her brain, and her heart, registered that this was quite an admission. One very unlike her, given her shut-off heart . . . if indeed it was, despite what Seth had done to her. And wasn't that what the quiet voice inside her had said during his attack? That no matter what he did to her body, he couldn't touch her heart or her soul? And wasn't she sitting here . . . thinking, feeling . . . proving it now?

Warming thoughts, hopeful thoughts. Thoughts that made her want to deal with something Jack'd said a moment ago. So, out loud, she queried, "You think the wolf considers me part of your family now? Why would she do that?" She wanted Jack to say it was because he loved her.

But he stared at her a moment, his expression becoming bleak . . . and unaccountably sad. "Why? Because you *are* a part of my family."

On the inside, Angel pulled back, looking again for that place where she used to hide. "You don't have to look so happy about it."

Jack gestured, shrugging. "I can't help it. Because I'm not happy about it. For what it means to you. You've seen enough of us to know we're not a good family to be a part of."

Not finding that hiding place, but feeling his words healing her, Angel, suddenly shy, told him, "Well, I think you are. You, anyway. And your father. I liked him . . . too."

Jack surprised her by covering his face with his hand and muttering, "Jesus." Then he looked up at her, his face pale, haggard. "My father." He huffed out his breath. "The Daltrys. What a sorry lot for you to be mixed up with."

Angel's hands fisted atop the chair's back. "I don't understand."

"I know you don't. And I wish I could let you go on not understanding. But I can't, not if I ever hope to—All right, here it is. You may not be blood kin, Angel, but you—your life, your mother's—have been tangled up with my family since you were five years old. Only you haven't known it."

"My mother?" His words hit her like bullets. Something awful—something he knew and she didn't—was going to be said. Her mouth suddenly dry, her heart's thumping no more than a shallow beat-beat-beat in her chest, Angel rasped out, "What . . . what do you mean?"

Jack cocked his head, ran his gaze up and down, assessing her. "How're you feeling, Angel?"

It was going to be bad, what he had to say. Very bad. But impatience with his stalling had Angel shoving to her feet, pushing away from the chair, and gesturing widely. "I'm fine. Tell me what you have to say. I won't break. I've been through hell, and I haven't broken yet."

His eyebrows rose, but he said, "All right." But maddeningly, that was all he said. He pulled away from the sink and paced across the kitchen, stepping out into the hallway and checking up and down its length. He didn't want Boots or Lou to hear him, Angel realized, scared now all the way to her toes. Apparently satisfied that they were alone, Jack turned back to her, saying, "You might want to sit back down."

Angel did want to—desperately—but she stiffened her knees, bracing herself, remained standing. Although she clutched at the chair back to her right. "I'm fine. Just say it."

Jack nodded . . . and looked suddenly tired, haggard. Clearly anguished, he paused before saying, "I found some things, Angel, at Seth's hideout, some things that were missing from here."

Her heart skipped a beat. "The papers?" she blurted.

He nodded. "Yes. And a knife—Seth's knife—stabbed through them. You were right. Pa did want you to have the place."

She couldn't stop herself. She had to see them. "Where are they?"

Jack eyed her, sobering even more. "They're here. I'll get them in a minute. But there was a . . . a letter with them, too. A letter to you . . . from my father."

"A letter?" she asked, puzzled. But then she knew. This letter contained the *why* of everything. Wallace Daltry'd written it all out. That's what he meant when he said the answers were here. Angel's blood pulsed with anticipation as she forced herself to wait for Jack's explanations. Why didn't he just give her the papers and the letter and be done with it? "Well?" she prompted when he remained silent. "What about the letter?"

A peeved look crossed his face. "This isn't easy, Angel. What I have to say is going to hurt. And hurt bad."

"Me or you?" Instantly, seeing the fleeting hurt replace his peevishness, Angel regretted her abrupt words . . . another first for her. Before a few weeks ago, she hadn't cared how anyone took anything she had to say. But now she did. She wanted to say she was sorry, but didn't have the words . . . or the courage.

"Both, Angel. They'll hurt both of us. But in different ways. And I don't know how we can ever survive this—well, let me just say it. My father—" He stopped, swallowed, and said, "Killed yours. By accident."

Angel's blood . . . every drop of it . . . went to her feet. She collapsed onto the chair, sitting sideways on it and staring straight ahead, breathing laboriously. She put a hand to her chest, held it there. It was all she could do for long, painful seconds. But then she whipped around, found Jack, her hair flying around her shoulders and stinging across her cheek. "How do you kill a man by accident, Jack? There're accidents and there're killings. They don't go together."

"Yes, they do," he said, sounding to her ears as if he'd moved about a hundred yards away, when in reality he hadn't moved an inch. "They did, Angel. Thirteen years ago. When your father was walking by the Silver Star and my father was inside in a fight over a card game that broke out into gunplay. He shot and missed the man he meant to hit—and got your father, instead. It's all in the letter."

Angel heard him, believed him, but couldn't take it all in. She stared at his face, a face she was just coming to believe she loved . . . and would always. If only she could get past the burgeoning hatred for all things Daltry that was taking seed in her heart as she sat there . . . staring at him, blinking, swallowing. "Wallace Daltry," she said, thinking she'd pronounced his name as if she'd never heard of him. And suddenly wished she hadn't.

"And here all this time," she went on, hearing the note of crushing wonder in her voice, "I was thinking he was such a good man. I carried his body back here and buried it. Even put flowers on his grave. And he killed my father?" Fierce anger, a building rage, now tore through her, tightening her chest, raising her voice. "*That's* why my mother wouldn't take his money. That's why she had to become a whore. To feed me, Jack. To *feed* me."

Angel jumped up, her hands fisted at her sides as she advanced on him, as if he'd done something wrong. "Do you know how that makes me feel? Do you? Her life, my life . . . *shot* to hell, right along with my father's. My father—a good and kind man. Dead. Because of a Daltry. A goddamned Daltry. I worked day in and day out in that stinking hotel, Jack, since I was twelve years old, cleaning up other people's slop. And my mother sold her body and her soul in a way that finally killed her. And all because *your* father couldn't abide the outcome of a *card game*?"

It was too much to bear. Angel suddenly realized she was standing in front of Jack and hitting him with her fists . . .

pounding on his chest. He gripped her arms, but wasn't trying to stop her. Even that was too much. "Fight me, damn you. Fight me. Your father paid my way all these years out of guilt, Jack. Guilt. Not kindness. But guilt. He brought me here—why? So I could be—"

"Stop it, Angel." Jack shook her, enough to get Angel's attention. She stared up at him. "Stop it. He tried to make it up to her. To your mother. He offered to marry her—"

"*Marry* her?" she spat out. "He'd just killed my father and the next words out of his mouth are marriage? Had he lost his mind?"

"It wasn't like that. It was a while later when he asked. But yes, he was out of his mind. With grief over what he'd done. He wanted to take you both in. He tried. He hated what he'd done. Every damned day of his life, according to his own words. But he *was* the man you saw, the one you knew. He was. No matter what went before, Angel . . . in the end, he saved your life."

"Why?" she screamed, her voice rending, tearing on a jagged sob. "So he could bring me here and I could be raped by his bastard of a son?"

Jack's grip on her tightened, his face reddened. "No, god-dammit, no. Listen to me, Angel. He brought you here because he *cared*. It ate at him, you and your mother's predicament. It ate at him. Ate and ate until it became a cancer inside him, a cancer that was killing him anyway, killing him—until Seth—"

Jack abruptly broke off, staring down into Angel's face with a deep and dark look of the purest hatred she'd ever seen. Her breath caught. She opened her mouth with her need for more air and nearly choked when he rasped out, "What the hell am I doing standing here?"

His voice—cold, flat, dead—chilled Angel. He pushed her back, practically flinging her aside as he stalked over to the kitchen table, jerked up his gunbelt and flung it around his waist, buckling it as he made for the back door to the kitchen. There, he jerked it open and stepped outside, slamming it closed behind him.

"No!" Angel screamed, not done with him. She took a step toward the door, saw Boots appear in the kitchen's entryway, the Winchester gripped in his hands. "We heard the yelling," the old man said. "Is everything—"

Jerking toward him, Angel pointed, warning, "Stay out of this."

The old man pulled up short, looking scared and confused. "Yes, ma'am," he said, staying where he was. Only then did Angel see Lou's wide-eyed little face peeking around from behind Boots.

She'd scared the heck out of them. Even in her frantic, angry state, she couldn't live with being mean to such defenseless old creatures as they were. So she forced a calm into her voice she didn't feel, and reassured them. "It's okay. I'll be right back."

They nodded. With that, Angel dismissed them from her mind. She charged over to the back door and, mimicking Jack's actions of only a moment ago, jerked it open, tore through it, and slammed it shut behind herself. Outside, only marginally aware of the day's quiet and warmth and bird-chirping sunshine, she looked this way and that, hunting for— There he was, loping for the barn with an intensity that spoke of purpose. He wasn't running away from her, she realized. He was running to something. His horse?

Seth. He means to go after Seth. Angel couldn't let him do that, for reasons all her own. She took off after him, ignoring her body's many aches and sorenesses—as well as the stinging, jarring, jabbing pain of running barefoot over the sandy, gravelly ground, softened only slightly by last night's rain.

"Jack?" she called out, running, fearing she'd fall and twist an ankle, but still not sparing herself. "Jack?" she called out again, hardly pulling any closer to him, given his head start, and his longer legs and loping gait. "Damn you, Jack Daltry," she cried out. "Wait for me."

He didn't wait for her. Or even act as if he'd heard her. She knew he had to have. She wasn't that far away. And even her horse had its ears pricked. The roan had heard her. Because it ambled over to the corral's split-rail fence and stared at her and then at Jack. Just then, Jack veered toward the corral, heading for her horse. The roan backed up, tossing its mane as it skittered to the other side of the enclosure and circled it at a canter. *He means to take my horse. No, he's not*, came Angel's realization and her protest.

She ran faster, her air-starved lungs burning, the stitch in her side forcing her finally to slow down. But then she was at the corral, braking, her hands out to stop her from colliding with the fence. Pushed up against it, she saw that Jack had already vaulted it and was reaching for a rope, no doubt to lasso the skittish roan. "Where are you going?" came Angel's breathless demand, even though she already knew.

Without turning around, just handling the braided *reata*, forming a looped knot in it, his gaze not leaving his handiwork, Jack ignored her question to ask his own. "What are you doing out here, Angel?"

"I'm asking you where you're going."

His hands stilled, but he didn't turn to look at her. "What difference does it make to you? You made your position clear. And I don't blame you one bit for hating the lot of us. Just go on back inside and let me take care of my business."

Ignoring what he told her to do, her emotions roiling, Angel's heart thumped wildly. "I don't hate you, Jack," she said softly. He turned his head, not enough to look at her, but enough to show he was listening. Angel tipped her tongue out to wet her lips and hurried on. "I don't even hate your father. Maybe I should. I thought I did a minute ago, back inside the house when you told me about him and my father. But now I'm thinking, what good would it do? He's gone."

A sniff came from Jack. He scrubbed a sleeve under his nose, turned his back more fully to her.

And Angel hurt for him, felt compelled to add, "The man saved my life, Jack. Like you said, no matter what else he did, he stepped in when he didn't have to. And he did try to make up to my mother, and even to me, for his . . . mistake. I don't know, maybe I could hate him if I hadn't gotten to know him. But I did. And he was a good man. I saw that for myself. And I can see now, with what you just told me, that he was hurting for what he did. That says a lot for him. I don't take that away from him."

Several wordless seconds ticked by. Then Jack said, just as softly, "I think he'd feel better knowing you felt that way. It's a lot for you to forgive, Angel. I know that, and I thank you for it."

Angel shrugged, shaking her head, uncomfortable with her own goodness. "Don't make too much of it. It's just the way I feel. Now will you tell me where you're going?"

Again ignoring her question, he said, "I'm taking your horse. I rode mine all night. He's worn out."

"So are you," Angel accused. Jack jerked around and stared, his burning eyes accusing her of caring. Her chin suddenly quivered, giving her away. Angel struggled for control, blurting, "You're liable to get my horse killed, riding him when you're that tired." It was true, that could happen, but . . . it was not her real concern. Jack didn't say anything, just turned away. She drew in a deep breath and let it out. "*Where* are you going?"

Jack arrowed her a sidelong glance over his shoulder. "Where do you think?"

"I don't know," Angel lied again, wanting only to stall him, to maybe change his mind. "That's why I'm asking. But you're not taking my horse."

"Yes. I am." He swung the rope above his head, threw the looped end, and expertly caught the roan. He then began hauling in the rope and making soothing noises to the white-eyed, struggling horse.

"Dammit, Jack, no you're not." Angel began climbing the rails, gritting her teeth against the splintery wood poking into her hands and her bare feet. "He's mine. Let him go."

With the horse under control, Jack turned to her, his eyes narrowing as she came over the fence, landing lightly on her feet. "What are you doing out here dressed like that?"

She looked down at herself, at his checked shirt and her bloomers, and then threw her arms wide, facing him. "What differenece does it make? Who's going to see me who hasn't already, Jack? You? Boots and Lou? Seth? I have no secrets.''

His knuckles whitened around the rope he held, and his expression clouded. ''Don't talk like that.''

Avoiding the horse apples dotting the enclosure, Angel advanced on him across the mushy, churned-up ground, feeling the cool earth squish between her toes. ''Why not? It's the truth, isn't it? Tell me, since you haven't said yet, Jack . . . how *do* you feel about what happened to me? What does it mean to you?''

His expression hardened, seemed to make the bones underneath stand out more, like rocky outcroppings pinning up a tan and wintery desert. ''What does it mean?'' Jack gritted out. ''It means that Seth won't live to see the sun go down, Angel. I'll kill him for what he did to you, just like I meant to kill him for what he did to my father. My only regret is I can't kill him twice, once for each of you, the two people I love the most.''

Angel stopped, frozen, suddenly feeling every bruise and scratch she had, every sore muscle, every torn bit of heart . . . knitting, healing. He loved her. She wondered, though, if he'd even heard himself say the words. Because he stood there, glaring, holding her roan still, as much as daring her to try to stop him. Which she intended to do. But how? Well, she knew one way. ''You can't kill him, Jack.''

He tilted his head, as if he weren't sure he'd heard her right. ''The hell I can't. I can, and I will.''

''No. You won't.''

His face took on a peevish expression. ''You already said that. Don't tell me you don't think he deserves to die.''

''He does. But are you just going to ride out again, not knowing where he is? Because we've been through this before.''

His stricken look touched Angel's heart. But she couldn't afford to soften any right now. Too much was at stake. Then he said, ''Angel, up to and including the day I die, I'll regret my leaving yesterday. And my leaving four months ago. I can't bring back Pa or undo what happened to you. But I can do this. Because this time, I know where Seth is. He left his own note with Pa's letter and the Circle D papers. He said if I wanted him and the money he took from the safe, he'd be at a place only I'd know."

Hungry for this one piece of information, Angel licked at her lips. "And where's that?"

Jack must have seen something in the way she looked or the way she suddenly straightened up because he asked pointedly, "Why're you asking?"

Angel shifted her weight, her stance. "I have a right to know."

"Why?"

"Because you're not going to kill him. I am."

Nineteen

Shock poured through Jack, stiffening his knees, tightening his grip on the lead rope holding Angel's roan at his side. "No you're not," he heard himself saying.

"Yes I am," she came right back, her now clearly visible eyes snapping, her hands at her waist, her body all but lost in his flannel shirt, under which her bloomers, bare legs, and muddied feet shone. "What's the difference to you? You want him dead. So do I."

"The difference is," Jack argued, "you wouldn't stand a chance against him."

An abrupt chuckle escaped her. "You haven't done so well yourself against him, cowboy. I had to save your ass the last time you faced him."

That's what he needed to hear right now, came his sour thought, sour despite her calling him cowboy, when about an hour ago he'd been praying to hear her say it. But now? "Dammit, Angel."

"Dammit, Jack."

Impasse. "You don't know what it's like to kill a man," he argued, meaning it. "What that does to your soul. I do."

"So do I. Why do you think I was being strung up? Because I killed Jeb Kennedy, that's why."

"Jeb Kennedy?" The man's hateful name spewed out of his mouth. Jack's heart sank for her. He could only imagine under what circumstances she'd been forced to kill him.

"John Henton's trail boss? I knew him. A worthless shit. But why'd you kill him?"

He saw Angel's chin come up, her throat work. "Because he tried to . . . he thought he could do to me what your brother did. And on the same day I buried my mother. So I killed him. With his own knife."

"Damn." Flashing images of Seth killing their father with a knife, just as Angel had Jeb Kennedy, filtered through Jack's consciousness, made him grimace. But her circumstance had been different. She'd been defending herself. Against yet another man. Suddenly, Jack felt about two inches tall for even being one. What the hell was wrong with the whole breed, himself included? "*Damn* him, Angel. He deserved to die. I'm glad you did it."

"That's what your father said."

"He did?" Jack's chuckle held no humor, but he was comforted to know that he and Pa obviously felt the same way about at least one thing. "Still, I'm sorry. I wish I'd known."

"Why? There was no need for you to know," she said, adopting that tough-girl attitude she always wore, Jack knew, when he'd get too close to the core of a deep hurt inside her.

"Well, still . . . I'm sorry." In the face of her calm and her sober expression, and jolted by the roan's impatient toss of its head, Jack spoke up. "But that doesn't change anything. You're crazy if you think I'm going to sit by while you ride out and face my brother. What kind of a man would that make me?"

"And what kind of a woman would it make me if I don't try to right a wrong that's been done to me? Just like you can't bring your father back, I can't bring my mother back. Seth was . . . with her, too. He hurt my mother, just like he hurt me. So I have as much call as you do to have my face be the last one he sees."

Hearing her words only brought home to Jack just how much there was between them to overcome, if indeed there even remained any hope of them having something together. He wasn't so sure anymore that they could get around this. But he knew he had to try. Because without her, he had no reason to go on. But how could he stop her? Then it came to him. He'd agree with her. "You know what, Angel? You're right."

She stood up straighter, looking wary. "I am? About what?"

"About Seth. About a lot of other things, too. You're right. You have as much reason as I do to see this through to the end. I don't want you running off after him. And you don't want me to go, either. So . . . let's do it together. What do you want to do? And how do you want to do it? What's your plan?"

Frowning, her eyes narrowed, she looked at him as if she didn't believe him. "My plan?" Then she looked around, not at anything specifically, just as if she were thinking. Then, she refocused on him and pointed to her horse. "Start with turning him loose."

"All right." Jack loosened the noose and slipped the *reata* over the roan's head, making a noise that sent the horse dashing away. "There. Now what?"

Angel eyed him. "There is no 'now what,' the way I see it. It's just plain crazy to go chasing after Seth. It could be a trap. His whole gang could be waiting on you."

"Yeah, that's true," Jack agreed, nodding. He'd already thought of that, but in his fierce anger of a few moments ago, he hadn't cared, had felt as if his rage and his six-shooter would be all he needed to outgun his brother's entire gang, seven men at last count. "So, do we wait here for him?"

Angel nodded now. "Yeah. We wait here. When you don't show up, he'll get curious and come see what's going on."

"Yep. That's true. That's what he did with Pa . . . came to see for himself." Jack liked the way she thought.

"How long you think it'll take for him to realize you're not coming and head for here?"

That got a shrug out of him as he thought about it. "Could be tonight. But I doubt it. He'll wait a bit, try to draw me out again. But I don't think he has the patience to go beyond a day or two, at the most, if I don't show up in a hurry. And he's not that far away. It's an old abandoned line shack about three hours from here. We used to go out there as kids. But he knows what he did''—Jack meant what Seth'd done to her—''and how much I'll want to kill him for it.'' His eyes narrowed with his hatred. ''Oh, yeah, he'll show up soon enough.''

''Good. Then we'll keep an eye out and see if he rides in alone. If he does, then we can . . . you can . . . well, we'll deal with that. But if he's not alone—How many men you suppose he'll have with him?''

Jack felt as if he were being questioned by a general right before a major battle. ''Hard to say. But my best guess is as many as seven.''

''That many? Whew. Well, at least there's me and Boots to help you out.''

She was on his side. That warmed Jack, had him grinning and saying, ''Don't forget Lou. He's simple-minded, but a hell of a shot.''

Angel gave him an answering grin . . . a fleeting one, but a grin nonetheless. ''Yeah? Well, I'll be. Okay, then there'd be the four of us. We can face Seth—and his men, if he brings them—right here. Together. On your own land.''

''On your land, Angel.''

Some emotion flicked within her eyes. ''No. Your land. It's yours, Jack.''

''It's yours.''

She put her hands to her waist. ''Dammit, Jack.''

Still clutching the thick looped rope, Jack put his fists to his waist. ''Dammit, Angel.''

She cocked her head. ''What are you doing . . . and I mean really?''

He cocked his head, feigning innocence. ''Agreeing with you.''

''Are you?''

''Yes.''

She frowned. ''It doesn't bother you that we're standing here talking about killing your brother?''

Jack's heart squeezed, but then it hardened. ''No. He's not my brother. Not after what he did to you. And my father.

And your mother. I hate him as much as you do."

"But still, Jack, he's blood kin."

Jack shifted his weight, ran a hand through his hair. "You know, you're right. It does bother me that we're standing here talking about this. In the middle of a danged horse corral . . . with you barefoot and in your bloomers. Can we at least go to the verandah?"

She shrugged, turning around, already walking away when she said, "Fine by me."

Jack stood there, handling the *reata*, watching her go. He shook his head, and despite everything, despite the whole damned mess, he grinned, barely holding back a chuckle. *Damned little spitfire. She's beat to hell—and tough as hell. Look at her. Muddied feet, bloomers, and a flannel shirt. But walking with more grace and fineness than any high-society lady in any parlor anywhere.* As he started out after her, looping the rope over a fence post, Jack knew he'd never forget the sight she made right now.

And knew he'd probably never love her more than he did at this moment. The realization staggered him, had him standing still, stiff-legged and watching her slender back and shapely calves. Any other woman who'd been through what she had would've taken to her bed, never to get up again. But not Angel Devlin. No, she was marching through horse apples, her long black hair swinging with every movement, and climbing a split-rail fence, getting ready to put the final touches to her plans for a war.

And suddenly Jack couldn't stand it, couldn't keep his hands off her. He caught up to her, capturing her around her waist—startled, she gasped, lost her hold on the fence—and pulled her down, turning her to face him.

Perturbed, she took him to task. "Jack Daltry, what's got into you—"

"You have," he said, cutting her off. And then he kissed her, softly, taking great care with her bruised and tender flesh.

He pulled her to him, enfolded her in his arms and reveled in her warmth, her sweet smell, his heart aching for her fragile slenderness, his body hungry for the feel of her against him.

Alert to her reaction, ready to free her at the slightest sign
she didn't want this, Jack gently swirled his tongue and lips
over hers, kissing her ... nearly dying when she melted
against him, when her arms shyly encircled his waist, when
she returned his kiss.

Such powerful emotions surged through Jack that he
wanted to get down on his knees and kiss the ground, mud
and all, out of thankfulness for Angel's presence in his life.
But to do that, he'd have to release her. And he wasn't about
to do that. But he did finally break their kiss and pull back,
breathing hard, one hand encircling her ribs, his other cupping
her jaw, raising her face until she stared into his eyes. "You,"
he repeated. "You got to me, Angel. I love you. I've never
said that to a woman before. But I do—I love you. And I
always will."

With that, he slipped his other hand around her back and
kissed her forehead, her cheeks, her nose. Angel closed her
eyes, her mouth opened slightly. Smiling, adoring her all the
more for her warm and innocent reaction, Jack felt emboldened enough to say, "No matter what happens here today,
Angel, or tomorrow, or next year ... I will always love you.
And it doesn't even matter if you don't feel the same about
me, because I—"

She reached up, covering his mouth with her fingers. "I
feel the same, Jack. At least, I think I do. I—" She lowered
her hand to his chest, resting it there. Her gaze followed her
hand. She stared at his shirtfront. Finally she raised her head,
looking into his eyes. "This is hard for me," she began. "I've
never felt this way before. I've never said ... these words
before. And I'm glad you haven't, either. That makes it easier
for me."

Tenderness and love gripping him, Jack smiled as he ca-
ressed her ribs under that shirt of his she wore. "Take your
time. I've waited all my life for you. And I believe I'd wait
the rest of it to hear you say you love me."

A sweet half-smile lit her features. She again lowered her
gaze to his shirtfront, but not before he saw her deepening
color. She was shy. He loved that about her. She raised her

head, saying, "I . . . do love you, Jack." As she said that, his heart soared. "I tried to tell myself I didn't know what it was that I'm feeling. But it has to be, this aching to be with you, to see you and hear your voice . . . and to touch you." A sudden anxious expression captured her features, widened her eyes. "That is love, isn't it?"

Beside himself with happiness, Jack chuckled. "God, I hope so."

But she didn't return his grin. No, instead, she soberly added, "Me, too. But I do, Jack—I love you. I don't know how I can. Or what we can do about it. I mean, I don't know how to get past everything that's gone on here—and I mean now or for the past twelve or thirteen years. And there's still more . . . bad stuff to go. I just hope that what I feel . . . what we feel when it's all over is enough. In the end."

Sober himself now, Jack said, "Me, too, Angel. Me, too." Because he knew, standing there with his arms around her, that if he lost her, there'd be no reason to go on. None.

Two warm, muggy, overcast days passed. With no sign of Seth. With no drop of rain to relieve the overhead battalion of low-hanging, disgruntled, full-bellied clouds. With each lagging hour, the tension in the main house at the Circle D escalated, finally becoming a living thing, the fifth presence among them. During the day, only Jack dared go outside alone. And inside, at night, none of them wanted to be alone.

Second-floor opened windows provided the only breeze, and the best vantage points for watching the hills and the surrounding prairie for interlopers. But maddeningly, none rode over the horizon. As much as trapped inside, lest they become unwitting targets at any moment, the four armed occupants moved through their days quietly. Even at mealtimes. Maybe especially at mealtimes. Because the food supplies were running low. They made do with what they had. And were grateful. But quiet. And edgy . . . not one meal passing without one or the other of them jumping up to look out a window, certain of a movement seen or a sound heard.

But no one was ever there.

As bad as the days were, the nights were worse. The sky remained cloudy, gave no quarter to the moon, no illumination to the ground. Evening's sheltering shadows slowly, reluctantly, gave way to night's black and funereal drapings. Outside, the dark and the shadows conspired only with those needing stealth . . . such as the occasional coyote going after a remaining chicken. But inside was no better, no safer. Because when day's light faded, no lamps could be lit and movements, by necessity, were few.

Why make it easy for any hostile gunman who might lurk outside?

The only relief, the only surcease from the constant tension, for Jack and Angel, was lying in each other's arms when one or the other of them wasn't taking a turn guarding. That first night after Seth's attack, Angel had shyly, with great embarrassment, come to his room, asking if he'd hold her. With open arms, Jack had welcomed her sweet presence in his bed, his heart warmed by her need for him. There'd been no loving beyond the embracing, given her bruising and soreness. But the love was there . . . and it was enough.

And so, the third day dawned, became several hours old, as Angel cleared away their lunch remains, as she held on to the memory of Jack's warm and solid body at her back all the night before, recalled his muscled arm around her, holding her close, his breath in her hair. *Drat his patience*, she found herself thinking . . . and grinning. Maybe tonight she could tell him she—She what? Angel's movements stilled.

Tell him what? Tell him that wearing his clothes, like she was now, only made her want to get him out of his? Angel's grin became wicked and had her nibbling at her lower lip. Oh, yes, she knew what she wanted him to do. She just didn't have the words for it. Then she blinked. Something white darting by outside captured her attention, crossed her consciousness . . . and was gone.

What was that? came her startled, knee-stiffening thought. *And what am I—? When did I—?* Only now did she realize that, at some point in her daydreaming, she'd come over to the kitchen window, was even now staring out of it . . . only now aware of what she was seeing.

Out at the corral, Jack was shirtless and wiping down Buffalo. Angel relaxed, melted. A sigh of longing escaped her. Gone was all thought of ghostly images flitting about. Something else filled her vision now. Angel didn't know which one she believed to be more finely muscled. The man or his horse. Both of them rippled and glistened, dark and tanned, each movement they made a display meant for appreciating.

Slowly, mechanicallly, not even glancing down, acting as if she feared that even the slightest noise from her would end this magical moment, Angel placed the dishes she still held into the sink and continued staring at Jack's bare back, at his long, muscular legs, at his spare and precise movements.

She couldn't believe the love welling up in her heart, the letting go of all her hurts, the forgiveness in her . . . all because of Jack. His love gave her a reason to go on, to live and to be happy. For once, and finally. A smile all the way from her soul lit Angel's face as she cocked her head, crossing her arms, and filling her eyes with his presence. Without him—if something were to happen to him—why, she couldn't go on, couldn't draw another breath, couldn't—

A wolf howled . . . mournfully. In the same instant, a single shot rang out, cracking the waiting day. Buffalo reared. Jack went down. Angel froze, clutched the sink's rim, thought she heard an animal's vicious snarling, but couldn't be sure—because of her own scream. "Jack!"

She jerked around, making for the kitchen door, already tearing off her apron, wanting nothing between her and the Colt strapped to her left hip. She'd not gone two steps before the sound of running footsteps in the hallway brought her up short—friend or foe?—and had her pulling the gun from its holster and aiming it. Boots and Lou rounded into the kitchen. Their gazes locked with hers. She pulled her gun up, exhaling her terror.

Then Boots, his eyes widened, his expression grim, mouthed, "Seth."

Angel knew that, knew it was Seth outside, knew he'd

fired that shot, but still . . . it was all she needed to hear. The man's name. Her expression contorting with the hatred in her heart, Angel said, "I'll kill him. He's shot Jack."

Boots's and Lou's mouths popped open, their expressions crumpling. But Angel was already on her way to the door. Suddenly her arm was grabbed and she was spun around, her hair tangling around her face and shoulders. Boots had a hold of her. "No. You cain't just hightail it out there. If he . . . got Jack, he can get you. You cain't do no good if you're—"

"Let go, Boots." Angel jerked her arm free, yanked the kitchen door open, and spewed out her words to the older man. "If Jack's dead, then I may as well be, too. Stay here and cover me, you hear?"

It was Lou who answered. "I do." With that, he sprinted over to the open window and aimed Wallace Daltry's Winchester out it. He cocked the rifle and then pivoted to face Angel, his expression hardened. "Go on. I got you."

Sudden tears blurred Angel's vision. She blinked them back, didn't have time for them. *Jack could be bleeding to death*, her heart and mind screamed. *Get out there.* She turned to Boots. "Watch out this door here. And don't you come outside. Either one of you."

And then, she was outside herself, bounding off the landing and running as low to the muddy ground as she could, but all too soon out in the open, away from the sheltering bulk of the main house. A chicken or two squawked, flew up as Angel slinked by, startling her as much as she had them. Her back heated by the day's sudden sunshine, and her Colt clutched in her sweat-slippery palm . . . all she could think was, *I'll kill him . . . I'll kill him . . . I'll kill him.*

Even so, even as she flew for the barn, for the corral next to it, she expected to be taken down at any moment by another shot. But none rang out. She knew she was in range, wondered why Seth didn't end her life right now. And then, alive, unharmed, she was at the barn, all but colliding with its lumbering wooden side. Her back to it, her right hand smoothing over the weathered boards with each step of hers, her left hand raised, the Colt clutched in it, Angel slouched along the building's length, past its open main doors, half expecting to be grabbed.

But she wasn't and then, her breath catching, she reached its edge. Her limbs leaded with fear, she peeked around the corner. And sucked in a breath. Jack was gone. Buffalo was there, unharmed. Jack's Stetson lay trampled in the churned-up ground. But Jack was gone. There was no blood. She frowned, not knowing what to make of this—

She was grabbed from behind. Her gun flew from her grip. Wrenching fright slammed through her as a big, rough hand clamped down over her mouth. An iron-banded arm encircled her waist as she was hauled up against a warm and solid wall. A man's chest. Her scream died in her lungs, her limbs went rigid. Her eyes felt as if they'd pop out of their sockets. And then she was being dragged backward . . . back and back.

Into the barn, she suddenly realized. Into its covering darkness. To her death. *Why don't Boots and Lou fire?* was her mind's anguished scream.

But she was no more than inside the hay- and manure-scented building, when a tense whispering filled her ear. "Shhh, Angel, it's me. Jack. What the hell do you think you're doing out here? Trying to get us both killed?"

The fight bled from Angel. She collapsed back against him, whimpering. He was alive. Then he released her, turning her to face him and grabbing her into his embrace. "Damn, you scared me," he spat out, his voice still low. Quickly he kissed the top of her head and then held her out at arm's length, running his gaze over her, as if checking her for wounds. "You all right? Yeah? I about passed out when I saw you scoot by these doors. Jesus, Angel!"

"I thought you were shot," she cried out, her vision filled with the blessed sight of him.

Jack clamped his hand back over her mouth. "Shhh. I fell down to make Seth think he'd got me." She nodded. He removed his hand from her mouth, his gaze flitting all around them, taking in everything, assessing, ordering. Then he looked down at her. "It worked, too. He's closing in some-where out there right now. I think he's alone. But he'll be here any second. And will you look at who's out here with me?''

He meant her. And he wasn't happy about it, either. But she didn't care as she stared up at him, her heart pounding with relief and with love for him. ''This is the only place I can be right now, Jack. With you.''

Jack chuckled, shook his head and cupped her chin, pulling her to him for a quick kiss. ''I'm glad you feel that way. Because you're stuck now.''

As if to prove it, another shot rang out, startling them both into stiffening and jerking around, making for the large, airy entrance formed by the open barn doors. Jack pushed Angel behind him as, his bare back to the thick wall, he peered out. ''That sounded like it came from the house.''

''Lou and Boots are in the kitchen,'' Angel told him. ''They probably saw something.''

''Or someone. Come on.'' With that, Jack turned around, tugging her hand, trying to pull her along with him into the barn's interior.

Angel resisted. ''Wait. My gun. It's outside.''

Jack stared down at her, as if having trouble deciphering what she'd said. Then, it clicked. ''Shit. Okay, stay here.'' Before she could protest, or divine his intentions, Jack let go of her and, staying low, dove around the door, flitting around to his right and out of sight. Left standing there, and stiff with fright—he seemed so much more vulnerable without a shirt on—Angel's mouth opened—Bullets flew, pinging into the wooden walls, forcing her to dive for the safety of a hay bale. Shaking to the bone, peeking over its top, Angel cursed that damned Jack Daltry for being so stupid as to—

Scrambling crablike on all fours, and covered with mud, Jack zipped back around the doorway, Angel's gun in his hand, his blue eyes wide. A grin appeared on his sweating face as he spotted her. Rolling over and over—bullets still flying and pinging into the ground no more than mere inches from him—and collecting hay bits atop the mud daubing his torso, looking somewhat like a plucked and breaded chicken, Jack reached Angel and held the Colt out to her.

"Here," he said, winking at her as he came up into a crouch, his weight on the balls of his booted feet. Then, sounding like a ten-year-old boy, he proudly told her, "There's more than one out there. But they all missed me."

"Give me that." Angel snatched her weapon from him, glaring at him—even though she realized he was putting on a show so she wouldn't be so scared. "Well, I won't miss you, Jack Daltry," she assured him. "If you ever do something that stupid again, I'll—"

"Shoot my ass, I know. Right now, you'd have to get in line, sweetheart." He finally sobered, saying, "There're about three or four men out there, I'd guess, wanting to do the same thing." The words no more than out of his mouth, Jack hauled Angel up by her arm and ran with her down the barn's center aisle, away from the gunfire outside.

If he had a specific destination or location in mind, he didn't stop to tell her. She had no choice but to keep up or be dragged. But this time, she held tightly to her gun. Almost to the end of the long aisle . . . Angel finally realized he was making for the ladder that led up to the hayloft. But Angel was somewhat behind Jack, her vision blocked by his tall, muscled frame, and she slammed into his bare back when he stopped suddenly.

Huffing out her breath and her shock—he was like hitting a tree trunk, one she had no effect on—Angel had no time even to regain her equilibrium before Jack grabbed her by her shirt and shoved her brutally into an empty stall.

Turned loose by him, her mouth opening with her shock, Angel windmilled her arms, slipping and sliding on the hay and slamming shoulder first against the narrow enclosure's side wall. Losing her grip on her gun, having no idea where it landed, she bounced off, her feet came out from under her, and she lost her balance, only to land spread-eagled on her belly. The impact took her air. She lay there—stunned and blinking and staring at . . . a horse stall. All by herself.

Where was Jack? And why had he shoved her in here? Angel rolled over onto her back, jackknifing to a sitting position and pulling long pieces of hay out of her hair, pieces

that poked against her face, irritated her eyes. And then . . .
she heard them talking, yelling. Outside the stall. Jack and
Seth. Her heart stopped beating, or seemed to. She froze, her
blood chilled. *Seth.* She couldn't move, couldn't seem to hear
them now, what with the roaring in her ears. Then . . . she
had another horrible thought. Where was her gun?

She needed her gun. Slowly, quietly, on her knees and
shoving her hair back, her heart tripping over its own suc-
cessive beats, Angel moved around the stall, patting down the
hay . . . hunting for her weapon, waiting only for a chance to
help Jack. And to kill Seth.

Twenty

Jack was of two minds right now. One part of his brain remained alert to the danger facing him. His younger brother. This part saw Seth's twisted grin, listened to him telling him how much he hated him, and all the reasons why. This part had Jack flexing his fingers over his holster, had him pronouncing himself ready to kill his brother. Or ready to die himself, was more like it, since Seth had the drop on him, had his gun pointed at Jack's heart. But it didn't matter about himself. Just Angel.

That other part of his brain, at the back of his mind, said he'd saved her by shoving her into that stall before Seth had seen her. Damn Seth, anyway, for slipping in through that side window. But thank God he'd seen Seth coming through it, had seen him land on his feet and turn around, a split second before Seth saw them. But his taking that moment to push her out of view, to save her, had given Seth time to turn around, his gun already out, and he'd had that extra second to spot Jack and freeze him in place with his pointed weapon. Well, so be it. If his life was the price for saving hers, then he could die happy.

Now if only she'd have enough sense to figure out why he'd sent her flying like that. That part, about her having sense, he didn't doubt. But the sense to stay put? He feared she wouldn't, once she heard Seth's voice. Being the scrapper that he knew she was, he expected her at any moment to pop up in that stall and start firing away at anything that moved.

That's what he needed right now, this other part of his brain commented. More to worry about. And with Seth right in front of him and getting more belligerent, Jack knew he couldn't even afford to look in her direction. All he could do was trust to the Almighty that she'd keep her head down, and stay out of the way.

"You don't have much to say for yourself, big brother," Seth snapped.

That drew Jack's full attention, his thoughts no longer divided, his hearing now attuned to the continuing gun battle outside the barn. He spared a thought for Boots and Lou, thankful for their loyalty and their skill with guns.

"What's to say, Seth? Either you're going to kill me. Or I'm going to kill you. Besides, you're the one doing all the talking, dredging up all that old, tired crap between us. You're also the one with the drop on me. So, my question is ... what're you waiting on? If it was the other way around, you worthless turd, you'd already be dead. So, go ahead. Do what you came here to do. Get it over with."

Seth cocked his head, narrowing his eyes. "Is that so? I'd already be dead, huh? You think I can't outdraw you in a gunfight? Like hell." Seth holstered his gun, spread his legs, settled his weight. "A fair fight, Jack. Me and you. It's been a long time coming, hasn't it?"

"Only because you've wanted it. I never did, Seth. Well, not until now. Not until Pa. And Angel—"

"Whew-wee ... Angel. Now there's a fine piece, huh, big brother? I had me a good time there."

A muscle jumped in Jack's jaw. His hands fisted, he started for Seth. "You little son of a—"

Seth pulled and cocked his pistol. "Uh-uh, big brother. Stay put. I'm not through with you yet."

Jack stopped, clenched his teeth, ready to jump for Seth anyway, ready to beat the life out of him with his bare hands. But how could he? Seth would shoot him before he took two steps. And if Jack got himself killed, how long would it be before Seth went after Angel again? So, forced to control himself, to stay put and put up with Seth's mouth, Jack said,

"Fine. I'm more than glad to play your game, Seth. I'll face you. More than glad. Whenever you're ready."

Brave words, words he meant, but Jack felt the sweat pop out on his upper lip as he watched his brother again holster his gun. Jack had never outdrawn Seth. Never. In all their mock battles growing up, once Seth got to be of gun-toting age, he'd proven himself a natural quick-draw, always beating Jack. And Jack had no reason to believe that that had changed. Which meant that Seth was just toying with him . . . like always.

Jack also knew Seth well enough to know he'd not kill him with the first shot. Where was the fun in that? No, Seth would hit his gun arm first, disable him . . . then shoot a leg . . . maybe his other arm . . . his shoulder, and so on, until he was on the ground, shot up and bloody, and there was only one bullet left. And that last one, Jack knew, Seth would put either in his victim's heart, or his head. Fine. Anything. As long as he could somehow first make sure Angel would forever be safe from Seth.

Just then, Seth shifted his gaze to Jack's left . . . and grinned, saying, "Well, will you look what we have here? Afternoon, Miss Devlin. Nice to see you up and around . . . although I like you better on your back."

Jack stiffened, turned to stone. The blood left his head, rushing to pool at his feet, staggering him. *No!* He jerked to his left, his heart now pounding. Sure enough, there stood his worst nightmare. Angel. Her gun drawn, her right hand holding her left one steady as she faced Seth. Blinking, sober to a point beyond grim, she acknowledged Jack not at all, her concentration focused completely on his brother.

"Afternoon, Seth," she finally gritted out. "On my back, huh? You know, that's one position I'd like to see you in, too. Only there'd be a bullet in your heart. And you'd be dead."

"Why, you little bitch," Seth snarled, his face a contorted mask of evil. "Don't think I mind killing you. Remember, the first woman I killed was my own mother." With that, Seth drew his gun and swung its muzzle in Angel's direction.

"No!" Jack screamed, the word welling up from his soul.

With that one word, time slowed . . . made Jack feel as if he were swimming against syrupy molasses, each movement heavy and forced. He reached for his gun . . . Seth's gun barked fire . . . Angel's returned it . . . Seth clutched his left arm, spun slowly around, blood seeping out from between his fingers . . . Jack pulled his gun out, aimed at Seth, fired—and missed when his brother spun as Angel fell to the ground, limp, pale, a spreading patch of bright red seeping over her chest.

"No!" Jack screamed again, seeing her drop, horrified, dying himself. This time, his yell sped up time, moving them through it as if they were atop racing horses. He rounded on his brother, walking toward him, firing, emptying his gun, hardly aiming, just shooting. But Seth—hit more than once, even doubled over and bleeding—fired back. But still, Jack kept coming. He felt the sting and the thud of being hit himself . . . in his shoulder, his arm.

But a blessed numbness insulated him. And rage kept him strong, kept him firing . . . until his brother lay on his back, on the barn floor, gut-shot, heart-shot, bleeding . . . and dead.

Angel called that one, was Jack's first thought as, grim, hating, he stood over his brother and stared down at him. He was almost afraid to turn to her, afraid to see her lying there. But he had no tears, no remorse, for his brother. Maybe later they'd come. Maybe for the little boy Seth had been, the one who used to tag after him, who had so many questions, so many fears. But for the cruel man Seth had become? No. Seth had made his choices. He'd had loving folks who cared about him. But he'd cared for no one in return. And for him, for that man, Jack felt nothing. But relief for his passing.

On an impulse, Jack threw his empty gun down beside Seth, as much as to say it was finally over. And wondered why he didn't feel his own wounds. He guessed he was beyond feeling at the moment. No doubt, the pain would come later. Already his wounds stung. But he could tell they were only superficial. Right now, he just didn't care. Not about himself. Not about his brother.

Only about Angel. And if Seth had taken the life of one woman in all the world that he, Jack Eugene Daltry, could or would ever love . . . well, then, he hoped there was a gun lying hereabouts with another bullet in it. All he needed was one.

With that thought anchoring him, Jack decided he was ready to face what lay behind him. Aware now of the quiet outside—so that battle was done, too, one way or the other—Jack raised his head, closing his eyes and drawing in a deep breath, steeling himself for what he had to do. And that was to see to Angel. He had to face it. Had to face her. Jack lowered his head, and feeling wooden, turned to her . . . his angel.

And froze with what he saw. She was still lying there . . . but propped up now on her uninjured arm, on her elbow, one knee bent, her black hair fanned out around her, her dark eyes clear, her shirtfront bloodstained. She'd apparently been silently watching him. "Is he dead?" she asked. "Or did you just run out of bullets, cowboy?"

Jack's heart soared, a watery laugh escaped him. He ran a hand over his mouth, and grinned at her. "Both. He's dead. And I ran out of bullets."

Angel nodded, her black eyes liquid, caring, hurting. "Yeah, I saw that. You okay?"

Knowing she referred to his brother's death, Jack nodded in return. He wanted so much to go to her. But he couldn't seem to get his feet moving, felt as if he'd grown roots where he stood. And so, all he did was say, "I thought you were dead."

"I thought I was, too." Then she edged her chin up, indicating his wounds. "You're bleeding, cowboy."

Cowboy. Jack looked at his bleeding arm, at his shoulder. "Just nicked me. I'll live. Too ornery to die." Then he pointed at her. "So are you."

She blinked, grimaced. "What? Ornery? Or bleeding?"

"Both." Jack chuckled at this conversation. It wasn't anything he ever could have imagined. And yet, he'd never lived through anything more real.

She looked down at herself. "Yeah. I noticed that. It's my shoulder. And you know what? It hurts like hell."

"I reckon it does." Jack wanted to cry. Or laugh. He didn't know which. He was just so damned relieved. He wanted to hold her, never let her go. But still, as if he'd been told to do so, he stood where he was, nodding and talking to her, as if nothing out of the ordinary was going on. "You want me to take a look at it for you?"

She nodded. "I wish you would. Before anyone else comes back here and tries to kill us."

"Yeah, I thought of that, too. I just hope Lou and Boots are okay." With that, Jack went to her, squatting down beside her, not wanting to hurt her further by wrenching her into his arms and pressing her to his chest . . . for the rest of their lives. Unbuttoning her shirt's top two buttons, Jack gingerly pulled the flannel material away from her wound, and peered at it, frowning.

"Is it that bad?"

Jack shook his head, making a dismissive face. "Naw. Looks like the bullet grazed your shoulder. Just skinned you, made you bleed a lot. You ought to be up and cooking and cleaning in a day or two." He grinned at her, finally chuckling at her pain-glazed but peevish expression.

"Cooking and cleaning, huh? Is that all you can think to do with me?"

Just as Jack opened his mouth, preparatory to telling her all the bedroom details of the things he could think to do with her, he heard his name being called out from the front of the barn. His name and Angel's. He tensed, listened, and then relaxed, grinned down at Angel, saw the white lines of pain at either side of her mouth . . . and yet she grinned right back.

Together they said, "Lou and Boots."

The sun was shining. The world was quiet. Or perhaps it was just the morning hush inside the Circle D main house . . .

Whatever it was . . . *What a difference three days can make*, Angel decided, as she moved against Jack in his wide bed, as she felt him take her in his arms, felt his mouth on her flesh, on her neck . . . and then lower. When he captured a nipple, his tongue swirling and suckling the sensitive bud, Angel was seized by a burning, stinging desire. It coursed through her, capturing her senses, had her clutching at Jack's shoulder, had her fingers tangled in his thick, black hair. Had her calling out his name.

Lying atop her, between her bent legs, his warm, naked length covering hers, Jack raised his head. "Am I hurting you?" His gaze went to her shoulder, to the patchwork stripping of bandage that was the product of Boots's fussing and clucking over her.

A slow grin spread across Angel's mouth. She gently ran her hand over Jack's matching bandages, one on his arm, one on his shoulder. And said, "No. You're not hurting me, Jack. You're making me whole again." Then she sobered, almost afraid she wouldn't have the words she needed to tell him what he meant to her, what she wanted him to do to her. "I . . . I need you, Jack. I don't want to wait any longer. I want you to do this. I want you to . . . make me yours . . . again."

She could see in his eyes, in his expression, that he knew what she meant. She wanted him to erase from her heart, from her body, any memory of Seth's ugliness toward her. She didn't doubt either that maybe just for a flash of a second, he saw himself and her and the unharmed Boots and Lou burying Seth and the three of his men who'd ridden in with him . . . not next to his mother and father, because he didn't deserve that, but on a remote part of the Circle D.

Jack blinked, and it was gone . . . that haunted look. It was then that Angel realized he needed her healing touch as much as she needed his. And that made the words suddenly come easy. She reached down, capturing his strong and handsome face in her hands, and looked deep into his blue eyes. "I love you, Jack. I always will. We . . . did what we had to do. It couldn't be helped."

His expression softened. "I know that. There was no other way. It's just that . . . when I think of how close I came to losing you, Angel. When I realize how much I love you and need you—well, it scares the hell out of me. To have you here now, and safe and saying you love me—'' He broke off speaking and lowered his head . . . he held his lips to her chest, just above her heart, kissing her there with all the tenderness she could ever want.

And then, with that gesture, the time for talking passed, became a time for celebration of their love. Jack again lowered his head, this time capturing her other nipple, this time burning her flesh with his touch, with the hot feel of his mouth on her. Angel's back arched as she pushed herself into him. Her toes clutched at the sheets under them. She held his head, wanting . . . wanting so much more. And Jack gave it to her.

Slipping down her, his hands never leaving her sides, his mouth never leaving her skin, her hungry body, he kissed his way down to her most intimate of places. Angel's breath caught, she stilled, a ragged gasp escaped her, had her staring at the ceiling . . . and then tossing her head, moaning, her eyes closed. The liquid-fire sensations scorched her, touched the very center of her. ''Oh, God, Jack,'' she muttered. ''What are you. . . .''

She couldn't finish her thought. Her entire body clamped down, needing what he was doing, existing only for the hot sensations that his mouth, his kiss, his swirling tongue, were awakening in her. This hunger . . . it required her total concentration, a complete giving of herself. It was an endless, aching need at her very center, at the core of her being. And then, she felt it . . . growing, burning, running hot and sweet, consuming her.

The rhythmic sensations seized her, held her immobile in his clutching hands, against his deliciously heated mouth as she moved her hips against him, increasing her own pleasure, never wanting this to end—even as at the same moment she believed she'd die if it didn't. Rigid with desire, she cried out . . . from the back of her throat, from the bottom of her soul, from the depths of her heart.

And then Jack was pulling himself up over her, covering her . . . sliding into her slickness . . . completing her. Angel exhaled, wrapped her arms around his neck, accepting him, encircling his hips with her legs, and loving him in return. "God, I love you, Angel," he whispered into her ear, his thrusts into her working their own magic, igniting the fire inside her yet again, even as he sought her mouth . . . and she tasted her honeyed self on his lips.

And it was enough, this loving between them, this closeness, this intimacy. It was enough to heal them both, to give them back hope. . . .

Lou and Boots would ride as far as Red River Station with her and Jack. There they'd pick up much-needed supplies, mostly foodstuffs, and then come on back here to the Circle D to keep the place going until she and Jack could get back from Wichita Falls. Back from the county seat. From filing those papers that Wallace Daltry'd had drawn up . . . and that Jack insisted she sign, saying he hadn't been much of a son to his father and that he wanted to honor this last wish of his by making the Circle D hers.

And he wanted her to be his. They'd agreed to be married by a justice of the peace while in town. Jack had then told her that she deserved to know that when they married, the laws being what they were, the property would revert back to him, anyway. But Angel hadn't cared . . . the name on some legal papers didn't matter. They both loved the land. It wasn't hers, wasn't his. It was theirs.

And speaking of the land, and their future on it, Jack meant to wire Abilene from Wichita Falls, hoping for some word from that railhead city on his men and the Circle D cattle. If they'd escaped Seth's treachery, if they'd gotten the herd through—and Jack had every reason to believe they had, he'd told her, given the size of the herd and the number of loyal and experienced men riding with them—then, he and she had all the money they needed for next year's herd.

But if not, if they hadn't made it through—the thought saddened them both—then there was the money from the safe that Jack had ridden out to retrieve from his and Seth's childhood hideout. With it, they could buy more breeding stock to replace those killed along with Tex and Calvin and the cow dogs. It'd be tough for a while, but it was a way of starting over. With Lou and Boots, a lot of hard work and patience, and their love for each other, as well as the land . . . they could do this.

Making a last-minute check to see if she'd forgotten anything, and knowing how pressed they were for time, how anxious Jack was to get started, Angel smiled as she looked around her bedroom—well, it was Old Mother's bedroom again. Because now, no longer wanting or needing to be alone, Angel slept with Jack in his room. Perhaps it was just being in here, thinking about Old Mother, that made Angel remember, that had her sitting weakly on the side of the narrow bed. Whatever the reason, she suddenly recalled that snarling she had heard on the day Seth came back.

Five days ago now. Maybe one day—she hoped soon— she could quit counting the days, could let go of those times. But for now, and needing to work through this, Angel sat, staring at nothing in particular, and suddenly remembered the white streak that had flown by outside the window that day. Or maybe it had just flitted across her vision, across her soul. Angel didn't know which, nor did she care. The truth was, the white wolf had warned them again. But had she been more spirit than flesh that time? Because she'd not left a mark on anyone. Where had she been going? Who was her snarling for?

Angel sat in the sunlit quiet, not receiving any answers. She smoothed a hand over the colorful Indian blanket that covered the bed, and murmured, "Thank you, Old Mother. I believe in you. I do."

Approaching footsteps stopped at the door to her room and had Angel looking up. Jack stood there, leaning his shoulder against the doorjamb. Angel's heart leaped, her pulse raced . . . at just the sight of him. She smiled at him. He returned it, saying warmly, "Hey, you. What're you doing?"

Angel shrugged her shoulders, looking down, suddenly embarrassed. She heard Jack's approach, flicked her gaze to him as he sat beside her on the bed and put an arm around her, kissing her temple. "It's okay. I come in here and talk to her sometimes, too."

Angel cocked her head, giving him a sidelong glance. "You do?"

"Yep." His blue eyes were sincere, his expression calm. "She's good for me. Just like you are."

Her heart melting, Angel's thought was that she loved him best when he was like this. Open and warm and caring, willing to tell her his thoughts, not afraid to let her know he wasn't always strong, that he too needed someone . . . needed her, as she needed him. "I'm going to miss her," Angel said suddenly into the quiet.

"Yeah. Me, too."

His words saddened Angel. "Then, you don't think she'll be back, either?"

Jack shrugged. "I don't know. It's hard to say." Then he shot her a glance Angel couldn't interpret . . . until he spoke again. "My mother said she saw a white wolf both times she was expecting a child. You may, too."

"A child?" Shock had Angel sitting up straight and turning to him. She hadn't thought of that, that she may already be carrying a child. But whose? "It may not be yours, Jack," she said quietly.

Without hesitation, Jack said, "It's yours, Angel. And that's enough for me. I'll love it as I do you."

Could she love him any more than she did at this moment? But then, his first words came back to her. With them, came shock. "Your mother saw the white wolf, too? But, how? I thought Old Mother—"

Jack feigned innocence. "Didn't I tell you? My mother was part Comanche. Which probably explains Old Mother and why the white wolf comes to us Daltrys."

Angel smacked at his arm. "Damn you, Jack Daltry. You know good and well you never told me that."

"I didn't? Well, you don't mind being hitched to a mixed-blood breed, do you? You know what folks say."

Angel shook her head slowly, her expression sincere.

"And you know what folks say about me. Will it bother you?"

"Yep. I may have to kill them, if they say one word about you."

Chuckling, Angel reached out to caress his cheek. He captured her hand, taking it to his lips, kissing her palm. Angel's throat thickened with emotion. She could barely get her words out. "You can't kill them all. Or stop them, Jack. They're going to talk. But you know what? I love you, Jack Daltry. And that's all that matters to me."

Jack stood up, pulling her to her feet. "That's all that matters to me, too," he said, enfolding her in his embrace, laying his cheek atop her head, and holding her.

Never before had Angel known such contentment. To be nestled against his warm strength, to be safe and happy, to be able to let her breath out and her guard down. To have this man's love. It meant everything. Into the ensuing quiet, she said, "I'm glad you told me about your mother. You don't ever talk about her."

Jack pulled back, capturing her arms and looking down into her face. Angel swallowed, felt tears prick her eyes ... even before he spoke.

"Neither do you ... talk about your mother. But there's a lot you need to say to her, Angel."

She looked down, stared at a button on his chambray shirt. "I know. I just don't. . . ." She turned her face up to his, saw the tender smile he had for her. And felt emboldened enough to ask him, "Will you go with me?"

Jack stroked her cheek. "Sure I will. You're not alone anymore, Angel. I'll do whatever you want." Then he smiled. "However, this day isn't getting any younger. You ready to get started?"

And suddenly, Angel realized she wasn't. She shook her head and stepped out of his embrace. "No." Turning away, she stepped over to the window and opened it, looking out onto the meadow, seeing the field of bluebonnets, the wolf flowers, waving in the warm and gentle breeze. A dart of disappointment assailed her, telling her she'd half expected to see the white wolf there.

Angel folded her arms under her bosom, felt Jack's arms encircle her from behind. She leaned her head back against him. "There's something I have to do first."

"All right."

His total acceptance, his patience, his unquestioning trust in her, the faith he placed in her, warmed Angel, made her feel no longer a captive to her fears. She smiled, reveling in his love, but still felt shy about saying what she wanted to do. So she just asked, "You think my mother would like bluebonnets, Jack?"

His hold on her tightened. "I think your mother would love bluebonnets, Angel. Why don't we go pick some to take to her?"

"All right," Angel said, turning with him to leave the room. But not his life.

Outside, in the meadow, reposing among the bluebonnets, the white wolf arose, her tail wagging, her muzzle parting in a grin as she turned away . . . as she faded away. "It is good." The wind carried her words, Old Mother's benediction.

The white wolf's children would survive.

Survey

TELL US WHAT YOU THINK AND YOU COULD WIN

A YEAR OF ROMANCE!
(That's 12 books!)

Fill out the survey below, send it back to us, and you'll be eligible to win a year's worth of romance novels. That's one book a month for a year—from St. Martin's Paperbacks.

Name _____

Street Address _____

City, State, Zip Code _____

Email address _____

1. How many romance books have you bought in the last year?
   (Check one.)
   __0-3
   __4-7
   __8-12
   __13-20
   __20 or more

2. Where do you MOST often buy books? *(limit to two choices)*
   __Independent bookstore
   __Chain stores *(Please specify)*
       __Barnes and Noble
       __B. Dalton
       __Books-a-Million
       __Borders
       __Crown
       __Lauriat's
       __Media Play
       __Waldenbooks
   __Supermarket
   __Department store *(Please specify)*
       __Caldor
       __Target
       __Kmart
       __Walmart
   __Pharmacy/Drug store
   __Warehouse Club
   __Airport

3. Which of the following promotions would MOST influence your decision to purchase a ROMANCE paperback? *(Check one.)*
       __Discount coupon

      __Free preview of the first chapter
      __Second book at half price
      __Contribution to charity
      __Sweepstakes or contest

4. Which promotions would LEAST influence your decision to purchase a ROMANCE book? (Check one.)
      __Discount coupon
      __Free preview of the first chapter
      __Second book at half price
      __Contribution to charity
      __Sweepstakes or contest

5. When a new ROMANCE paperback is released, what is MOST influential in your finding out about the book and in helping you to decide to buy the book? (Check one.)
      __TV advertisement
      __Radio advertisement
      __Print advertising in newspaper or magazine
      __Book review in newspaper or magazine
      __Author interview in newspaper or magazine
      __Author interview on radio
      __Author appearance on TV
      __Personal appearance by author at bookstore
      __In-store publicity (poster, flyer, floor display, etc.)
      __Online promotion (author feature, banner advertising, giveaway)
      __Word of Mouth
      __Other (please specify)_____

6. Have you ever purchased a book online?
      __Yes
      __No

7. Have you visited our website?
      __Yes
      __No

8. Would you visit our website in the future to find out about new releases or author interviews?
      __Yes
      __No

9. What publication do you read most?
      __Newspapers *(check one)*
      __*USA Today*
      __*New York Times*
      __Your local newspaper
      __Magazines *(check one)*

   __*People*
   __*Entertainment Weekly*
   __Women's magazine *(Please specify:_____)*
   __*Romantic Times*
   __Romance newsletters

10. What type of TV program do you watch most? *(Check one.)*
   __Morning News Programs (ie. "Today Show")
   (Please specify:_____)
   __Afternoon Talk Shows (ie. "Oprah")
   (Please specify: _____)
   __All news (such as CNN)
   __Soap operas   *(Please specify: _____)*
   __Lifetime cable station
   __E! cable station
   __Evening magazine programs (ie. "Entertainment Tonight")
   (Please specify: _____)
   __Your local news

11. What radio stations do you listen to most? *(Check one.)*
   __Talk Radio
   __Easy Listening/Classical
   __Top 40
   __Country
   __Rock
   __Lite rock/Adult contemporary
   __CBS radio network
   __National Public Radio
   __WESTWOOD ONE radio network

12. What time of day do you listen to the radio MOST?
   __6am-10am
   __10am-noon
   __Noon-4pm
   __4pm-7pm
   __7pm-10pm
   __10pm-midnight
   __Midnight-6am

13. Would you like to receive email announcing new releases and special promotions?
   __Yes
   __No

14. Would you like to receive postcards announcing new releases and special promotions?
   __Yes
   __No

15. Who is your favorite romance author? _____

WIN A YEAR OF ROMANCE FROM SMP
(That's 12 Books!)
No Purchase Necessary

OFFICIAL RULES

1. To Enter: Complete the Official Entry Form and Survey and mail it to: Win a Year of Romance from SMP Sweepstakes, c/o St. Martin's Paperbacks, 175 Fifth Avenue, Suite 1615, New York, NY 10010-7848, Attention JP. For a copy of the Official Entry Form and Survey, send a self-addressed, stamped envelope to: Entry Form/Survey, c/o St. Martin's Paperbacks at the address stated above. Entries with the completed surveys must be received by February 1, 2000 (February 22, 2000 for entry forms requested by mail). Limit one entry per person. No mechanically reproduced or illegible entries accepted. Not responsible for lost, misdirected, mutilated or late entries.

2. Random Drawing. Winner will be determined in a random drawing to be held on or about March 1, 2000 from all eligible entries received. Odds of winning depend on the number of eligible entries received. Potential winner will be notified by mail on or about March 22, 2000 and will be asked to execute and return an Affidavit of Eligibility/Release/Prize Acceptance Form within fourteen (14) days of attempted notification. Non-compliance within this time may result in disqualification and the selection of an alternate winner. Return of any prize/prize notification as undeliverable will result in disqualification and an alternate winner will be selected.

3. Prize and approximate Retail Value: Winner will receive a copy of a different romance novel each month from April 2000 through March 2001. Approximate retail value $84.00 (U.S. dollars).

4. Eligibility. Open to U.S. and Canadian residents (excluding residents of the province of Quebec) who are 18 at the time of entry. Employees of St. Martin's and its parent, affiliates and subsidiaries, its and their directors, officers and agents, and their immediate families or those living in the same household, are ineligible to enter. Potential Canadian winners will be required to correctly answer a time-limited arithmetic skill question by mail. Void in Puerto Rico and wherever else prohibited by law.

5. General Conditions: Winner is responsible for all federal, state and local taxes. No substitution or cash redemption of prize permitted by winner. Prize is not transferable. Acceptance of prize constitutes permission to use the winner's name, photograph and likeness for purposes of advertising and promotion without additional compensation or permission, unless prohibited by law.

6. All entries become the property of sponsor, and will not be returned. By participating in this sweepstakes, entrants agree to be bound by these official rules and the decision of the judges, which are final in all respects.

7. For the name of the winner, available after March 22, 2000, send by May 1, 2000 a stamped, self-addressed envelope to Winner's List, Win a Year of Romance from SMP Sweepstakes, St. Martin's Paperbacks, 175 Fifth Avenue, Suite 1615, New York, NY 10010-7848, Attention JP.

KATHLEEN KANE

"[HAS] REMARKABLE TALENT FOR UNUSUAL,
POIGNANT PLOTS AND CAPTIVATING
CHARACTERS."

—*PUBLISHERS WEEKLY*

A Pocketful of Paradise

A spirit whose job it was to usher souls into the afterlife, Zach
had angered the powers that be. Sent to Earth to live as a
human for a month, Zach never expected the beautiful Rebecca
to ignite in him such earthly emotions.
0-312-96090-5 _____ $5.99 U.S. _____ $7.99 Can.

This Time for Keeps

After eight disastrous lives, Tracy Hill is determined to get it
right. But Heaven's "Resettlement Committee" has other
plans—to send her to a 19th century cattle ranch, where a
rugged cowboy makes her wonder if the ninth time is *finally* the
charm.
0-312-96509-5 _____ $5.99 U.S. _____ $7.99 Can.

Still Close to Heaven

No man stood a ghost of a chance in Rachel Morgan's heart, for
the man she loved was an angel who she hadn't seen in fifteen
years. Jackson Tate has one more chance at heaven—if he finds
a good husband for Rachel…and makes her forget a love that
he himself still holds dear.
0-312-96268-1 _____ $5.99 U.S. _____ $7.99 Can.

KAT MARTIN

Award-winning author of *Creole Fires*

GYPSY LORD
_____ 92878-5 $6.50 U.S./$8.50 Can.

SWEET VENGEANCE
_____ 95095-0 $6.50 U.S./$8.50 Can.

BOLD ANGEL
_____ 95303-8 $6.50 U.S./$8.50 Can.

DEVIL'S PRIZE
_____ 95478-6 $6.99 U.S./$8.99 Can.

MIDNIGHT RIDER
_____ 95774-2 $5.99 U.S./$6.99 Can.

INNOCENCE UNDONE
_____ 96089-1 $6.50 U.S./$8.50 Can.